Uncertain Refuge

Tales of the Kashallans, Volume 4

Celu Amberstone

published by Kashallan Press, 2022

I0524673

Uncertain Refuge

Tales of the Kashallans, Volume 4

Celu Amberstone

Published by Kashallan Press, 2022.

UNCERTAIN REFUGE

First edition. March 22, 2022.

ISBN: 978-1777537982

Written by Celu Amberstone.

Prologue

The russet twilight was deepening into full dark, when a lone Warlinga runner limped up to the gate of Meh'gach Keep. As yet unnoticed by the keep's inhabitants, the lizardman allowed himself a shameful luxury and leaned his bulk against the unyielding stone of the outer wall, for uncounted moments, he surrendered to his weakness; his scaly face contorted with the agony of his injuries. He had made it this far, but he needed a little time to collect himself before facing the people within and relaying his message.

The Hunt Leader, and the matriarch of Ticca, Ima Ngeal, sent him on this desperate mission days ago. Through the haze of pain that engulfed him, he still understood his duty—he must not fail them. Ticca Keep's safety might depend on a well-armed hunting pack returning with help in time. In the pouch at his waist, he carried a letter from Ima Ngeal to the High Council at Riath.

With the poisonous Sorin storms coming any time now, the situation at the keep was a desperate one. If reinforcements didn't arrive soon, the outlaws at the Swamp Gate might become desperate enough to invade the keep. There was not much danger of them succeeding, of course. Ticca's walls were thick, and the Hunt Leader was on guard against an attack—still, who knew what the renegades were capable of. Especially if there was any truth to the Dingay assertions of Umwira magics being involved.

As the keep's fastest runner, he, Temull, was entrusted with this most dangerous task, and, like a cowardly Begta slave, he had failed them. Knowing the need for haste, he'd foolishly continued his run over the treacherous Shaden River Trail in the dark. And as ill luck would have it, he slipped on a loose rock and tumbled down a steep embankment, just missing being carried headlong into the foaming river below.

Temull lay on the ledge for sun-marks—or perhaps even days—listening to the pounding roar of the falls, and drifting in and out of consciousness.

Finally he regained enough strength to climb up the steep slope and continue on his journey, much hampered by his wounds and a leg he feared might be broken.

With mudslides and tumbled boulders choking the narrow trail, the rugged country around the falls was a challenge for a well-seasoned hunter, let alone someone in his condition.

But he had limped on over the portage, each step one of flaming agony, praying that a pack of scavenging beasts wouldn't scent his blood trail and come after him. *That would be very bad—don't think about it—just keep moving*, he'd told himself over and over, *damn you, keep moving*.

Temull had stumbled on, at last coming down into the gentler slopes of the Yeyen Banai Valley beyond. Here the land was a little kinder, but no less desolate. Sun mark after sun mark he continued with only the moss covered hills and the thorn for company.

Temull feared that he was doing irreversible damage to his injured limb, but it didn't matter—he would fulfill his duty or die in the process. And if he ended his task as a disabled hunter—well then, he would give himself to the mercy of the knife, and allow brother Warlinga to feast on his flesh. At least he would have the satisfaction of knowing that his kinsmen would praise him. He would have saved his people and done his duty.

Duty, but, by the Great Hunt Leader, he *hadn't* done his duty, now had he. It had taken him much too long, even to get this far. There was so little time left; could help reach Ticca before the storms cut it off from any hope of rescue? The Hated Enemy drew their foul magics from the storms. If Ticca was cut off; then surely the Umwira wizards and the outlaws would destroy the keep, as Ima Ngeal feared.

At some point in the haze of weariness and pain that never left him, Temull realized that he wouldn't make it to Riath in time. Turning aside from the main path he decided to head for Meh'gach Keep. K'San Yargal was on the High Council. If there was any chance of sending hunting packs to rescue Ticca before the Sorins struck, they must come from Meh'gach—and may the Gods be praised he had made it.

Trembling violently, Temull sank to the ground, his clawed hands carving long furrows in the dirt of the wall beside the gate. As he fell he realized with dismay that he should not have waited; he should not have tried to rest before announcing his presence to the keep. Instead of adding to his strength, this delay had totally drained him. In helpless frustration, Temull banged weakly with his spear on the gate a few times, then lay back and lost consciousness.

The light gone from the sky at last, the night enveloped him like a shroud.

Part One: The Sorin Storms

Chapter One

Aju'an ignored the noise of his kinsmen in the main hall of Meh'gach Keep, and stared moodily down at the purple froth on his third bowl of mushroom beer. He was well on his way to getting drunk, and he knew it. Though drowning his troubles in beer wasn't his usual manner of dealing with things; tonight, it seemed most appropriate.

The Sorins would be here soon, and that, in itself, was a good reason to feel low. The forced inactivity while the storms ravaged outside, was hard on all Warlinga, at the best of times. And this, he thought, taking another drink, was hardly the best of times for him, now was it? His father had sent him home from Riath in disgrace. And it wasn't even his fault—he had been sorely provoked. That loathsome piece of Begta vomit, Combaron had—

He sighed. Once again, his quick wit and sharp tongue were to blame for his current troubles. Without stopping to consider the consequences, he spoke out against the Dingay—and in a semi-public place. Such an act could have cost him, and maybe even his family, their lives, the way things were going these days, but he had had to respond. What Combaron Dingay implied was outrageous.

Aju'an deeply resented this chastisement. Combaron Dingay was a sniveling little pervert—everyone knew it. He had been deliberately making snide assertions about the loyalty of the Meh'gach clan for days, before Aju'an had finally lost his temper and returned the man's insults in kind.

When the story got back to his father, neither he nor Aju'an's older brother Varrod had been very amused by Aju'an's cutting wit. In fact, Yargal was so definitely unimpressed by his son's behavior that he had sent Aju'an out of Riath that very night, to await further punishment when he got home.

The weather had shifted days ago; Yargal's arrival was emanate. His father would want to be safely home before the first storm hit, so his hunting pack should have already left the Capital. They would be here any time now and then...

He took another long drink of his beer.

Sometime later Aju'an was startled out of his brooding when his twin sister sat down at the table across from him. He scowled, his head crest lowered in annoyance. With father away, she was wearing her warrior woman's garb again.

Years ago, Chelka had seen a picture of an ancient Warlinga woman warrior in one of the household priest's oldest books. Both the story about this ancient heroine and the drawing of her had stuck in the young girl's imagination. In the picture, the woman had been carrying a spear and wearing a heavy leather apron, inlaid with polished bone scales, to cover and protect her vulnerable breeding pouch.

When she was older, Chelka had pestered Overn, father's retired Hunt Leader, who could refuse her nothing, until he made her a copy of the ancient apron of her own to ware.

The youngest children of a well-loved wife, who had died soon after their weaning, both twins had been spoiled shamelessly in their early childhood. Their father and many of Meh'gach's inhabitants, especially the men in the hunting packs, doted upon Chelka, most of all. She had grown up indulged and allowed liberties, out here in the wilderness that would not have been permitted a highborn woman if they had lived closer to the Capital.

Beautiful, and ever adventurous, Chelka had coaxed the men into allowing her to train with Aju'an when they were younger. Being the only children of their age group in the keep at the time, it seemed like a logical solution to the problem of obtaining a sparring partner for the young Aju'an, until he was old enough and strong enough to train with his more mature cousins.

For years Chelka reveled in the physical combats. Being as quick and agile as Aju'an himself, she became skilled at the warrior's art. She bitterly resented it when her father, now horrified by her wild ways, forbade her further sparring bouts, fearing he would never be able to find her a bridegroom if her training continued.

Aju'an suspected that his sister secretly managed to coax some of the old veterans into still sparring with her on occasion. He'd been persuaded a few times himself—but they had to be very careful about it. If his father were to find out...

Grinning, Chelka reached over and poured herself a bowl of beer from his nearly empty pitcher. Aju'an glared at her balefully. "What are you doing out here at this time of night, little sister? You should be in the Accavett with the rest of the women,"

Chelka glanced around the torch-lit hall, taking in the knots of drinking men and the noisy dice game in the back corner. Her head crest rose. "Should I, but why, Dear Brother? Am I bothering you? I could always go drink with somebody else, or maybe join the game over there. Mar promised me a rematch; I could take him up on his offer."

Aju'an's scales darkened to a murky green, and he growled a curse under his breath. Was she deliberately trying to provoke him? Probably.

Chelka drank more of her beer then gave him another toothy grin. "Besides, the women in the accavett are boring. They talk only of babies, embroidery, and adorning themselves for their husbands' pleasure. But, since I am neither breeding nor married, it is all rather tiresome. Why would I want to stay and listen to that sort of drivel, hmm?"

"You might learn something that could help you when you *do* marry and start breeding," he muttered, then reached for the pitcher, scowling murderously when he found it was empty.

Chelka snorted. "Who said I want to get married or have babies, hmm? And besides, if you keep insulting our illustrious allies, neither of us will be getting any red kavay for breeding to carry on the proud family name, now will we?"

Aju'an's color deepened, and his shoulders sagged. That barb had stung, as she knew it would—damn her.

Chelka sighed, reached out a clawed hand and stroked his arm. "Aju'an, I'm sorry—I didn't mean it like that—I wasn't thinking. You made me angry just now, with your talk about a woman's place. You know how I hate that kind of talk. I'm sorry. I forgot for the moment about Latiya. Maybe when father gets home he will have some red kavay for you to consummate your marriage. The High Matri couldn't be that cruel. We won't have to return her to her family—surely not—the marriage contract has been signed. I don't care much for myself—in fact, I'm grateful for the reprieve, but I can guess what a trial this is for you both. Latiya is such a gentle woman, and I know you care for her already."

Motioning for a Loti servant to bring them another pitcher, Aju'an said thickly, "Forget it. I know you didn't mean anything by it." Taking a big gulp of his new beer, he belched then smirked. "I am fully aware that I'm not the only one born into this family with the curse of a sharp tongue and not enough brains to know when to keep silent." He drank some more, then added morosely, "So maybe it's a good thing that neither of us will be doing much to further the next generation, hmm?"

Chelka's head crest rose; she laughed mirthlessly, raised her bowl, and saluted him. "Shut up and drink—you can be such a dolt at times."

When she'd emptied her bowl Chelka set it aside and looked at him, her eyes troubled, her head crest dipping. "Aju'an, what's wrong—I mean, *really* what's wrong? This isn't like you, to be sitting here getting drunk like one of the men in the hunting packs. You haven't been yourself for months now. Can't you tell me about it?"

Aju'an sighed, the tip of his tail curled and uncurled on the floor by his feet. "It isn't that simple, little sister." At her scowl, he added, "It isn't that I don't want to tell you—it's just I can't put it into words even for myself. I feel this vague sense of impending disaster. If we don't abandon our present course, something will happen that will destroy us. I'm sure of it, but father and Varrod won't listen to me when I try to warn them."

"You're talking about our alliance with the Dingay again, aren't you?"

"Yes," he admitted. "Oh, I know all the arguments—Varrod and father have thrown them back at me often enough, so please spare me. But damn it, there is something wrong with that whole clan of Avairei!"

"Though I'm not sure I would go so far as to align ourselves with the Caltia cause, they do have some good arguments. And we can't deny that the Dingay rise to power has been rather sudden, and not without its *convenient* accidents for those who oppose them."

Aju'an stared moodily down into his beer, watching its lavender froth spiral round the interior of the bowl. As if forgetting for the moment that his sister was even there to listen, he said, "They wield too much power for one clan—Avairei or Warlinga. Only a council of *all* the clans should have so much influence, not just one among us. And father refuses to admit to me that he sees what is staring him in the face, but I think he does know, and is worried, too.

"My own and your breeding situations are cases in point. He will not accept the truth when I tell him that our breeding problems only began after our blind support for the Dingay cause began to wane. And I don't believe for a moment that the sacred Khutani have anything to do with the matter, as the Dingay claim.

"The Dingay are doing this deliberately, to punish us. It's a threat, pure and simple—do as we tell you, or be destroyed in one generation." He broke off, unable to continue a subject that was altogether too personal and too painful to speak of, even to her.

Chelka's head crest drooped. She let him drink in silence for a while, but finally she said very carefully, "Brother mine, you are getting very drunk at the moment. You are safe here, among your own loyal kinsmen, but if you had the foolhardiness to mention even a fraction of what you've just said in Riath, even in our private suite there, I can see why our father rushed you home. That kind of talk has gotten more than one person killed."

He laughed bitterly. "Yes, it has, and I know it as well as you, or anyone else, for that matter." Aju'an slammed his bowl down on the table, splashing half its contents onto himself and the floor. He never even noticed.

"But damn it, Chelka, that's the whole problem! Everyone is either too afraid of the Dingay, or out to curry their favor at the expense of their neighbors. All the clans are going around whispering in corners, looking over their shoulders, scared a spy will tell the Dingay what they really think about them.

"So what if they do tell the Dingay? If we all stood together and confronted them—but no, we all continue to cower like Begta, each of us worrying about our own scales, afraid to act as a united front. And in the meantime, the Dingay and their pet Warlinga, like K'San Drucas Segoi, continue to pick us off one by one, until soon there will be no one strong enough or brave enough to oppose their will."

Chelka shuddered, and fell silent. It was a depressing but all too believable situation that he was describing, and nothing she could think of to say would either cheer him or alter his predictions. She lifted her bowl and took a long drink.

SOMETIME LATER, AS they both sat moodily drinking, Hunt Leader Fergannal approached them. He bowed to Chelka, then addressed Aju'an. "Young K'San, I think you should come see this—there has been an unfortunate death." He glanced warily at Chelka, as if unwilling to speak of the matter in her presence.

Not noticing the man's difficulty, Aju'an put down his bowl and snapped impatiently, "Come, speak, Fergannal. Out with it—has there been a fight?"

The man sighed, lowering his head crest in resignation. "No, San Aju'an, there hasn't been a fight; that isn't the problem. A few minutes ago, one of the sentries on duty thought he heard a pack of vistri fighting over something outside our gate. Curious, he went to investigate, and found that the vicious beasts had killed a lone Warlinga, and were fighting over the carcass.

"He called for help and drove off the vermin, but the man was dead. Perhaps you should come, and see for yourself," he suggested, giving Chelka another significant look.

Ignoring him, Chelka rose, along with her brother. Aju'an swayed, steadied himself on the edge of the table, and gave his sister a sour look. Chelka stuck out her long brown tongue at him and followed the men out into the night.

In the shelter near the gate, the guards had laid out the man's mangled corpse on a long stone table for Aju'an's viewing. The flickering torchlight showed, in grizzly detail how the man died. Suddenly cold sober, Aju'an stared down at the man—damned vistri.

Chelka let out a startled gasp. Maybe seeing this would make her forget about her warrior woman fantasies at last, Aju'an thought. "Anyone hurt driving off the beasts?"

"No, K'San."

Aju'an reached out and touched the bony forehead, stroking back the man's torn head crest. The face was almost intact. "By the Great Hunt Leader, what was he doing at our gate, alone, in the dark, like that? Anyone know him, or was he carrying anything that will tell us who he was?"

"Mar thinks he saw him on a visit to Ticca earlier this year," Fergannal said. "He is probably one of Hagar's kin, because we found this near the body when we drove off the vistri." Fergannal held up a belt strung with the man's belongings. It had been halfheartedly chewed, then abandoned for a juicier morsel. On the belt were a bone knife in its sheath, a punctured water bladder, a torn food sack, and what looked like a message pouch of some kind.

Aju'an pointed to the symbol on the pouch. "That does look like Ticca's emblem all right. Let me see it."

Fergannal slipped the pack from the tattered belt and handed it over. Aju'an stepped closer to the torch, Chelka crowding in to see as well. Opening the pouch, he pulled out a thick tube sealed at both ends. On the leather bottom of the scroll case the symbol of Ticca's island fortress was burnt into the hide. On the other end, where wax had been dripped over the leather cap to seal it, the symbol for the High Council at Riath was stamped.

Aju'an tapped the case thoughtfully with a clawed forefinger. Hmm, why would Ima Ngeal send off a lone runner at this time of year? Was Ticca in danger from the Hated Enemy? The tribes of the western Umwira had become very bold of late, but surely they weren't strong enough to pose any real threat to a fortress like Ticca.

Aju'an slipped the scroll case back into the bag, and then turned to his father's Hunt Leader. "Have someone carve out some of his bones for his relatives' death strands. The damned beasts have poisoned the meat for all but their own loathsome consumption, so have a hunting party bury the corpse away from the keep after first light tomorrow." He paused, then added, "And then send the priest to me in my chamber."

"Tonight, San Aju'an? He has already gone to bed," Fergannal said.

"Then wake him, Fergannal. I want to know what has happened at Ticca, now, tonight. It is obvious that this man's news was important; otherwise Ima Ngeal wouldn't have sent a runner to the Capital so close to the Sorins. If there is trouble I want to know—there may be no time to waste." Fergannal bowed, then motioned for Mar to go wake the priest.

ON THEIR WAY BACK TO his chamber, Chelka remained silent, not drawing attention to herself. In his room, she settled comfortably on one of his padded stools out of the way and waited, watching silently while Aju'an paced the brightly colored carpet, lost in his own thoughts. Finally there was a knock at the door, and the priest, followed by Hunt Leader Fergannal entered.

The old priest yawned, blinked, and bowed to Aju'an. "How may I serve you, San Aju'an?"

Aju'an pointed to the sealed scroll case on the table and explained, "That was taken from the body of a messenger who was attacked and killed tonight by a pack of vistri outside our gate. I need to know what news it contains."

Neyall crossed to the table and examined the case. He looked up in surprise. "This is addressed to the High Council, San Aju'an. I cannot—"

"Neyall, old friend, I can see that," Aju'an interrupted. "I know enough of your priestly glyphs to figure out who sent it and where it is bound. But the messenger who was carrying this is dead; I have no way to question him."

"But—"

"Oh, wake up and think, Ata," Aju'an snapped. "There is no time for me to send this on to the Capital before the storms hit. If there is trouble at Ticca—which obviously there is, or the Ima Matri wouldn't have sent off a runner. Then, as my father's representative, it is my duty to know what this scroll contains and send aid, if I can."

The priest considered, then nodded. Reaching forward, he broke the seal and read them the message it contained.

When he was gone, Aju'an slumped onto a stool, staring blindly at the far wall. A pity the woman had been so vague. There was talk in the Capital about Sagas Caltia turning renegade and destroying her own keep, with the aid of Umwira sorcerers. Aju'an dismissed such nonsense as just another of the Dingay slanders against their hated rivals.

But if these strange travelers that Ngeal made mention of were the outlawed priestess and her followers it might be very interesting to discover her version of what happened at Sulas.

In the interest of fairness, the High Council needed to know both sides of this issue before a judgment could be made. But if they waited to send aid till after the Sorins, Ticca Keep could already be destroyed, if the Dingay claims about the woman were true.

And if they weren't—well, another hunting pack sent from Riath might not care to discover the truth behind those outrageous Dingay claims, before the priestess had a most unfortunate accident.

Following this line of reasoning, Aju'an convinced himself that his father would want him to go to Ticca and seek out the truth of these terrible accusations, without delay. And, if it was indeed Sagas Caltia, and she truly was the traitor the Dingay had said—then, as acting head of the only available Warlinga force that could possibly make it to Ticca in time, it was his duty to reach the threatened keep before the Sorins struck.

It was a gamble to be sure. The storms could overtake them while they were still traveling—but that was what he determined to do. And he kept telling himself that, if his father were here, he would probably do the same thing.

When he expressed his decision to Fergannal, the man didn't like it. "I agree with your reasoning, young K'San, but you yourself should stay here. I will lead the hunt."

Aju'an tightened his jaw and gave him a stern look. "I think not, Hunt Leader. My father left you in charge of Meh'gach in his absence. You can't be spared for this hunt. There are too many last minute details needing your attention before the Long Confinement. I will lead this hunt myself. I'm the only one that can be spared to do it."

Reluctantly, Fergannal agreed and left to gather supplies and a strong, well-armed hunting pack, so that Aju'an could leave at first light.

When the Hunt Leader had gone about his errands, Chelka rose from her place and faced him. "Aju'an, let me come with you."

He had forgotten all about her being here, and stared at her stupidly for a moment, then, head crest flattening in annoyance, he said, "No! What are you talking about? Of course not. This is a hunt, not a renewal outing—we have no idea what we will find when we get to Ticca. Don't be stupid!"

Tail lashing the carpet she swore a vial barracks oath and snapped, "I know very well it isn't going to be an outing, and I'm not being stupid. I'm perfectly capable of taking care of myself if there's a fight."

"No! Absolutely not. Father would never forgive me."

"And since when have our father's opinions ever stopped you before?" she countered.

"No, Chelka, the answer is no," he growled. "No matter what you say, the answer will remain no, so save your breath."

"Aju'an, please," she begged, trying hard not to break down, "this may be my only chance to know what it's like, before father locks me away in some K'San's accavett. Please, brother, let me come!"

"No, I can't and I won't. I love you too much. If anything happened to you I would never forgive myself—never mind facing father's wrath. The answer is no, and that's the end of it." Taking her hand, he ran his tongue over its glossy scales. "Now get out of here and go to bed. I have a lot to do before I can sleep."

Furious, Chelka jerked her hand out of his grasp and stomped from the room, slamming the door as she went. Aju'an sighed, then dismissed her from his mind and went to check his gear.

MUCH LATER, IN THE stillness before dawn, two shadowy figures slipped silently out Meh'gach's side gate into the gloom.

Chapter Two

Dunnagh-Tani yawned and stretched, enjoying the sensuous feel of the water in Ticca's kashallan pool against his bare skin. He was lying in the shallows, head resting on the padded pool rim, the faintly phosphorescent blue liquid amercing him to the neck in its comforting warmth. This pool, like all Khutani-inhabited pools, lay in a large cavern deep within the bedrock. Glowing fungus in many colors ran in luminous streaks down the rock walls and hung from long crystal formations dripping from the shadowy darkness above.

He took in a deep breath and smelled the aromatic, spicy scent of the mists hovering above the water. Mm, it was a comforting, homey smell—at least to Tani, the Khutani symbiont part of him. Far out in the darkness, Dunnagh heard a pod of the young cousins splashing and playing. In his middle the dozing young symbiont stirred in response. He stroked his middle in a soothing gesture. He'd no wish to spoil his mood by joining in a boisterous game of tag at the moment.

Ticca Keep. They had made it at last. He and his band of human and native followers had overcome the hardships of a trek across the Great Swamp, battled with the keep's misguided defenders, and won Ticca for their own. They'd claimed their Sorin sanctuary. While the poisoned winds scoured the land, his people would be safe and protected. He felt good, able to relax for the first time since fleeing Sulas Keep months before.

Swimming up to him in the shallows, a long, sinuous body coiled itself loosely about his pale legs, and nuzzled its sleek, gray head against the chest of the symbiont's human host. Dunnagh-Tani reached out a tentacled hand and formed the link, letting his new guardian know that he was well—yes, very well. He yawned again, and reached out to run his free hand down the flank of his other companion.

Curled up beside him, head resting on the cushioned pool rim, his long brown hair had come loose from its braid, and floated about his muscular torso in feathery tendrils. Nathan still slept soundly. Dunnagh studied that well-loved face with its high cheekbones, strong nose, full lips, and listened to his slow, even breathing. It was so good to have Nathan here with him in the pools; he wished Nathan wasn't so unwilling to make a kashallan bond.

Nathan needed someone to love and take care of him. After losing his family so young, he'd always been terrified of being alone. But he couldn't stay with Tessa much longer. Her spirit bondmate's demands were taking their toll.

Nathan was being stubborn of course, and paying a high price for his loyalty. It would be hard for him to let go. But with a bondmate of his own, he would never be lonely—and the two kashallans could share so much—maybe even more than they once had. Well, for now at least, he would have to be content with his dreams.

Dunnagh let out a wistful sigh; it was hard being the only kashallan. They expected so much of him—the elders and the Avairei were always fussing...

He'd been such a fool to break off their physical closeness years ago. And now? Well, as Nathan kept pointing out to him, things were too complicated to resume that part of their friendship. *But at least*, he thought, *our love in other ways has withstood the tests of time.*

From somewhere on the latticework of stone walkways that allowed the keep's inhabitants access to this watery realm, Dunnagh listened to an Avairei priest rap a beater-stick against a stone pool rim, calling the young Khutani to a meal. The young broke off their play, squealing in excitement as they raced towards the sound.

Fully awakened by the noise, Tani writhed, hunger aroused by the clamor—and his own hunger too. The Khutani encircling him raised its head; delicate mouth tentacles brushed over his human face.

<<Are you hungry, child? I will feed you. >>

Personally, Dunnagh would have rather sat down to a nice meal of roast meat, masa root cakes hot off the griddle, and a bowl of cool mushroom beer. He *was* hungry, but he wasn't going anywhere for the moment, so he might as well take his nursemaid/protector, up on its offer. He obediently opened his mouth and allowed the Khutani to insert a rubbery feeding tube between his lips. As the Khutani regurgitated a creamy blue liquid that tasted to Dunnagh something like a lemony coconut milkshake.

As he swallowed his meal, he tried not to think about the actual process needed to secure their refuge. They had had to take Ticca by force, because of Dingay lies. Using the high-tech weaponry they'd brought with them, the Kashallan and his human warriors scaled the outer wall of the keep at night and fought a quick and bloody battle with Ticca's defenders. By the time he made his way to the underground pools where his Khutani kin lived, the symbiont, Tani, was so upset that it vomited, in all its gory detail, the whole story of their ordeal since fleeing Sulas.

In hindsight both bondmates realized that that had been a bad mistake. What their tale of woe did was get everyone upset. The young Khutani had attacked a Dingay priestess without cause, and his outraged Khutani elders had confined him to the pools, until they were assured of his safety in the keep above.

That restriction hadn't been part of the plan, and Dunnagh had worked very hard to ease Maker Dievris's mind about his safety. Having everyone in Ticca come down to the pool so the Khutani elder could "Taste" them and take their oaths of fealty helped. Dunnagh also suggested that the Maker form a link with his best friend, Nathan, who was one of his military commanders as well.

As Dunnagh expected, Nathan was nervous when he entered the pool. But once Maker Dievris obtained his submission to its will, and wrapped him in its massive coils; it had been surprisingly gentle with him.

The bondmates secretly congratulated themselves, when the Maker told them later how pleased it was after tasting Nathan. They had suspected that he would be a good choice as the first one of Dunnagh's human kin, who now called themselves the Speir'dina, to be examined by such an unyielding ancient.

Dievris spoke with Nathan a long time, and seemed to respond with both surprise and pleasure when it learned of the caring that now bound host, symbiont, and Speir'dina warrior to each other. It had even concluded its time with the big man by doing a healing on his injuries itself, rather than leaving such a task to the Kashallan, or to others of the younger kindred.

The Maker showed another mark of its favor by treating Nathan as if he were a young kashallan, and put him to sleep in the pool where he had lain for the healing. Later, after the oath taking was over, it made the exhausted Dunnagh-Tani lie beside him to rest as well. Before it left them, it gave Dunnagh-Tani a mild sedative and posted another one of the kindred to watch over the sleepers.

SOMETIME LATER AS A full and sleepy Dunnagh-Tani was drifting back to sleep, his Khutani guard tightened its coils protectively around him, raised its head out of the water and gave out a menacing hiss. The Kashallan opened his eyes and looked around. A washed and cleaned-up Oglas stood by the pool's edge. He reached out a hand and reassured the Khutani. The guardian lowered its head and stopped hissing, but remained with its coils still wrapped about his legs. "What is it, Oglas?"

The armachd saluted. "Sorry to wake you, Ce'awn, (chieftain) but the Commander wants to know if you'll be coming up anytime soon. He sent for the rest of our people a while ago, and one of the guards on the wall has just sighted them approaching the Swamp causeway. He thought you would want to be there to greet them."

"Mm, yes, I would, thank you, armachd. What time is it?"

"Late afternoon, Ce'awn."

Dunnagh rubbed a hand across his face. "Gods, why didn't someone wake me earlier? What's been going on? Have you people had any rest?"

"Yes, Ce'awn, we've been trading off our duties and getting our share of rest. The Ima Sagas, she said not to wake you; said she and the Commander could take care of what needed to be done. She was most insistent-like."

"Mm, I bet. Well, tell the Commander that I'll be up shortly."

Oglas saluted then paused, his glance shifting to the still sleeping Nathan. "Is Nathan all right?"

The Kashallan glanced down at the sleeping man and nodded. "Yeah, he's all right. He got his ribs busted again from a well-aimed Warlinga tail during the fight. The Maker put him to sleep so the injuries could begin healing. I'll wake him up and bring him along. Go on upstairs and tell them we're coming. And, Oglas—if the Imas Ngeal and Sagas aren't too tired ask them to join us."

"They're already there waiting for you, Ce'awn, as are most of Ticca's inhabitants,"

When Oglas was gone, the Kashallan explained to his Khutani protector that he and Nathan would be going into the keep soon. Dievris had already given its permission. It had conceded that the Chosen, Dunnagh, had a responsibility to his followers and his family, and needed to be with them.

The bondmates had won their freedom, but with the proviso that they come back frequently to communicate with the Council within the pools. The Elders dreams had warned them that the Kashallan was still in danger. Even though the keep had sworn them fealty, the Khutani were worried about this unknown threat.

Information given, the Kashallan broke the link. Leaning over his friend he kissed the sleeping man. "Wake up," he breathed next to his ear. "Tizu has sent for the Speir'dina; we need to get up now. They'll be here soon."

Nathan stirred and yawned. He grunted a noncommittal reply, and settled himself more comfortably against the pool's headrest.

"Come on, it's time to get up." Still smiling, Dunnagh bent down to kiss him again, but as their lips met Nathan reached out and pulled him roughly atop him, and returned the kiss with rising passion. The movement must have jarred his healing ribs, because suddenly he broke off both kiss and embrace with a gasp, and opened his eyes.

Nathan pushed him away and sat up, blinking, as if not sure where he was. "Sorry, I didn't mean to do that—I was still half asleep." His voice trailed off and he looked away, reddening in embarrassment.

The Kashallan took in several deep breaths, trying to stop his natural response to that kiss. Damn him—keeping his newly-found resolve to stop trying to seduce him was going to be harder than he expected if Nathan did that again. "I didn't mean to startle you," Dunnagh said, when he could speak once more.

Back turned to him Nathan grunted. The Kashallan let him sit for a long moment, then reached over and began untangling the mess of his wet brown hair. At his touch, Nathan stiffened, but didn't pull away. "Don't worry; your virtue is safe with me. I just want to re-braid your hair a bit. We have to go up soon; the clan is coming. Tizu sent Oglas down to fetch us."

Nathan grunted again, then relaxed and leaned into the rhythmic combing motions Dunnagh was making. He closed his eyes and sighed.

Then he felt a mild sexual arousal. Nathan's eyes flew open. "Hey, I thought you said—" Across his lap a gray, sinewy form slid, then twined itself around his hips. He heard Dunnagh laugh softly behind him, and let out a slow, ragged breath. "Damn you anyway. I bet you planned this," Nathan grumbled.

Still laughing Dunnagh said, "No I didn't—but I know what you're feeling. Relax; it just wants to check on your injuries."

When he felt the Khutani's mouth tentacles gently sink into his side, Nathan jumped in spite of Dunnagh's warning. <<Sorry, young one,>> came the hollow Khutani voice into his mind. <<I didn't mean to startle you. I know you will be leaving soon, and I want to taste your injuries one last time so I will know how the healing is progressing. Now take in some deep breaths and let me know if your ribs still hurt.>>

Nathan did as it asked, all erotic thoughts driven from his mind by the Khutani's clinical manner. He took in several deep breaths, and had to admit that, though they felt much better, his ribs still hurt a little. No sooner had he mentally voiced that, than he felt a soothing warmth penetrating the affected area and easing the pain. When the soreness was completely gone, he gave the Khutani his thanks, and it disentangled itself from around his waist.

The Kashallan retied the end of Nathan's braid and stood up. He looked down at his friend, and raised an inquiring eyebrow. "You coming?"

Nathan nodded and slowly stood up, gingerly feeling his ribs. The pain was indeed gone. "Yeah, I'm coming. Where are my clothes?" Already at the edge of the pool, the Kashallan pointed to a dark pile heaped up beside the cavern's wall. Nathan grimaced, hating to put the filthy things back on, but he saw no way around it, unless he wanted to go up there naked.

When he picked up the first article of his clothes, he received a pleasant surprise. Someone had washed out the worst of the blood from his things while he slept. They were still damp, but he put them on gratefully. He strapped his weapons belt around his waist and looked around. The

Kashallan was straightening a few folds on his kilt. He glanced up and smiled. "You about ready?"

Nathan nodded.

The Kashallan's smile widened. "Then let's go welcome them. We've worked long and hard to get here, and I feel like celebrating and forgetting about the past for a while. We have our refuge for the Sorin season, so we might as well enjoy it—the Gods alone know what will happen afterwards." Nathan gave him a conspiratorial grin and they headed up the stairs.

Chapter Three

The matriarch of Ticca, Ima Ngeal Maveth stood with her councilors, Hobral and Quellyn on the steps outside the inner keep, waiting for the rest of the outlawed band to arrive. They had dressed in their best ceremonial garb for the occasion. Ngeal wore the heavy metal inlaied collar and long red kilt with its lacy blue embroidery around its hem that was the outward trappings of her office as Ima Matri here.

Pushing back her mane of ornamented braidlets she tried to keep the worry she felt from showing on her cat-like Avairei face. Nearby, Ima Sagas, beads of moisture still clinging to her velvety brown fur from her bath, talked in a low voice to the ugly black-clad figure of the Speir'dina Hunt Leader, Tizu. Sagas was still wearing the patched and stained kilt she'd worn when she came along with the raiders, but she had made some attempt to wash out the worst of the blood and grime. What were they talking about so intently?

Ngeal looked away, glancing out into the courtyard instead. She had no wish to be drawn into their conversation—whatever it was. She'd had enough of their company for a while, that was for certain. Out in the courtyard, she searched the animated faces of Ticca's inhabitants. Nearly everyone was gathered here waiting for the arrival of the outlaws who hadn't come with the Kashallan. Were they truly that excited, [r were they merely concealing their true feelings as she was herself.

Fear still gnawed at her heart, in spite of Khutani assurances and her curiosity about the host's kin. She had seen the dead after the battle. And, as Amril had pointed out to her, Speir'dina weaponry was similar to the great technology possessed by the ancient race that had almost destroyed their world in the past.

Yet the Speir'dina did have the favor of the Holy Ones in the pools—that was obvious. She truly believed that the Khutani, with their powerful magics, had called them here to become the new host race for their symbiont children. Surely the Makers, the oldest and wisest of the Khutani, must have known about their weapons and their other disturbing qualities. Oh, Mother, surely.

As the new host race, the Speir'dina deserved her loyalty and respect, although they were definitely going to take some getting used to, Sagas was right about that. And, her former student was also telling the truth about another thing—the Speir'dina were a stubborn, strong-willed people, with their own ways of doing things.

Unlike the Timornan Warlinga posted to defend an Avairei keep, these creatures weren't about to bow to any Avairei's will unless they could see the sense in it. It hadn't taken long for her and the one called Tizu to clash. Ngeal wasn't used to explaining her decisions to any *Hunt Leader*, and found she resented it.

When she gave an order to some of the guards, which he disapproved of, he had demanded an explanation from her. She had, naturally, out of habit, refused to give it. That had been a big mistake, she later realized. He made it very clear to her, in ways that none of *her* Warlinga would ever have dared to do, that from now on she *would* be required to explain herself when it came to matters concerning the defense and safety of Ticca Keep.

"It's *my* duty to protect this fortress and its inhabitants, Ima, and I'm damn good at my job. Ima Matri or not, you will explain your *recommendations* to me, and I will decide whether to implement them or not. In matters of security, you will take orders like the rest of the civilians, or else. And I don't care one bit whether you like it or not, because you *will* do it, just the same."

Ngeal was astounded by his bullying attitude towards someone in her position. Her species, her authority, and her outrage meant nothing to him. As tough-minded as any Ima Matri, he held his ground and refused to change his position.

Catching sight of Sagas's amusement at one point in their heated confrontation, Ngeal was furious with the woman for not coming to her defense, as a good Avairei Ima should, when her authority was being threatened by such an insolent male. She told Sagas so right then and there, but, to her further astonishment, the younger priestess heatedly sided with the Speir'dina.

"San Tizu is a very experienced Hunt Leader, Ima; he will know what is best for us. You must stop trying to interfere."

That stopped Ngeal cold. "Have you lost your mind along with your keep? A stupid Warlinga telling Avairei what to do!"

"Tizu isn't a stupid Warlinga," Sagas snapped. "He can read and write in his own language as good as any Avairei can in ours."

Ngeal gaped. After that revelation, she was unable to continue the argument. Shocked by her former student's attitude, as much as she was by the fact that the Speir'dina could read, she could think of nothing further to say. Truly these outlaws were an unconventional bunch.

Their loyalty to the Kashallan bound them together in a revolutionary way. No matter what their original clan or race, they defended one another fiercely when challenged by an outsider. Among them, an Avairei might even defend a thieving Begta, if the disgusting little creature was one of them. Truly, they were an odd bunch, and not just the Speir'dina. That Avairei who came on the raid and wore his mane in one braid like the warriors, was just as alien as the rest of the band.

What would the remainder of these wild outlaws be like? Ngeal's glance turned to the off-duty Speir'dina clustered near the open gate. Dressed in black clothing of an alien design, they talked and joked with one another in an unknown language, their ugly faces animated with their triumph.

She shivered, and pulled her cloak a little closer around her shoulders. It was getting late, the light was waning and the mist coming in from the lake. Where were the others? This waiting was intolerable.

Dismissing those unsettling thoughts, Ngeal focused her attention on the people waiting in the courtyard below her. The younger Avairei seemed excited about meeting the rest of the outlaws. All thoughts of the deaths put aside, they were laughing and talking animatedly among themselves, braid ornaments jingling in the heavy evening air. The older Avairei, like herself, stood quietly, still cautious.

Hmm, where was Amril? Ngeal noticed that he wasn't among the excited young folk, as she would have expected. At first she thought he might have been too tired from his ordeal, and was just sleeping in his cell. But, upon another survey of the courtyard, she finally located him, over by the open gate among the outlaws.

He was talking to the old Ata named Temog, who was the Speir'dina healer, and that insolent young Avairei, Tama, or Timil, or something like that, who had come with the warriors. That young man was a disgrace. She gave them a sour look. Why, by the Great Mother, was Amril over there with that bunch of misfits?

She would have to have a talk with that young Ata. He was definitely not going to start behaving like that disgraceful lot—not if she had anything to say about it.

After the oath taking, Ngeal sought out Amril Caltia for a private talk. She had always had a special affection for Sagas and her younger brother. Amril was a student here at Ticca, before he ran away from the keep to join his sister and the Kashallan. She had found Amril, working with the Speir'dina healers. Calling Amril away from them, Ngeal shepherded him out of the cavern. In her chambers, she had demanded to know as much as he could tell her about the outlaws and their ways.

Granted, the young Ata had only been in their camp for a short time, but what he had observed was very disturbing, to say the least. The blue-eyed creature who was now the Kashallan had warned her that there would be changes. He had joked with her about it at the oath taking, saying that this Sorin season would be *interesting*.

Appalled by his flippancy at the time, she was now afraid he might be right. She could only hope that most of these changes would be for the good of her world, and not the beginnings of its near destruction once again.

Thinking of the outlaws made her consider the woman who had listened to the Khutani and helped create this new kashallan, her former student, Sagas. She glanced out of the corner of her eye at her. The woman's recent behavior caused her mouth to tighten with worry. Right now the woman was standing unusually close to the black-clad, Tizu. They were talking too quietly to be heard from where she stood, but the light in her eyes disturbed Ngeal as she listened to the man.

There was something odd about those two. Sagas was behaving almost like a young woman in love—but with him? An ugly, flat-faced alien? No, that kind of perversion was too disgusting to be believed. Surely Sagas hadn't lost all sense of decency, and changed *that* much—she couldn't be in love—she was too old for breeding.

Oh, well, that was a problem for another day. Right now there were other things to think about. On the far side of the courtyard near the Warlinga barracks, a dejected group of the lizardmen slouched against the outer wall.

She had learned from Amril, to her dismay, that Hunt Leader Hagar had been one of the casualties. That had deeply grieved her. He had been a good and loyal defender, and they had worked well together—which was more than she could say about Ticca's present Hunt Leader. Their flattened head crests and bewildered faces, told Ngeal that Hagar's surviving kinsmen were taking his death very hard indeed.

No matter what their personal feelings, like everyone else in Ticca, they were *made* to swear fealty to the new kashallan—or die. For the moment, they were cowed by their experiences, and by their fear of the Speir'dina's powerful weaponry. But something would have to be done about them, because, left on their own without direction, their mood could quickly sour into violence.

Out of the corner of her eye Ngeal noticed Tizu also eyeing them speculatively. *Hmm, perhaps he does know his job. He seems to be aware of the potential for trouble there, if the expression on his ugly, alien face is any indication.*

How odd this Tizu was; how did he gain such respect among his people—did he have magical powers? Hairless golden skin, dark eyes and black maned, he was one of the smallest of his species, no bigger than an Avairei male—only a bit more muscular than the slimly-built men of her own race.

And yet the other, mostly larger and stronger, male and female Speir'dina warriors all obeyed him without question, in spite of his size and lack of powerful teeth and claws to enforce his will. That was just another enigma about these strangers that needed answering.

Suddenly, from the shore of the lake, Ngeal heard an eerie sound. At first she wasn't sure if it was real, or just some of the weird effects the Swamp made at times. As the sound came closer she thought she heard drums beating out a lively rhythm, accompanying the wailing noise. Straining to hear, Ngeal held up her hand for silence. Around her, the others on the steps broke off their own conversations to listen. "What is that strange noise?" Ngeal finally asked of no one in particular.

Tizu listened for a moment longer, then cursed in his own language. Turning to Sagas, he growled, "Now I know why that fool Tarla was so eager to be sent back to the camp. He and one of the Begta must have fixed his pipes for this occasion. Shit! I'm going to make him eat that thing when I get hold of him."

From behind them, the sound of delighted laughter made the waiting group turn in surprise. In the doorway, the Kashallan and Nathan stood, listening to the music of the Caldoni pipes.

Away from the Maker's confining coils, Ngeal could now see all of him for the first time. Almost as tall and muscular as the Warlinga lizardmen, he wore several votive necklaces on his pale, furless chest, and a kilt made of the same black material as his warrior's uniforms. His red-gold hair was braided into many long, thin braidlets, like an Avairei instead of the one braid his warriors favored. Flung loosely around his shoulders was an Avairei-furred cape.

He was standing beside his brown-maned kinsman, listening to the sounds coming from the causeway and grinning happily. Like a child in a man's body, she thought, then started at that description, for, in a way, that was indeed exactly what he was.

This Kashallan-bonded pair was a strange blending of the mature and the young—an adult male host and a Khutani child. Now they were both bound by the Kashallan oath and bond, the two parts of himself striving for some kind of balance with one another. She guessed that each traded the dominance of their shared flesh, as the expertise of one or the other was needed.

Coming down onto the steps beside the already assembled group, the Kashallan nodded a greeting to the Avairei then laughed again at Tizu's sour expression. "Why, Hukiyo, all your years among the Lann Gheal Caldoni, and we still haven't managed to teach you any musical appreciation?"

Tizu snorted. "Music? Sounds like two tomcats fighting to me," he grumbled.

"The man has no musical *taste*," Nathan quipped, and then he and the Kashallan started laughing, even more boisterously.

"Ha, ha, a little Khutani humor there, Nathan. My, my, getting a little cozy with the snaky folk, aren't we? Planning on a lifestyle change sometime soon, hmm?"

At Nathan's startled expression, Tizu gave him a wolfish grin.

The Kashallan chortled, doubling over with his mirth.

Nathan scowled. "That isn't funny and you know it—the Geish is off, I'm not making a bond."

"Hey, what is it with you two?" Glaring at the Kashallan, Tizu asked gruffly, "Did those big, snaky relatives of yours make you and this other idiot here eat some kind of funny food, or what? You're acting like assholes, the pair of you."

Ngeal's nostrils flared with indignation. The impertinence of this arrogant, overbearing man was intolerable. How dare he speak to one of the Sacred Khutani and its host in such a manner? Near her, she could feel the outrage of her councilors building. She was about to blast Tizu, and Nathan too, for their disrespect; when Sagas laid a restraining hand on her arm.

"Don't interfere with them," she warned in a low voice, staring fiercely at each Avairei in turn. "The Chosen and his kin talk like that to each other all the time, and the symbiont doesn't mind—really it doesn't. Tani even joins them in their insulting banter at times, so leave it alone.

"If you try to reprimand the Hunt Leader or any of the other Speir'dina for their insolence, the Khutani will be more likely to reprimand you for *your* interference, rather than thank you for coming to its defense."

Ngeal stared incredulously, but reluctantly heeded her former student's guidance. However strange her advice seemed to her, Sagas had been right about her warnings before.

The Kashallan glanced at the Avairei. In a lower voice he said, "Maybe you're right, Commander. I guess we aren't setting a very *dignified* example, are we?"

"Damn right. You two laughing amadans and Tarla and his pipes—who, I might add, is going to be pulling the shittiest duty I can think up for him, after this. All of you are giving me and everyone else around here a headache, so behave yourselves."

"If you really do have a headache, San Tizu, and are not just teasing my Kasha, I would be glad to help you get rid of it," Tani offered, extending a tentacled hand.

Nathan doubled over as Tizu's face froze into a horrified mask.

"No, thanks, Tani, I *was* just teasing your—uh—Kasha," Tizu muttered.

Giving Tizu an anxious glance, Sagas said hastily, "You seem happy, Holy One. Your time among your kindred must have been very pleasant. Did you rest well?"

The Kashallan smiled and put an arm around her shoulders. He kissed her forehead. "Very well, Dear Ima. I think the Ancient One must have given Nathan and me something special, as Hukiyo suggested, for I do feel wonderful. But perhaps it is just the relief of finally being safely here, after so much trouble and pain. I'm not sure what is the cause of my mood, but it feels good to be alive." He hugged her close, and smiled down at her affectionately.

Sagas returned his smile for a moment, then sobered. "I am glad that you are happy, and safe, but, Kashallan, don't forget the Sweh'an's warning. There may still be danger for you here."

You will have what you hunger for, Khutani, but be careful what you taste. Soon your enemies will know you for what you really are, and they will not be as easy to rise above as the stonewalls of the keep.

The Kashallan's face clouded, the lines of his mouth taking on a grim expression. "I haven't forgotten that most infuriating demon spirit's words to me. Not any of them," he said. "But, for the moment, I would like to enjoy this day, and my hard-won feelings of peace. Do you begrudge me this brief respite from my worries and responsibilities, Sagas?"

Startled, she stepped back, shaking her head. "No, Kashallan, no indeed. I am sorry." Her voice trailed off in confusion.

The Kashallan chuckled and pulled her close again. "It's all right. I know you meant well, but just let it be for now, Sagas, all right?"

Nathan tapped him on the shoulder. "Look, here they come," he said and jumped down the last few steps to the ground.

Ngeal had been distracted by the troubling interaction between the Kashallan and his Hunt Leaders, and missed the approaching clan's arrival until Nathan spoke. Now she stared open-mouthed, like the rest of Ticca's inhabitants. The Speir'dina, this keep would be their home during the Sorins—and maybe longer.

Before the plague Ticca had housed a much larger population than now, so at least there were several unused wings that the outlaws could take over as their own. That would minimize tension between her people and the newcomers—she hoped. Living with them during The Confinement was going to be a test of endurance, Ngeal could see that already.

Chapter Four

The first inside Ticca's gate were more of the black-clad warriors, the drummers and a large male playing the strange musical instrument at the front of the column. They marched in, two abreast, singing a wild, triumphant song in an alien tongue, the words of which Ngeal couldn't understand, but whose intent was unmistakable.

As they entered they fanned out, giving the assembled people a good look at their exotic alienness. After the warriors, the other Speir'dina men and women, and the native Timornans of their band, came in, also singing and keeping time with the drums.

The Speir'dina males and females who were not in black were dressed in a mixture of bizarre, bright clothing, with their manes elaborately styled. Even the native Timornans had adorned themselves for this occasion. Ngeal scowled, noticing with distaste a few Begta among the newcomers, their necks weighed down under the many shiny objects they wore. She sighed, wondering how much mischief the horrid things would cause, and knowing that, under the circumstances, she couldn't make them leave.

As they filed by, Ngeal noticed that even the usually sensible Loti among these outlaws wore woven headbands and bright strips of cloth braided into their long tails. Nestled in the shaggy fur of their upper torsos, Ngeal saw the usual bone and seed necklaces, but around their arms and on all four clawed feet they were wearing colored bracelets as well.

Watching the flamboyant display, it was obvious to Ngeal that this entrance into Ticca had been well-staged and planned in advance to create a specific impression upon their audience. This show had definitely been designed to make a statement in which this people's alien uniqueness was enhanced, rather than minimized.

The Speir'dina seemed to be saying, "We are here, and we will host the Khutani, but we are not the docile Bebech. We will still remain ourselves.

Timornans we may be now, and we will accept that reality; we will work with you, and fight alongside you, but we will not be ruled by any of you. We are the Speir'dina, the people from out of the sky, and we are a power to be reckoned with in your society from now on."

Ngeal shuddered—it was a challenging declaration. Tearing her eyes away from the scene in the courtyard, she glanced over at the outlaws clustered around her. Judging by their astonished, yet delighted, faces, and Tizu's muttered comment about show-off Dymarians corrupting his troops (whatever that meant), this performance had not been expected by them.

Turning once more to the entrance, Ngeal caught sight of another strange phenomenon. Near the end of the line, she saw three women, two Speir'dina and one Avairei, sitting astride their Loti companions in a way she had never seen before. The gentle Loti, whose duties sometimes included carrying a high-ranking priest or priestess in a litter, often carried Avairei. But to sit astride their backs—why, she had never seen nor heard of such a thing. More changes, she thought grimly.

Their torsos bare, they were dressed in Avairei women's kilts with cloaks fastened about their shoulders. The Speir'dina women's manes were twined with bright strips of cloth, and the young priestess with them was attired just as outrageously. As regal as any High Matri attending a fair, they entered Ticca surrounded by a laughing, dancing chorus of their outlaw kindred. Ngeal saw that the light-haired Speir'dina female and the Avairei priestess were far along in their breeding cycles.

The Kashallan and Nathan saw the approaching women at about the same time as she did. With glad cries, and all semblance of dignity forgotten, they hurried across the courtyard, to greet them.

Ngeal frowned, then touched Sagas's arm, drawing her slightly away from the Hunt Leader and the other Avairei. "Who are those women?" she asked in a low voice.

Startled, Sagas turned. "Which women, teacher?"

Ngeal hissed in exasperation. "Don't be dense, Sagas. "I'm talking about the three women sitting in that odd way atop the Loti."

Sagas sighed. "I'm not being *dense*, Ima. I am just so used to seeing the Kashallan and others of his kin ride the Loti in that manner that I forgot for a moment how strange they must seem to you, that's all." She looked back to the courtyard, then added, "The two who are breeding are the Kashallan's wives. The dark-maned one—well, she is sort of mated to San Nathan, at the moment."

Ngeal heard Sagas's hesitation, but let it pass, more intrigued by the prospect of Avairei matings with the new host species. "I would not have expected such an alien race to be fertile with us."

Sagas gave a short bark of a laugh. "Under normal circumstances, I doubt if the Speir'dina are fertile with any of the native Timornans. But now that they have the kavay in their blood, they are like the rest of us—their fertility cycle, if not their erotic urges, will be controlled by the red kavay's dictates. As to this particular mating, the host has a lively interest in erotic couplings, and enjoys his partners. And as for the breeding, the Khutani symbiont, with the aid of the red kavay, took care of any incompatibilities that may have been there to start with."

"And what of the other Speir'dina female?"

"She and her child were an unexpected gift. I gather from my priestess that she was the host's mate, and already carrying his child before they were separated—when he was brought to Sulas for the bonding. We didn't know about her at the time, because the host believed she was dead, but she has made the transition to our ways quite well. She and Pela have even sworn the sister-wife bond together."

Ngeal looked at her sharply, but said nothing. It was Sagas's right to oversee such a breeding—but to *Pela*? *Oh, my poor Amril, finding out that your promised love was the bride of another must have been terrible for you.*

WHEN THE KASHALLAN and Nathan approached, the music stopped and the outlaws gathered round their leaders. Holding his hands out wide to them, the Kashallan threw back his head and laughed. "Oh, welcome, my people, welcome."

They cheered him with great exuberance, and for the next few minutes the courtyard was awash in a chaotic flow of sound and color as the Speir'dina greeted the Kashallan, and exclaimed over their new home. Unsure what was expected of them, Ima Ngeal and her councilors remained where they were on the steps. Ngeal heard Tizu swearing softly as he watched the disorderly scene.

Stepping close to Sagas, Tizu glanced out of the corner of his eye at the bewildered Avairei and murmured, "I think we had better have Arishim or Bennett give our boy down there some badly-needed lessons in diplomacy. This display may be great for *our* people, but your Ima friend there seems pretty unsettled.

"I'll be the first to admit that we're a weird bunch, but out in the Swamp it didn't matter. We're going to have a rough time of it here during the Sorin storms, even with Khutani backing, if we can't win these people's love and co-operation." He motioned with a jerk of his head to the scene below. "And this little show isn't making a good impression, I'm thinking."

Sagas sighed, also glancing round at their companions. "Mm, I think you're probably right, Hukiyo. But Ngeal is very loyal, to the Khutani, at least, and once she understands a bit more of our story, she will be willing to put up with quite a bit."

Tizu grunted, unconvinced. "If you can get the Ima and her councilors to move away from the steps and go down to him, so they can meet Arishim, Bennett, and some of the others, I'll start getting the rest of these idiots organized and into the quarters that have already been arranged for them."

Sagas nodded. "Good idea."

COMING UP TO HIS STILL-mounted wives, finally, the Kashallan greeted the Loti, Berren and Mashen, then smiled up happily at the women. "Hello, loves, enjoy your ride?" Reaching up, he helped Pela from Mashen's back, enfolded her in his arms, bent, and kissed her. A moment later he did the same for Sairsa, then, with an arm about each of them, he looked around to see how the settling-in was progressing.

To his relief, Tizu seemed to have things well under control. Nearby, clan elders, Arishim and Bennett were talking quietly with Tessa and Nathan. He smiled to himself; even in their travel-worn robes, they looked festive in the woven headbands. In the next moment a troubled look came into his eyes.

Where was Singey? The Kashallan glanced around, trying to find his friend in the confusion.

"Kashallan?" Sagas called. She was heading towards him across the congested courtyard; the Avairei dignitaries trailing along uncertainly in her wake.

With some dismay, he suddenly realized that, in the excitement of the arriving Speir'dina, he had forgotten all about the Ima Matri and her councilors. <<Tani, Clan elder Arishim is going to give us the sharp side of her tongue for this one.>>

<<Mm, true enough, Kasha, we did forget.>>

Reddening in shame, he waved to Sagas, then, catching Bennett's eye, he motioned for him and Arishim to join him.

Coming up to the Avairei, wives in tow, he bowed deeply to them. "Ima Ngeal, please forgive me. Neither Tani nor I are used to playing this type of role," Dunnagh explained. "I am sorry; I meant no disrespect by abandoning you and your councilors."

Ngeal bowed as well, accepting his apology with good grace. As she straightened, she became aware of two newcomers making their way towards them. The gray of their manes and their dignified manner alerted her to their high rank among the outlaws. The weariness around their eyes and the lines etched into their hairless faces told another story. This trek across the Great Swamp must have been an exhausting trial for them.

The Kashallan glanced quickly around, once more looking for Singey. Still not locating the missing scientist, he sighed, and returned his attention to the group around him. "Clan elders, Bennett, Arishim, I'd like you to meet Ima Matri Ngeal. And this is her Ata Leyas, Ata Hobral, and Ticca's Lore Mistress, Ima Quellyn. Imas, Ata, I'd like you to meet two of our Speir'dina clan elders, Sa Meldra Arishim, and San Hyram Bennett.

"These two were both highly respected people in our old home. San Bennett was a famous healer, among other things, and Sa Arishim—" He paused, considering. "Our traditions are quite different, you must understand, but I guess you might say she was something like a High Matri among us."

Arishim chuckled, but shook her head. "My Ce'awn does me an undeserved honor, Ima Ngeal. My former role would be better described as being one of the people chosen to sit on the High Council that ruled my world, rather than filling the important position of the High Matri's seat."

Giving Ngeal one of his famous winning smiles, Bennett said, "And I, too, would have to add that my Ce'awn gives me more credit than I deserve. True, I once was considered a fair enough healer, but our ways of practicing medicine are so different from how things are done here that I have had to begin as a student, and learn my craft all over again. On Timorna, Ima, I am no more than one of the Kashallan's and Ata Temog's apprentices."

Giving her another smile, he added, "And as soon as my grasp of the Timornan written language improves, I hope to continue my studies here at Ticca."

Ngeal bowed. "My former student, Sagas has already mentioned to me that many among the Speir'dina are taught skills similar to an Avairei's. I understand that even your warriors can read. There will be plenty of time over the Sorin season to study. I am sure that some of our teachers can be persuaded to help you, and anyone else among the Chosen's kindred who wish to take lessons from us. Our library is one of the oldest and best on Timorna."

"That is a very gracious offer, Ima," Arishim said, "and there will be many among us who will wish to take advantage of such an opportunity." She smiled, a mischievous gleam in her dark eyes. "I think maybe we can offer something in exchange for the teaching, however. Ima Sagas has told me that the Sorin seasons can be long and confining.

"Among the Speir'dina there are many who are skilled artists, musicians, and actors. Though our crafts may be a bit different from what you are used to, we can perhaps make the time pass a little more pleasantly for all of us, by offering you and your people some entertainment."

"Hmm, that is a novel idea. During the Sorins, the Umwira are especially active with their magics. We native Timornans rarely think about entertainment at such a time. At Ticca, the Avairei usually spend the Sorins in prayer, ceremony, or just in sleep.

"As to what my Hunt Leader and his Warlinga kin did when they weren't in their drug-induced hibernation, I never asked. Having some entertainment would certainly be an interesting experiment."

Ngeal nodded. "Yes, that is an excellent suggestion, clan elder, which I'm sure we will all appreciate during The Confinement. Since your people aren't used to being restricted to underground quarters for long periods, it will give them a way to channel their energies creatively."

The Kashallan beamed at Arishim. He hadn't even liked the woman upon their first few encounters, but now he could see what an asset she would be to him, as he floundered through the morass of Timornan politics—an occupation in which neither bondmate had any expertise, or much interest.

"This seems like a very good plan. I know you will enjoy their entertainment, Ima; the Dymarian members of my clan are famous for their artistic talents throughout the galaxy."

He sighed wistfully. "And I hope there will be time for me to learn to read and write as well. Ata Temog has already told us about the library here, and I know San Bennett and San Singey have been looking forward to exploring its treasures."

Frowning, he stood on tiptoe and glanced around the emptying courtyard. Still not spying his friend, he finally asked, "Where is Philip, by the way? I wanted to introduce him to the Ima as well."

Silence...

The Kashallan glanced from one Speir'dina face to the other. No one would look him in the eye or answer his question. Suddenly he had the feeling that they were concealing something from him. "What has happened? Where is Singey?"

Into the strained silence Sairsa finally said, "He's gone, Love."

"What! Where?"

She shrugged. "We don't know for sure."

Maybe they didn't know, or maybe they were too frightened to tell him what they suspected. Catching sight of Nathan and Tessa still standing nearby, he muttered a curse under his breath, then pushed his way unceremoniously between Bennett and Ata Hobral.

Storming over to the unsuspecting couple, he grabbed Tessa roughly by the arm, yanked her out of Nathan's embrace and swung her around to face him. Face twisted with rage, he demanded, "Where is he, Demon? Damn you, what did you do to Philip?"

Terrified, Tessa tried to pull away then began to cry hysterically. "Please, Ce'awn," she begged, "I don't know what happened—I didn't do anything to him!"

Ignoring her pleas, he shook her. "Don't lie to me, Spirit, what did you do to him?"

Nathan cursed and gave the Kashallan a stinging blow on the arm that broke his hold. Pushing Tessa behind him, he balled up his fists and faced the enraged bondmates, his face contorted by his conflicting loyalties.

"Dunnagh, if you try that again, I'll knock you flat. I'm warning you. This is Tessa! Do you hear me, you stupid ass? TESSA!"

The Kashallan moaned, covering his face with his hands. "I'm sorry," he breathed. "Oh Gods, Nathan, Tessa, I'm so sorry. Philip's gone, and—" His voice trailed off as he choked on a sob.

Stepping quickly to his side, Bennett put an arm around his shoulder. "Ce'awn, I'm not sure what this is all about, but I'll tell you what I know—which, unfortunately, isn't much. Ever since his visit with you to the wild pool in the Swamp, I've been anxious about him. Philip's been—upset about something.

"The night, you left on the raid, I found him sitting by our fire instead of resting, as he should have been doing, after offering you the blood gift. I asked him if he wanted to talk about what was bothering him. He thanked me for my concern, but said that, before he could talk to anyone about it, he needed more time to figure the problem out for himself. Just after that Conal Taleish came by to have me look at his stump.

"I went to bed after that, and Philip said he would be going to bed, too. I thought no more about it, but the next morning he woke me early to tell me that he wasn't coming with us into Ticca. He looked terrible, but he refused to tell me anything further. Later McLaren told me Philip left with Headman Banno and his people. I'm afraid that's all I can tell you."

"Singey went with the Begta?"

Bennett nodded. "Apparently so, but I haven't a clue why—nor does anyone else that I've talked to."

The Kashallan sighed. Turning back to Nathan, he said, "I have to ask the Spirit—please understand."

Nathan nodded reluctantly, then, turning to the still-sobbing woman, he embraced her and spoke to her quietly for a few minutes. At last she nodded, then, head bowed, she stepped forward.

The Kashallan's eyes flicked to the ugly marks he had just made on the pale skin of her arms; his face reddened. "Tessa, I'm so very, very sorry. I—" He shook his head, swallowed hard, and tried again. "There's no excuse for the shameful thing I just did, and I won't insult you by offering one, but would you at least let me take away some of the pain that I've just caused you?"

Hesitantly she approached and held out her hands, palms downward. Extending his tentacles, the Kashallan reached out, took her wrists, and formed the link the symbiont needed to do its healing. When it was over, he looked deep into her soft, dark eyes, and asked, "Tessa, did the Sweh'an have anything to do with Philip's leaving?" She nodded. "Do you know why he's left?"

Tessa shook her head, then reddened and looked away. "I don't know exactly. Sometimes the spirit likes me to stay—it wants me to feel what it's making my body feel when—" She glanced at Nathan, reddened, then continued, "I don't know what my bondmate saw in our future that made it go to him—it doesn't always tell me. I just know he had to make a decision, and he had to do it that night. So it went to him, and—" She broke off, flushing an even deeper shade of red.

The Kashallan grimaced. "Tessa," he said in a quiet but firm voice, "I need to know what's happened. You'll have to let the Sweh'an come through."

Biting her lip, she finally nodded. "All right, Ce'awn, I understand." Closing her eyes, she moved her lips as she soundlessly repeated the invocation to summon her bondmate.

For a long moment, nothing happened; then, suddenly, the atmosphere around the group changed, as the eerie presence of the Sweh'an came into its host.

Ngeal shuddered, feeling the fur at the back of her neck rise. "A Sweh'an Spirit—oh, Holy Mother," she murmured under her breath. Glaring at Sagas she mouthed, "How could you have been so stupid?"

Sagas's expression hardened, then Ngeal's attention was drawn violently back to the Kashallan. With a growl of rage, the Sweh'an lunged forward, hands clawing for his face. Taken totally off guard, he barely managed to control her before she did him serious damage.

"You hurt my H'an," the spirit screeched. "You're going to pay for that, Khutani slimeworm!"

Wrestling her arms to her sides and pinning them there, Dunnagh leaned forward and laughed into her face. "What's the matter, Spirit—jealous, hmm? Sorry you weren't here to *experience* the pain? Ah, too bad," he taunted.

"Too bad for you, slime," she hissed. "You hurt my H'an, and I won't allow anyone to do that."

"Anyone but you," he shot back. "Is that how it is, Demon? Tessa can't be hurt unless you're there to have your fun? Is that the way of it? Hmm, is it?"

Growling deep in her throat, she jerked herself forward like a striking snake and caught his lower lip between her teeth, biting down hard.

Tasting his own blood in his mouth, the Kashallan let out a startled cry and tried to pull away, but she held on, sinking her teeth even deeper into his flesh.

He struggled a moment longer, then went limp, giving up the fight. Extending his tentacles, he injected a fast-acting numbing substance into Tessa's body. In a short time it took effect, and he stepped away from the amazed Tess-weh. Wiping the blood from his mouth, the Kashallan gave her a toothy smile.

"It will wear off in a minute or so, but if you come after me again, Demon, I'll just give you more of the same till you start behaving."

He waited. When she remained quiet and just glared at him, he nodded, and continued, "Good. Now I want some answers, and I don't want any more games. You swore fealty to me, and by that oath I demand that you answer me. What did you do to Philip Singey to make him leave?"

"I didn't *do* anything to your precious Singey," Tess-weh snapped. "If he's gone, then it was his choice."

His face darkened, and he took a few deep breaths to calm himself before he spoke again. "I know you're trying to bait me, so stop it. There's more to it than that. What happened to him, Spirit?"

"He had a decision to make. He paid my price, so I told him what he needed to know. What he did with the information I gave him was *his* choice,"

"You're trying my patience," he warned. "That doesn't explain why he deserted us and went back to the Swamp with the Begta."

"If you're too stupid to figure it out, that's just too bad, Khutani, I've told you enough to fulfill my part of the agreement." She gave him a sly yet triumphant smile.

With a strangled cry, he advanced on her. Before he could do or say anything further, however, Sairsa stepped between them, her face livid. "Stop it right now, both of you. STOP IT!" Giving him a vigorous shove backwards, she placed herself between the demon-possessed woman and a very startled Kashallan.

Sairsa took a deep breath, letting it out slowly; the pair stared at her dumbfounded. Stepping aside so she could see them both Sairsa said in a more even tone. "This has got to stop. I don't know why you two act like this, and—" She held up her hand to silence them, "I don't want to know why. It's not important.

"What *is* important is that you are both behaving like spoiled brats, and this recent episode in your on-going battle with each other tells me how dangerous this is getting. Everyone else in our band has had to swallow their pride, accept each other, and work together. Everyone else has done it, but not you two."

She faced her husband, hands on her broad hips, her green eyes solemn. "Dunnagh-Tani, the Sweh'an has given you its pledge of fealty. You yourself admit that a Sweh'an keeps its oaths. So stop trying to challenge and bully it every time it tries to fulfill its part of the bargain. The Spirit *is* doing what it agreed to do, and you know it.

"The Sweh'an doesn't have to give you its messages in grammar school language; it just has to tell you enough so you can use your brain to figure out the answer for yourself.

"Were the meanings of your grandfather's stories always spelled out for you, or did the old man make you *think*. And, when you did understand, didn't they mean more to you because you had to *work* for the answers?"

At his startled expression, Sairsa nodded. "I thought so, and." Pointing her finger at him as she warmed to her subject, "Did you ever stop to consider that there may be certain laws of the universe governing what the Spirit can and can't say, because of how its knowledge could take away our free will, if its power isn't held in check?"

Catching the Sweh'an smirking at the Kashallan out of the corner of her eye, she next rounded on that pair of bondmates. "This problem isn't totally his to lay blame on or solve. It's as much your doing as his, Tess-weh," she announced. "Yes, you too, and you know it." Softening her tone, she continued, "Spirit, you bait him all the time. I know you don't like being bound like this, and I know that it amuses you to watch him so stupidly fall into your traps over and over, but you have to stop. If you make him so frustrated and angry that he can't listen to your warnings, then, if something happens—"

"If he doesn't listen, that's his fault, not mine," Tess-weh said in a petulant voice, but she refused to meet Sairsa's eyes.

"Are you so sure that the Great Ones who judge your service will see it like that?" she asked quietly. "Are you willing to risk so much on that opinion? Are you, Spirit?"

Tess-weh blinked. She looked down at the ground and reluctantly mumbled, "No."

"Then will you answer the Kashallan's questions about our friend Philip?"

"No." When Sairsa continued to stare at her, Tess-weh added, "I have told the Khutani enough to satisfy the requirements of my oath—this time." She looked at Sairsa slyly. "But for you I will say more, Sairsa-meh—for a price."

"And that is, Spirit?"

"That you kiss me. And, let me feel the baby again."

Striking a dramatic pose, Sairsa considered. "All right, first I will give you a kiss—a sisterly kiss, mind. Then you answer my questions, and, if what you say is informative, then you can touch the baby."

The Kashallan choked off a cry then opened his mouth to protest. Beside him his Avairei wife, Pela, dug her claws into his arm, and shook her head.

Tess-weh folded her arms across her creamy breasts. "I will only answer three questions."

Sairsa sighed her face miming her disappointment. "Only three," she agreed, and stepped closer to offer her kiss.

The kiss began as Sairsa had intended, a kiss between sisters or friends, but Tess-weh pulled her closer, forcing upon her a more passionate version. Sairsa pulled away. "No, Tess-weh, no." Catching her breath, she continued, as if talking to a slow-learning child, "Tess-weh, remember, we talked about this before. You and I aren't going to do that kind of thing together."

"Why?" the spirit pouted. Looking over at the Kashallan's darkening face, she gave him a malicious grin. "He shares his other love with me. I want to share you too."

Unable to stop herself, Sairsa's eyes flicked to Nathan and away. Her face reddened and she sighed. "Spirit, you can have many lovers, that is one part of our physical experiences that you have indulged yourself in often before. But what I'm offering you is something different, something very special. I'm offering you my friendship. Have you ever, in all your many bondings, had a real *friend* before?"

"No," it admitted.

Sairsa nodded. "It's like I've been trying to teach you, Spirit. Pleasure and pain are very intense and easily come by physical acts, but they are not the only expressions of our physical reality. If you are wise and careful with your use of your host, and if the Gods are kind to you both, you and your H'an will have a long and rich life together.

"This is an excellent opportunity for you to explore other aspects of our reality that you haven't had a chance to experience before. One of those very special things is having a friend."

Sairsa smiled at her. "So we will do this kissing again, and this time we will do it like friends. Physically it may not be as exciting as passion, but emotionally it can be very rewarding." Sairsa leaned forward and gave Tess-weh the kiss of a friend. When that was over, she said. "Now for my first question." Tess-weh nodded.

"Where did Philip Singey go with the Begta?"

"He went back to their village with them."

Sairsa frowned. That wasn't very helpful, I already guessed that." Tess-weh gave her a toothy smile. "With only two questions left, I can see that I will have to be very careful how I phrase them. What did you tell Philip that helped him decide to do that?"

"He was a Chosen One—the Maker marked him the first time he went to the wild pool. I told him that if he wanted what the Khutani had to offer, he must not enter Ticca. If he really wanted a kashallan bond, he must go back with the Begta to the wild pool."

"But why?" the Kashallan blurted. "I suspected that was what was on his mind, but he could have done that here at Ticca. I would have helped him, and there is a Maker here to—"

"No, he could not," Tess-weh snapped. "And I know which of your slimy relatives are here, Khutani, so—" At a warning sound from Sairsa, Tess-weh subsided. "Singey couldn't enter this keep if he wished to make a kashallan bond. If he tried to bond here, the future would spin itself out in different ways that could cause all to be lost.

"I told him he had to choose—if he wanted a kashallan bond, ever, he must go back to the Swamp. If he didn't want it, then it mattered little if he entered the keep or not. That's all I can say about this, and I'm not playing any game."

"But the Sorins!" the Kashallan protested.

She snorted. "He will have time to reach the pools, if he doesn't lose his nerve. And have you so little faith in your own kind, Khutani, hmm? A host willing to bond is a jewel beyond price. Don't you think your slimy relatives will do all in their power to protect such a treasure? He'll be all right, if he acts quickly enough." She smirked. "Otherwise he'll be spending the Sorin season with the Begta, which will test even his scientific curiosity."

"But—"

"My last question," Sairsa interrupted.

Tess-weh folded her arms across her chest again. "I have already answered more than three."

Sairsa shook her head. "Those last ones were the Kashallan's questions. Your agreement was with me."

Tess-weh glared murderously at the Kashallan, but at last relented and nodded for Sairsa to continue.

"Thank you, Tess-weh. My last question is: now that we have reached Ticca, will we still be in danger from our enemies during the Sorins?"

Tess-weh sighed. "This is a very important question. I couldn't possibly answer such an important question, not for such a small price. You must—"

Sairsa chuckled, shaking her head. "No, no, you agreed to three questions from me. You didn't say what kind of questions, or how important they had to be."

"Hmm, you are very good at this bargaining," the Demon grumbled. "I am glad that you don't wish to bond with one of us—you might prove to be a very difficult H'an."

Sairsa bowed. "Thank you, Honored Spirit. Will you answer that question?"

The Sweh'an considered, then smiled slyly and turned to face the Kashallan. "From without and within, your safety will not be won. A pledge betrayed, an unseen blade. Both the bitter and the sweet you will taste before the Sorins are done." When she finished she gave Sairsa a triumphant grin.

Sairsa bowed deeply. "Thank you, Honored Spirit." Tess-weh's face took on a confused look; she glanced expectantly from Sairsa to the Kashallan. The Kashallan's face was a deep red, but he only glared. Tess-weh sighed; then she brightened. "Now I get to touch the baby again,"

Sairsa moved up to her, lowering her kilt slightly, the better to expose her rounded belly. "Yes, it is, as we agreed, but he's probably asleep right now. Riding on the Loti rocks him to sleep, usually, so don't be too disappointed if you don't feel much. Next time you come to us you can feel the baby again, if he doesn't wake up now, I promise."

The Sweh'an looked up from its contemplation of Sairsa's enlarged abdomen, studying her face carefully. Deciding at last that she did mean it, the Demon nodded, satisfied. "Oh, he will wake up for me—he likes me," Tess-weh said, unable to resist a taunting glance at the Kashallan. Then, placing her hand upon her friend's swollen belly, Tess-weh traced one of the spiraling blue kavay brands that crawled across its expanse.

As her finger reached a point near the top of a blue curve, she felt it. A sharp lump protruded outward from the rest of the mass under her hand. It disappeared then came up again in a slightly different spot. Tess-weh laughed. "He's moving! Is he waking up?"

"Could be."

Tess-weh placed both hands on Sairsa's belly, very excited now. The baby moved around a few more times, then, settling himself again, he became quiescent. Tess-weh's face fell. "Ah, he's sleeping again."

Sairsa patted her shoulder. "Never mind. Because you are my friend, the next time you come to us, if he is still inside me, you can touch him again."

"You are very kind to me, and I know you watch out for my H'an when I am not with her, so I will give you a present that is just for you." Leaning forward, the spirit whispered next to her ear.

"When you are in doubt, always trust your inner feelings. No matter what others do or say, trust in yourself, for you do have some of the gift, my Sairsa-meh. Always believe that." Then the Sweh'an kissed her gently, and was gone.

Letting out a long breath, Tessa collapsed into her friend's arms. "Thank you, Sairsa, thank you," she breathed.

Sairsa hugged her, then looked around at the rest of her audience, feeling suddenly exhausted and a bit self-conscious. Catching Nathan's eye she said, "Nathan, she's all right, but have you any place set aside where we could go? I know Tessa's usually exhausted after the spirit leaves her, and I could use a rest, too."

Ngeal cleared her throat. These Speir'dina intrigued her. The little scene she had just witnessed between the Sweh'an and the Kashallan's alien wife was fascinating. It certainly wasn't the usual way to handle such a spirit, but the woman had done it very well indeed. She wanted more time to talk to these most interesting creatures. They were obviously from a far different class than the black-clad warriors.

When she had their attention, she said, "Clan elders, daughters, there may still be quite a bit of confusion inside, as your people get settled. May I offer you refreshments in my suite in the meantime?"

Chapter Five

The Kashallan and Nathan were about to follow the women inside, when Rhys approached them and saluted. Dunnagh's eyes flicked towards the Warlinga barracks, becoming aware of the loud growls and angry voices for the first time. "What is it, Rhys? Is there trouble with them already?"

"Sort of, Ce'awn, but it's not a discipline problem. The Commander could handle that, even with those big brutes. No, it's about what to do with their dead, Ce'awn, that's why we need you. Commander Tizu hopes that if they'll listen to anyone it would be you."

"What's the problem?" Nathan muttered. "If the bodies are dead, they're dead."

"Yes, Sir," Rhys agreed. "The problem is that some of them want to hold the usual feast of the dead, but some of the others say that these dead kinsmen were traitors to the Khutani, and should be dumped into the waste pit with no honor. That's why the Commander needs the Ce'awn to settle it."

"Hmm."

The Kashallan paused in the doorway of the barracks, surveying the situation. Yes, things were definitely getting out of hand here. As he watched, one of the larger Warlinga, with head crest raised, loomed over the smaller Speir'dina commander in a threatening manner. Before the Kashallan could say or do anything, however, Tizu stepped back a pace and jumped up. With a front kick, he planted the steel toe of his combat boot squarely on a sensitive nerve spot just under the man's jaw. The blow was well-aimed and solid, and the big Warlinga's eyes rolled back as he hit the floor with a resounding crash.

Beside him in the doorway, Nathan murmured, "Pretty good for an old man."

"Mm, very good."

"How'd he know where to hit him, though?"

The Kashallan grinned, displaying his sharp white teeth. "I figured, with his small size, he might have trouble with them, so I showed him a few things. He's a quick learner."

"Mm, has to be, or end up on the dinner menu," Nathan commented.

"It was his choice to take on this job," the Kashallan reminded him. "I hope he can manage it. But once they figure out his size doesn't mean he can't handle things, they'll settle down."

Inside the barracks, there was a stunned silence. Tizu eyed the Warlinga warily, his attention flicking from his opponent to the rest of the assembled lizardmen. On the floor the Warlinga roused. He growled deep in his throat, coming up with red eyes blazing, Tizu kicked him hard again, sending him sprawling.

When the Warlinga opened his eyes a second time, Tizu drew his sidearm and pointed it at the lizardman's chest. "Now, this time, if you try to come at me, you piece of Begta filth, you're a dead man. You got that?"

The man nodded, feeling his jaw gingerly. "All right, then. Sit up slowly and stay put." When the Warlinga complied, taking a belligerent stance, Tizu faced the rest of the barracks's inhabitants. "Any of you other shit-for-brains Begta want to continue this little discussion?"

When no one spoke, he said, "All right, as I said before; we wait for the Kashallan."

"I'm here, Hunt Leader," the Kashallan announced as he and Nathan entered. He gave the Warlinga a stern look. "One of my men has already explained the problem to me, and I'll get to that in a moment. First I want to say that I am very displeased by what I observed just now." His eerie, ice-blue eyes raked over them. "Before coming to this world, the part of me that is the host was a Warlinga among my own people. At that time, San Tizu was *my*," he thumped his chest, "Hunt Leader.

"Don't judge any of my Speir'dina clansmen by their size alone—if you do, that mistake may cost you your lives. My Hunt Leaders are both skilled at their craft. Since coming to Timorna, we have already fought the Umwira and won." That got their attention, he noted, smiling inwardly at that slight bending of the truth.

"If you co-operate with Hunt Leader Tizu we can combine our knowledge and together become a powerful fighting force against the Umwira and other enemies.

"You have all sworn fealty to my Khutani kin and me. Since your Hunt Leader is dead, I require you to accept the leadership of the most skilled commander among us, and that is, in my opinion, San Tizu. When there is time, officers from among you will be chosen to work with my Speir'dina warriors. I wish the two hunting packs to be united.

"During the Sorins, Ticca will be left alone, but afterwards—" He shrugged. "Well, a runner was sent to Riath, and who knows what will come of that. You are part of my people now, and, to those at Riath, Ticca will be an outlawed keep. We are in this struggle together, and there is no turning back, not for any of us. Do you understand what I am saying to you?"

He waited, and when he received their grudging assent, he continued, "Now to the other matter. I have been told that there is a dispute among you about what to do with your dead. Is that indeed the problem?"

Once again they murmured their agreement. "Though I didn't have the pleasure of knowing Hunt Leader Hagar in life, I honor him and the others who met their deaths defending this keep.

"Hagar and his kin died doing what they mistakenly thought was their duty to this keep and the Khutani. I deeply respect them for that, and there will be no more talk about throwing their remains into the waste pool. The feast for an honored kinsman will be performed as usual. Neither I, myself, nor my Khutani relatives are angered by these men doing their sworn duty to the best of their ability."

Letting go of his cool aloofness, he added, "Your Hunt Leader was a loyal and brave man. Those are admirable qualities to be reminded of at any time, and especially now. We all can learn from such men." He looked down, suddenly shy, as a new idea came to him. At last he ventured, "I know it isn't the usual custom, but, if his kinsmen will permit, I would ask that my two Speir'dina Hunt Leaders and I be allowed to partake in the feast of the dead."

He held up his own death strand for them to see, its bone beads showing up clearly in the flickering green lamplight. "And, if you permit, we will wear a bead of him on our death strands, to remember such courage and loyalty."

That pleased them, he could tell, listening to the low murmur of conversation as they talked it out among themselves. The Kashallan waited. At last, the one called Fadir bowed to him and his two Hunt Leaders, then said, "Holy One, it would please us if you and your Hunt Leaders would join us later. You do our kinsman a great honor, and we will share Hagar's bone beads with you, as well."

Breathing an inward sigh of relief, the Kashallan bowed to Fadir. "Thank you. We will await your summons. When all is ready, you need only send for us."

CONAL TALEISH LEANED against the parapet and stared moodily out into the darkness. It was getting late; his watch had just ended and he should go to bed, but why bother? He wouldn't sleep anyway. No, it was better to stay up here in the concealing gloom, with the damp night air cool upon his face, rather than go back inside the keep.

After the Umwira attack that lost him his hand, it had been hard enough to get used to the pity he saw in his comrades' eyes, but now, here at the keep, there were so many new faces—and all of them stared at him again, as if he were some kind of freak. Their regard, a mixture of pity and horrified fascination, followed him wherever he went. There was no escape, and it made his skin crawl.

That's why he had asked for this lonely night guard duty—it was so peaceful out here, with no one staring. He could do his job, and pretend he was just like everyone else. On this Gods-cursed world, a "cripple," would have been on his relatives' dinner menu long before now.

He had heard what the native Timornans said about him behind his back—and he knew what they counseled the Ce'awn to do about him. Yes, he knew. In the harsh reality of Timornan society, there was no place for a disabled warrior like himself.

He ground his teeth at the memory. Gods, how he hated this—it was so unfair. One stupid, careless mistake—just letting down his guard for a second—and the big Umwira brute came out of nowhere, bit off his hand at the wrist, and ran away. Oh, by the Gods, why? There had been no sense to it—just a cruel malicious joke. That was the way he saw it. Their leader had been defeated; they were running away. A joke that had left him at the mercy of other people's charity, a cripple for the rest of his life.

If he had been back home on Caldon when he received such an injury, it would have been bad, of course. But at least there, he could have been fitted with a cybernetic hand that would have been almost as good as his own—but here there was no such saving technology to free him from the nightmare.

From the courtyard below, a high, piercing wail of grief shattered the stillness. Conal shivered; its poignant sound was an echo of his morbid mood. The sound came from the Warlinga barracks; the feast for the Warlinga dead must be still going on. He smirked. What a great way to spend the evening, dining on half-raw Warlinga and listening to the dead men's kinsmen lament and tell lies about how great their dear departed were.

Conal leaned against the outer wall, and idly fingered the handle of his dagger. If he were to take out the blade and slit his throat right here and now, would his own kindred mourn and carry on about his passing? Would they lift up their voices in the traditional Caldoni keen? Or would they say good riddance, and toss him over the wall, to be eaten by one of the Swamp's many predators?

Conal blinked, feeling the sting of unwanted tears in his eyes. "Damn!" He swore and rubbed at his eyes with his remaining hand. His body trembled with the effort of holding back his sobs, grateful for the darkness that hid him away from pitying eyes. Gods, what was he going to do? The journey was over; they were finally at Ticca Keep—

"Poor, poor little cripple, feeling sorry for yourself—want to jump?" a low, throaty voice asked.

Startled, Conal spun round, instinctively dropping into a fighter's crouch. A woman stepped out from the shadows, her lovely heart-shaped face now visible in the torchlight from the courtyard below. Conal relaxed his stance, letting his breath out slowly.

What did *she* want? He felt his face burn, as a mixture of fear and desire welled up within him. Conal had no doubt about who was addressing him. Tessa, the lovely young society woman who was the spirit's host, would never have come to any man alone in the darkness like this—only the demon spirit who sometimes shared her flesh would be so bold. He shuddered, as his loins throbbed with longing.

Eyeing him coolly, she laughed again and stepped closer, as if aware of the turmoil she was causing him. "Poor, poor cripple, what will you do with yourself now that we've reached Ticca, hmm? All the new people to pity you—and asking themselves, why is he still alive? Ah, poor cripple, only one hand—only half a man, perhaps? Are you only half a man, hmm?"

Stifling an angry sob, Conal swung back to the darkness so that she couldn't see his face. He stared blindly out over the lake, trembling violently. He'd like to smash her face in for that—or slam her down on the hard stone walkway and show her how much of a man he really was.

Gritting his teeth, he held himself back, not wanting to make more trouble. Nathan, while not exactly a friend, was a good officer. "Leave me alone, Demon Bitch."

Cocking her head to one side, she studied him curiously for a moment then asked, "Why should I? Poor, poor Conal—such a tragedy—lost his hand to the Umwira—can't do the simplest things without help. Poor, poor cripple." She shook her head and clicked her tongue in mock sympathy. Then, her voice hardening, she snapped, "Answer my question, Cripple—are you half a man?"

Letting out a strangled cry, Conal swung back to face her, breathing raggedly, eyes wild. "What do you want with me, Spirit?"

Tess-weh smiled, licking her lips, and stepped closer. "What do you think, Cripple?" Cupping one heavy breast, she held it out to him. "Are you half a man?"

"Bitch," he growled. Lunging forward unexpectedly, he hit her hard across the chest with the stump of his arm. Tess-weh stumbled, falling to her knees. Before she could rise, he was on her, slamming her down against the rough walkway and pinning her between himself and the stone. He slapped her again. She let out a startled cry, then smiled.

Green eyes ablaze, Conal laughed. "Want more?" Tess-weh stared up at him without speaking, as if measuring how much further she could push him. "Demon Bitch," he spat. Pressing her against the hard stone with his body; he kissed her savagely.

With his one good hand, he tore open his pants, freeing his straining phallus. His whole body felt like it was on fire. Grunting in his eagerness, he kneed her legs apart, impatiently yanked aside her kilt, and thrust himself deep into the moist heat between her thighs. He groaned with pleasure, hoping he was hurting her, his rage goading his lust to even greater heights.

"Ah, My Treasure, you are a man who truly knows how to use your anger. What a sweet surprise." Lifting her arms she entwined them behind his neck and pushed his face towards the erect nipples of her breasts.

"What do I want with you—a crippled man? Ah, ah, My Jewel, that remains to be discovered, does it not?" Running her nails cruelly down his back, she thrust her hips forward to meet his frenzied strokes.

"Mm, mm, yes. I could tell you how to solve this problem of yours—how you could have an honored place here. I could tell you how you could be more than the cripple you are now." She tangled her hand in his disheveled warrior's braid, and jerked his head up so that she could look into his tormented eyes. "Yes, I could do all that," she purred, "if you pay my price."

His rhythm slowed. "Can you give me back my hand?"

"Perhaps."

With a curse, he hit her in the face with his stump. "Don't play games with me, Demon Bitch. Tell me, or I'll throw you off this wall and save all of us a lot of grief. Can you give me back my hand?"

Tess-weh tasted her own blood in her mouth, and shuddered with orgasm. Staring up at the still enraged Conal, she finally said, "I can't give you back your hand, but I can tell you how it can be returned to you."

"How?"

Reaching up a hand, Tess-weh pushed his head back down to her breast and held it there, till he began to suck. Feeling his teeth nip at her flesh, Tess-weh arched her back in pleasure. "That, My Treasure, I will only tell you when you have paid for it."

LATER AFTER SHE LEFT him Tess-weh lay on the bed she shared with Nathan and stretched, her body lazy with the afterglow of multiple orgasms. She laughed softly to herself. How very interesting. She had definitely underestimated him. Her experiences with Nathan, and Singey hadn't prepared her for the raw violence and primal passions of Conal Taleish.

To get any pleasure out of her earlier lovers at all, she had to work hard to break down the "civilized" facade behind which their passions hid. But Conal—ah, he was a rare jewel indeed. Filled with resentment, pent-up rage, and an unfulfilled need for vengeance, he could truly hate, and express it violently.

She resolved to toy with him for as long as he pleased her before telling him what he needed to know. There was time. But she would have to be careful, too; he was strong, and could turn on her in an unguarded moment, even kill her perhaps. Ah, but the unpredictability of his passions was part of his appeal.

Tess-weh licked her lips and smiled. She was getting tired of Nathan. Tessa might want to simper and stare dreamily into his troubled eyes when they made love, but he was becoming much too tame and boring for her bondmate's tastes. The Sweh'an craved a far more rough and passionate coupling than he was willing to give it.

The demon had tried to break down his resistance, but thus far she had failed, and now—why bother? Let Dunnagh-Tani have its leavings. Why should it care, when here was one far more amenable to the spirit's guiding hand than Nathan ever would be.

Chapter Six

I ma Tomina Dingay threw back the blanket on her bed and sat up. There was no point in trying to sleep any longer: the pain in her injured arm made that impossible. She picked up the sack of burning-sand on the table by her bed and sprinkled some into the top of the lamp sitting there. A moment later there was a faint hiss, and a flicker of silver-green light set the shadows to dancing in her windowless room.

She sighed and looked down at the raw, swollen bite marks that crisscrossed her furred arm. "Damn the Khutani slimeworms," she murmured, clutching her arm and rocking back and forth with the pain. "May they all rot in the black pit of oblivion where they belong!"

Tomina looked longingly at the medicines Ata Hobral had left for her. The potions would dull the pain, allow her to rest and heal—but she dared not take them. She needed more time—to think and to plan. No, healing was not for her, not yet. Unpleasant as the pain in her arm was, it would be nothing compared to the pain in store for her if she should fail the Master's trust.

When she used the crystal and contacted him after the Khutani's attack, Barak had given her his orders and she must not displease him—not now when their hated enemies' destruction was almost at hand. She must consider her discomfort as a goad to help her think; she was living on borrowed time, and she knew it. This creature that called himself the Kashallan had made it mandatory for every inhabitant in Ticca to swear an oath of fealty to him and his slimy relatives.

So far she had been spared that indignity, but that couldn't last much longer. Soon enough he, or Ngeal would begin to question why she didn't come forward, of her own will, to take the oath. But she couldn't take that chance; in the link, he might be able to *taste* the falseness in her words, and the punishment for that would be a painful death, she was sure.

That loathsome cousin of hers, Combaron, had already put this Kashallan and the Caltia witch on their guard against her with his bungling—may he be flayed alive for his stupidity. She dared not take the chance—but how could she avoid it and do what the Master demanded? There were guards outside her door—she couldn't leave her room until she had complied with the Kashallan's command.

By The Fires, why now—why did the kashallan bond have to be re-formed? The wizards' plans were so close to their fulfillment. How could there be a new host race come to carry the damned worms out of their pools? "Damn the Makers and their magics," she cursed through gritted teeth.

Who were these ugly, flat-faced creatures, the Speir'dina, anyway? Where had they come from—had the Khutani called them from the stars, as Hobral claimed? Was that possible? Probably not.

They were more likely to be mutants bred by a rival wizard from one of the clans across the Shallow Sea. Many were jealous of her Master. One of his rivals must want to seize the southern lands for his people, instead of waiting for the alliance to conquer it. If that were so, then all the years that had gone into the Ghostland wizards' careful planning could all be for naught.

Tomina needed more information—and more time. She must find a way to get out of this room. She could do little to bring about the Kashallan's death while still confined. And he must be destroyed—there was no doubt in her mind about that. She must find a way to make these outlaws trust her. Standing up she began to pace. How? How could she mislead him? Was there a way to lie while in the link? Perhaps the Master might know, but she certainly didn't.

Tomina paused, looking wistfully towards the hiding place by her bed where the communication crystal lay. Barak had warned her about contacting him again. He had given her an order; she must kill this Kashallan—there was no need of further discussion in the matter, as far as he was concerned.

And there were risks—who knew what the Khutani were capable of—could they detect her communications with her master, as the Umwira feared? But he didn't seem to understand how her confinement left her without any means of eliminating their enemies. Without swearing the oath, she would never be allowed to leave her cell. Tomina ground her teeth in frustration. What should she do?

Startled, she spun around. Had that been a knock at her door, so early? Ah, yes, there it was again. She shuddered. Were they coming for her already?

Moving quickly to her bed, Tomina slipped beneath the covers. "Come in," she called in a trembling voice.

In the next moment, the door was opened by one of her black-clad guards, and Nona, her personal maid, walked in carrying a pitcher of hot water and some washing rags. The guard gave Tomina a sour look, then closed the door behind the maid.

Tomina glared right back at him, then, turning, smiled at Nona as she set the pitcher down on the table beside her bed. "You're up early, my dear."

"Yes, Ima, I know, but I couldn't sleep. And," she added shyly, "I was so worried about you."

"How kind. My arm is still very sore, dear child."

"I am sorry to hear that, Ima." Setting down the pitcher and towels, Nona took Tomina's basin from the shelf under the table and poured some of the steaming liquid into the clay bowl, then handed her mistress a cloth. "I thought you might wish to bathe, Ima. It might make you feel better."

Tomina took the rag, dipped it into the bowl, and mopped her face. She let out a deep sigh. Yes, the warm water did help. As she bathed, she studied her young maid covertly. Nona was a pretty young thing, just reaching her maturity. She would be looking for a mate soon—a possible candidate for one of Tomina's own sons in the Ghostlands perhaps.

The girl had been her personal maid for several months now, and she was starting to know her well. Nona did her work without slacking, and was biddable to the point of timidity at times. It would appear that she was also kind, and loyal—hmm.

The girl came from a branch of Ngeal's own clan, which meant that her bloodline was of the best—for an Avairei slave. Yes, she might be a good match, indeed. Oh, she would never willingly allow herself to be bred to an Umwira changeling, as Tomina had done, but there were drugs that could solve that problem.

Perhaps. Tomina almost dropped the rag as a new thought came to her. It would mean giving up any hopes of using the girl as a breeder. But under the circumstances—it might be worth it.

Letting the cloth slip back into the cooling water, she smiled at the waiting girl. "Thank you, Nona, I feel a little better," Tomina cooed. "Would you be so kind as to empty my chamber pot, and see if you can find me anything in the kitchen to eat at this early hour? I wasn't feeling like eating much last night, and now I find myself a bit hungry.

"I don't want much; just something hot to drink, and perhaps a piece of masa root cake, if there is any. Could you do that for me, hmm?"

Nona beamed. "Certainly, Ima, I can do that." Picking up the bowl, she poured its contents into the chamber pot, then picked up the pot and the wet rags. Bowing, she walked to the door and knocked. "I'll be right back," she promised.

"Take your time, dear, I'm in no rush."

When the girl was gone, Tomina hurried to the door and bolted it from the inside. There; that would prevent any unwanted intrusion for a few minutes.

Returning to her bedside, Tomina moved the tiny wicker table beside her bed away from the wall. Then she removed the loose stone that the table concealed and drew out the tightly wrapped bundle from its hiding place within the wall. Returning the table to its former position, she sat down upon the edge of her bed, the bundle in her lap.

Then she hesitated; her plump body trembled with indecision. It was dangerous to disobey—but she had little choice—the Master must reconsider the situation here. This was too important. Unwrapping the bundle she took out the darkly glowing crystal and held it between her palms. For a long moment, she stared into its inky depths, watching the ominous play of its swirling indigo and violet patterns. Tomina shivered, then closed her eyes and made the call.

Suddenly pain exploded behind her eyes. She gasped, almost dropping the precious stone, and bit her lip to keep from crying out. <<Master, please,>> she cried. <<I know I am disobeying, but please hear me, PLEASE, OH, PLEASE!>>

As suddenly as it had come, the pain was gone. <<Speak then, worthless half-bred slave of the Khutani,>> Barak snarled into her mind. <<Tell me what is so important that you risk my wrath. I will have no patience with your stupidity, Avairei filth, if I am not pleased—you will know the strength of my disapproval.>>

As always when speaking to her beloved Master, or any of the other Ghostlanders, Tomina felt her heart burn with shame. She knew she was worthless—only a half-bred slave. Her tainted Avairei blood cursed her forever. She was despicable, not fit for more than to serve and blindly obey the commands of the Real People.

<<Master, I am still confined to my room, and I have learned that I will not be allowed out until I take an oath of allegiance to the new Kashallan and his kin. When I spoke to you before of him and the Caltia woman, you ordered me to kill them, but I don't see how I can while I am imprisoned.

<<There is no getting around this. To obtain my release, I must take the oath—but if I do, he will taste the falseness of my words. And if I don't swear, and soon, they may guess my true loyalties, and perhaps have me killed anyway.

<<Is there a way—some spell, perhaps—that would allow me to lie while in the link? If I was free—even for a little while—I'm sure I could bring about their destruction.>>

Within the distortion of the jewel, Barak's withered face scowled in concentration. <<Perhaps. The symbiont is still young, inexperienced—there may be a way to deceive it. If you drink some of the ull powder we gave you in a little water, just before the swearing, it should mask the taste of your deception enough to get you through a simple oath taking.>>

Barak's rasping laugh rang in her mind. <<The powder will get you out of your cell, Filth—now tell me what you plan to do with your freedom.>>

<<I—I'm not sure—>> Tomina stammered.

Pain!

<<Please, Master,>> she begged, trying to ignore the pain and think. There was something else she wanted to tell him. Something—ah, now she remembered. <<Master, there is a young girl—a student of mine. She is very pretty—and marriageable. She is also very easily controlled.

<<From what I have learned, this new kashallan has very perverted appetites. He still couples with his women, even though his two wives are both breeding. One of his wives is an Avairei woman, so it is said. I—I thought, if he had a taste for Avairei, perhaps he might like a new companion for his bed?>>

<<Hmm. Perhaps. If the girl is as docile as you claim, she could be very useful. Is she of the Dingay clan?>>

<<No, Master, that's why she is so perfect for our use. She is of Ima Ngeal's own clan, and she has already given her oath. No one will suspect her. Nona could be assigned as maid to his suite—then, who knows what she might learn? Does this please you?>> Tomina asked hopefully.

<<This affair is too important to leave solely in your hands, Slave. I must have access to the woman at will myself. You must give her your black crystal pendant to wear, so that I can communicate with her or control her as I see fit. You *have* pleased me with this, Tomina; though your blood is tainted, your heritage from The People is strong.>>

Tomina felt her heart soar. She had been forgiven, even been praised—Oh, by the Blessed Fires, her beloved Master was pleased with her again—

There was a soft knock at the door. <<Master,>> Tomina said hurriedly, <<the girl is here now. Do you wish to speak with her yourself?>>

<<Yes.>>

Breaking off the contact, Tomina shoved the crystal under her covers, and quickly walked to the door and opened it. She eyed her grim-faced guard, and ushered the girl into her room, closing and bolting the door behind her.

Tomina returned to her bed and sat down on the edge. "Thank you so much, Nona, for bringing me that." She motioned to the full tray the maid placed on her table. "It looks wonderful."

Nona smiled, and uncovered the meal. "It was all I could manage this early—Cook just got up."

"It's fine," Tomina assured her, then patted the bed beside her. "Come, sit. I'm lonely, all cooped up in here—I would appreciate a little conversation while I eat. You can tell me the news."

Nona gave her a puzzled look, then sat gingerly on the edge of the bed. "Will you not eat, My Ima?"

"Mm, in a minute, but first I have something very special that I'd like to show you," Tomina said. Reaching out with her uninjured hand, she peeled back the bed covers, exposing the darkly glowing gem.

Nona gasped, her eyes widening, caught and held by the hypnotic play of colors within its shadowy depths. She let out a long sigh. "Beautiful!"

"Yes, isn't it." Tomina picked up the jewel, and held it closer to the girl's face, allowing her to delight in its patterns. "Very beautiful, would you like to hold it?"

"Y-yes-s."

The priestess smiled. "Good, that's very good. Here, my dear, let us hold it together—just like this...."

Chapter Seven

Aju'an yawned and surveyed the final preparations for their journey with a critical eye. Everything seemed in order. They would be traveling fast and light, so there hadn't been much to arrange. Though there was barely enough light in the east to see by, the courtyard was a bustle with activity. Loti servants built up the cooking fire and passed around roasted strips of meat and freshly baked masa root cakes. His hunters wolfed down their last hot meal for a while and checked their weapons and gear.

At Fergannal's suggestion, he was taking a small but well-armed hunting pack—some of Meh'gach's best fighters, men who were fit and knew the country. They would have to be quick, or the first Sorin storm of the season would catch them in the open. Aju'an shuddered; he didn't want to think about their fate if the poisonous winds caught them. He turned his face to the south, nostrils flaring. Inhaling deeply, he let out his breath in a long sigh. The air still had a bit of moisture in it—they probably had time.

Each year when the rainy season ended the winds shifted direction, and came straight down from the Dead Lands to the north. As these violent dust storms headed south they picked up what was left of the toxic waste from the Great War that had almost destroyed the planet. During this season, the life forms that the Khutani reintroduced to the surface world either confined themselves to underground dwellings, or went into a dormant stage in their life cycle. Only the Umwira risked the storms and the horrible mutations they could cause.

Aju'an swallowed the last of his breakfast and walked over to where Fergannal was talking to his cousin Mar. He gave the older hunter a solemn bow, then grinned at his cousin. "Good morning, ready for a little exercise?"

Mar grinned back, his tail lashing with excitement. Fergannal gave the two young hunters a scowling look. "This isn't a game you pair of idiots," he growled.

Aju'an laid a hand on the older man's shoulder. "I know, Fergannal, I'm not a child anymore. You don't have to lecture me. It's too early in the morning for that—please, I know you aren't happy about my leading the pack, but Meh'gach can't spare you right now, so it's only logical that I go. Ticca needs help; that is clear to both of us. As my father's son, it is my duty to go."

"Mm, and what will I tell your father when he comes home, finds you gone, and tries to rip my heart out? I doubt if K'San Yargal will be any happier about your decision than I am."

Aju'an's lips curved into a smile. "He may not be happy about it, but I'm sure you will think of something to explain why it was necessary—you always do."

"Insolent brat, get out of here. I've survived your father's displeasure before; I suppose I can do it again."

Aju'an sobered, giving the Hunt Leader a troubled look. "Seriously, mentor, I feel it is my duty to go. If there is trouble at Ticca..."

"I know. Just be careful. Yargal *will* rip my heart out if something happens to you—remember that."

The men were lining up by the gate. Aju'an gathered his weapons, and took his place at their head.

"Open the gate," Fergannal shouted.

Aju'an glanced around the courtyard one last time as they headed out the gate. Chelka really must be angry with him, he thought. She hadn't even come out to say good bye. He'd expected her to show up with spear in hand and demand to go along. Of course she couldn't, both he and Fergannal would have stopped her, but in a perverse way he was a little miffed at her for not trying. Oh well, it was better this way—she would have to set aside her silly fancies soon enough, so no sense on making it hard on everyone by causing a scene.

I T WAS LATE AFTERNOON when Aju'an came upon the first disturbing setback of the day. Topping a small rise in the trail, they stared down on such a scene of savagery in the ravine below that it chilled him to the bone. Vistri. Snarling under his breath, he halted; his men fanned out protectively around him.

The carnage they'd wrought was all too plain, but where were the loathsome beasts at the moment. They listened, ears straining for the slightest sound, nostrils flaring to catch any lingering scent upon the wind. At last satisfied that the vistri were indeed gone from the area, they headed down the slope.

The harvest was late this year, and that meant that many of the far-flung Loti holdings were later than usual getting in their crops. Yargal, like any good Warlinga K'San, always sent out his hunting packs to guard the harvesters and escort the peasants safely into the fortress at these times. Aju'an knew that Fergannal had been doing just that in his father's absence, but this particular family must have been afraid they'd been forgotten, and so they had started for the keep on their own.

Unfortunately for them, they encountered a large pack of the vistri, instead of the hunters sent to escort them. Hopelessly outnumbered, they had been torn apart by the ever ravenous beasts. They'd tried valiantly to defend themselves.

Surrounding their children and old folks, the adults had lashed out with powerful kicks, and beat at their enemies with wooden and bone farming tools. Several dead vistri were a gruesome testimony to their courage, but it had been a hopeless struggle from the start, and Aju'an mourned their loss, both as their K'San's son and as a man.

It was going to be hard to convince another Loti family to farm such a distant holding after this tragedy, and that meant less food available for everyone on Meh'gach lands, for perhaps years to come.

He growled, grinding his teeth in anger as he surveyed the remnants of the vistri's meal and the wreckage of toppled farm carts and torn sacks of food. Around him, he heard the curses of his men as they sifted through the debris for usable items they could take with them.

If he had had the time, he would have liked to set a trap for this pack of beasts; after they slept off their feast, they would be back. There was too much tempting flesh still left here on which to gorge for them to abandon the kill this soon.

But that hunt, enticing as it was, would have to wait. After the Sorins, this particular pack would have to be destroyed. They were far too large and daring for the safety of Meh'gach's folk. The Warlinga couldn't afford to ignore them for another season. With a deep sense of regret, Aju'an abandoned the bodies to their grisly fate, and motioned to his men to move on.

Not long afterward, his second grim setback appeared, stunning him like a hammer blow. In a clearing by a small creek, where they planned to make camp and rest a while, he found his sister and old Overn sitting on the bank waiting for him.

Sputtering with rage, he loomed over her and roared, "WHAT ARE YOU DOING OUT HERE?"

"I told you I wanted to come with you," Chelka said, in a strained, brittle voice. "I knew you would only say no if I asked again, so I snuck out late last night. I—" Her voice trailed off. She shuddered, then looked down at her feet, her tail making small circles in the dust.

"San Aju'an, please," Overn began, "she hasn't had an easy time of it. We barely missed being caught by that vistri pack back there—"

Rounding on the old veteran, Aju'an knocked Overn to the ground with a murderous sweep of his tail. "Be silent, Begta Vomit! Why did you let her do this, you old fool?" he roared. "Why?"

He would have hit the old man again, but Chelka, eyes ablaze, jumped to her feet and whipped her own tail across his chest. Caught by surprise and off-balance, he staggered and almost joined the old man on the ground.

"Don't you dare touch him again," she warned, "or you'll have to fight me too. He came with me because he knew that, if he didn't, I would have come alone, that's why, damn you! So stop acting like a child having a temper tantrum. I'm here, and I'm coming with you."

"By the Great Hunt Leader, you're not," he spluttered, "you're going home right now. Fergannal will be worried sick about you. You could get a lot of good men killed with this little stunt. Those vistri back there—"

"He won't be looking for me, Aju'an. I told my maid that you had secretly allowed me to accompany you. To avoid trouble, I was to meet you outside the keep this morning. She was to tell Fergannal that just before the noon meal. Nobody's going to get killed because of me, so stop worrying,"

Head crest flattened, he stared openmouthed. He was so furious he couldn't speak, and yet he had to admire both her slyness and her daring. Before he could find his voice, Mar touched his shoulder. "Might I have a word with you, Cousin?"

Motioning Aju'an away from his sister and the pack, Mar led him a short distance downstream. When they were out of earshot of the others, he said, "Cousin, it is unfortunate that Chelka has chosen to disobey you, but it would be unwise, to send her back. To do that, we would have to split up the pack to give her a proper escort. Old Overn alone couldn't defend her against the vistri, or any other predator that was determined on the kill. They escaped today only by the favor of the Gods, I think; they mightn't be so lucky again."

That was true enough, Aju'an realized, but splitting up his men had its own dangers, as he well knew. If this vistri pack was as large and as hungry as it seemed from the evidence of its last kill, then separating his force could put one or possibly both groups in danger of being attacked.

Mar nodded solemnly when he saw his cousin follow the path of his own reasoning.

It hurt Aju'an's pride to give in to her like this, but Mar was right—they had better bring her along. His father might kill both of them if they survived this little venture, but she would be safer if she remained with the pack rather than going back. He sighed. "All right, you have a point, Cousin. We'll keep the hunting pack together and bring them both along."

Returning to his men, he growled, "All right, we'll eat and rest here for a time, then move on." Grimly, he grabbed his sister's arm and hauled her back down the creek out of earshot of the others.

When they were alone, he said, "Mar has convinced me that it would be foolhardy to split up and escort you back, so you're going to get your wish, Little Sister. From now on, you will be treated just like any other member of the hunting pack. No special favors, and we won't slow down for you, understand? And if I have to kill you because you can't keep up—" Voice quavering, he turned away from her, and swallowed hard.

Putting a hand on his shoulder, she said gently, "Aju'an, don't. I'm sorry I had to do it this way, but I had to come, and I will keep up. I'm as fit as you are, probably. Overn has been training me in secret. Really, you don't have to worry—"

Oh, damn her and the old fool. Overn never could refuse her anything, and this false sense of confidence could cost all of them their lives. "Damn you," he snarled, turning round to face her once more, head crest raised and eyes flashing. "It's not just you I'm worried about here. You're right; you are young and strong, and just maybe you will be able to keep up with the pack, so we don't all die in the storms. But what about the old man, hmm? What about Overn—can he keep up—can he?

"Is this how you repay his love and loyalty all these years? A slit throat on a deserted trail, left for the beasts and the storms? I probably will have to kill him somewhere between here and Ticca, you know.

"And, damn you, if I do—I'll never forgive you for that. Nor, I think, will you be able to live with yourself, either. So I hope playing out this little fantasy of yours is going to be worth the price, because it may be a high one."

Looking at her flattened head crest and stricken face, he knew he had wounded her deeply with his harsh truths, but he wasn't sorry. If she wanted to play at being a warrior, she was going to have to learn the rules of the game.

Part Two: Sorin Confinement

Chapter One

The Kashallan sighed and rolled over on his back staring up at the pitted ceiling. What time was it—how could he tell with no windows to let in the daylight? The suite he and his wives had been given was spacious and comfortable, but windowless, and a bit gloomy to Dunnagh's way of thinking.

This close to the Sorin Season, the airy chambers of the upper keep that overlooked the lake were abandoned. Everyone had moved into the rooms underground to wait out the storms.

The Avairei had given him the best they had; his suite was luxuriously furnished with thick carpets on the floors, fine wicker furniture, and skillfully woven tapestries covering the stone walls. With only the burning powder and fungus lamps for light, however, even the bright colors on the walls looked somber. It was going to be hard getting used to being closed in down here, Dunnagh thought.

He sighed again; now that he was fully awake the treadmill of his worries had started whirling around in his head once more. What to do about Pela and Amril? How to keep his people from going crazy during their long confinement? What would happen to his people after the Sorin season? And what should be done about the Dingay woman? So much to think about—it was no wonder he couldn't sleep.

Dunnagh was about to ask Tani to make him some kind of sedative, when the door opened and Pela walked in. He smiled up at her, and, throwing back the covers, patted the bed beside him. Setting her cloak down on a nearby chair, she crawled onto the bed and into his warm embrace. He settled her comfortably in the crook of one arm, pulled the blanket back over them, and kissed her. "Your fur is cold. Are you all right, my sweet?"

She sighed with contentment, and hugged him. "I'm fine. It feels good to be back in a keep again. I just wanted to pray with the others this morning—as I used to do back at Sulas."

"Mm." Tentacles extended, he ran a hand down her silky flank. In spite of his worry over other matters, he felt a growing interest in his loins at the feel of her soft, sleek fur under his hand. Before they pursued that course too far, however, he formed the link to check on her pregnancy.

When he released her, Pela watched him warily through half-closed eyes. He continued to study her with his unnerving blue stare. Pela looked away. Finally she ventured in a tiny voice, "Have I done something to displease you, husband?"

Bending down he kissed her, then said, "Pela, sweet, we need to talk. There has been so little time—and so much else to do—and well, you know I care about you, and I want you to be happy."

She nodded solemnly. "I know. You have been very kind to me, Dunnagh-Tani. I am very grateful for your concern."

In his arms he felt her tense. Damn, this was going to be more difficult than he imagined. He cleared his throat and began again, "Pela, I truly want you to be happy, believe me. You realize I didn't know about you and Amril before Sagas gave you to me. If I had known, I would never have agreed—"

She was watching him intently now; he wasn't saying this very well. He took a deep breath, then blurted in a rush, "Pela, after the baby comes, if you want to leave me and marry Amril, I would understand. We could—"

Pela gasped. Eyes wild, she pushed herself out of his arms and sat straight up in bed. Mouth quivering, she turned to face him. In a trembling voice she asked, "You want to divorce me?"

"Well—yes," he stammered, "if you would be happier that way. I thought you and Amril could—"

She didn't let him finish, but covered her face with her hands and burst into loud sobbing.

Stunned, he reached awkwardly to comfort her. "Pela, Pela, sweet, what did I say? Whatever it was, I didn't mean it—don't cry, Love—oh, please stop!"

He tried to pull her into his embrace, but she pulled away from him, refusing to listen or be consoled.

<<Gods, Tani, what did I do wrong? This definitely wasn't one of our greatest ideas. What do we do now?>>

The symbiont gave a mental noise of disgust. <<How should I know? You're supposed to be the one with so much experience where females are concerned. And what's this about *our* idea, hmm?>>

<<All right, all right, it was my idea,>> the host admitted, <<but you didn't disagree with me! As I recall, Shalla, you thought it was the best thing to do under the circumstances.>>

Tani gave a mental snort. <<And as a child, what do I know about such things, hmm?>>

AT HIS BACK, SAIRSA sat up abruptly, rubbing the sleep from her eyes. She blinked, and would have smiled, if the problem didn't appear to be so serious. Her sister-wife was in tears, and a frantic Kashallan was trying to soothe her. Her lip twitched; in spite of herself; he looked so desperate. "What did you do to her?" she demanded.

Startled, he turned to her, eyes pleading. "I—I don't know what made her so upset, really! When she came back from chapel—when I tasted her—she seemed so sad. I just wanted her to be happy—Sweetheart, I didn't know she was going to cry. I—"

"What did you say to her?"

"I—I said if she wanted to, after the baby came—that I would understand if she wanted to leave and marry Amril."

"Oh, Sairsa'meh, our husband wants to divorce me!" Pela wailed. "I have angered him with my bad moods and willful behavior, and now he doesn't want me! I must leave you! And the babies. Oh, I will be shamed forever!" As she proclaimed her terrible fate, Pela began to cry even louder.

"No! Oh, no, Pela!" he protested, "I didn't mean that—I'm not angry with you, My Sweet, and I don't want you to leave us—I just thought you would be happier with—" He looked desperately at his human wife, eyes begging for help.

Sairsa sighed in exasperation. Pushing him roughly aside, she said, "Oh, move over, you Big Boob, and let me try to talk to her. Why did you tell her that? Now look what you've done!"

"But I—" Sairsa growled in exasperation and he moved out of her way, allowing her to crawl over to sit beside the hysterical Avairei. Taking the smaller woman in her arms, Sairsa stroked her gently. "There, there, stop crying, Pela—stop. Our husband isn't angry with you—you misunderstood."

She eyed the Kashallan, and said, a little louder, "He isn't going to divorce you, so stop it. If he tries to divorce you—I'll leave him, too."

Seeing the Kashallan's astonished face at that revelation, Sairsa almost laughed. "Now stop all this nonsense. You're not going anywhere," she assured her. Sairsa brushed the tears away with the corner of the blanket and kissed her.

"There, that's better. You misunderstood him—he isn't going to shame you, so don't worry."

Pela sniffed. Still clinging to Sairsa, she glanced fearfully at the Kashallan, then back to her sister-wife, and asked in a quavering voice, "If our husband isn't angry with me and doesn't want me to leave, then why did he say such a terrible thing to me?"

Sairsa sighed. "Because he's a big idiot who means well, but doesn't know what he's doing half the time. He knows how much you care for Amril and he wants you to be happy, that's all."

"But I wouldn't be happy if I had to leave you, or our husband, and the babies—even if I could have Amril for my own. But the Imas never would let me have him, not if I was divorced by one of the Khutani! I would be a disgraced woman—they would never let me breed with anyone else. Oh, Sairsa'meh," she wailed, starting to cry all over again.

Sairsa pushed the braidlets off Pela's forehead. "Now stop, Love, you're getting yourself worked up over nothing," she said, more sternly this time. "I don't know which one of the bondmates' idea this was—Dunnagh's, most like, the amadan—but times like this, I think neither of them has a whole brain between them." She glared at him, her green eyes demanding that he say something to reassure the frightened woman.

"Pela, please, Love, forgive me. I'm so sorry—I never meant to hurt you, never!" Tears coming to his own eyes, he said, "It wasn't fair, what Sagas did to you—making you marry me. I didn't want you to have to grieve for your lost love.

"You gave me back my Sairsa when I thought she was lost to me forever. I just wanted to do the same thing for you, give you back your lost love—so you could be happy, too."

Over her sister-wife's head, Sairsa mouthed, "Show her!" He nodded and reached for his Avairei wife.

WHEN IT WAS OVER, THE three lay together replete and content, Pela nestling snugly between her two larger mates. Inwardly, Dunnagh breathed a sigh of relief, thankful to have at least one of the day's crises settled so amiably. It had been close, though—Gods, he didn't even want to think about it if—

As he was just drifting off into an exhausted doze, Tani roused him with an idea of its own. He sighed.

Into the drowsy silence, the Kashallan hesitantly spoke. "Loves, can I talk to you for a moment. I have another idea."

Sairsa groaned dramatically. "Please, haven't we had enough inspirations for one day?"

"No, please listen," Tani said. "You were right, Sairsa—that last plan was Dunnagh's, but this idea is mine. It is a much better plan, I promise you—it will make everything turn out well—I think."

"All right, Tani, if we must, let's hear your brilliant inspiration. It can't be any stupider than Dunnagh's," she muttered under her breath.

From the cradle of their encircling arms, Pela looked up at her husband with moist brown eyes. She took a deep breath. "What is it you want to tell us, Tani? I will listen."

"Thank you, My Sweet. Both Kasha-Dunnagh and I do want you to be happy. So, before I explain my idea, let me ask you a question first." When she nodded, the symbiont continued, "As the Kashallan, it would seem to me that many of the conventions of Timornan society don't apply to us—is that correct?"

"I—I don't know, maybe."

The Kashallan frowned and closed his eyes—how to make them understand? <<Kasha, this is harder to explain than I thought,>> Tani complained.

A mental laugh. <<Oh, no, this is your idea—you tell it. I'm staying out of this one.>>

The Kashallan opened his eyes once more. Both women were watching him warily. Tani began again. "What I mean is that, as the first Kashallan, we are different—because there has been no other bonded pair like us. So, as the first of the new kashallans, we can choose our own ways of doing things—provided we don't break our sworn oath, of course."

"Tani, Dear, get to the point," Sairsa said.

"All right—the point is that since we are the Kashallan—I think it's time, that we took a new wife."

"A what!"

He nodded, trying to hold back a grin. <<Well, that got their attention,>> Dunnagh said.

"Yes," Tani said, "a new wife. And, if I understand Avairei custom correctly, I must ask my first wife to do my negotiating for me. Is that not so, Sweet?" Blue eyes alight with mischief, he smiled down at Pela's bewildered face.

Sairsa's eyes narrowed with suspicion. Rising up on one elbow, she gave him a warning look. "What's going on here? That look on Dunnagh's face tells me that you two are up to some devilment. What is it?"

"No devilment, I am perfectly serious."

Pela was starting to get that wild, frightened look again. Sairsa gave him a warning frown. He was definitely looking too smug and pleased with himself for her liking. "All right," she said hesitantly, "I'll rise to your bait. Who's the *lucky* girl?"

"Amril Caltia."

"What? Amril—" Sairsa stared at him openmouthed, then flopped over on her back and laughed.

Pela glanced from one of her spouses to the other, totally confused. "I don't understand what either of you are trying to tell me. Please. Why are you laughing Sairsa'meh?"

The Kashallan hugged her tight. Eyes twinkling, he said, "Pela, Love, you already have a sister-wife—wouldn't you like to have a brother-wife, too?" This brought another peal of laughter from Sairsa.

Pela gave Sairsa a troubled look, then returned her attention to the Kashallan. "But why would you want Amril for your wife? You and he—he can't have your children—why?"

The Kashallan chuckled and kissed her on the forehead. "No, Amril can't give me any children, not directly anyway. But he can give *you* children, Pela, Love. Wouldn't you like that? If I marry him, you could love him and have his children. I would care for and claim as mine all our babies, no matter who fathered them. We would be one big family, and there would be no disgrace for you, hmm?"

She stared at him incredulous.

"Oh, Pela, think," Sairsa said. Then, turning to her husband, she smiled. "Well, Tani My Dear, I have to admit this is a most inspired plan, but what about your kindred? Would they agree to this—and Amril himself? Such a relationship is rather *unconventional*; he may not want to become anybody's 'wife,' even if it was only in name—people might mock him, or worse."

"Where a breeding is concerned, it isn't up to Amril to decide," Pela said firmly, her eyes now alight with hope. "It is the Imas who determine a prospective match—and the Khutani," she added, giving him a grateful, look.

Tani chuckled, and with tentacles extended stroked her soft flank. "Yes, Sweet, I know. And at least this Khutani agrees."

"Thank you, husband. I don't know if the Khutani Elders or the Imas will agree, but I thank you for thinking of me and worrying about my happiness. As your first wife, I will begin the negotiations for your new bride as soon as possible."

Chapter Two

Ngeal frowned. Sagas had just asked her a question about something—but she hadn't been listening, caught up in her own musings about Tomina. The woman should have been well enough by now to come out of her room and take the Kashallan's oath, yet Hobral claimed she was still convalescing—

"I'm sorry, Sagas, I was thinking about something else. What did you just say?"

They were sitting companionably in the comfortable chairs of Ngeal's outer chamber, a pitcher of spiced tea on the low table between them. From the chapel down the hall came the melodic sounds of a praise song to the Great Mother.

Sagas poured more tea from the pitcher into both their bowls. "I said, do you think your message will get to Riath before the Sorins begin?"

Ngeal shook her head, a worried expression crossing her face. So much had happened since she sent that runner off to the Capital. When her superiors in Riath found out about Ticca's change of allegiance they would consider Ticca an outlawed keep.

She made that decision out of fear—before she truly understood what the Khutani wanted of them. But by her action, she had inadvertently endangered them all. Should the High Matri decide to send her Warlinga in force to retake the fortress, there could be many lives lost.

Unlike Sagas, Ngeal had little faith in the obnoxious little Speir'dina Hunt Leader's ability to withstand an attack by such well-trained troops. "I don't know if Hagar's man got there, and even if he did, I'm not sure a hunting pack would have the time to come all the way here before the storms. The rains stopped days ago, and the wind will shift soon. It won't be long now before the Sorins come."

"Yes, I know, but I'm still worried. I don't trust Enaju Dingay to do anything predictable."

"Mm, perhaps. But I think we will be left alone here until after the blue snows have cleansed the land, but then we should be prepared for anything—"At a knock at the door she broke off.

Ngeal's maid Sondi put down her sewing and rose to answer it. Sondi opened the door a crack, spoke to someone briefly then turned back to Ima Ngeal. "It's the Kashallan's wives. They say they would like to speak to you, Ima."

Sagas scowled. "What is wrong now?" she muttered, and glanced warily at her old mentor's face.

Ngeal lifted a hand in a noncommittal gesture. "Invite them in, Sondi, and bring some more tea."

Sondi bowed, holding the door open for the two women. As they entered, Pela's eyes widened when she saw Amril's sister Sagas sitting next to her. Ngeal surveyed them through half closed eyes. They were nervous about something, especially the young Avairei—Pela. "Well, daughters, what brings you to seek me out today?"

Pela glanced at her sister-wife, and took a deep breath. "Thank you for seeing us, Ima Ngeal. I am sure you are very busy, so we won't stay long. As first wife of our husband the Kashallan, it is my duty to come to you on his behalf."

Face a blank mask, Ngeal nodded. "Mm, it is a pleasure to know that a young person like yourself respects our traditions," she said. "So how may I be of service to your husband?"

Pela took a sip of her tea, her eyes once more seeking out her sister-wife. Sairsa gave her an encouraging nod. "Our husband has informed me that he feels it is time for him to take a new wife. He has spoken to the Holy Ones in the pools about his choice—and they have agreed. He has sent us to ask for the approval of the Ima Matri of Ticca, so that the preparations for the marriage may proceed."

Ngeal sipped her tea, thinking. This was a possibility that hadn't occurred to her. One that could be of great advantage to her clan. She knew about this strange half-alien, half-Khutani creature's sexual appetites. Already they were the talk of the keep.

By her people's standards, his ongoing interest in his breeding wives was a shocking revelation. If he had been an Avairei—well, such behavior would have been considered a shameful perversion. Being this strange mixture, however—well, no one knew what to think. And now he wanted *another* wife!

It did make a strange kind of sense. These two were far along in their breeding cycles, and it was his duty to father many children who might make the bonding someday. Hmm. Nona was about the right age—if he chose a woman of her clan...

Ngeal studied the women carefully. There was something else going on here, she decided. They seemed too happy about this. Maybe they were just relieved that he would be taking his lust elsewhere, but she didn't think so. She had observed what she believed to be genuine love and caring between those three, so why would these women risk shattering that harmony by allowing him to lust after another unknown woman?

"Hmm. He wishes to take another wife, does he, and you say the Khutani approve—most interesting. And who, may I ask, has been chosen for this great honor?"

"Amril Caltia."

Beside Ngeal Sagas choked. "My idiot brother!" Then, narrowing her eyes, she demanded, "Pela, is this some kind of game? Which one of you foolish young women thought up this scheme? Because if it is—"

Ngeal put a hand on her shoulder to quiet her. "Sagas, be still. This isn't your concern. I am Ima Matri here, and I decide the breeding arrangements for the people within Ticca.

"As head of the Caltia clan in this keep, you will naturally, out of courtesy, be the first to be informed of my final decision. But as Ima Matri here, it is *my* right and duty to rule on this matter."

Sagas scowled, but kept her peace. Ngeal considered the women sitting anxiously before her. They were both big with child, yet how different they were.—a*h, Khutani, you have truly brought a great change to our world*. Ngeal fixed them with obsidian eyes. "Before I give any answer about this marriage, I want to hear more about this rather—shall we say, *unconventional* proposal."

Returning her look calmly, Sairsa said, "This isn't either Pela's or my idea, Ima, I assure you. It is the Khutani itself who makes this request." She smiled, giving Ngeal a knowing wink. "Tani has taken a liking to the young man in question, and feels that he could become a valued member of our family."

"I see. And, what would your husband be willing to give to this keep, and to the Caltia clan, for the loss to us of such a *valuable* young priest, hmm?"

Sairsa looked bewildered, and turned helplessly to Pela. The Avairei cleared her throat, glanced at her sister-wife, then said, "He—uh—will personally make for the Caltia five marriage bottles of red kavay and seven flasks of the yellow," she offered.

"Mm and for Ticca?"

Pela's expression grew desperate and she hastily turned to consult with her sister-wife in a low whisper.

Though she kept her face expressionless, inwardly Ngeal smiled to herself. These two hadn't been prepared for things to go this far, so quickly. *They probably expected to have to plead their case for a much longer time before contract negotiations were considered. I doubt if they have even discussed the trade items with their husband yet. What will they do now?* Sagas gave her a withering stare, but Ngeal ignored her.

Conference over at last, Pela took a deep breath and turned back to Ngeal. "For Ticca he will make the same. And he will personally taste, to make sure that their lineages are compatible, all the prospective couples in this keep for the next two renewal seasons."

"Ten bottles of red kavay for Ticca, eight for the Caltia, fifteen bottles of the yellow for Ticca, ten for the Caltia, and four seasons of the couple suitability, and eight of the green for Ticca," Ngeal countered.

"But—" Pela stammered.

Sairsa threw up her hands in dismay. "Oh, Ima, our poor husband—how could you be so cruel!" she wailed. "His symbiont is so young—and they are still so weak from our long, harsh journey! How could Tani possibly do so much without endangering its so-delicate health?

"Oh, Ima Ngeal, would you cause the death of one of the Khutani by your unreasoning demands? Oh, oh, what are we to do—our children will be orphaned before they are even born!" she moaned.

"Six of the red, eight of the yellow, and only four of the green. And two seasons, no more, please, Ima—you will kill him!"

Ngeal's mouth twitched. She glanced at Sagas. The poor woman was staring, mouth agape. Well, this dramatic bargaining wasn't the way these things were usually done—but why not play the game. This wasn't your usual marriage contract, either.

As before, when she had observed this young Speir'dina woman dealing with the Sweh'an, Ngeal found herself unexpectedly drawn to the alien. What a fascinating treasure she was.

Ngeal sighed. "All right, daughter, I wouldn't want to be the cause of leaving you a widow. Six of the red for the Caltia, nine for Ticca. Only eight of the yellow for the Caltia and ten for Ticca, five green, and three seasons. He will have plenty of time in three seasons to finish such a task," she said trying to hide her smile.

"Done," Sairsa agreed.

Ngeal nodded. "Very well. I will inform the young man of his betrothal and upcoming wedding. When do you and your husband wish this marriage to take place?"

"Uh.—" The women glanced at each other. Pela shifted nervously. "Ima Ngeal, under the circumstances we thought it would be best to have the ceremony a private affair, and soon?"

"Mm, I see. Well, in this case you may be right," Ngeal conceded. She sighed. "All right—Sagas and I will make the necessary arrangements."

Looking relieved, the two wives stood up to leave. They bowed, and headed for the door. Before they could reach it, however, Ngeal stopped them. "One other thing, be sure to advise your husband that he is also responsible for making his new bride the marriage flask of red kavay that he must have before the wedding night."

Pela's eyes widened in surprise. Normally it was the woman's job to take charge of the red kavay that made all Timornans fertile.

"But surely, Ima," Sairsa protested, "under the circumstances that won't be neces—"

Ngeal shook her head, cutting her off. "There you are wrong, daughters. I can guess the intent behind this proposal, and under the circumstances it is a very honorable and generous offer. But in making this contract, you have bargained for a *wife*, and a wife is what you will be getting, remember that!

"What goes on in your bed is your business, but in the eyes of the world Amril Caltia will be the *wife* of the Kashallan, and he will dress and act the part, or he will bring shame down upon all of us."

Ngeal studied their shocked faces, and nodded. "Hadn't thought of that, had you. Do you want to withdraw your offer?"

They looked at each other again. Finally Pela stammered, "I—I don't know."

"Ima," Sairsa suggested, "if this is the way it will have to be—shouldn't we ask Amril what he wants—"

Ngeal shook her head. "You are new to our ways, daughter, but that isn't how things are done here. Amril will accept the will of his Ima Matri in this matter—it isn't up to him to decide. Now, do you wish to withdraw your offer?"

For a long moment they were silent, then Pela spoke. "No."

"Very well, so be it then. We will make the necessary arrangements."

When the women were gone, Sagas turned to her old teacher angrily. "Ngeal, how could you—why did you do this?"

Ngeal took a sip of her tea and stared at her for a long moment. Setting down her bowl, she shook her head. "Sometimes I despair of you, Sagas. You really don't understand?"

When Sagas gazed at her blankly, Ngeal sighed. "All right—it's really rather touching, actually. The Kashallan didn't know about Amril when you arranged for Pela to marry him. Now that he *does* know about our young lovers he wants to make amends in the only way he can.

"I doubt if he wants Amril for himself, if that's what you were thinking. No, he wants Amril for Pela, don't you see? If he divorced Pela, she would be shamed and never allowed to marry, so he will marry the man instead."

Sagas stared, incredulous.

Ngeal chuckled. "Think, Sagas, think! It isn't for sentiment that I am doing this. You will thank me for this one day—if we live that long. Granted, the relationship is unconventional, but if we all survive these next few seasons, what a coup for your family this marriage will be. To have one of your clan in the first kashallan's own family! If he is as lusty a young male as you claim, I may try to persuade him to take one of my own young nieces in time."

Sagas snorted. "He is that. Like the rest of his kin, the host is very interested, and the Khutani—well, it certainly does nothing to discourage its partner's activities in that direction." She sighed, giving in. "All right, I see your point—and theirs. I will agree to this marriage."

She stood up. "I guess I should go find the brat and tell him of his betrothal."

"Will you tell him who he is marrying?" Ngeal asked.

Sagas considered, then smiled, a wicked gleam in her eye. "No, not just yet. I think I'll let him squirm for a while first."

Chapter Three

Amril sat at the end of a long bench in the keep's large dining hall and picked at his food. The room was congested with hungry diners, and Avairei novices hurrying to and from the kitchen with large trays of food in their arms. Around him was the sound of muted conversation, and the click of eating sticks against clay bowls and plates. At the other end of his table several Speir'dina sat together, talking quietly in their own language.

He sat alone at his end of the table. He picked up a ball of spiced masa root, then dropped it back on his plate with a sigh. How could his sister do this to him? Oh, Holy Mother, he was still grieving for his lost love—the last thing he wanted right now was to get married!

This morning, Sagas sought him out as he was studying in the library and informed him that he was getting married tomorrow. Just like that—and she wouldn't even tell him to whom. All she would say was that the Khutani and Ima Ngeal had agreed to the mating, and that he would be told more when the arrangements were made.

Why now, and who? The only girls in the keep who were marriageable at the moment were Nona and Gressa. Nona was kind of nice, but he doubted if it could be her. He had overheard Ngeal say once that she already had plans for her clanswoman. No, it had to be Gressa. Oh, Mother, he would definitely need the red kavay to mate with her!

Her family and bloodline were among the best, true enough, but—how could the Imas do this to him? Amril buried his face in his hands in despair. At a touch on his shoulder, he looked up.

"You look like someone has told you some bad news, my friend. Can I help?" Timma asked, and sat down at the table across from him.

Amril shook his head. "Thanks for offering, Timma, but I'm doomed, and nobody can save me." He sighed dramatically and pushed the food around on his plate, unwilling to look the other Avairei in the face.

"Sounds pretty bad," Timma observed. "Are the others still treating you like an outcast because of your role in the raid?"

Startled, Amril looked up. "No, it isn't that—and I don't care about those silly fools, anyway," he grumbled. Then, hoping to change the subject, he asked, "How about you? I haven't seen much of you the last while—are you still getting the disapproving comments from the Avairei here, yourself?"

Timma pulled the long four-ply warrior's braid around from his back and studied it critically. Without looking at his friend, he said quietly, "Oh, yes, but I expected that." He flipped the braid back over his shoulder and gave Amril a lopsided grin. "I knew it wouldn't be easy, but I can't go back to what I was before, Amril, you know that."

In spite of his brave words, Timma's eyes pleaded for understanding. Amril nodded.

With the Kashallan's permission, of course, Timma had chosen to become the first of the Kashallan's new native Timornan medics. The medics were healers who would also be trained in a warrior's skills as well as medicine. This new type of healer would go with the Warlinga, to treat the wounded on the hunt, rather than waiting till the injured could be returned to a keep for healing—or death rites—as was the usual custom.

Amril studied his friend. There was something different about him today. "Timma." He reached out and touched a new medallion around the young man's neck. "When did this happen? You are a full Ata now—I am very happy for you."

Then, feeling a bit hurt, he added, "Why didn't you tell me? I would have liked to go to your coming-of-age celebration!"

Timma made a face, then shrugged. "I didn't tell you about the party—because there wasn't any. Amril, don't look so hurt—of course I would have told you, if I'd had one. No, it wasn't like that. After Ata Hobral saw my work, he agreed with Ata Temog that I was far more experienced than most of his students who were much older than me, so why not give me in name what I had already earned?

"And as for the other part of our duty—feeding and caring for the Khutani—" He held out his scarred arm, "Well, I've already been giving Tani the Blood Gift for months now—so there was no point in making a big deal of it. They just gave me the medallion."

He fingered his braid again and made a sour face. "They probably didn't want to make too big a thing of it because of this," he said, "but I don't care; I'm an Ata now, and Ata Temog is my teacher as before. That's what matters." He gave his friend a crooked grin and held up the medallion.

"But this does make things a bit easier. All those young idiots around here who were looking down their noses at me and trying to give me orders have stopped."

But it did matter, Amril thought; he could see it in Timma's eyes. The coming-of-age ceremony for all young Avairei was the highlight of a young person's life. They were ushered into adulthood by being formally introduced to the Khutani, making their first blood gift and forming the link. Later, friends and relatives congratulated them during the feast and celebration that followed.

Like Amril himself, circumstances conspired to deny Timma what should have been his right. "Well, don't feel too bad. I never got my coming-of-age celebration either—and you're right, it doesn't matter." Then changing the subject, he said morosely, "I'm doomed anyway. They can celebrate at my funeral tomorrow—I don't care!"

Timma sat back, eyes widening in astonishment. "Your what? My, my, you're in a great mood today. Amril, By The Goddess, what is the matter? Please tell me."

Amril pushed his plate away and stood up. "Come on, let's get out of here. I need to go down to the pools for some medicines Ata Hobral wants. Come with me and I'll tell you, if you really *want* to know."

Timma shrugged. "Sure. I was supposed to meet San Bennett there soon, anyway. I'm to instruct him in the color coding of the different kavay ponds," Timma said, as he fell into step beside the other priest.

At the bottom of the stairs leading into the main cavern, Amril paused. He took in a deep calming breath; the warm spicy air had a soothing quality, even in his troubled state. He scraped a bit of the glowing wall-fungus into the bowl of a lantern, and then picked up several clean, empty bottles that were stacked by the wall and put them into a carrying net.

From somewhere out in the darkness the young Khutani splashed and squealed as they played. Timma laughed, his attention drawn to the sound. "The Holy Ones seem very happy. I wonder if Tani is playing with them."

"Mm." Amril stepped onto the nearest causeway and headed for the kavay ponds, where he began listlessly filling the carved stone flasks from the shallow pools.

Timma crouched down beside him. "All right, we're alone now. What's this all about?"

Amril put down the flask he had just filled and sighed. Then in a tight voice, he said, "My sister informed me earlier today that I'm to be married tomorrow."

Timma stared open-mouthed. "You're what?"

Amril nodded gloomily.

"Oh, My Friend, to who?"

"I don't know," Amril said. "And Sagas is playing the inscrutable Ima and won't tell me—and Ima Ngeal won't tell me, either. But there's only one girl it could be, and she's—" He took a deep breath, then picked up another bottle, moved over to the next pond and began dipping its frothy liquid into the vessel. "I'm doomed."

Timma followed, stunned. At last he murmured, "I take it that this woman isn't to your liking."

Amril sighed. "I don't particularly care for Gressa—she's a bit bossy—but she's not a bad sort. And her bloodline is impeccable, but—" She's not Pela, his heart cried, but he couldn't say that out loud, not even to Timma.

"Mm, this is one aspect of adulthood that I'd forgotten about when I was in such a hurry to be recognized as an Ata. I guess they will be considering me for betrothal sometime soon, as well."

Amril laughed. "Probably, but don't look so glum. You'll most likely keep your freedom for a while—your warrior's braid will see to that. Ima Ngeal still isn't sure how she feels about you, so don't worry just yet."

Timma chuckled. "Well, that's one advantage to my new appearance and training that I never thought of." Stroking his braid again, he said thoughtfully, "You know, Amril, times are changing. If this marriage is truly not to your liking; why not ask the Kashallan to get you out of it? He needs more Timornan medics for his Warlinga, and—"

Ask the Kashallan for help, Amril thought. Oh, Goddess, what would he say to him? "Please help me. I don't want to do my duty and marry Gressa, because I'd rather have one of *your* wives instead!" Oh, Holy Mother, no. What a laugh.

He shook his head. "No. Thank you for your concern, Timma, but I can't—it wouldn't be right. No, I will do my duty—the breeding time isn't forever—if we don't suit, after the children we can separate. I—"

"My, my, this seems like a very serious discussion. You two look like the future of Timorna has just been lost," a cheerful voice from behind them said. "What's wrong?"

Startled, the two young Atas looked around. Eyes twinkling, a smiling Kashallan watched them.

Hastily, the Avairei got to their feet and bowed, but remained silent. He waited, obviously wanting an answer to his question. At last, Amril mumbled, "It's nothing, Holy One, I'm—not feeling well, that's all."

"Ah, I see." His eerie blue eyes still fixing them with an amused stare he extended a tentacled hand. "In that case, perhaps I should offer my services as healer—"

Amril stepped back, shoving his hands hastily behind him. "No! Oh, no, I'll be fine. Really—I'm not sick in that way. It's just—" He broke off, looking down, unable to meet the Kashallan's gaze any longer.

"His sister just told him he's getting married tomorrow," Timma supplied, "and he doesn't care for the girl that they have chosen for him."

The Kashallan blinked, then his eyes widened. He stared at Amril curiously for a long moment, then he asked, "You don't care for your intended? Is this true, Ata?"

Amril shifted nervously. "I—I don't particularly like the one I think the Imas have chosen for me, but I will do my duty, Holy One. I will go through with this marriage, as my elders and the sacred Khutani have commanded me," Amril assured him.

"Mm, that's good to know; I am glad to hear that."

Then, changing the subject, he held out two beautiful red kavay marriage flasks. "I have been asked to make the red kavay for the occasion, Amril. When I saw you and Timma over here just now, I thought I'd come and ask you which one of these flasks you'd prefer."

Amril stared stupidly at the vessels, his stomach churning. *I really am doomed*, he thought. The marriage flask that contained the kavay that made couples fertile on Timorna was a highly valued item to his people. A new wife received a flask upon her marriage, and wore it at her waist as a sign of her new status as a breeding woman. Later, when she was older, she would pass it on to a daughter, or another valued member of her family, as a mark of her favor.

These two were both beautiful examples of their kind, and he should feel very honored that the Kashallan himself would be doing this for him and his spouse to be—but he was so depressed at the prospect of this marriage that he didn't want to think about it, let alone decide which should be Gressa's flask.

He shrugged. "I don't know—they are both beautiful."

"Mm, you're not being very helpful today, are you?" Turning to Timma, he said, "Care to help your friend out?"

Timma considered, then pointed to the one on the left. "That one's prettier."

The Kashallan held it up, examining it critically. "Hmm, I think maybe you're right. I'll make the red kavay to fill this one. Thank you."

He started to turn away, when shyly, Timma asked, "Holy One, the Imas haven't told Amril who he is to marry—and there is this one girl here—but since you are making the red kavay for the wedding, surely you know the identity of Amril's intended."

"Yes, I know."

Amril looked up sharply. "Holy One, my sister is playing some stupid, cruel game with me," he complained. "She won't tell me who I am to wed—but it has to be Gressa—she's practically the only one here—and Ima Ngeal said, when I asked her, that it's my duty to do what is expected of me, no matter who it is." Eyes moist with unshed tears of frustration, he pleaded, "I just want to know—if it's Gressa—I—I won't mind *too* much if I have some time to prepare myself. Sagas won't tell me—will you?"

The Kashallan chuckled. "Sounds to me like you are considering this marriage something akin to a fate worse than death. I'm sorry to hear that," he said, eyes still studying the young priest with a strange gleam in their kavay-blue depths. "I had hoped your betrothal would please you more than it apparently does."

Afraid that he had angered or offended this august personage, Amril bowed and hastily said, "Holy One, I meant no offense to the sacred Khutani or my elders—I will do what is required of me. I—I—" He broke off, hanging his head in shame.

Oh, Mother, this was awful. He glared at Timma murderously. Even though Timma had meant well— Oh, but why did he have to open his big mouth. He couldn't explain—not to the Kashallan—this was terrible!

"Cheer up, Ata, things may not be as bad as they seem," the Kashallan said.

Amril looked up hopefully. Maybe they were going to let him marry Nona—maybe Ngeal felt sorry for him after he lost Pela. Maybe. "Will you tell me then?"

"Well, perhaps that's only fair. Sagas is being a bit high-handed with you, I suppose. Maybe you're right. All right, I'll tell you, if you really think it will help you prepare. It isn't Gressa you're wedding—it's me."

Amril's mouth dropped open. He stared, incredulous, unable to speak. The Kashallan chuckled, unable to hold back his amusement any longer. "Oh, yes, it's quite true—and, as my new wife I'm very happy to know that you are so willing to do your *duty*—very glad."

He gave Amril another toothy smile, then, seeing Nathan coming down the steps, he excused himself and left.

Body trembling, Amril sank down to the walkway, blindly staring out across the cavern. He shook his head, trying to clear it. Goddess, had he heard him correctly?

Timma stared after the retreating Kashallan, then returned his regard to Amril. Almost as stunned by the news as his friend, he said, "Holy Goddess, Amril."

Amril turned round to face him. "Why are you staring at me like that?" he demanded. *Get used to it*, a small voice in his head warned. *When they dress you in a woman's kilt and tie the marriage flask at your waist, everybody'll be staring at you*. Wife—to him!

Amril clenched his fists. Suddenly, he felt like he wanted to hit someone, or cry, and he wasn't sure which. A man formally being given as wife to another male...

When the Avairei here thought him a traitor, their contempt had been hard enough to bear—but this—well, they wouldn't know what to think, and why should they? He didn't know himself. Wife! And the Kashallan— He shivered. He was so—big!

Chapter Four

As they climbed the stairs, the Kashallan asked, "Why were you looking for me? Is there anything wrong?"

Nathan shook his head. "No—Tizu sent me to find you. He thinks he has a good candidate for his second-in-command among the Warlinga. He wanted to make sure that you approved of his man, that's all."

"Mm, so who'd he choose?"

"Someone named Fadir. Evidently he was Hagar's unofficial heir. Tizu thinks that the rest of the Warlinga will fall into line a little easier if this man is his second, and the one they take orders from most of the time."

"Fadir," the Kashallan murmured to himself, trying to remember his taste, or to place him among so many new faces.

"He was the young officer at the funeral feast who did most of the talking for the rest of them," Nathan supplied. "Tizu said he remembered him from that day when he and the Imas tried to enter Ticca as pilgrims. Fadir evidently was in charge at the Swamp gate that time. Tizu said he almost had to kill him, because he was too good at his job."

"Mm, just as well he didn't."

Nathan grunted. "Yeah, right."

They walked along companionably in silence a while longer, then Nathan asked, "So, what was going on down there with you and those two? Amril looked like you could have knocked him over with a feather, and Timma didn't seem much steadier."

The Kashallan continued walking in silence, glancing at him out of the corner of his eye from time to time.

Nathan allowed the silence to go on for a while then demanded, "All right, what's up? When you get that *look*, I know there's something going on—what is it?"

Dunnagh sighed. "Well, I guess I'd better tell you, before you hear about it elsewhere, and get the wrong idea."

"Shit! Out with it."

"...I'm getting married again tomorrow."

Nathan stopped and gaped. For just a moment, Dunnagh thought he saw a look of hurt in his gray eyes then it was gone. Nathan began walking again, quickening his pace. "Getting quite the little harem, aren't you? Who?"

"It isn't what you're thinking, Nathan," Dunnagh protested. "It's not for me that I'm doing this—"

Nathan snorted. "Right."

"It isn't, damn it!"

"Sure."

"It isn't—it's for Pela."

Nathan stopped again, and stared, incredulous. "Let me see if I've got this straight. You're going to marry another woman tomorrow—for Pela. She given up on men these days?"

Dunnagh let out a long-suffering sigh. "No, she hasn't given up on men—at least I hope not—I'm not marrying another woman, anyway. I'm marrying Amril Caltia—for Pela, like I said."

At Nathan's uncomprehending look, he explained, "Pela and Amril had been promised to each other since they were children. I can taste that they still love each other—and the way Sagas treated them was unfair. I can't divorce Pela because she'd be shamed, so I'm marrying Amril instead so they can be together."

Nathan laughed, shaking his head in consternation, then he began walking again. "You certainly like to go out of your way looking for trouble. Gods, which one of you two idiots thought up this *brilliant* scheme?"

"Actually it was me. And my idea was much better than my Kasha's, just for your information," Tani added smugly.

Nathan grunted. "That wouldn't be hard. I can believe that, Tani."

They continued on down the corridor, Nathan stealing sidelong glances at the Kashallan. At last he blurted, "So if this marrying Amril is only for Pela's benefit, why were you so afraid to tell me about it, hmm?"

"Because I was afraid you'd take it the wrong way, just like you're doing—I didn't want you to be hurt, or angry with me."

Nathan snorted. "What's it to me who you marry, or sleep with? Marry half the keep if you want to. You're the Kashallan—do what you want. What do I care?"

Dunnagh stopped, spinning Nathan around to face him. "Because you *do* care," he said fiercely. "I saw it in your eyes just now, and I want you to know it isn't like that. *You're* the only one I've ever wanted, or will want, in that way, please believe me!"

Nathan pushed his hand away, and started walking again. "Yeah, right, *Holy One.*"

"Nathan, stop it! You know what I'm saying is true. You're the only—"

"And what have I told you about that, hmm? I told you no, didn't I, Dunnagh? Ever since you and Tani started playing this stupid little game with me again, the answer is no—and is going to stay no. There are too many other problems in our lives, too many other people involved who might be hurt."

"So was I asking?" Dunnagh countered. "I heard you, and I agree with you—or were you hoping I *would* start asking again?"

Nathan swore viciously in Caldoni, earning him the startled looks of two Avairei passing them in the corridor at the time. When the priests were gone, he said, still in Caldoni, "Look, we swore the oath of the Ca'Companachda—battle companions—to each other years ago, and that isn't going to change.

"But we also haven't been physical lovers to each other in years either—so why do you think I'd start caring now who you sleep with, damn it? In spite of both you and Tani trying to seduce me every chance you get, Dunnagh, I don't care about Amril!"

"I've never taken another man to my bed,, Nathan," Dunnagh said quietly in the same language, "nor, I think, have you."

"Shit." Nathan sighed. "Even if you are doing this for Pela—and maybe you are, sleep with him too—for all I care," Nathan growled. "I don't want to hear it—and I don't give a shit what you do, or don't do, all right? So just drop it."

"Damn it, Nathan, are you deliberately trying to be difficult?" Dunnagh shot back, his temper and his voice beginning to rise. "I know you, remember—when you're afraid of getting hurt, you try to get people angry with you, so you can feel justified in pulling away first. So stop it, it's not going to work! I love you, I always will, and I'm telling you, it isn't like that with Amril. You're the only man that I've ever loved like that, or wanted so—"

"And does that pretty speech go for Tani too, hmm?" he interrupted. "What about your bondmate, Dunnagh?" At his shocked look, Nathan snorted. "Yeah, just what I figured."

"No, Nathan, it's not like that—"

Nathan put out a hand to stop him, then folded his arms across his chest. "You mean to tell me that the symbiont isn't curious—doesn't want to find out what it would feel and *taste* like to make love to another male? You gonna stand there and lie to me, right to my face?"

"I—I—"

"Right," he said, seeing the answer plain upon Dunnagh's startled face. "So damn it, just shut up," Nathan growled. "I don't want to hear it—and I don't give a shit what you do."

Lowering his eyes, Dunnagh said, "Fine, I will then—believe what you like."

"Damn right I will," Nathan muttered and began walking again.

TICCA'S NEW HUNT LEADER had set up his command post in a room adjacent to the wings where the Warlinga and Speir'dina would be quartered during the Sorins. This part of the keep was set apart from the chambers of the Avairei in the inner sanctum. As they approached, Oglas and Goronwy saluted. Nathan knocked, then, at a muffled reply, they entered.

Tizu was sitting at a long wickerwork table, a few maps and stacks of papers spread out in front of him. As they came in, he looked up, then went back to the report he was studying. Nathan remained near the door, but the Kashallan walked over and pulled out a chair and sat. Tizu glanced up when he finished reading. The tension in the room was thick enough to cut with a knife. "So, what's with you two, have a lover's quarrel?"

That had just been a smart-assed remark—he hadn't meant anything by it, but the withering look Nathan gave him, made Tizu's eyes open wide. Damn, what was going on?

Before he could ask, Oglas opened the door and ushered a Warlinga still liberally plastered in yellow kavay scabs into the room. The man saluted, clawed hand to his chest, and then stood with head crest slightly raised. Tail tip twitching he warily eyed the three humans, waiting further orders.

Nathan cleared his throat. "Commander, you got anything you want me for? Otherwise I'll be going, I—"

"Yeah, as a matter of fact I do." He rummaged in the pile of papers on the table in front of him, then, picking one up, he held it out to Nathan. "Here's the duty schedule I made up for the guard stationed outside the Dingay woman's door. See that it gets posted in our meeting room, and make sure those idiots *read* it. I want no slip-ups because somebody didn't think to look at the sheet."

Nathan saluted, then giving the Kashallan one last unreadable look he left.

Seeing the look of astonishment on Fadir's face, Tizu snapped, "What's wrong with you? And sit down, damn it, before you give me a neck-ache. This is an informal meeting—you're not being disciplined for anything."

Fadir bowed, grabbed a stool from near the wall, and sat. Red eyes wide with wonder, he continued to stare at the Speir'dina Hunt Leader.

Annoyed with the man's look, Tizu scowled. "What?"

Fadir's face greened in embarrassment. "I'm sorry, Honored Hunt Leader, Holy One, I—I meant no offense—but you can read!"

Tizu nodded. "Yeah, so?" Fadir dropped his eyes, confused. Tizu's scowl deepened.

The Kashallan leaned forward, and said into the silence, "On Timorna, Hunt Leader, only the Avairei have that skill. Here Warlinga don't read or write. Though I would like to see that change, if there are those who would be interested in learning such skills."

Fadir nodded, tail tip flicking back and forth. "Yes, Holy One, there are many of us who would like to know how to read, but the priests—they will not teach us."

Tizu swore in an undertone, and pushed aside several papers on his worktable. "So much for the orders I've been trying to write down with the glyphs Timma's been teaching me." He sighed, and picking up a pen, jotted down a note to himself.

"If they won't teach you, then *I'll* teach you myself," he said. "Our written language is different than the Timornan glyphs, but it will work. And, it's simpler to learn, actually. I think it should be an important part of the new training I have in mind.

"All my Speir'dina armachda can read and write, and it'll make things much easier if everybody can communicate that way."

"Yes, Hunt Leader," Fadir murmured, his tail increasing its rhythm. "Hunt Leader, you wished to see me?"

Tizu folded his arms on the table in front of him. "Yes, I did. As you may remember, the Kashallan and I mentioned at the death feast that I would be looking for a Second Hunter to work with me as my next in command." Fadir nodded. "Well, I've had my eye on you for a while, and I'd like you for that position. Are you interested?"

Fadir raised his head crest in surprise. "I am still quite young for such an honor," the Warlinga hedged.

Tizu snorted. "You were Hagar's unofficial heir, weren't you?" Tizu countered. "And the question of how old you are isn't important at the moment. What I want to know is whether you can handle the job." He ran his eye over the Warlinga, expertly appraising the man.

"You look strong enough and tough enough to handle yourself well if you're crossed. And you trust your instincts and can think under pressure—I already know that."

Fadir's head crest rose even higher. "I am confused—how could you know that? Is this more Speir'dina magic?"

Tizu chuckled softly. "How do I know? I was afraid I was going to have to kill you that day on the causeway, when I came with the Imas. You were too alert, too suspicious—you impressed me then, and you still do. I think you're the man for the position. The question is, do you? Will your kinsmen take your orders, and, just as important, will you take mine?"

Fadir considered. He glanced surreptitiously from Tizu to the Kashallan, tail tip flicking rhythmically. At last he nodded. "Yes," he said slowly, "as you say, I was Hagar's heir, unofficially. The others will take my orders. And, I will take yours."

"Good."

Fadir hesitated, then asked, "Hunt Leader Tizu, you and the Holy One spoke at the funeral about combining our two hunting packs—if I am to be your Second, will the Speir'dina take *my* orders, or will that not be a part of my duties?"

Tizu grinned at the Kashallan. "What did I tell you—smart, right?" Turning to the Warlinga, he nodded his approval. "Good point. Yes, if this is to be a combined fighting force—and it is—then most definitely the Speir'dina will be taking orders from you. And they *will* take your orders," Tizu growled, "or I'll know the reason why not."

Relaxing a bit on his stool, the Warlinga nodded. "That's good. The other night there was talk about a combined pack, but I wasn't sure if it was just that—talk. Apparently not."

The Kashallan beamed at Fadir, then started to rise. "Good. I can't think of a better man for the job. Now, I'm sure you and Hunt Leader Tizu have a lot to work out, so I'll—"

"Ah, ah, ah." Tizu shook his head and waved him back to his seat. "Not so fast, boyo. There are still a couple other things I need you for."

The Kashallan made a face, then sat obediently. Catching sight of Fadir's shocked expression, he chuckled, then, in a stage whisper, said, "Remember I told you, Fadir, that San Tizu was *my* superior when I was a warrior? Well, sometimes he still thinks he is."

Tizu glanced up from the papers he was sorting, and snorted. "Damn right." Then, finding what he was looking for, he handed over a paper and explained, "A few of the beam rifles and side arms are just about useless. We took all the extra recharge packs from the base, but we'll still have to be careful how they are used from now on.

"One of Briyenn's hobbies is studying ancient weaponry, so I set him the task of designing a weapon that we could make with the materials available on this planet. He thinks a crossbow made of laminated bone and those bamboo-like reeds would be our best bet."

The Kashallan studied the diagram, then nodded. "Sounds good to me—with almost no metals and very little wood to work with, a crossbow would be good for us to start making and using. Get the Begta to help Briyenn gather some materials before the storms lock us in," he suggested, then smiled at Fadir and handed him the sheet.

Fadir took the paper reverently. When he saw the diagram, he hissed in surprise. Head crest flattened and red eyes narrowed, he stared at the other men in disbelief.

"What?" Tizu demanded.

Fadir flung the paper back on the table as if it had burned him. In a tight, controlled voice, he said, "That—that filth is an Umwira weapon!"

Tizu leaned back, placing his hands behind his neck and smiled to himself. "Well, well, well, that's very interesting."

"Hmm, interesting," Dunnagh echoed. Then remembering something he asked the Warlinga. "When we fought the Umwira in the underground passages near Sulas, I didn't see them using such weaponry. Those monsters fought only with tooth and claw—and the mind magics of course."

"I don't know much about the Ghostlanders, but I think they are different from the tribes who live by the Shallow Sea. The amount of mutation is not the same perhaps. I only know that the western tribes that come here to raid and steal our folk use such things."

He pointed with disgust at the discarded paper. "Hunt Leader, you can't possibly be serious about using an Umwira weapon—it wouldn't be right—"

"Fadir," Dunnagh said, interrupting him in mid-flow, "my Speir'dina kindred will need some type of weaponry to replace what we brought with us from our old home. Our gear will not last forever, and we were not bred, as your people were, with any natural defenses.

"The Speir'dina are a tool-using people. We will have to adapt ourselves, and the tools we use, to what is available on Timorna, but we must find some way to defend ourselves here. In our ancient past, we used such a weapon as this." He pointed to the diagram. "We even have a word for it in our language. It isn't just an Umwira creation, but belongs naturally to us, as well.

"Though it *is* very interesting that both the Hated Enemy and my people have come up with the same solution to a similar problem," Dunnagh said. "Hmm." Then, recovering himself, he added, "We will have to use *something*. The spears that your men make will do for some of my people, but for others—" he shrugged.

"The Hunt Leader and I are open to other suggestions, so if you have a better idea, I'm interested in hearing it."

Fadir lowered his eyes and his head crest, shamed. "No, Hunt Leader, Holy One, forgive me—I don't."

"Well, give it some thought," Tizu said. "I'll be depending on you to give me more information on the local environment and battle tactics, so maybe you can figure out ways of adapting what we know to better meet Timornan conditions.

"I want to set up some practice bouts so I can see how your kinsmen fight, and you can see how my people fight. Then maybe we both will have a better idea to enhance each other's skills."

His expression intense, Tizu leaned forward, and placed his hands atop the table. "Fadir, I don't want you just to 'yes, sir' me without giving any comments. There will be times when I will expect unquestioning obedience from you or anybody else, but most of the time, I want us to work together. I will answer your questions when you don't understand something, and I expect your suggestions when you have any, all right?"

FADIR SIGHED WITH RELIEF. Well, that would be an unexpected blessing. Hagar had always been so set in his ways that he resented the younger man's comments, more often than not. Maybe it wouldn't be so bad working with this Speir'dina, after all. If he was willing to accept that he had things to learn about Timorna, they would probably be able to work together quite well. "Yes, Hunt Leader, I understand. Thank you."

This Tizu would be a hard man to get used to, perhaps—but the Kashallan had been right, as an outlawed keep they would need all their fighting men, come the renewal season. He resolved then and there to do his best to see that they did form an effective fighting unit during the Sorins.

In spite of himself, he was impressed. Even though he knew the Kashallan approved of the man, it was still hard for him, and the rest of his kinsmen, to accept this small, seemingly defenseless creature as their new Hunt Leader.

His cousin Hagar had been a large, powerful man for his race, who had ruled this keep with strict discipline and had enforced his will, when necessary, with tooth and claw. His people expected that in a leader, and, though San Tizu had shown some skill in fighting in the barracks the other day—that wouldn't be enough if there was a serious discipline problem to deal with.

But teaching them to read and write—himself! Well, that was something that would definitely impress his clansmen, in spite of the man's size. And he would be there to see that the Hunt Leader's will was enforced. It was going to take a lot of work, all these new things, but they could do it.

Chapter Five

Opening the door to his own suite, the Kashallan was surprised to find a strange Avairei setting down a tea tray on the table by the wall. What was she doing here? Then he remembered. This must be the new maid Ngeal said she would be sending them.

At the sound of the door opening, the girl jumped, nearly dropping the tray she was holding. "Oh, Holy One, you startled me." Setting the tea things down carefully on the table, she put a hand to her breast. Braid ornaments tinkling, her lithe body sank into a low obeisance.

The Kashallan gave her a reassuring smile. "I'm sorry. I didn't mean to frighten you." When he'd come into the room and closed the door, he hesitated, suddenly feeling vaguely uneasy. Everything seemed normal, and yet—where were Pela and Sairsa?

The young priestess was watching him intently, her hand clutching a dark stone pendant that hung from a leather cord around her neck. Her fur was a rich brown in color, her eyes soft and luminous. She gave him a shy, dreamy smile, and went back to dusting the furniture. Dunnagh took in a deep breath—something was wrong, he felt— <<Tani, what's going on? I feel so-so weird—are we getting sick?>>

A mental chuckle. <<We can't be sick, Kasha; Khutani never get sick.>>

Dunnagh moved further into the room. What was a matter with him? There was no danger here—just the maid sent by Ngeal to clean up for them. Shying at shadows, he thought in disgust. Trying to act normal, he crossed to a comfortable chair and sat down. No danger, but there was an unfamiliar, musky smell in the room. It wasn't unpleasant, just—odd. He took in a deep breath, and felt his pulse quicken. The maid moved around the room with a sensuous grace, managing to catch his eye from time to time as she worked.

Feeling disconcerted and a little foolish, Dunnagh cleared his throat and asked, "Uh, do you know where my wives are?"

The girl put down the dust cloth she was using and approached him. Her fur shimmered like satin in the lamplight, her faint smile enticing. In spite of himself, Dunnagh felt his sex begin to harden. Within his middle, Tani stirred. <<She's very beautiful, isn't she, Kasha?>>

<<Yes,>> he agreed, mesmerized by her every move.

Standing beside his chair she bowed low before him, her soft, brown eyes never leaving his face. In a low, melodious voice she said, "Your Avairei wife has gone to the chapel, and your Speir'dina wife has gone to visit some of her kinswomen."

"Mm, thank you." Suddenly embarrassed, he didn't know what to say next. She was staring at him so intently—he should say something—she was so—beautiful!

"You look tired, Holy One. May I offer you some refreshment?"

He blinked. "Ye-es, thank you that would be nice."

Never taking his eyes off her, Dunnagh watched her cross the room, her kilt swaying gently with the motion of her hips as she moved. She was like liquid satin, all shimmering curves and a sweet promise. He felt his phallus stiffen further and hastily draped another fold of his own garment across his lap. She poured some of the pitcher's contents into a large bowl, then, returning to his side, she offered him the brimming vessel. He motioned for her to set it down on a nearby end table.

The maid complied, then, she laid a hand gently upon his arm. "What is it you wish, Kashallan? I am here only to serve you."

"Uh." Dunnagh shuddered, swallowed, then looked away. A wealth of sensations coursed through his body with that touch, confusing his mind. Tani writhed, its desire definitely aroused. Dunnagh swallowed hard again. <<Tani, please, this isn't right—>>

Then unable to resist he reached out a tentacled hand and stroked her furred arm—warm, velvet under his hand. "Uh. What's your name?" he asked, trying to resist both her strange allure and his bondmate's overwhelming interest.

"My name is Nona, Holy One, and I am yours to command." Without warning she sat down on his knee. He took in a ragged breath. Her nearness and her musky scent were intoxicating, overpowering his reason. Dunnagh stroked the silky fur of her shoulder. Oh, Gods—his head felt like it was full of cotton, but his loins were on fire. Cupping a small, round breast, he moaned with pleasure. "So soft, pretty Nona," he breathed, feeling as if he were drowning in a flood of desire.

Nona laughed, and gave him a knowing smile. Reaching down, she slipped her hand under his kilt and caressed his straining manhood. Looking deep into his eyes, she repeated, "You look tired, Holy One. Come into the bedroom and let me give you a massage, hmm?" Molding her hand around his shaft, she stroked him rhythmically. "I'm sure I will please you," she purred. "My touch will relax you and let you sleep *most deeply.*"

When he made no protest, Nona settled herself more comfortably on his lap, then she handed him the brimming bowl once more. "Drink," she coaxed. "Then let me please you, hmm?"

He let out his breath in a long dreamy sigh. "Ye-es, mm, ye-ess." The feel of her was so inviting; it promised endless delights. He groaned in eager anticipation. Ah, she was so beautiful! A tiny voice in the back of Dunnagh's mind warned that there was something wrong here—the drink. Oh, he couldn't think, not now—

Nona gave him a lingering kiss; then, bringing the bowl to his lips, she urged, "Drink—"

"Ahem! Dunnagh-Tani—what are you doing?" Sairsa stood in the doorway, her cool voice snapped like a whip.

Startled, the two sitting in the chair looked up. Then, recognizing who it was, the Kashallan jumped to his feet, spilling the surprised Nona onto the floor. He set the sloshing bowl back on the end-table, and took a few steps toward her. The look in her eyes brought him up short.

He swallowed, then stammered, "Uh—Nona was just offering me some tea—I was thirsty—and tired, and I—" Under her protracted scrutiny, his voice trailed off and he turned a deep red. "Sairsa, please, I—"

He felt so ashamed. Behind the anger in her green eyes, he could see the hurt. <<Oh, Gods, Tani, what were we thinking of—what did we almost do—how could we have been so stupid?>>

The Kashallan glanced down at the shivering girl huddled sobbing on the floor. He was a beast! She was so young—and so innocent. An Avairei priestess, just awakening into her womanhood, she was—how could he have almost—oh, Gods, he was such a brute. He shook his head, trying to clear it.

"Sairsa, I'm so s-sorry. I don't know what came over me. I—please don't look at me like that. I love you—please—"

"Ce'awn, oh, Ce'awn, come quick! There's a fight. Please come!" Oglas gasped from the doorway.

Oh, thank you, Oglas. I think you just saved my life. Already on his way to the door, Dunnagh demanded, "Who?"

"Nathan and Conal."

Swearing a colorful, Caldoni oath under his breath, Dunnagh followed Oglas into the hall. At the last moment, he turned back. "Sairsa, I have to go now, but I'll be back—I love you—" His eyes pleaded with her not to be angry, to wait; he would explain. They would talk later and get it worked out—but he had to go now.

━━━━✦✦✦✦✦━━━━

WHEN THE MEN WERE GONE, Nona turned off her sobbing, uncoiled herself from the floor, and stood up. She faced Sairsa with sly, downcast eyes. She said nothing, merely stood there, but Sairsa felt the other woman's challenge, ringing clear as a bell between them.

Sairsa folded her arms across her chest and fixed the maid with angry green eyes. "So. Just exactly what were you doing in here with him?" Alarm bells had been going off in her head ever since Nona showed up today and announced that she was their new maid. Sairsa felt a dark undercurrent about the girl that belied her tender young exterior.

Holding onto a pendant around her neck, Nona smiled, her eyes as hard as the stone she wore. "Why, I was only doing my duty, Speir'van Sairsa."

"Your duty is to bring our meals and clean up around here, not sit on my man's lap."

Nona's eyes flicked contemptuously over Sairsa's enlarged belly, her overripe breasts, and the purple kavay brands, spiraling across her pale skin like livid bruises. She curled her lip in disgust. "My duty is to serve the Holy One, in whatever way *pleases* him."

Sairsa's eyes widened and her mouth dropped open in shock. *The little bitch, how dare she speak to me like that?*

Nona looked deep into her eyes, catching and holding her gaze. Without warning, Sairsa reeled, as a flood of unwanted images cascaded into her mind. Suddenly she felt so fat, so ugly, and oh, so unwanted. She hated herself and the way she looked—no wonder Dunnagh wanted someone else. Someone younger, prettier—

Choking on a sob, she grabbed onto the doorframe for support. She was too ugly to live, she felt like— "Stop it!" Sairsa cried. "Whatever you're trying to do to me, it isn't going to work!"

"I am doing nothing to you, Speir'van. What are you talking about?"

Sairsa shook her head; it was gone now. Oh, the girl was pretending not to know what she meant, but that was a joke. She wasn't imagining this; she *had* felt those things, and she *had* seen the maid on Dunnagh's lap with her hand under his kilt.

The Avairei were usually so—so conservative about sex—no wonder that big boob of a man of hers had acted like a fool just now. He wouldn't have expected that kind of blatant sexual behavior from such a young priestess—he would have been like dough in her hands.

Who was she—what was she, really? Sairsa didn't know, and a chill of foreboding ran down her spine at the thought. Confused, she glared at the maid. Then, with all her protective instincts aroused, she stepped away from the door. "You've done enough in here for one day. Get out. Now!"

The girl gave her a graceful bow. "Your will, Speir'van," she said, and glided from the room.

When she was gone, Sairsa slammed the door hard. Feeling totally drained, she trembled with the aftershock of their confrontation. Unable to stand any longer, she crossed to the chair the Kashallan had just vacated and flopped into it. She brushed at the tears that were flowing down her cheeks. Safe from prying eyes, she buried her face in her hands and sobbed. *Oh, Dunnagh-Tani, how could you!*

Knowing that Pela would soon have Amril to love, Sairsa realized that secretly she had been glad of that fact for a very selfish reason. It would mean that she could have her beloved Dunnagh more to herself. But now—with that horrible girl gone—she had to admit to herself that she wasn't sure about Dunnagh's affections. Maybe she'd just assumed—maybe he really did want another pretty Avairei to share his bed.

No, she shook her head, furious with herself for even considering it. That couldn't be—that was stupid—she wouldn't believe it. No! Sairsa pushed those frightening thoughts aside. There had to be another reason for what she just witnessed—there was something else going on here. She could feel it. Hadn't the spirit told her that she had the Sight. She had to trust her feelings—no matter what?

Sairsa wiped her eyes. Her throat ached from all that crying. Blinking, she noticed the forgotten tea-bowl on the table and reached for it. Sairsa raised it to her lips then stopped. She sniffed. What is in this? It looked like ordinary tea, spicy and cool, like they made it here at Ticca. It looked all right and yet— She sniffed again, then frowned. Taking a fingertip, she dipped it into the liquid then brought it to her lips.

Suddenly she gagged, alarm bells chiming in her head once more. Unable to stand the thought of tasting even that small amount, Sairsa rose to her feet, and bowl in hand, walked to the chamber-pot and dumped the tea in. Returning to the side-table, she retrieved the pitcher and poured its contents as well into the foaming mass.

Sairsa didn't want to believe what her instincts were telling her. Could that arrogant little chit have been trying to poison them? Gods, how was that possible? The girl was Ngeal's clanswoman, and she had sworn her oath of allegiance to the Kashallan. Surely if she were false, Tani would have detected it. Who could she tell her suspicions to—who would believe her?

Suddenly she couldn't stand being alone in this room any more. Washing the pitcher and the bowls as thoroughly as she could with the water they had in the suite, she crossed to the door and flung it open. She needed to find Pela—she must talk to her—there was something strange going on here, and she needed the support of her sister-wife very badly right now.

Chapter Six

By the time the Kashallan and Oglas reached the hallway where the disturbance had started, the fight was over. Tizu and some of his Warlinga had gotten there before them, and separated the combatants. Nathan was standing between Tarla and Briyenn. They each held an arm, but he wasn't putting up a fuss about it.

Conal, on the other hand, was giving Fadir and one of his kinsmen more trouble. Half naked and bloody he was screaming Caldoni curses at the top of his voice. He was incoherent with rage, and desperately trying to free himself to continue the dispute.

The fight occurred just down from a main intersection near the Speir'dina wing of the keep, and the noise was drawing quite a crowd. He could see shocked Avairei faces peering from the shadows, and several more were hurrying towards the commotion. He sighed. Just what they needed—more trouble. The Avairei already thought they were a bunch of barbarians, and now this—how could Nathan be so stupid?

Pushing through the knot of onlookers, he stepped into the cleared space around the two adversaries. In the dim light, it was difficult to tell the extent of their injuries, but neither of them seemed to be seriously damaged by their fracas. What could this possibly be about?

Nathan had been in a foul mood lately, but even so, it wasn't like him to get in a fight—especially not with Conal. And Conal—well, the man had a quick temper, but still, going after Nathan—that was suicidal.

Folding his arms across his chest Dunnagh shouted, "All right, that's enough, Armachd, settle down," Conal quieted, though a murderous look remained in his eyes. "What's this all about?" he demanded. When neither man volunteered any explanation, his face darkened as his own temper rose.

"Nathan?" Nathan gave him a sullen look, but stubbornly refused to speak.

Dunnagh opened his mouth to repeat his demand, when Conal blurted, "Damned interfering shit, he had no right! No right, Ce'awn—I paid her damned price, and he—"

"What are you talk—" Breaking off in mid-sentence, Dunnagh peered into the gloom behind the knot of warriors. Yes, someone was there—who?

Then he saw her, and everything fell into place. Muttering a curse under his breath, he brushed past the warriors and dragged Tess-weh out into the light. "I should have known you were behind this," he said. Then, taken aback by the woman's battered appearance and complacent expression, he stared, mouth agape. So this was how the demon liked her "payments." He had suspected—but never knew for sure. Dunnagh felt his gorge rise in disgust.

"Let go of me, Khutani slime," Tess-weh hissed.

She tried to pull away, but he firmed up his hold on her arm. Looming over her, he growled, "I warned you, Demon, I told you that if you caused trouble among my men—or if you hurt *him*—I would—"

"Kashallan, please, allow me to deal with this," Ngeal said, placing a restraining hand on his arm. Ngeal had come up to him unnoticed, two sturdy young Atas by her side. When he hesitated, she fixed him with a determined look.

Now cloaked in her role as the Ima Matri of Ticca, she repeated, "Please, Holy One. Here at Ticca we are far more experienced in dealing with the Sweh'an-bonded than are you and your Speir'dina kinsmen. Let us do what is necessary to restore order here."

Tess-weh snorted and gave Ngeal a contemptuous look. "You, mortal, handle *me*?"

"Ye-es," Ngeal said, "I think I can manage that." She surveyed the circle of onlookers, lingering for a moment on the two combatants and the guards holding them. "We are acquainted with your kind here, Honored Spirit."

Following her gaze, the demon gave her a toothy grin. "You aren't happy, Spirit," Ngeal continued, "you should let me help you. Your pleasures are causing a disruption among your H'an's kin; you must stop this—"

"My *pleasures* are my own affair."

At the Kashallan's strangled growl, Ngeal tightened her grip on his arm. She shook her head, then, addressing Tess-weh once more, she said, "No, Honored Spirit, it isn't that simple. Your H'an is too young, too inexperienced, and the balance of the bond is unequal. So it is my duty to step in and do what is necessary to restore harmony."

Tess-weh smirked, her dark eyes challenging the older woman.

"There are limits," Ngeal said sternly. "You will learn that I am Ima Matri here, and you will comport yourself in a proper manner while within this keep. In your many lives among us, spirit, have you encountered the discipline of the Ba'etchat'seh?"

The demon froze. "No," Tess-weh muttered, but she looked away, unable to meet Ngeal's eyes.

"Oh yes, you have, I can see it on your host's face—you know what I'm talking about." Ngeal motioned her two attendants forward. "I think it is time you taste the flavor of our chamber for the Ba'etchat'seh, hmm?"

Motioning for the Atas to take charge of the possessed woman, Ngeal stepped back, nodding to the puzzled Kashallan to release her. Tess-weh screamed and tried to fight them, but, with the help of one of Tizu's men, the priests hustled her out of sight down the corridor.

"NO!" Conal shouted, "you can't do this to me—she owes me—NO, please, Ce'awn!"

"Shut up, Taleish," Tizu said, "you've caused enough trouble for one day." The rest of the struggling man's words were cut off, as Tizu motioned for Conal's guards to take him back to the Speir'dina quarters. "Keep the stupid shit locked up and guarded till he cools down," Tizu shouted after his retreating men.

Walking over to the Kashallan and the priestess, he gave the Ima a curt bow, then nodded his head towards the still-restrained Nathan. "What do you want me to do with our other brave warrior?"

Glancing over at his friend, the Kashallan sighed. Nathan was watching them sullenly, but seemed under control. "I'll talk to him."

Tizu grunted, then, giving the Kashallan one last searching look, he ordered Briyenn and Tarla to release their prisoner. Motioning for his remaining men to clear the corridor of onlookers, Tizu headed back to HQ.

The Kashallan stared after him, then without looking at Ngeal, he asked, "Will this Ba'etcha—whatever you said—hurt her?"

"No, Holy One. The spirit will hate where they are taking it, because the Ba'etchat'seh is a tiny, darkened room with no furniture, only padded walls and floor, but no harm will be done to either bondmate."

"Thank you that does ease my mind. I don't want Tessa to suffer—the demon puts her through enough." Then he grinned. The demon was definitely not going to be pleased with its new accommodations.

Giving Ngeal an appreciative look, he bowed. "Thank you, Ima, I will leave this matter in your hands with relief."

He glanced at Nathan then returned his attention to the Ima. "If you will excuse me, Ima, I should talk to my kinsman—"

Ngeal laid a restraining hand on his arm and drew him aside to speak privately. "Kashallan, I can't say that I approve of what Sagas and Surrel did. Suggesting to one such as your Tessa that she host the spirit was wrong in my opinion, but—" she motioned towards the waiting Nathan, "*he* must not stay with her any longer.

"I have been told that he and the host were betrothed before—but that union changed with the bonding. He is too young and inexperienced to handle the spirit, or to control what is happening to both himself and the H'an. He must leave her to me, and others who I will choose to take care of her. They have been trained for this work, and will be able to control her excesses with much more success. Do you understand me, young one?"

The Kashallan nodded. "I understand—and you are right. I've been trying to tell him that. It isn't good for him to be with her, but he's stubborn—he won't listen, he—"

"He must listen this time," Ngeal insisted. "He must." She hesitated, then gave him a secretive smile. "And I think if the spirit accepts my offer, Tess-weh herself will insist on the break." At his puzzled look, she chuckled. "In good time you will know, young one, but for now allow an old woman her mysteries, hmm?" She bowed. "And now I must leave you and see to my *honored guest.*"

Walking over to Nathan, Dunnagh asked, "You all right?"

"Yeah, I'm all right," Nathan muttered. He stared after the retreating Ima then asked, "What are they going to do with her?"

"Don't worry about Tessa; she'll be fine. They have something in this keep that is the Timornan version of a padded cell, Ngeal tells me. They plan to keep her in there till the demon decides it will behave."

Nathan grunted and started to walk away, but the Kashallan stopped him. "Nathan," he said, a note of annoyance tingeing his words in spite of his resolve to stay objective about this. "Ngeal agrees with me. It's over—you've got to let go. This is tearing you apart inside; you can't stay with her. No matter what you once felt for Tessa, you've got to let her go—she's not the same woman you fell in love with."

"And whose bloody fault is that," he spat back. At Dunnagh's stricken look, Nathan snorted. "Yeah, whose, Dunnagh, whose? And don't give me that 'oh, I'm so sorry, Nathan,' look of yours, either. Just leave me alone—and stay out of my business, damn you. Go back to your harem and leave me alone!" Pushing past him, Nathan stormed blindly down a deserted corridor.

"Nathan!" The man gave no sign that he heard, and continued walking. Swearing under his breath, Dunnagh started after him, but stopped as someone grabbed his arm. He swung round; a sharp response choked off as he recognized Sairsa.

"No, Love, let him go."

He hesitated. Intent on resolving the fight, he hadn't noticed the arrival of his wives. Had Sairsa told Pela yet about the maid? Oh, Gods, what was he going to do about that mess? His face contorted with indecision, he stared at his wives, torn between his desire to follow Nathan, and his need to explain to them.

Sairsa patted his arm. "I'll go talk to Nathan. You and Pela go on back to our suite."

The Kashallan watched her out of sight, trying to swallow the ache that was choking him.

"Husband, come, we should go now," Pela whispered, taking his arm.

He searched her face—yes, she knew. Pulling her into a desperate embrace, he buried his face in the musky fragrance of her braided mane. "I'm sorry, Pela, I'm sorry." For a long moment, he held her close, body trembling with emotion. Then he released her and shook his head. He couldn't go back to their rooms—not just yet—that look in her eye—and the memory of what he had almost done was too raw, too painful.

"No, sweet, I—I need to go to the pools right now, not back to our suite. Can you understand—can you forgive me?"

"There is nothing to forgive, Dunnagh-Tani, you must do what you think best."

Her gentle words didn't comfort him—the look in her eyes had hardened. *Later, when my sister-wife returns you will have some explaining to do,* those eyes seemed to be telling him.

Pela put an arm around his waist. "Come, I will walk with you as far as the chapel. Go to your relatives and I will pray to the Mother for all of us."

"Thank you," he breathed, and together they started down the shadowed corridor.

Chapter Seven

In a darkened alcove, Nathan leaned his face against the cold stone, and slammed his fist against the rough wall, trying not to think. The pain of his bloodied hand was intense, but he kept up his pounding; it was nothing compared to the pain that was tearing him apart inside. *Oh, Gods, I want to die—Tessa—Dunnagh—oh it hurts so bad.*

"Don't, Nathan, please stop," a soft, feminine voice said from just behind him. He froze.

Sairsa stepped closer, and took his injured hand in her own. Gently, she cradled the bloody mess between her palms and looked up at him. "This isn't the way to make it feel better, Nathan. Hurting yourself like this isn't going to make things right."

Retrieving his hand, Nathan leaned heavily against the wall and turned his head away, unable to face her. He wished she'd go away and leave him alone. Her compassion right now was destroying his resolve not to break down. He didn't want to think, or to feel— "Sairsa, what are you doing here? Did *he* send you after me?"

"No. I came because I was worried."

Nathan sighed. "Thanks, but I'm all right, Sairsa. You can go now—I'll be fine."

Taking up his hand again, she said, "Come, sit with me a while; I have to rest before I can start back." Without giving him time to protest, she led him to a stone bench, carved out of the wall, and drew him down beside her.

Sairsa settled herself in a more comfortable position, leaned back against the wall and took several deep breaths as the baby repositioned in her swollen abdomen. For a long time they sat together, and when she spoke at last, her low voice made him jump.

"I wanted to find you, and talk to you if I could, because I care about all of us, Dunnagh, you, me—and Tessa."

Gripping his hand a little tighter, she turned to him, her green eyes pleading with him to listen—understand. "Nathan, what I'm going to say isn't easy, believe me, but I need to say it, and I think you need to hear it, too." At his puzzled look she sighed and leaned her head back against the cool stone once more.

"I had dreams too, you know. Dunnagh and I were going back to Caldon, marry and—well, never mind—I know what it's like to want things to be different. You love Dunnagh—and after having him for your own for so long, I can imagine how hard it is for you."

He stiffened, his face molding into an expressionless mask. She let out an ironic laugh. "Oh, I know how you feel, believe me. So many to share your loves with, when all you want is to claim Dunnagh or Tessa, or both of them, for your own. It hasn't been easy for me, you know. Tani, Pela, then there are the Spirit's none too subtle hints suggesting that you and Dunnagh are something more than friends."

Nathan opened his mouth to speak, but she waved him into silence and continued. "No, not easy, but I have learned so much from Pela. Her love, her compassion, and her courage—she has taught me so much.

"When Sagas forced her to marry Dunnagh-Tani, she gave up Amril, her childhood sweetheart for the good of her people. And when she learned about me, instead of being jealous or possessive, she saved my life and made me her sister-wife.

"She showed me how I could have at least a part of my dreams back, even though without Amril, she could never be truly happy herself. With such an example to guide me I'm trying very hard to put aside my own worries about being alone and abandoned, and really love another person, without fear. Do you understand what I'm trying to say to you?"

Silence. Then a mumbled reply, "I'm not sure." Then, "Sairsa, he probably told you about us swearing the Ca'Companachda oath when we were younger—and that still holds—but we haven't been—"

"It doesn't matter to me what you are to each other. I would like to believe that Dunnagh's love for me won't change—no matter who else he loves.

"Unconditional love. Think about what I've said." She gave him a hesitant smile. "It's hard to read your expression in the dim light. Have I startled you? Ah, well it needed to be said." Then as if to herself, she said, "Such a tangled web of relationships we have made for ourselves, since being stranded on this world. It's a wonder any of us is still sane."

"Maybe we're not."

She laughed, then kissed his injured hand, tasting the salt of his blood on her tongue. "You're probably right."

They sat together in companionable silence for a time, Nathan unconsciously shifting his body to lean against her. Finally he said, "When I saw them—when I saw what he was doing to her—and how she was enjoying it—she always wanted me—" He choked, his voice trailing off into the darkness.

"That wasn't Tessa, Nathan, you know that," Sairsa said, and brushed the hair back from his forehead with a soothing gesture.

He reached over and took hold of her other hand, clinging to it desperately. "Oh, I know. It was that damned thing—that—that demon, but—"

"Nathan," Sairsa said. "There is no 'buts' about it any longer. I know it won't be easy, but you have to let her go. There are things—hurtful things—that the spirit must do to discharge its vow, and collect its payments. You can't stay with her and keep your sanity!"

He sighed. "Yeah, I know."

She patted his hand again, a mischievous gleam in her eye. "I know you care for her so it will be painful at first, but it isn't the end, Nathan. There are several ladies just waiting for a chance to show you just how much they're interested."

Startled he looked up. "Who?"

"Well, Briya for one. Haven't you caught those sorrowful looks of hers directed your way?"

He grunted and smiled to himself. Then he shook his head, his whole body trembling. When he spoke again his voice shook with suppressed tears. "Oh, damn it why? First Dunnagh, and now Tessa—why does everything I do turn out so wrong? Oh, Sairsa—why does everyone I love die, or change—and leave me?"

For answer she took him in her arms and held him tight, murmuring to him softly, like a mother with a hurt child. Nathan laid his head against her warm, ample bosom, and cried.

TAKING UP THE LEATHER wrapped bundle, Fadir bowed to Ngeal. "It will be as you command, Ima. I must tell hunt Leader Tizu, but I'm sure he will see the wisdom in letting us decide this among ourselves."

Ngeal grimaced, folded her arm upon the surface of her worktable and gave the Warlinga a stern look. "Whether Hunt Leader Tizu agrees or not, my orders must be carried out. This doesn't concern our defense; he has no say in the matter. If you choose to inform him; that is your own affair."

When the door closed behind him Fadir glanced down once more with a mixture of horror and fascination at what he had been given. San Tizu was a good commander; surely he would allow the Warlinga to work out the problem among themselves, but by the Great Hunt Leader, what a thing to have to ask one of them to do. None of them were going to like the Ima's orders, but it must be done, and soon, or there would be more trouble.

Throughout Timorna's long history it had always been a Warlinga's duty to become a Wa'chassey'ul whenever a Sweh'an bonded pair had been formed. A Warlinga's bond with the demon was a mixed blessing. The Wa'chassey'ul was magically bound until his death. As its mortal guardian, he would gain almost supernatural strength and endurance. As its submissive lover, his ecstasy would be unimaginable.

In payment, however, he must surrender to its will in everything, like any Begta slave. No longer to go on the hunt—never to breed—feared and shunned by his kin—truly a mixed blessing, he thought. Who amongst his kinsmen would be suited for this dubious honor?

Lost in his own dark musings, he didn't at first notice the lanky figure that stepped out of the shadows and fell into step beside him. When Fadir halted, the man bowed to him. Head crest flattening, the Second Hunter narrowed his eyes. Who? Ah, yes, the troublemaker who caused the fight—the cripple. Feeling his gorge rise at this poor excuse for a warrior, Fadir fixed him with a cool, red-eyed stare. "What do *you* want?"

Conal's face darkened, his green eyes stormy. Tossing his raggedy braid over his shoulder he took a deep breath then said, "May I speak with you, Second Hunter?"

Fadir considered. What could the man possibly want with him? Standing here bruised and ragged, his long, oily hair tangled around his face and shoulders—the man was a disgrace and a coward. He should have let his kinsmen feast on his flesh months ago. "If there is a problem, perhaps you should speak to Hunt Leader Tizu."

Fadir started to brush past, when Conal grabbed his arm. "Please, Sir," he begged. "Tizu can't help me with this—and besides, if we are supposed to be combining the units as everybody says, why shouldn't I come to you?"

Well, the man had him there, Fadir conceded. He nodded, then motioned for the Speir'dina to follow him further down the corridor, away from the Ima Matri's suite. When they were far enough into a deserted side passage, Fadir turned and faced the crippled man. "All right, say what you have to say. Tell me why I should handle this *problem* of yours, rather than the Hunt Leader."

"I came to you for two reasons." Conal hesitated, then, when Fadir glared at him impatiently, he said, "The Hunt Leader and me—well, let's just say we've had our differences. But that's not the point." He waved his good hand in dismissal. "Mostly I came to you because you're a native Timornan, and the way I see it, the help I need has got to come from a *native* Timornan, 'cause only a *native* would understand."

Fadir flattened his head crest, unable to mask his disgust any longer. The man was making no sense, and he was getting tired of all this. "I doubt if a *native* Timornan could understand anything about *you*, but go ahead and ask."

Conal's green eyes flashed. For just a moment, pure hatred contorted his Caldoni features then he took a deep breath and controlled himself. "I need to see Tess-weh."

Fadir's head crest rose in astonishment—the nerve of the insolent little slime. He curled his lip in a sneer. "No. Get out of my way before I discipline you for your insolence, the way I would one of my kinsmen."

With a growl of frustration, Conal stepped in front of the lizardman and held up his stump for the other's inspection. "Damn you, I need to see her." He shook the stump in Fadir's face.

"Oh, I know what you 'mighty warriors' think of me. I should have been on my kinsmen's dinner table a long time ago—I know. Well, damn you, *He* wouldn't let me—and I'd given him my oath, hadn't I? Damn you, all of you. I need to see her. Tess-weh promised me, if I paid her price, she'd tell me how I could get my hand back—how I could be a whole man again."

Conal lowered his arm, but remained blocking Fadir's path. Still defiant he said, "Would you have done any different if it was you, Warlinga? Would you? I didn't want to start any trouble between me and Nathan—he's a good officer, and I don't care about the woman. I just want what's owing to me!"

Fadir considered. At last he said, "All right, I will let you see her, briefly, tonight during the late watch. If she owes you, as you say, you will have your chance to *speak* to her. I will tell my kinsmen that you have my permission. Now get out of my way."

Stepping quickly aside, Conal bowed and let the Warlinga pass, a gleam of triumph in his green eyes.

Chapter Eight

In the dim light coming into the Ba'etchat'seh cell from the hall behind him, Doyan studied the sad figure huddled up in the gloom. To be Sweh'an bonded so young, his heart lurched at the sight of her. Oh, Holy Mother, How cruelly fate had dealt with this poor young woman.

In his youth, he had been apprenticed to the Cha'Han at Shaden Keep, when they had a bonded pair there. The priestess who was host for that spirit died before his training was needed, but he was the best Ngeal had to offer.

Watching the woman cringe away from the light, the stink of old blood and filth a thick miasma in the tiny cell, he wondered if he would still be capable of fulfilling his duty. He felt so ill prepared; he'd never dreamed that after so long he would be called upon to use those neglected skills.

She wasn't even of his own species—and she was so young—nothing he had been taught would seem to apply to this situation. But Ngeal was right—there was no one else, and she would need him. He would just have to trust his instincts and do the best he could. And seeing her now for the first time, he thought that wouldn't be too hard; already he could feel pity coming to his aid.

Crossing the small distance between them, he crouched and touched her shoulder. "Speir'van—Tessa," he said gently. "Don't be afraid—I've come to take you out of here. My name is Doyan. I am to be your new companion, your Cha'Han."

At his touch she flinched, but she was listening, he was sure of that. Finally she turned to face him, her moist brown eyes staring at him in a bewildered appeal. "My companion," she repeated, blinking as if she was having trouble making any sense of his words.

Doyan inwardly sighed, controlling a flare of annoyance. Damn Quellyn—he had *told* her that it had been too long. And judging by the woman's listless behavior, they should have let him come for her some time ago. It was apparent that the treacherous spirit had abandoned its bondmate to the dark and to her fears hours before.

"Yes, Speir'van, I am your new companion. I wish only to serve and care for you. I will stay with you from now on."

Tessa nodded. "Doyan? Is that what you said your name was? I don't understand, you want to take care of me—but why? Where's N-Nathan?"

"My dear, he will not be coming," Doyan said gently. "It is better this way—for both of you. There are others who will care for you now. San Nathan is not suited, or trained—can you not see that? Try to understand and accept what is inevitable."

Tessa's face crumpled. In a voice barely above a whisper she said, "I know you're right—staying with Nathan this long was a mistake. It is destroying him, but I was so selfish—and afraid. I will miss him—letting him go—it hurts." Her tears fell in glistening droplets down her cheeks.

Ah, Mother, Doyan thought, *this is awful*. He was moved, in spite of himself. *Oh, how cruel, what a shame. And how courageous she is, to sacrifice so much for her people—for all of us.* He touched her cheek, feeling her tears damp upon his fingertips.

His own heart aching in sympathy, he cupped her face between his palms, bent, and kissed her tear-stained cheeks, tasting their saltiness upon his tongue. They told him that these strangers from the stars had different customs about love, customs that any decent Avairei would shun as basest perversion. Ah, well, if that was what would be required to ease her heart, he would comfort her, if need be, in that way—it was his duty, was it not? They would see.

Taking her hand, he stood, drawing her to her feet beside him. Removing his cape, he put it around her shoulders and fastened the clasp. "Come, my dear, you will feel better when you have bathed and eaten," he said. "The Ima Matri has given you your own suite. I myself, your kinswoman Moraga, and others, will be there to attend you, so come. Let me take you out of this place. You have stayed here too long as it is."

Outside her new suite, a strange Warlinga bowed and opened the door for them to enter. He stepped inside after them and closed the door behind himself. At a sharp shake of the head from Doyan, the lizardman nodded and remained by the entrance.

Doyan led Tessa across the well-furnished outer chamber and into a comfortable looking bedroom. In the center of the floor a large wooden tub had been placed, and Tessa recognized the person pouring water into the tub. "Moraga," Tessa cried, and flung herself sobbing into the big Caldoni's arms.

"There, there," Moraga soothed, "don't take on so. I told them you couldn't stay by yourself among all these strangers. I told them you needed one of your kin, and a woman, to be with you—so don't cry. I'll be staying with you," the big woman announced, giving Doyan a challenging, grey-eyed stare.

Ignoring the Speir'dina's implied challenge for the moment, Doyan poured another bucket of water into the tub, then invited, "Come, Tessa, you will feel better when you have bathed. The water is quite delightful."

"I can do for Tessa," Moraga said. "You can wait outside till we're done, Ata."

Doyan bowed, his face a controlled mask. The woman was giving him that look, well aware that as an Avairei, he found her odd-colored eyes disconcerting. He hoped he wasn't going to have trouble with this one. He had agreed that the young host would probably be grateful for one of her kinswomen to attend her, but this warrior woman needed to learn her place. It was he, and he alone, who was responsible for the H'an's wellbeing, and he would do his job.

In a quiet but firm voice he said, "I will stay and help you. Tessa must get used to me. It is my duty to see to her needs, and I intend to do just that, Sa Moraga."

Over Tessa's bowed head, Moraga's face set into a stubborn mask of resistance. Doyan met and held her gaze. *It will be you who leaves, woman, not me.* At last she lowered her eyes and backed down. Making gentle cooing sounds, she assisted Doyan in helping Tessa into the bath, and together they washed their new charge.

Doyan sent for a substantial meal, and when Tessa had eaten, he had the tub and water taken away. Then he excused Moraga from the room, and put the H'an to bed.

Crawling in beside her, he covered the stone lamp on the table beside the bed. As the green light dimmed and went out, Doyan took her into his silken arms. Sighing, Tessa snuggled closer, but she seemed not to want the coupling that he had been warned about, so he just held her until she fell asleep.

WHEN TESSA AWOKE, SHE had no idea where she was or how long she'd slept. Was it morning? Suddenly afraid to open her eyes and find out; she listened. From somewhere beyond the door, she could hear the sound of Avairei singing. The sound was vaguely soothing, but too indistinct for her to make out the prayer song itself, and thus the time.

Tessa yawned and stretched. Eyes still closed, she reached out a hand and realized that she was now alone in the big bed. The place next to her was still warm. Idly she wondered why Nathan hadn't awakened her before he left—then she remembered, and choked down a sob. Nathan hadn't been here—it had been another, a stranger, who had slept beside her. Nathan was gone. She was alone.

Feeling a flutter of panic Tessa rolled over and opened her eyes. Moraga looked up from her mending and smiled. "Good morning. How are you feeling, My Dear?"

Tessa breathed a sigh of relief and sat up slowly. "I'm fine I guess. Where is—" She groped for the priest's name.

"Ata Doyan," Moraga supplied. "He's gone on some priestly errand, he didn't say what—but he said to tell you he would be back as soon as he could. Are you hungry?"

Tessa considered. "Yes, a little."

Moraga put down her sewing and stood. "Good—Doyan was having something sent up for us. I'll go ask Cadrach if it's come yet." Pointing to some folded garments on another chair, she added, "There's some water for washing in the pitcher by the bed. Get dressed and come out when you're ready, and call me if you need anything."

Tessa nodded as the door closed behind her. She picked up the folded kilt; her hands running over the finely crafted cloth. The kilt was a deep red in color with embroidered yellow flowers along its lower border. She knew enough about Timornan customs to know that only a high ranking woman would be given such a rich gift to wear. Why? Tessa glanced around the bedroom, for the first time noticing the heavy braided rug covering the stone floor, and the well-crafted tapestries covering the walls. The bed too, now that she thought of it was soft, wide and covered with fine fur blankets.

Tessa unfolded the kilt and began listlessly pleating it about her hips. This was all rather nice, but didn't change the fact that Nathan was gone. What was going to happen to her now—did she care? She felt so detached, like all of this was happening to someone else.

Too bad that wasn't the case. It had been a surprise to find Moraga in her new suite last night, but she was glad of it. Being alone with all these strangers would be too much to bear. Good, solid, dependable Moraga, but she wished Nathan—no, best not think about him, or she'd start crying, and that wouldn't do any good. It was so hard, and she was so frightened.

When Doyan hadn't returned by the time she'd finished her meal, Tessa told Moraga she was still tired, and drifted back into her bedroom to rest. Tessa wasn't exactly sleepy, as she claimed—no, she felt more depressed and anxious than sleepy, but it was too much effort to carry on a conversation. She just wanted to be alone.

In spite of herself, she must have dozed off, because she was startled awake when someone sat down on the bed beside her. Tessa shuddered and pulled back.

"Did I startle you, my dear?" Doyan's gentle voice asked. "If so, I am sorry."

Tessa sat up and threw her legs over the edge of the bed, rubbing the sleep from her eyes. "I must have been more tired than I thought," she said. Remembering his silken arms around her last night, she felt suddenly shy and dropped her eyes.

He surveyed her for a long moment, then said, "Perhaps, but I would guess what you are feeling right now is more a sense of loss for your Speir'dina mate, and maybe a little fear about being in a new place with strangers, hmm? And, if I were you, I would be wondering what is going to happen to me now. Is that how it is, My Dear?"

Startled she glanced up, then nodded. He chuckled. "I can see by your expression that I am right, hmm?" He patted her hand. "Don't be ashamed, Tessa—it is perfectly natural. As I told you before, I have been given to you by Ima Ngeal, to serve and take care of you. Here at Ticca, we have had some experience with the Sweh'an-bonded. We know what is needed for your comfort. The Kashallan has agreed with my Ima that you and your spirit bondmate will be much happier among those who will love and understand you, than if you were to remain among your Speir'dina kindred.

"That is why you are here—not to punish you. We only want what is best for both of you. We want you and the Honored Spirit to be contented while you are among us, and we will try our best to see that you are," he assured her.

She had to admit that, in a way, she would be glad to be here among the Avairei. When they had been traveling across the Great Swamp, she often felt uncomfortable among her Speir'dina kindred. It would be a relief now not to feel their fear, or the men's lustful eyes following her wherever she went. But what was she, Tessa, going to do with her time when the Sweh'an wasn't with her? Tessa voiced that question to the kindly priest.

Doyan smiled. "For the most part, whatever pleases you, Tessa. Ima Sagas has already told me that among your people, before you came here, you were trained as a scholar. She also said that Ima Nansa, before her death, was teaching you our ways. If you would like, I will continue with your studies. Perhaps you would like to share with me and other scholars, things about your old life that will be of use to us in the future.

"We native Timornans will need someone trained as you have been to help us understand your people, I think. Your work will be of great benefit to everyone, my dear, I promise you that.

"And your kinfolk haven't abandoned you," he confided. "The Kashallan's wives and a few others have been asking about you. They hope to see you whenever you feel well enough for a visit. You are not without friends or those who care about you. So you see there will be plenty of new things to occupy your mind and ease your heart."

Suddenly becoming shy himself, he gave her a tentative smile and patted her arm. "And if you become lonely, as your sworn companion, I am here to do whatever will please you." He glanced significantly at the bed behind them.

Tessa blushed and looked down at her hands, taking his meaning. "Thank you."

Doyan leaned forward and kissed her cheek. "Yes, I see that we have made a good beginning already, and with time I'm sure we shall become quite fond of one another. But now it is time for you to meet another who will be sharing our life together. You must meet the one who has agreed to be bound as the Wa'chassey'ul."

Turning, Doyan motioned to the shadowy figure by the closed bedroom door to come forward. Startled, Tessa blinked; she hadn't been aware of his presence until Doyan drew her attention to him. The big Warlinga glided forward and knelt down on the carpet in front of her. Curious, Tessa studied the scarred veteran, then glanced at Doyan. "I don't understand."

"This is Cadrach, Tessa. He has come forward from among his kinsmen to make the bond of the Wa'chassey'ul," Doyan announced.

Tessa returned her attention to the lizardman. He was watching her attentively with solemn red eyes. When he saw that he had her attention, Cadrach bowed his head and handed her a leather-wrapped bundle. Bemused, she took the package, then, at the priest's urging, Tessa opened it, laying out what it contained on the bed beside her.

Tessa stared; she'd never seen such things before—what did all this have to do with her? Among the items on the bed, there was a scourge, leather hobbles, something that reminded her of a dog muzzle, and a pair of oddly-padded gloves suited for a large, four-fingered hand. There were also other things whose use she couldn't even imagine. She looked at each man in turn, bewildered. "I don't understand—"

"Tessa," Doyan said gently, "it is time for you to call your spirit bondmate to join us. The Sweh'an, I am sure, will know what is needed here. It will be pleased, I believe, with the gift that is being offered it."

When she continued to stare at the implements spread out on the bed, Doyan said, "Just as I am sworn as the life-long companion of the host, the Warlinga will become the life-long companion of the Spirit. He will be its submissive lover and mortal protector when it is with you. Cadrach here has chosen to bind himself as a Wa'chassey'ul to the spirit's will."

"No!" Tessa glanced up sharply and looked into the Warlinga's eyes. Cadrach held her gaze unblinking, only a slight nervous flicking of his tail betraying his inner agitation. At last Tessa lowered her eyes. "Do you know what that would mean—do you really want to do this?"

He nodded. "I know. It is of my own will that I do this, Sa Tessa. Please call your bondmate."

Still she hesitated, knowing better than anyone what it meant to be bound to the Demon's capricious will.

"Tessa," Doyan said more firmly, "you must call it. Over many long centuries, the Wa'chassey'ul have made the gift of themselves to these powerful but troublesome spirits. He will give it the pleasure and obedience for which it has been looking. Having a Wa'chassey'ul will prevent more trouble among your kindred in future. Giving the demon a Wa'chassey'ul to be with is the best way—please believe me. It is how we have always done this in the past, and we should do so now."

Tessa vaguely remembered that there were times, when the demon was with her that it had exerted considerable power over Nathan, trying to bind him to its will. Once or twice he had almost given in, for love of her. But instinctively she had fought her bondmate's urgings, and won. Nathan never agreed to the binding. Now seeing these things, and suspecting how this bond would warp the one who had been bound, she was glad she stood up to the spirit, for his sake.

Tessa shivered, and, before she made the call, she reached out and gathered the Warlinga's hand between her own. With tears in her eyes, she brought his battle-scarred hand to her lips and kissed it tenderly. "Thank you, Cadrach," Tessa said. Then, before either of them could lose their nerve, she closed her eyes and made the call.

DOYAN SWALLOWED HARD. As Sagas had also told him, these Speir'dina were capable of acts of unbelievable kindness and compassion. He hadn't expected such an intuitive insight from this young one. Ah, it would be a delightful and challenging adventure serving such a woman. Then he had no more time for speculation. He felt the atmosphere in the room shift as the demon entered into the body of its host. He shivered.

Opening her eyes, Tess-weh glanced around; her hard, dark eyes took in the room, with its opulent furnishings. She surveyed the priest beside her on the bed, and the big Warlinga kneeling at her feet. When her glance took in the objects spread out upon the bed, her eyes widened; then she smiled.

Doyan bowed his head. "Honored Spirit, my name is Doyan. I have been sworn to your host as Cha'Han. As my Ima has told you, we wish only to give you honor, and to make your time among us a pleasurable one. As proof of her regard, the Ima Matri asks you to accept the gift that she offers you. This man has come forward to make the Wa'chassey'ul bond, as is our custom."

Tess-weh's hard eyes raked over the big Warlinga kneeling in front of her. Under her penetrating gaze, Cadrach shuddered, then, tightening his jaw, he bowed. "It is as the priest says, Honored Spirit." Then, with one hand, he removed a bone knife from the sheath at his hip and offered it to her, unable, in spite of himself, to control a slight tremor in his hand as he did so.

Tess-weh gave a throaty laugh and took the blade. With this knife, she would carve the sigil of power onto his forehead—a mark that would magically bind him to her will. From henceforth, for as long as he lived, all would know that he had surrendered his free will to become her Wa'chassey'ul slave.

Turning to the priest, the demon said, "Leave us, priest. Tell your Ima that I *may* be pleased—we shall see."

Doyan stood and bowed. "As you will, Honored Spirit." Then, without looking back at the hapless lizardman, he left.

Chapter Nine

Conal leaned against the pitted rock wall, shuddered, and dragged his good hand across his forehead, trying to wipe away the cold sweat that was pouring into his eyes. It seemed like, he'd been wandering these deserted halls, alone, in the gloom for countless days, trying to decide what to do.

What to do? He laughed, the sound high-pitched, bordering on hysteria. Gods, what a joke—his laughter ended in a sob. Well, it served him right, didn't it? Yes, it did. He should have known—the damned bitch—she'd certainly got the better of him, now hadn't she?.

He had bullied them into letting him see her so he could get his hand back. Well, she told him how, damn her, and the witch was probably still laughing. Conal found his legs would no longer hold him, and he sank to the cold stone floor, burying his face in his arms.

If you truly want another hand—as you claim, My Treasure, you must go to the Khutani and make a kashallan bond. Only they can heal you, and they will only do it if you pay their price.

Eyes hard and mocking, she taunted him; amused by his fear and revulsion. Tess-weh laughed and laughed, and he hated her for that. If he had been alone with her then, he would have killed her. As it was, the Warlinga had to physically remove him from her cell, or he would have done her some great hurt. But they *had* thrown him out, and her taunting mirth pursued him, echoing down the hall as he ran.

Since then, he had wandered the empty places of this vast keep, a tormented, ghostly presence, unable to sleep or even to think clearly. Tears stinging his eyes, Conal lowered his arms and stared at his stump. Unnoticed, a tear splashed upon his scarred flesh.

Oh, Gods, he wanted his hand back—he hated living like this, helpless, scorned—but could he do it? Could he make the bond? Become only half human, sharing his flesh, forever, with another, alien, creature—could he?

That was the question that was torturing his soul, and he'd better make up his mind soon, or he was going to go totally insane.

Conal removed the long dagger he carried at his hip and stared balefully at its blade. Black as the pit of lost souls, deadly, its sharp edge promised a quick end to his torment. If he wasn't going to pay the Khutani's damned price, then he might as well kill himself and be done with it.

In disgust, he shoved the dagger back into its sheath. He was too much of a coward; he was afraid to go to the pools, and he was afraid to take his own life.

Growling with self-loathing, he got clumsily to his feet. This had to end—he *would* go to the pools—he didn't want to die. He would pay their price,. Lurching down the corridor, he headed for the entrance to the deep cavern where the Khutani's pools lay.

As he neared the pool entrance, he slowed, looking around for spying eyes. This particular portion of Ticca's vast underground fortress, the Avairei considered *their* exclusive domain. Though not exactly forbidden to the other inhabitants of the keep, his presence here would be frowned upon and reported to the Ima Matri, if he were discovered. But the hour was late, and he was getting very good at traveling these dim passageways without being noticed.

At the entrance to the pools, Conal paused, unsure what to do next. The cavern was so vast, with its many causeways and luminescent ponds—where should he go to make his offer? He supposed, if he were totally sane, he would go back to his bed, wait till morning, then ask the Kashallan to help him. But he wasn't totally sane—and if he waited, he might lose his nerve all together, and then he would be right back where he started. No, he had to go through with this, right now.

Conal, like most of the Speir'dina, had been down here on one supervised errand or another since their arrival. Thinking of the Kashallan gave him his destination. Before he could change his mind, he stepped out boldly and turned down the main walkway, heading for the kashallan pool.

He knew the basic layout of the caverns, and figured that the kashallan pool would be the best place to talk to one of the big Khutani about the bonding.

Unlike the small kavay ponds, where the Khutani deposited the medicines they made for the priest's collection, the kashallan pool was large enough for several people to enter and be immersed in its waters. At its far end it deepened into the channels where the Khutani lived, but along its sides, in the shallows were padded headrests and sunken shelves where the Kashallan and his patients could recline while the healing was taking place.

When Conal arrived at the pool, he hesitated looking out into the dimness. He could see little through the steamy mists that hovered above the water, but he thought he heard some of the young ones playing out there. At his feet, the faintly glowing liquid lapped against the pool's shallow rim. Ah, there they were. By the water's pale luminescence, he could just see their eel-like forms. Yes, they were there, and seemingly aware of him, too, if their nearness to the walkway at this late hour was any indication.

He shivered. Some of those sleek, gray bodies were huge, they could—so what if they did tear him apart? Did he really care? At least if they did, they would put him out of his misery. Besides, being devoured by some of Tani's relatives was maybe as good a way as any to go. Then, before he could lose his nerve, he clumsily pulled off his clothing, hid them in a darkened recess among the rocks, and stepped into the pool.

Conal waded out till the water was chest high before he was surrounded by a number of sinewy bodies of various sizes. They swam round and round him, churning the water to a phosphorescent foam as they tightened their circle.

He froze, unsure what to do next. In all his muddled reveries, he hadn't considered how he was going to communicate with these alien creatures. He knew the Kashallan did something with his tentacles—but that was hardly going to help *him* now was it?

Suddenly, he decided that this hadn't been one of his better ideas. Maybe he should leave and get the Kashallan to help him in the morning. Turning around, he found his escape route blocked by one of the largest of the pool's inhabitants. A flat reptilian head rose out of the water and swiveled to study him with knowing yellow eyes. Conal swallowed hard, trying not to let panic overwhelm him.

The Khutani lowered its head at last. Mouth tentacles fanning out in the water, it glided forward and slowly encircled him in its massive coils.

Conal felt the sinuous mass tighten around him. He shuddered, but held his ground. *This is what you came here for, fool,. So stop acting like a slimy coward and let it do what it wants with you.*

MAKER DIEVRIS WAS CURIOUS. Without even making the link, the Khutani could taste the man's fear. Why had the creature come here, alone in the quiet of the night? Surely not out of mere whim. No, there must be some other reason. Deciding to test this young one, Dievris lifted him off his feet and carried the trembling Speir'dina into deeper water.

As it expected, the man was terrified, but he controlled it well. Hmm. There was a grim determination to the flavor of his surrender that spiced the pungent taste of his terror. How very interesting, but it needed more information.

Rotating its large head around to face the man, Dievris explored his face, neck, and shoulders with the sensitive tentacles around its mouth. The young one shuddered, but made no objection to its touch. When it felt that the man was ready, the Maker took hold of his shoulder gently, bit down, and then placed a tentacle within the shallow wound to form the link. The man cried out, then relaxed when he realized Dievris wasn't going to eat him.

Within the link, Dievris tasted and considered. This Speir'dina was a far different example of his species than the others it had tasted. Yes, far different. This one had suffered, torments both of the body and spirit that hadn't been evident in his kinsman Dunnagh. In this one, dark currents of hatred and violence swam far nearer to the surface of consciousness than was desirable. And yet, under this layer, the basic taste of the man was not unpleasant.

Deciding it had learned enough for now, Dievris spoke into the waiting man's mind. <<So, Young One, I have tasted you. Why have you come alone and uninvited to our pools? Such an offense could have cost you your life—could still if I so choose. Speak now and tell me why you have come to us.>>

When, the question was repeated with a growing note of impatience in the mental voice, the man said, <<I came here at this time because, if I

waited, I might have lost my nerve and not come at all. I meant no offense, Elder.>>

<<Mm, so what is so important that it couldn't wait?>>

<<I came to make you a deal,>> he said boldly. <<A deal that I hope will get both of us what we want.>>

Deal? Here he lies, totally engulfed in my coils—with almost no effort at all, I could crush the life out of him—and he has the gall to talk to me about "a deal." The man was either very brave, or very foolish—or maybe a little of both. Dievris curbed its desire to discipline this insolent little slimeworm. <<What is this 'deal' you wish to make with me then? Speak, before your insolence earns you the discipline you deserve.>>

<<I'm sure your 'tasting' of me, as you put it, has informed you that I have lost a hand. I will agree to a kashallan bonding, if you agree to make a replacement hand for me.>>

Ah, so that was it; a kashallan bonding—an imaginative and daring plan—but would he suit? Dievris wasn't sure. It would have to take counsel with its peers about this one. Granted, there was a need for others of this man's species to come forward and make the bonding, but not just anyone who offered could be a Chosen. The candidate had to meet certain requirements, and the Maker wasn't sure if this man, with his dark currents of resentment and violence, would be suitable at all.

The Speir'dina had his good qualities, to be sure. He was courageous and basically honest, Dievris could taste that as well. He was also young, strong, and intelligent. And his injury had given him a ruthless pragmatism that was more like the attitude of a native Timornan than anything the rest of his pampered race had exhibited.

This one was a survivor, the Maker sensed. His unwanted tempering might be useful in a host, if the Khutani's goals were to be achieved on this world. But could he be controlled and channeled in the proper way? He would need strict supervision, to curb his violence and his destructive tendencies. And care would have to be taken in forming the Shalla for such a host.

To the waiting man, the Maker said, <<I will consider your offer, and take it to our Council. We will speak of this later.>>

Conal blinked in surprise. Had he heard the creature right? Damn, what was it talking about—consider his offer. He was the one that was going to have his guts eaten out here, wasn't he? He was the one who was going to suffer—to have to share his flesh with one of the slimy little worms—what did this Khutani mean, *consider* his offer?

In a flood of rage and resentment, Conal's feelings crashed down the link, letting the Maker know passionately how he felt about its counteroffer.

The Khutani removed its tentacle and hissed. Tightening its coils, it bit down into his shoulder, shaking him. Conal cried out, and slammed his fist into the side of the Maker's jaw. Dievris growled and squeezed. Conal choked on a curse, gasping for breath. He kicked and punched against the tightening coils.

When at last he lay quiescent and exhausted, the Maker reformed the link, and repeated, <<As I said, Young One, just because you offer doesn't mean you will be found worthy to host one of our symbiont children, but I will take your request to the Council.>>

Suddenly Conal felt his resolve crumble as a black despair took him. Like everyone else since he became disabled, even the Khutani were scorning him. If he couldn't make a kashallan bond—maybe he should just end it. <<Please, Elder, I can't go on like this any longer; let me make the bond. The Sweh'an said it was the only way—the Spirit said I should come—>>

<<Hmm, the Sweh'an. This adds a whole new spice to the offer,>> the Khutani said. <<I can taste the flavor of your anguish, but I don't understand it. You fought me bravely, but now you taste of bitter despair. You feel your cause is hopeless, but why?>>

<<Because nobody wants a cripple, not even the Khutani,>> Conal said, <<I might as well end it, like the Warlinga keep telling me I should, that's why.>>

<<That isn't at all the case, Young One. Your taste is not unpleasant to me, but as I told you, I cannot make such a decision without consulting the Council—and that has nothing to do with your worthiness. But I think I will keep you, until we have a chance to meet. You will remain here with us. You are exhausted; we will care for you until we can decide whether to accept your generous offer.>>

<<Thank you, Elder, I will gladly stay.>> Then, with unexpected insight, he said, <<And if you don't want me—I'd rather end it here, where at least my flesh will make the young ones a good meal. I don't want to go back up to the keep where they all despise me.>>

<<So be it then,>> the Maker intoned. <<I will take you to a place far back in the cavern. The kashallan birthing pool hasn't been used in centuries; no one will look for you there. You can rest there, and be safe. We will feed you and take care of you.>>

<<I would like that, Elder; I'm very tired.>> Conal relaxed and closed his eyes, as he felt the Maker swimming off with him into the darkness.

Chapter Ten

Amril walked stiffly into the small chapel that was the Ima Matri's private sanctuary. Glowing fungus lamps on the walls illuminated the brightly-colored tapestries and the solemn faces of the people waiting. The Avairei already in the room knelt with faces turned towards the altar, chanting a melodic hymn of blessing.

Beside him, Sagas growled under her breath, "Quit slouching. Stand up straight—and stop walking like that—you'll shame our family with your bad behavior. You act like you're going to a funeral, not your wedding."

"I can't help it—I'm sore," he hissed back. What did she expect? He might as well be going to a funeral—his own.

Sagas tightened her grip on his arm and hustled him further into the chapel where the rest of the wedding party was already waiting.

Oh, the humiliation of it. Today, they'd dressed him in a woman's kilt, then, like any young bride-to-be, they made him report to the Marriage Mistress for the necessary preparations for the first night of love. Though the dear old Ima had been kind—and her hands quite skilled—it had been an upsetting experience for both of them. Oh, Holy Mother, his bottom was so sore. Ah, well, he supposed, later he would be grateful for the priestess's efforts to *prepare* him.

Amril's stomach churned; he was so scared; he licked his lips. His eyes focused on the large, muscular form of his *bridegroom*, already kneeling by the altar awaiting him. Oh, why—how could they do this to him?

Trembling, he stumbled as a grim-faced Sagas pushed him down beside the Kashallan. Reaching out a pale, five-fingered hand, the host steadied him, patted his shoulder and smiled. Amril swallowed hard and tried to return the smile, but his face felt like it was carved out of stone. He swallowed again, as the Kashallan took his hand, kissed it, and then continued to cradle it in his own.

Had anyone noticed that kiss? Amril looked around furtively—maybe not. Standing over by the door, he saw San Nathan, Timma, Hunt Leader Tizu, and some other Speir'dina that he recognized by sight, though not by name. Now that the hymn was finished, the Avairei knelt quietly, their faces controlled, staring at the center altar.

There was Sagas, of course, and Ima Surrel, her chief assistant and Ata Temog, representing the outlaws. From Ticca's inhabitants, he noticed Lore Mistress Quellyn and his mentor Ata Hobral, among others. What had the Imas told Hobral? He seemed a bit stunned by it all. What must the poor old man be thinking—what were they all thinking? Oh, well, he'd know soon enough.

Just behind him, he felt the presence of two more kneeling figures, but he didn't dare turn his head to see. His co-wives, and that was the only bright spot in all of this insanity—at least he would be with Pela—sort of.

Gods, it felt so weird to think of Pela and himself, not as husband and wife, as he had always dreamed, but as co-wives to this strange creature. What would it be like? Could he endure this—knowing she and the Kashallan would be doing— *Never mind that*, a small voice in his mind said. *What about, what you and the Kashallan will be doing tonight?*

Suddenly there was no more time to worry, because at that moment Ngeal entered, resplendent in her scarlet robe and jeweled collar, her grizzled braidlets confined under the metal headdress of her office. She crossed to the altar, knelt, made her blood offering to the Mother and the Khutani, and then began the wedding ceremony.

The rest of the ritual passed for Amril as if he were in a dream.; he made the blood offering to the Gods, and repeated his vows along with the Kashallan. Mechanically, he did whatever was expected of him without protest. He was so nervous that he felt he was drifting in a fog of unreality, unable to think or feel anything.

When it was over, he stood blinking, his hand once more held by the Kashallan as the witnesses passed by to offer them their congratulations. Woodenly, Amril repeated his thanks for their best wishes over and over, but his thoughts were elsewhere.

They would be going back to the Kashallan's suite soon, and he wished he'd taken Timma up on his offer to sneak him some lamra brandy, instead of being such a prude. He had been too worried, at the time that Ngeal might find out, or that Sagas would smell it on his breath when she came to get him. But he was so nervous, he could have used some brandy now for certain.

Coming up to them, Ngeal smiled at Amril and his sister-wives, then gave the Kashallan her hand. "Thank you, Ima, for agreeing to do this," he murmured. "Under the circumstances it was the only thing I could think of to do to make things right."

"I know that, and it speaks highly of you to have proposed it." She smiled at him, then added, "Though this mating is rather unconventional, I am pleased, and I hope that all of you will be very happy together."

"Thank you, Ima, I value your opinion and your good wishes highly." Then, unable to stay serious any longer, he said, "And do your *good wishes* extend to lowering your demands on our marriage bargain?"

"They most certainly do not. The bride is well worth the price, and I will hold you to every bottle."

The Kashallan laughed and hugged his new bride. "He most certainly is, and as long as you don't expect the whole batch in one afternoon, I'll manage."

"I will give you till the end of the Sorin season—will that do?"

He bowed. "Your will, Ima, I am yours to command."

She chuckled and patted his shoulder. "Only when it suits you, I think. Sagas has already warned me about your stubbornness."

Grinning, he bowed again, and she passed on to speak to his wives.

Right behind Ngeal, Sagas glared at her brother, and mouthed, "Stand up straight—you're disgracing us." Before she could go further with her murmured diatribe, the Kashallan intercepted her. Kissing her lightly on the forehead, he smiled down at her, his eyes twinkling. "Ah, my new sister-in-law—you have made me a very happy man."

Sagas snorted, but the corner of her mouth twitched in spite of herself. Giving her brother a stern look, she said, "I am glad you are happy, Holy One. I hope this ungrateful brother of mine will do his duty and serve you properly, or I—"

"Now, dear Ima, don't fret." He hugged Amril close, and kissed him on the forehead. "Amril's a good lad, and we will get on just fine together, I'm sure. Won't we, Sweet?"

Sweet? Amril nodded.

The Kashallan smiled and hugged him again. "And I'm sure he's looking forward to 'doing his *duty*,' as you put it. He is a Caltia, after all—I know he will please me, won't you, My Dear?"

Amril nodded again. *Oh, Mother, he would do his duty. Sagas didn't have to chide him about that, but—* He touched the marriage bottle at his waist, suddenly grateful for its presence. *Ah, well, with the red kavay to help, maybe it won't be so bad—*he hoped.

Tizu gave Amril a quizzical look. Dark eyes alight with amusement, he said to the Kashallan, "The bride seems a bit nervous." As if noticing that fact for the first time, the Kashallan studied Amril carefully.

Aware that the Hunt Leader's comment had focused several people's attention directly upon him, Amril felt his guts knot up even tighter. He looked down at the floor, wishing the stone would open up and swallow him.

"Yes, Hunt Leader, I think you may be right," the Kashallan said. He squeezed Amril's hand. "Like most young brides on their wedding night, he does seem a bit nervous." He winked, then added, "But he needn't worry—I'll be very gentle, I promise."

Tizu snorted, then gave him a toothy grin. Next to Amril, Sairsa put her hand quickly over her mouth to stifle a laugh. She glanced at Nathan behind Tizu, who rolled his eyes, then grinned.

Pela frowned, noticing Ngeal's scowl, she stepped forward and said. "Come, husband, it's time to go. You may joke with your kinsmen another time."

"You're right, My Sweet, it isn't fair for us to keep our new bride standing here like this. He's probably tired, and I dare say he needs to go to—uh—bed, hmm? We should go." Then, tucking Amril's arm in his, he waved to the remaining guests and headed for the door, Pela and Sairsa in his wake.

Near the entrance, Nathan caught up to him. "I've got some lamra brandy in my room. Timma dropped it by earlier. I didn't ask where he got it—you want some?"

Dunnagh smiled. "Yeah, Sairsa and I will see you in a while—save us some." Giving Amril a conspiratorial wink, the big man passed out the door ahead of them.

The halls were nearly deserted at this time of the evening, most of the Avairei were in their rooms or keeping private vigil in the main chapel. Amril was relieved; it made things easier. No one spoke, and for that Amril was grateful—he doubted if he could have gotten a single word past the lump in his throat.

When the Kashallan entered their suite, he stared around him in amazement. Briya and Jerina jumped up from their chairs and faced the wedding party, grinning. On one wall, a tapestry had been removed, and a large, luminous painting took its place.

The artwork was composed of several abstract spiral designs drawn with the multi-colored, glowing fungi normally collected to light the hallway lamps.

"My what a surprise," the Kashallan said, and crossed to admire the artwork. "Very ingenious, I don't think anything like this has ever been attempted." He glanced at his Avairei wives for confirmation.

"It is very beautiful, and no, husband, I don't think any Avairei or Loti craftsman has ever thought to use the fungi so," Pela said. Then her face saddened. "All that beautiful work, but it won't last. Away from the moist, warm air of the pools they will die."

"So we were told, when we gathered it earlier today," Briya said. "But while it lasts, enjoy it. We wanted to do something nice for all of you. Though it's officially Amril's wedding night, the rest of you haven't really had any time for celebrating your weddings either, so this is our gift to all of you."

Sairsa sat in a comfortable wicker chair, and leaned back with a grateful sigh. Her large belly ballooned over her lap. She smiled at all of them contentedly, then closed her eyes.

The Kashallan turned to the Dymarians with unshed tears in his eyes. "That was very kind of you, and I thank you. You're right—with all the running and fighting to just stay alive, we haven't had time for much celebrating." He sat down beside his Speir'dina wife, and studied her carefully for a moment, then took her hand and made the link.

Sairsa raised her head and opened her eyes. "I'm all right, Love, though I will be glad when this little one decides to come out. I'm just a little tired that's all."

He held the link a moment longer, nodded and sat back, giving everyone a toothy grin.

Amril stood where the Kashallan left him and stared around in confusion. He had no idea what was going on, or what they expected of him. Taking his arm, Pela guided him to a chair and sat him down, then sat beside him, still holding his hand. Amril glanced down at their linked hands, then over at the Kashallan.

The Kashallan was watching; when he saw Amril's glance directed his way, he winked, but said nothing. Confused again, Amril looked down at the floor, only raising his eyes when a full bowl was pressed into his hand.

Sairsa's Dymarian friends had also decorated the room with fragrant incense and refreshments laid out on a scarlet tablecloth. Turning back to his friends, the Kashallan asked, "Jerina will you and Briya bring us drinks so we can toast the bride."

When Sairsa was handed her bowl, she gave Briya a questioning look. "It's all right. We got the refreshments ourselves," Briya murmured, "and one of us has been here the whole time."

Overhearing the remark, Pela frowned, then deciding to let it pass she returned her attention to the Kashallan.

He was saying, "A toast is a Speir'dina custom on special occasions. Hold up your tea-bowls." When they complied, he raised his bowl, and, trying to control a slight tremor in his voice, he said, "To life. May the Gods bless us always. May this marriage be filled with love, happiness, and," his eyes twinkling, he grinned at his female wives,' "many babies," then, he smiled at Amril. "May our children brighten all our days."

Raising their bowls to his, they drank. When he finished, the Kashallan set down his tea-bowl and stood, helping Sairsa to her feet beside him. The Dymarian women rose as well.

"And now, Love, before you get too comfortable in that chair, I think we should go." He smiled at the other two women. "Nathan said something about a flask of fine lamra brandy, so ladies, shall we take the party down the hall, hmm?"

Crossing to his two Avairei consorts Dunnagh-Tani bent down and kissed Pela tenderly, then he took both their hands. Addressing Amril first, he said, "I'm sorry that you've had a rough time of it. I couldn't resist teasing you a bit earlier, but I am glad you're here with us, Amril. I know Pela is very happy, and I hope you will be too."

He glanced down at the woman's kilt the young Avairei was wearing, and sighed. "That kilt was the Ima Matri's idea, not mine, and I hope we can straighten it out in time, but until then—" He shrugged helplessly.

He squeezed their hands. "Good night, Loves. Bright blessings and don't wait up for us. If Nathan and Tani let me, I plan to get very drunk," Dunnagh confided. "We'll probably sleep there, so enjoy this time together."

Sairsa bent and kissed her two co-wives. To Pela she said, "If we don't come back, I'll be here first thing in the morning for the sister-wife ceremony. Good night, Amril, sleep well." Then, taking the Kashallan by the arm, she headed for the door, the smiling Dymarian women trailing along behind them.

When they were gone, the silence in the room was deafening. Amril stared open-mouthed at the closed door. What was going on here? After all the Imas' preparations—after all he'd gone through—his new husband had just walked out—leaving him behind—and on their wedding night! He turned to Pela for an explanation. She was watching him intently, an unreadable emotion gleaming in her warm, brown eyes.

"Finish your drink, Amril, and let's go to bed," she murmured. Raising her own bowl to her lips, she drained it and set it down on the table between them, then looked at him expectantly.

Still confused, he emptied his bowl then set it down, looking at her wide-eyed, his pulse racing. She was so beautiful in her scarlet kilt, and tinkling hair ornaments. Even large with child as she was, she seemed like a dream come true. Her lustrous, silky fur, her soft, dark eyes, and the mischievous little smile she was giving him right now—she was *so* beautiful. He wanted her so much, but he was also afraid. Why had the Kashallan left him alone with her like this? Didn't the Holy One know how hard it would be for him to hold back—to restrain himself.

Seeing the longing plain on his well-loved face, Pela chuckled deep in her throat and stood, pulling him to his feet beside her. Then, still holding on to him firmly, she led him into the bedroom, closed the door, and took him over to their large bed.

In the dim light from the tiny votive lamp on her altar, she smiled up at him. Stepping into his arms, she kissed him. "Mm—I've been waiting for this night most of my life, and now, in spite of everything, I have you with me."

Feeling suddenly shy and awkward, he put his arms around her. She ran her hands down his warm brown fur, and kissed him again. When they came up for air, she reached down to his belt, untied its knot, and allowed his kilt to fall to the floor at their feet. She gazed at him for a long moment, her smile mysterious and inviting, then she guided his hands towards her own sash.

Stepping back from her, Amril said a little breathlessly, "Pela, please, we shouldn't be doing this—"

She stared at him incredulously. "Why not?"

"Well, uh—they might come back," he improvised hastily.

"So? If they do, they'll join us." She motioned to the large bed behind them. "It's a big bed, there's room for all of us." She giggled. "Besides, you heard our husband say they wouldn't be back till late, if at all."

Amril glanced nervously at the bed. Oh, yes, it was a big bed. Well, two of his new consorts were hardly small creatures, now were they—and if they were all going to sleep together—oh, Mother, what had the Imas gotten him into?

Out loud, he said, "Our—uh—husband, the Kashallan, he might be angry with me if we—you know—"

"Amril, what are you talking about? They left so we *could* be alone for this first night. Didn't the Imas tell you? He didn't marry you for himself, not really—he married you for me—so *we* could be together."

Amril gaped, unable to take it all in. Pela watched him a few moments longer, then her face crumpled. She sank down hard on the edge of the bed, buried her face in her hands, and began to cry. "After all our planning and our bargaining, all that work, and—and now you don't want me!"

Amril sank down on the bed beside her and patted her shoulder clumsily. Pela—his Pela was crying! "Oh, Pela, don't cry, of course I want you. I—the Imas, my sister, they told me nothing. I thought—they made me go to the Marriage Mistress today—I thought—oh, Pela, don't cry!"

Pela sniffed and wiped her eyes, then stared at him incredulously. "They made you go to the Marriage Mistress? But why?"

Embarrassed, he finally mumbled, "Because I was getting married today, and my new husband would want—well, you know—what husbands usually want from their new brides."

She gaped, then began to laugh. "Oh, my poor Love, we didn't know—oh, my poor, poor Love."

Amril scowled. "I fail to see what's so amusing, Pela. My backside is still sore, and—"

"Oh, Amril, never mind, just kiss me," she wheezed in between giggles; throwing her arms once more around his neck.

A little later she whispered, "Help me off with my kilt, Love."

Once again he hesitated. "Pela, should we be doing this?"

"Oh, what is it this time?" she said impatiently. "I told you he *wants* us to be together." Then, softening her tone to a seductive purr, she tapped a finger on his nose, and said, "And, as his first wife, it's my duty to see that my junior wife is worthy of our husband's regard."

Shocked by her wanton manner, he drew back. "I know you said he approves, but—but you're breeding, Pela—what about the baby—his baby? Won't it hurt you or the child if we—"

She giggled. "Oh, my Love, you have a lot to learn. No, it won't hurt me or the baby—we do it all the time."

Amril gasped. So it was true what the Avairei had been whispering about his new family's "perversions." And his sister had approved—

"Stop looking so—so like an old Ima. You look just like Sagas when you do that."

"Do what? I do not!"

"Oh, Amril, listen to me," she said, suddenly serious again. "I guess, when I think back, it was hard for me at first, too. Those who we will share our lives with aren't Avairei, Love, so don't judge them by Avairei customs. The Speir'dina are a confusing, sometimes frightening, people, but they are also very generous and loving. I have gotten used to this new lifestyle, so I don't see it as abnormal any more.

"Amril, you have got to set aside all your old prejudices. Think of being married to the Kashallan as a great adventure; we are doing something that has never been done before. There are no rules or customs to guide us. We are the first, and sometimes that isn't easy, but if we love each other it will all work out. Please, Love, for me, will you try to accept this new way?"

For her, he would try, and she was right. They weren't going to be living with Avairei; to judge their marriage by Avairei customs wasn't fair. "You're right. Pela, this is all so new—and I'm so scared and confused—but I'll try, because I do love you and want to be with you, no matter what."

Pela smiled then reached down, rummaging around in the folds of his kilt that lay discarded on the floor. At last, finding what she had been looking for, she held up the beautifully carved marriage flask and sat back on the bed. She turned it in her hands, admiring the carvings a moment, then handed it to him. She licked her lips. "Now, my Love, as our new *bride,* I can see you're going to need this."

"But Pela—"

"Amril, as first wife I see I am going to have to teach you to obey me. Now, shut up and drink your red kavay or we're never going to get anywhere tonight. Then you may kiss me."

Chapter Eleven

Awakened by a noise in the corridor, Dunnagh sat up then groaned, clutching his head. Oh, Gods, it felt like a sledgehammer was being used inside his skull. He stared blurry-eyed at the chaos around him. The room was littered with discarded bottles, empty bowls, clothing, and a variety of other, mostly unrecognizable objects. Scattered among the debris were a few unclothed sleeping bodies, also unrecognizable in his present condition. He groaned again.

<<I warned you, Kasha, that if I let you drink all that brandy without helping you, this would happen,>> Tani smugly reminded him.

<<A-ah, so you did, Shalla, but you don't have to rub it in—not now when my head hurts like this. Ah, Tani, can't you do something—please?>>

A mental chuckle from the symbiont. <<It was rather fun last night,>> Tani said. <<Humans are a most amusing species when they are—what did you call it, Kasha?>>

<<Drunk. Tani, please—>>

<<Drunk, yes, that's the word you and Nathan used. It's a most interesting experience. Kasha, weren't the Hunt Leader and Nathan funny when they were trying to show the women how to—>>

<<Tani, please, I'm begging. Please, Shalla, I'm dying!>>

Another mental chuckle. <<No, you're not, Kasha, your head just hurts a little.>> At another pitiful groan from its host, the symbiont relented and sent a painkiller and a restorative into his bloodstream.

When Dunnagh could think clearly, he breathed a sigh of relief and said, <<Shalla, if I ever want to do this again, remind me, please, what it will feel like the next morning.>>

<<I can try, Kasha, but you don't always listen. As Ima Sagas says, 'The Speir'dina are a stubborn, willful people.'>>

<<Mm, right.>>

The host stood and stretched, then adjusted his kilt and picked up his cloak. Smiling to himself he glanced around at the still-slumbering figures strewn about on the furniture and the floor. That brandy had been strong stuff; there was going to be more than one hangover lamented about later. Well, it had been fun, and they had all needed to relax. He would come back in a while and help them out.

Where was Sairsa? Then he remembered; she must have gone back to their suite for some kind of sister-wife ceremony they had to do with the new "bride." Well, that meant he couldn't go back to his room just yet and sleep some more, as he would like to do.

Maybe he should go down to the pools to see Maker Dievris and get that chore over with for the day. By then the women should be finished with Amril, and he could go back to bed.

Heading down the corridor, he ran into a distracted priest who was coming out of a side passage in front of him. The Kashallan smiled and steadied the startled man. "Good morning, Ata?"

Hobral blinked, then, recognizing who he had bumped into, he bowed low in embarrassment. "Forgive me, Holy One—I apologize for my clumsiness."

"It is nothing," the Kashallan said, falling into step with the older man. "You seemed quite lost in thought just now—is there a problem I can help you with?"

Hobral walked on a few paces considering, then said, "I haven't wanted to trouble you with this, because I know that there are so many other things needing your attention, and yet I am at a loss how to explain this enigma."

"I would be glad to help, Ata, if I can. Tell me what is bothering you."

Hobral sighed. "It's Tomina, Holy One. I have tried everything I can think of, but her arm refuses to heal."

At the mention of the Dingay priestess, Dunnagh's face hardened. The Khutani cousins had been angry when they chewed up her arm, but still—they hadn't done anything to the woman that shouldn't have responded long ago to the conventional treatments.

Dievris had been after him to bring the woman to answer its questions, but with so many other things to do, he had been deliberately avoiding that unwanted chore.

Reluctantly, he had to admit to himself that he liked things the way they were. Tomina was safe under guard where he could keep an eye on her, and she couldn't start any trouble. But he supposed he'd better go take a look at the woman.

Today was as good a time as any to see her, and if she was indeed still suffering from her wounds, then he could take her with him down to the pools, so the Elder could taste and question her after she was treated.

"I think I should come with you and have a look at her, Ata. I should have seen to the woman before now, anyway."

Hobral nodded, his relief plain upon his kindly face, and led the way down the hall to the priestess's room. "Thank you, Holy One, it would ease my mind if you had a look at her."

Outside Tomina's door, the Kashallan paused to speak to the Speir'dina on duty. "Anything to report?"

Marti and Marnez saluted, and shook their heads. "Her maid was here and brought her breakfast a little while ago," Marti said, "but she's alone at the moment."

"Good—keep it that way till the Ata and I finish with her." Hand on the door, he paused. "I'll be taking her down to the pools after I examine her arm. Let the duty officer know that, and see about a litter or chair, in case she is really too ill to walk, as she has told the Ata."

"Yes, Ce'awn." Marnez's lips moved silently as she spoke to the officer on duty through her communications implant.

Knocking peremptorily on the door, the Kashallan opened it and walked in, Hobral at his heels.

TOMINA JERKED HER HEAD up at the loud knock. She rose from the bed, eyes flashing. The angry retort she was about to make died on her lips when she saw the one who dared enter her room unbidden. Tomina had never seen him before, but, in spite of that, she knew him. Taking a deep breath, she faced him squarely and bowed. He was much as they had described him—a big male, with ugly, flattened features, a long, red mane, and startling blue eyes.

Stepping out from behind the Kashallan's bulk, Hobral smiled. "Good morning, Ima. On my way to see you, I met the Kashallan in the hall. I told him how worried I am about your injured arm, and he agreed to come with me and have a look at it."

Damn the interfering old fool, I'm not ready for this—my plans aren't in place yet. "Thank you, Ata, that was very kind, but it isn't really necessary to trouble the Holy One with such a minor problem. I feel much better today."

The Kashallan raised his eyebrows in polite disbelief. "I am glad to hear that you are on the mend, Ima Tomina, because we have some unfinished business to take care of, don't we? There is the little matter of your oath of fealty that needs to be settled."

Tomina bowed. "But of course, Holy One. After I have finished my meal and bathed, I will come to you for the oath taking." *That will give me time to use Barak's ull powder.*

"Mm, I think not," he countered. Then, before she knew what he planned, the Kashallan took her injured arm. "As long as I am here, Ima, I will have a taste of your injuries. I am curious why they aren't healing as they should." Not giving her time to pull away, he extended his tentacles and made the link.

"And before I can take your oath, the Maker Dievris wants to taste you. It has some questions it wants to ask you. Your answers will determine whether you will even be allowed to swear fealty."

Oh, by the Fires, they hadn't told her about that. A Maker! Oh, what to do now? Even with Barak's potion, she doubted she could fool a Maker.

Suddenly the Kashallan's eyes widened in surprise. "You're no Avairei! You're—you're an Umwira changeling! How?"

"No! not true, Holy One." *Oh, Master! How could this hated enemy know that? None of the other Khutani ever guessed.* Barak had assured her that none but the ancient Makers had ever tasted the Real People. With a strangled cry, she tried to pull away, but he tightened his hold, his blue eyes afire with hatred.

Tomina felt her hip bump up against the table where her breakfast tray lay forgotten. She had to escape—get out of here—tell the Master— With her free hand she reached behind her, groping for something to use as a weapon. Her fingers closed around the handle of her eating knife. Without taking time to think, she brought the makeshift weapon round and plunged it, hilt deep, into his exposed abdomen.

With a startled cry, the Kashallan released her, and crashed to the floor, clutching at his middle. Tomina brushed past the astonished Hobral, knocking him to the floor in her haste. Totally panicked, she flung open the door, plunged past the dumbfounded guards, and ran.

Marti took in the crumpled body of the Kashallan upon the floor, and the frightened priest crouching beside him. She bellowed the alarm in her foghorn voice, and took off after the fleeing Dingay priestess, leaving her partner to see to the Kashallan.

TOMINA RAN. SHE HAD no idea where she was, but the sounds from the inhabited portion of the keep were growing fainter. She needed time—somewhere to hide—catch her breath—think! Behind her, the pounding footsteps of the big Speir'dina female were coming closer. Damn her to the Fires! If she could just get rid of this one, she could hide in these deserted tunnels till things calmed down—later she could sneak out—get a message to the Master...

Without slowing her pace, Tomina glanced around wildly for something to use as a weapon. Spying a small stone figurine in a wall niche near a dimming fungi lamp, Tomina grabbed it, and backed into a shadowed doorway to wait.

FEAR AND ANGER WERE dual spurs goading Marti in pursuit. *Damn the Dingay woman! I should have gone with him into her room, I should have—*

Out of the corner of her eye, she caught a movement as she came up to a blackened doorway. Marti swerved, throwing up an instinctive block as a furred hand holding an unknown object lunged at her face. Marti grabbed the wrist, bending it backward.

Tomina staggered and dropped the statue with a cry of pain. Still holding on to the other woman's arm, she brought her free hand around in a fist, and delivered a hard blow to the priestess's abdomen. Tomina let out a grunt of surprise, and fell forward. Still acting totally on instinct, the Speir'dina next slammed the callused side of her hand against Tomina's exposed throat.

There was a strangled gurgling sound from Tomina, and the woman crumpled lifeless to the stone at her feet. Breathing hard, Marti loomed over the fallen woman, trying to catch her breath.

"That was nicely done, My Jewel," a cool voice said. Startled, Marti looked up; Tess-weh laughed. "Yes, very professional, wouldn't you agree, Cadrach?"

"Yes, Mistress."

"But perhaps not wise," Tess-weh continued. "For now that she's dead, there will be no way of knowing if she had other accomplices within the keep."

"Unless you tell us," Marti countered.

"True enough, My Beauty, but I think not. There are rules, you see." The demon smiled. "But perhaps we can come to a mutually satisfying arrangement—if you pay my price, hmm?"

Marti snarled a vile oath, and stomped away down the corridor. Giving vent to her own exasperation, Tess-weh shouted, "Come back here, you fool." When the woman paid no attention, Tess-weh told her slave, "Go get her. Don't hurt her over-much, but bring her back here."

Without a word, the Wa'chassey'ul bounded after the retreating woman. Catching up to her in a few quick strides, he flung his massive arms around her from behind, then picked her up as if she weighed nothing and carried her, swearing and struggling, back to his mistress. Setting her once more on her feet in front of the demon, he kept his hold on her and waited for further instructions.

Tess-weh scowled, her hard eyes still smoldering. "That was very stupid, but as my H'an reminded me just now, you were always a hot-tempered one, prone to act rather than think first."

Ignoring Tess-weh, Marti fought to free herself from the Warlinga's iron grasp. When she'd exhausted herself, she stood gasping, her eyes defiant. Tess-weh laughed. "You can't break his hold, you know. The strength of the Wa'chassey'ul is more than mortal."

Marti continued to glare, but said nothing. Tess-weh laughed again, then reached out a pale hand and stroked the dark woman's cheek, enjoying the play of contrast their skins made next to one another. "Mm, you really are quite beautiful when you are so *aroused*."

Snarling, Marti tried once more to free herself, then fell back gasping as the Wa'chassey'ul made it painfully clear to her that she would not succeed.

"Enough," the spirit snapped. "I grow tired of playing this game. Hear what I have to offer and pay my price, or let the blame for the coming disaster be yours."

"All right, I'm listening."

"Good. Now, as I was saying, My Jewel, there are rules—I can't tell you if there are others, or who they might be, but I can say that there are things in Tomina Dingay's room that must be found and destroyed, immediately, or there will be those who will die because of them."

Marti thought about it for a long moment then said sullenly, "What things? Will you come with me and show me?"

"I will come with you and tell you if what you find are the right things," the demon countered.

"What about the Kashallan?" Marti blurted. "Is he—"

Making an impatient hand gesture, Tess-weh snapped, "Enough questions—you are wasting valuable time. The Khutani will keep. You can't do anything for the Kashallan that is more important than what I am telling you to do. The bondmates are cared for at the moment."

"All right, I'll pay your damned price, let's go."

Motioning for Cadrach to release her, they headed back to Tomina's room.

Inside Tomina's chamber, Marti, with her partner Marnez's help uncovered an interesting array of potions, powders, and magical objects that the demon directed them to put in a growing pile in the middle of the floor.

When they hesitated, Tess-weh said, "Keep looking."

Marti placed her hands atop her broad hips and growled in frustration. "You keep saying there's something else, but we've been over this room four times now. And the last time, we didn't find anything new, so what—"

Tess-weh cut her off with an impatient wave of her hand, "You haven't much time; don't waste it on foolish chatter. Keep looking."

Suddenly Tess-weh turned her back on the irate Marti and closed her eyes. Her body stiffened as she focused her attention on the scene enacting outside the closed door, through her link with the Wa'chassey'ul left on guard.

Tess-weh saw Tomina's maid creeping up the hallway. She looked harmless enough, just a pretty young Avairei—ah, but looks could be deceiving. The maid held on to a dark stone, and the demon could feel its power. Yes-s, she was the one.

SOMETHING WAS WRONG; the wizard could feel it through the psychic link he shared with his minions within Ticca. Why didn't that fool Tomina respond when he called to her? At the earliest opportunity, she would feel the strength of his displeasure in payment for her inattention.

When he once again looked through the eyes of the girl, Nona, Barak hissed in surprise. A shiver of dread ran down his backbone. Wa'chassey'ul! He recognized the sigil of power carved on the big Warlinga's forehead. Damn these putrescent Avairei! Why hadn't they told him about such a creature? Damn the useless slaves to the Fires.

Approaching cautiously, Nona bowed to the Wa'chassey'ul. "Excuse me, Warlinga, but my Ima requires that I attend her. You may let me in—I have permission." For answer, the big brute only stared at her silently, unmoving.

Nona and the watching Barak waited. At last, growing impatient with this stalemate, Nona started forward, clutching her amulet. "Let me pass, slave," she snarled in a deep voice unlike her own. Cadrach remained, blocking the doorway.

Raising her free hand, Nona began to draw a glowing sigil of power in the vibrating air between them. Instantly the Wa'chassey'ul, responded with a countersign. The air around them exploded as the two glyphs collided. The Warlinga remained where he was, but Nona flew backwards across the hall. Slamming up against the far wall she crumpled, dazed, to the floor.

Coming to her senses a moment later, Nona stood, eyes flashing with rage. The wizard- would have pursued the attack, but from down the hall came a shout and the sound of running feet. Another confrontation with the guardian would have to wait; their battle hadn't gone unnoticed. Snarling in frustration, Barak directed the Avairei back down the corridor. Damn them, they would pay, Barak raged. When he got his claws into that fool of a Dingay filth...

STILL SPEAKING TO TESS-weh, Marti spun round; her argument dying on her lips as the sound of an explosion rattled the door in its frame. She started for the door, but Tess-weh seized her arm with an inhuman grip, spinning her around. "Quickly, there isn't much time—Cadrach will deal with the problem," the spirit hissed. "You must find it soon or it will be too late!"

"But what are we looking for?" Marti cried in desperation.

Over by Tomina's bed, Marnez had finished ripping apart the priestess's mattress. They had found some interesting things in and under it, but if the spirit wasn't satisfied, it might be worth another look, she reasoned. But after another check, there still wasn't anything in the bed to add to their pile.

Marnez let the disemboweled shell flop back on its frame, then, getting down on all fours, she pushed aside the tiny night table and peered under the edge of the bed once more. It was dark under there, and though the bed frame was attached to the wall, maybe they should—

As she raised herself from under the edge of the frame, Marnez noticed something odd. One of the stones in the wall that had been behind the table was a slightly different color from the rest. They had moved the table before, of course, but from this new angle she could see the stone's uniqueness much clearer. Hmm. Reaching out a hand, she tentatively grasped the stone and pulled. To her surprise, it came away easily into her hand. She gasped. "Marti, come here!"

Startled, Marti broke off her arguing and crossed hurriedly to her partner's side. "What?"

Marnez pointed, then reached into the tiny cavity and brought out a heavily wrapped bundle. Sitting back on her heels, she stared in amazement at the object in her hands.

"Mm, well done, My Treasure," Tess-weh purred softly as she came over to them.

The two women paid her little attention, suddenly mesmerized by the mysterious package. Marti reached out, took the thing, and began to untie the cord that bound it.

"That would not be wise, My Pearl," Tess-weh said and laid a hand on her shoulder.

Startled, Marti shook herself as if coming out of a trance. She held out the object for the demon's inspection. "Is this what we've been looking for?"

Tess-weh smiled. "I cannot say—the rules, you understand." As Marti's eyes began to smolder, she added, "But I can advise you that this and anything else that is in that hole should be destroyed—*immediately*."

Chapter Twelve

Tizu flattened himself against the wall as a blue flash of light and the sound of an explosion echoed from a side passage just ahead. *Shit! By all the gods, what was that?*

"Hunt Leader, was that one of your magic weapons?" Beside him, Fadir shuddered, head crest flattened.

Tizu shook his head, then, drawing his sidearm, he motioned for the Warlinga to follow him down the hall. They continued slowly along the corridor, but, other than passing a frightened young Avairei hurrying in the opposite direction, they neither heard nor saw anything else out of the ordinary.

Near the Dingay priestess's room, Tizu halted abruptly, frowning. Goronwy said Marti and Marnez were on duty outside the Dingay woman's door. The women were gone. Who was this big brute?

Annoyed, he started forward to demand an accounting of the man, but Fadir stopped him by roughly grabbing his arm. "No, Hunt Leader, you must not."

"Let go of me," Tizu muttered. "What do you think you're doing? I want to find out what's going on."

To his surprise, Fadir tightened his hold. "Please, San Tizu. I know I have sworn to take your orders, but you have also given me leave to do what I think is best, when there is reason. I assure you this is one of those times. There are things here that you don't understand—"

"What's to understand?" he snapped. "This man is—"

"Is not one of our hunting pack, Hunt Leader," Fadir interrupted in a hurried undertone. "He will not take your orders, and if he perceives you as a threat to himself or his Mistress, he will kill you."

Tizu stared at his Second, perplexed. "Look at his face, Hunt Leader," Fadir whispered. "He is the Wa'chassey'ul I told you about. And for him to be here at this time means that he is under orders from his Mistress, the Sweh'an. It would not be wise to cross him. Whatever has just happened here involves the power of the demon. We should tread carefully."

Shit, Tizu thought, *that's all I need right now, that crazy Tess-weh mucking about, stirring up more trouble.* "All right." He jerked his arm out of the other man's grasp. "I see your point, but I still need to find out what's been going on around here and what has happened to my guards—"

"That is true, Hunt Leader, so, if you will permit?"

Tizu sighed. "Go ahead."

Fadir approached the big Warlinga cautiously, Tizu trailing in his wake. At a respectful distance, he halted, in plain view of the door's guardian. "Cadrach," Fadir said, "are you permitted to speak to me?"

"I may speak to you, Cousin," the big Warlinga intoned in a hollow voice.

"Good, is your Mistress within?"

"Yes, Cousin."

"Is she alone?"

"No, Cousin."

"Are either of the Speir'dina women who were on guard duty here with her?"

"They are both with her."

"What are they doing?" Tizu blurted. Fadir hissed, and gave Tizu a warning look. Tizu ignored him, folded his arms across his chest and glared at the Wa'chassey'ul.

Cadrach eyed him with a cold inhuman gaze that sent chills down the Commander's spine. "I am not permitted to speak of that right now."

Tizu flushed and would have pressed the man, but Fadir quickly diverted the conversation in another direction. "Where is the Dingay priestess? Is she in there too?"

"No, Cousin, she is dead—the big female Warlinga has killed her."

"When and where?" Tizu demanded, and pushed passed Fadir. He was getting tired of this little question and answer game. He wanted to get to the bottom of this—right now!

Fadir quickly barred the commander's way with the weight of his tail across Tizu's chest. "Please Hunt Leader. We must go carefully here." There was such a troubled look in the man's red eyes that Tizu grunted and stepped back. "Where is she, Cadrach?"

Cadrach pointed back down the hall. "She lies in the side passage to the right, Cousin."

"Thank you, Cadrach, we will go find her now." Then, before the Hunt Leader could protest, Fadir took him firmly by the arm and led him back down the hallway. Tizu started to argue, but broke off as a nearly hysterical Sagas ran blindly into him.

Tizu grabbed her by the shoulders to keep her from falling. Braids tangled, eyes round and wild, he'd never seen her in such a state. She looked into his eyes without comprehension for a moment, then she recognized him, and slumped against him with a sob. "Oh, Hukiyo, what has happened? I heard—they said—the Kashallan—"

Tizu held her close for a moment longer than was necessary, then released her. "Calm down, Sagas, you won't do him any good by falling apart like this."

Sagas glanced at the staring Warlinga, took a deep breath, and smoothed her rumpled kilt with a trembling hand. In a calmer voice she said, "Is he—dead?"

"As far as I know—no. Fortunately some of the armachda were nearby. When they heard the call for help. They carried him to the Khutani straight away. Some of the priests are with him too, so if he can be saved—I'm sure they will do the best they can."

Sagas swallowed hard, and nodded. With a visible effort she took a few more deep breaths and pushed her mass of tangled braids over her shoulder. "May the Great Mother bless us and keep him safe." Then, her expression hardened. "I also heard that it was the Dingay woman that tried to kill him."

"It would seem so, Ima," Fadir said.

Sagas glared murderously down the dim hallway. "Damn all the Dingay," she said. "I'll kill her!"

Tizu gave her an appraising look, and a ghost of a smile curved his lips. "One of my armachd has saved you the trouble, Ima. Tess-weh's Wa'cha—whatever he's called, says her body's down this passage." He took her arm. "We were just on our way to find out. If it will make you feel better, come with me and see for yourself."

They found the Dingay priestess sprawled in an untidy heap near the end of the side passage, as the Wa'chassey'ul claimed. Fadir retrieved a fungus lantern from a bracket further down the passage, returned and held it high above the corpse

Tizu knelt and flipped the body over, feeling for a pulse. Hovering almost at his shoulder, Sagas gazed down at the body. "Is the verminous filth dead?"

Tizu stood up. "Yes." Turning to his Second, he said, "Go find a couple of the men and come back here with a litter. Put her in a vacant room until things settled down and we know what the Khutani want us to do with her."

Fadir hung the lantern on a nearby wall bracket and bowed. "Yes, Hunt Leader."

When he was gone Tizu returned his attention to Sagas. She was standing, statue-like, staring down at the lifeless body of her enemy. Coming up behind her, he enfolded her in his arms. "Sagas?"

She stiffened. He tightened his embrace, his lips brushing the scented mass of her braidlets. "Sagas, don't do this to yourself, please. It's not your fault."

Ignoring him she continued to stare at the corpse. After a long moment she said in a hollow voice, "This *is* my fault. I should have remembered—I should have told him. Now he may die and it's all because of me."

Tizu turned her in his arms to face him. "Sagas, what nonsense are you talking about? How could you have known the woman would do this, My Dear One?"

Sagas looked up at him, tears welling in the corners of her eyes. His expression softened and he hugged her close. For just a moment she relaxed against him. He kissed her hair again, his hands sliding over her silky fur. She shuddered, then stepped away from him. "Don't, Hukiyo, please—and it is my fault."

He sighed and folded his arms across his chest,. "OK, Little Miss Stubborn, why do you think this is your fault?"

Sagas bristled. A sharp retort died on her lips and she looked away from the longing in his eyes. Staring down at the corpse once more she said, "When we first arrived at Ticca—and we were down at the pools, I taunted

Tomina about her Umwira Master. I was just saying that to anger her—I don't know why, but when I saw her expression—she was afraid.

"Hukiyo—she thought I knew the truth, and she was afraid. But I didn't—but it was true, and I was too stupid to tell him." Her hands balled into fists, and she swore one of the armachda's barrack's oaths under her breath. "I forgot—Tomina was confined, and now—"

"Even so, this isn't your fault," he repeated and reached for her again.

She sidestepped his embrace. "Don't, please, Hukiyo, I know you care—and maybe I care for you too, but this isn't right—I can't—it isn't seemly for an Avairei of my age to—" She broke off and stepped further away from him as she heard the sounds of footsteps approaching.

"Too old, what kind of crap is that, too old? I told you before; I'm not interested in screaming babies."

"And, I told you, before, that your offer is insulting and disgusting," she hissed back.

Tizu swore and gave her a disgusted look. The woman both attracted and infuriated him in nearly equal measure.

They glared at one another for a long moment, then Sagas dropped her eyes. "I've got to go to the pools—I have to see him," she murmured, and before he could stop her; she was gone.

THE OATH TAKING AND lovemaking of the sister-wife ceremony completed, Sairsa nestled comfortably between her two furry co-wives. She yawned and pushed her ample backside up against her new brother-wife's crotch and sighed with a sleepy contentment. Shyly, Amril put his arm around her, glancing over at Pela for approval as he did so. She smiled, and snuggled closer into her sister-wife's embrace.

Sairsa hadn't slept well last night. Though Nathan had been chivalrous and let her lie down in his bed when she grew tired, it had still been noisy there with the party going on all about her. It would be nice to go back to sleep now. Warm and relaxed from their love, it felt so sensuous to lie here between her furry co-wives—mm, yes very nice, she decided as she drifted near the borders of sleep. Mm—

Suddenly she let out a startled cry and sat bolt upright in the bed, tumbling Amril unceremoniously to the floor. "OH, NO, DUNNAGH-TANI!" she screamed then doubled over sideways, clutching at her enlarged belly as a blinding pain tore through her abdomen. She screamed again and again.

Picking himself off the floor, Amril stared in stupefaction at the writhing woman on the bed. "The Holy One will kill me for this! I told you, Pela, we shouldn't do that—it would hurt the baby," he wailed.

"Shut up, Amril, don't be stupid. Something else is wrong with her." Shaking her head, Pela turned her back on him and reached for her sister-wife. "Sairsa'meh, talk to me—what is it? Tell me what's wrong."

When she couldn't get Sairsa to answer after a few more attempts she shouted at Amril, "Don't just stand there gawking like a fool, go get help!"

Amril stared at her for a moment longer then her words penetrated his stunned senses and he raced for the door. "Yes, I'm going—right now—I'll get help."

Through the pain, Sairsa heard Pela's frantic questions and tried desperately to respond. Ah, but the pain—it was so intense—it was so hard to speak— Finally, she managed to squeeze out in between the spasms, "Dunnagh-Tani—he's hurt—and oh, Pela, I think the baby's coming!"

Chapter Thirteen

The Kashallan awoke when he felt another human body lie down in the warm water at his back. The other placed a hand on his shoulder and slid it hesitantly down his arm. Without opening his eyes, he said, "I'm awake, Nathan."

After Tomina's attack, Dunnagh had been vaguely aware of the frightened Avairei and Speir'dina who came at Marti's bellow. They surrounded him, put him on a litter, and carried him, as gently as they could, down to the Khutani.

He thought he could recall Ata Hobral, or maybe it was Temog, removing the knife, and then an angry and impatient Maker Dievris cradled him in its massive coils, for the rest of the healing.

For immeasurable time Dunnagh swam in a sea of endless pain, alone and very frightened. He wondered if he were going to die, and decided he didn't care. Without the Shalla...

The hand stopped its progress, then withdrew. At last, a hesitant voice said, "It's not Nathan, Amsi. He was here until a little while ago making himself crazy with worry, but finally the Commander and Sairsa made him go get some rest in his room. I wanted to come see you while they were all gone—because I have been worried about you, too."

Nathan, Sairsa, the Commander? Apparently a lot had been going on while he was so weak. That voice was familiar, but he couldn't place it. And why would that person address him as "Amsi?" Even Nathan, as close as they were, didn't know the term the Khutani siblings used when addressing kin of the same age grouping. Puzzled, he eased himself slowly over onto his back so he could see his visitor.

The Kashallan gaped. Long, drooping mustache, brown hair plastered to his head so he looked more like a seal than a man, bright green eyes watching him anxiously—it was a face he remembered well. "Conal?"

The man chuckled then smiled, displaying sharp, triangular teeth. "Yes, Amsi, it's me, Conal-Tiel." Reaching out once more, he picked up the Kashallan's hand and clumsily made the link.

Dunnagh-Tani stared down dumbfounded at the pink tentacles in his arm. "You? A kashallan—how—when?" Then, remembering the fight, he asked, "Amsi, does this have anything to do with your fight with Nathan?"

Closing his eyes, Conal-Tiel took a moment to taste the extent of Tani's injuries before answering. Finally he said, "In a way, I guess the fight was about my making the bond—though I didn't know it at the time. Soon after we got to Ticca, Tess-weh came to me claiming she could tell me how to get my hand back—if I paid her price. I did, and more than once—but each time she kept saying it wasn't enough. She was making me crazy.

"Later, I went to Second Hunter Fadir and explained my situation. He let me in to see her. When she told me that the only way to get another hand was to make a kashallan bond, I went even more crazy for a while. Finally I got up the nerve to come down here on my own and try to make a deal with our Elders myself."

He grinned ruefully. "That, too, wasn't one of my brighter plans—my amla, Maker Dievris almost put me out of my misery then and there for my impudence."

Yes, Dunnagh could believe that. Dievris wasn't a creature to toy with. Gingerly the Kashallan raised himself to a sitting position, swinging round to face his new cousin. "Let me see them," Tani begged.

Conal-Tiel held up his hand, displaying his new acquisitions proudly for Dunnagh-Tani's inspection. "I only have one set, as yet," Tiel explained. "I still have to do much more reconstruction on my Kasha's other hand before we can have two pairs like you."

Dunnagh-Tani reached out and took both of Conal-Tiel's wrists in his own hands. He examined first the stump where a bulge of new tissue was already growing.

Next he turned his attention to the other hand, with its new, delicate pink appendages. "Aren't they wonderful," Tani said. "When could you extend and contract them for the first time?"

"Not long ago, but it's hard to tell time down here. I've been so weak from the bonding and all the adaptations, myself, that I haven't been doing much but eating and resting until now.

"They are still very sore, but you're right, Amsi—they are wonderful. I begged the Elders to let me come to you while no one else was around, so I could taste you for myself."

Tani laughed delightedly. "I remember, when I first could extend and retract mine, I was very sore, because I couldn't stop bringing them out to admire them."

Extending his own tentacles, the Kashallan formed the link on Conal's arm just above his growing hand. Reversing his good hand in the Kashallan's grasp, Conal-Tiel proceeded to re-establish his own link. For a long time, the two hosts just sat and grinned at each other, as their symbiont bondmates carried on a rapid conversation of their own.

When the two symbionts were talked out for the moment, Dunnagh brought the conversation back to an earlier topic. "Why would it matter if you came to me when others were around? I don't understand."

Conal-Tiel shrugged. "I'm not sure, Amsi. I just know that, for now, the Makers want to keep my bonding a secret." He glanced anxiously back down the walkway towards the entrance to the keep above. "They are still worried about our safety."

"Hmm. Maybe they haven't caught the Dingay priestess yet."

"No, I don't think that's it. I'm sure Nathan or one of the priests told amla Dievris that she was dead. No; there is some other reason they are worried, and feel it isn't safe for us up there yet. Perhaps she had accomplices that haven't been found."

"Hmm, I suppose that's possible," the Kashallan conceded, "but the Maker and I tasted everyone else in the keep before the oath taking. I can't see how such a one would have escaped our notice. Surely if I didn't catch the falseness, the Maker would have."

The Kashallan shook his head and frowned. "There is one thing I would like to know, however. If Tomina is dead, what did they do with her corpse?"

"What? They threw the filth in the waste pool where it belonged, of course. You didn't expect us or anyone else to eat it, did you?"

"No, but I do wish the Elders, at least, had been allowed to taste her, before the Avairei disposed of the body."

"By all the Gods, why, Amsi?"

"Because when I examined her, I was sure I tasted the flavor of the Umwira about her. I would have liked the Makers to have had a chance to verify my assumption."

"Umwira, here! How could you know that, Amsi?"

"During the fight under the mountain when the Ghostlanders attacked us, I had the occasion to taste one of the Hated Enemy. Tomina carried traces of the same flavor, but I was so startled, I let her know what I suspected before I had a chance to think. That's why she panicked and stabbed me."

Conal swore in Caldoni, his green eyes suddenly hard. "You must tell the Elders, Amsi, this is very important."

"Mm, I know, and I will, as soon as Elder Dievris or one of the other k'amsi comes by to check on me."

Conal-Tiel nodded. Then he looked up, over the Kashallan's shoulder, and smiled. "I should go, amsi, or the Elders will discipline me. You have another late-night visitor, who has, I think, a special surprise for you. I'll come back if and when they let me." Leaning forward, he touched the Kashallan's cheek with an extended pink appendage, then bent and kissed him. Smiling at the Kashallan's bemused expression, Conal-Tiel slipped below the surface of the pool and was gone.

Who would be coming for a visit so late? Carefully, he shifted around to see, then, he smiled and held out his arms in welcome. Sairsa grinned back. She slipped off her clothes quickly, then waded out into the water, a squirming Tameh held firmly in her arms. Sitting down beside him in the warm liquid, she placed his young son in his arms, and lay back on her side with a contented sigh.

"Mm, I'm glad to see you finally awake, Love, how do you feel? I've been waiting impatiently to introduce you to this little fellow for some time now."

He laughed in delight, and stared down in wonder at the baby he held in his arms. "He's so beautiful," Dunnagh-Tani said. With his cap of curly, red-gold hair, unfocussed green eyes, and pink bow of a mouth, the baby was a wonder to behold. Extending a tentacled finger, he traced the baby's face, marveling at the softness of his smooth, pink skin. He gently allowed the tip of that sensitive organ to penetrate the baby's flesh. Tameh screwed up his face for a moment but made no further objection to his father's examination. "Oh, Love, he's so—beautiful," he breathed. "When?"

"I guess you don't remember, but it was quite chaotic down here for a while," she explained. "I think I felt it when Tomina tried to kill you—I got this white-hot pain right here." She pointed to a place on her now deflated abdomen. "The next thing I knew, I was in labor. Dr. B wasn't sure if the Khutani would want me here while you were being treated, but when he sent Timma down to ask, they said yes.

"After the birthing, Maker Dievris let me stay near you. I just went upstairs a few hours ago, when we finally coaxed Nathan out of here." She smiled to herself thinking about it. "He wouldn't go unless I did."

Screwing up his little face, the baby began to make impatient sucking noises. Tameh turned his head and nuzzled his father's bare chest. Reluctantly, the Kashallan handed him back to his mother. Sairsa settled Tameh in the crook of one arm, and positioned an erect pink nipple by his searching mouth. As the baby sucked, Dunnagh-Tani watched the procedure with rapt attention.

Finally tearing his eyes away from the baby, he asked, "It must be late, Love, what are you doing down here? Why aren't you in bed sleeping?"

Sairsa chuckled. "Sleep! What's that?" In her arms, Tameh had only sucked for a short time, then stopped. Nipple still in his mouth, he stared up myopically at his mother, definitely wide-awake in spite of the late hour. "Just like before his birth, this little fellow still hasn't figured out the nights are for sleeping, not playing.

"Rather than keeping my co-wives awake any more than necessary, I decided to come back down here, check on you, and let some of your cousins play with him till he gets sleepy again."

She lifted the baby up, nuzzling his belly with her nose, then held him out once more to look at him. "Isn't that right, My Little Seal? And I see your playmates are already here waiting for you, so away you go."

The Kashallan gasped as his wife calmly placed the squirming baby down in the pool and let go of him. Instead of half drowning as he feared, the baby swam after a young Khutani who nuzzled him, and looped a coil around his middle to steady him.

Glancing at Dunnagh's shocked face, Sairsa laughed and patted his hand. "He's fine, really. What do you think he's been doing for the last nine months, Love, hmm?"

"Swimming?"

"Mm-hm."

"But—"

"It's all right," Sairsa assured him. "I'd heard about this before, on Dymar but never thought one of my children could swim like this so soon after birth. But it just seemed to happen quite naturally, really. It would seem that if babies are exposed to a watery environment soon after their birth, they don't forget how to hold their breaths till they come to the surface for air.

"And this little fellow was born in this pool, and we stayed right here at first, so it's natural he should be as much at home here as on land—if not more so. And the Khutani do a good job of caring for him when he's with them,"

He shook his head in amazement. "If I wasn't seeing it with my own eyes, I don't know if I would have believed it." Leaning over carefully, he kissed her. "You are a wonder to me." He kissed her again. "And you make beautiful babies."

She laughed and kissed him back. "I had a little help, remember."

"Mm, I do indeed," and he kissed her again.

They watched the baby play for a while in companionable silence, then Sairsa repeated, "I don't know if you are avoiding my earlier question, or you just forgot when you saw your new son, but how are you, Love, really?"

"I guess I was doing a little of both," he admitted, "but I'm getting better. I'm still in some pain, and I'm not sure when the Maker is going to let me get out of here, but other than that I'm fine."

She surveyed him critically for a moment longer, then nodded and relaxed.

Sometime later, a now sleepy Tameh was pushed into her arms by his Khutani playmates. Sairsa gathered him to her ample breast and settled him down for a bedtime feed. When he was sound asleep, she gave him to his adoring father while she dressed, then she took him back and left to seek her own bed in the keep above.

Exhausted himself, the Kashallan let her go, and, after his own feeding, he lay back and slept as contentedly as his new son.

Chapter Fourteen

Aju'an motioned for his hunting pack to go on by, and slackened his pace to come alongside his sister. They'd been running flat out since leaving the ruined keep at Ha'limra this morning. How much longer could she keep on running like this?

After a moment, Chelka herself became aware of his solicitous regard. She glared at him, curling her lip in a silent snarl, and motioned with a jerk of her head for him to get back up to the head of the pack where he belonged. He hesitated, then caught the eye of his cousin Mar, who was running slightly behind her. Mar nodded for him to go on.

The two men exchanged worried glances, but Aju'an felt satisfied that Mar would look out for her, no matter what happened. Relieved, Aju'an nodded to his sister and pressed forward to resume his position at the head of the pack.

In spite of his worry, he had to admire her. Chelka's naive confidence in her training with the old hunt leader had dissolved by the end of the second day. She'd been bruised and sore, but she hadn't complained. Doing her share, and stoically pushing herself on to the limits of her endurance, Chelka had never asked to be treated any differently than other members of the pack.

The country between Meh'gach and the Shaden Falls Portage was rough, composed mostly of thorny thickets and rock-strewn rolling hills, crisscrossed by deep, eroded ravines where the land rose in elevation towards the falls. Recent floods had wiped out the trail in places, which had meant more delays as they retraced their steps and sought out alternative routes around the obstacles.

They had traveled fast, with long hours at a steady trot, little rest, and less food. Twice they had also been unexpectedly attacked by packs of hungry predators, and had to fight their way clear before being encircled and devoured.

Chelka was certainly finding out what it was like to be a Warlinga hunter. She was fitter than he expected, and yet between her, the old man, and the weather, they'd hadn't made as good time as he'd hoped. The first Sorin storm of the season overtook them before they'd reached Ticca. Seeing the front coming, and knowing they wouldn't reach Ticca in time, they veered off the main trail and headed for the abandoned keep of Ha'limra. With the storm nipping at their heels, the pack just made it to Ha'limra before it hit.

Barricading themselves in a large inner room, the Warlinga settled down to wait out the blow. When the weather cleared, they would have to try once more to make it to Ticca, because they didn't have enough food with them to last through the Sorin season at this abandoned keep.

SITTING MOROSELY BY a tiny fire, Aju'an had been considering various possibilities when Overn approached him. The old Hunt Leader bowed, knelt in front of him, drew his long bone knife and held it out to him.

Chelka saw the gesture and knew what it meant. Shaking her head in disbelief, she quickly knelt by the old hunter. "No, uncle, please, you can make it."

He glanced at her fondly, and stroked her scaly cheek with a scarred hand. His calm resignation was an impenetrable wall of acceptance. "No, child, it is better this way."

"But I never meant—oh, Overn, please—" Her voice trailed off as she choked on a sob.

"I know that, My Dear, so please don't blame yourself. I knew the risks much better than you, when I agreed to come with you. I wanted you to have what you always dreamed about, even if it meant I wouldn't reach Ticca myself."

He smiled and traced a clawed finger across her jaw line. "And I was glad to have the chance to come, believe me. For what better death could an old hunter like me wish for than to die on the hunt? And with my gift, I will be serving my kinfolk, now, won't I? Dear Child, you gave me what I thought would never come again, and for that I am truly grateful to you."

He chuckled and, turning back to Aju'an once again, he added, "And I haven't done too badly keeping up with you young bloods, now, have I?"

"No, honored kinsman, you have not," Aju'an agreed.

Overn smiled with satisfaction and proffered the knife once more. "If the weather breaks in time, the pack will need all its strength to make it to Ticca before the next storm hits. I could never make such a run, but I offer the gift of myself, so that my kin will be strong enough to finish the journey in time."

Glancing at the hunting pack that had gathered solemnly around them, Overn said, "Feast well, my kinsmen, and, if it pleases you, carry my bones in remembrance of me. Rest and eat well of me, then make a run for Ticca—that is what I advise."

Aju'an took the knife with a hand that trembled. "It will be as you wish, Honored Elder, and we will wear your bones on our death strands with pride, always." There was a murmur of agreement from the pack.

Aju'an did what was necessary.

THE STORM RAGED FOR three days, while the hunting pack rested and waited. Finally, the weather cleared. Judging that it was now or never, the pack began their final run for Ticca that morning.

The day had started out fine, the orange sun burning off the russet clouds, but in the early afternoon, the wind picked up, and dark clouds massed once more on the northern horizon. Could they make it in time? He didn't want to think about it. *Just run,* he told himself. *Just focus on putting one foot in front of the other, and don't worry about anything else. Not far now—can smell the lake—keep running.*

Rounding a bend in the trail, he skidded to a halt, mouthing a curse. The angry wind-whipped waters of Lake Ticca stretched out before him. He could make out the dark silhouette of its island fortress; it was a tantalizing promise of sanctuary. Unfortunately, just ahead the causeway was already awash, as waves driven by the coming storm smashed against its raised stone pilings.

To the north, the sky was a livid bruise, alive with swirling patterns of unnatural color as jagged streaks of heat lightning tore through the menacing clouds of dust and poisonous debris. He shivered as a stray gust of wind hit him full in the face. Gods, they were so close! But dared they risk the half-submerged walkway out to the island now?

Did they have a choice? Whoever controlled the keep, even be they outlaws or the Hated Umwira, they would have to seek shelter there, or die out here in the storm.

Taking out a coil of rope from his pack, he tied a loop around his waist, then handed the loose end to the man beside him, motioning for the others to follow his example. Aju'an glanced at his sister one last time. She was, at the moment, being tied securely between Mar and another sturdy kinsman.

Chelka raised her head crest in encouragement. She was frightened, he could tell—by the Great Hunt Leader, he was afraid himself, but he could also see in her eyes that she was telling him not to worry about her. She would make it, if any of them did. Turning away, he stared out across the lake once more; his eyes blurred with unshed tears. By the Gods, he loved her.

BOOM, BOOM, BOOM! IN the large stone room that was their makeshift HQ, Hunt Leader, Tizu, Nathan, and Second Hunter Fadir broke off their conversation and listened. The Speir'dina and Warlinga studying at the long worktable or huddled over a bone game in the corner froze.

"What, by all the Gods, is that sound?" Nathan grumbled as he picked up the map he'd dropped on the floor.

Fadir's head crest flattened in dismay. When they could hear him over the echoes, he said, "That's the sound of the alarm drum. We have visitors, Hunt Leader."

"Shit! Who?" Tizu said. "But how? The storm season has already started. I didn't think anybody but the Umwira would be out in weather like this. And, I doubt if they'd be dropping by for tea, now, would they?"

Missing the sarcasm in his commander's remark, Fadir said. "That is true, it would not be the Hated Enemy. But the Sorins, aren't bad yet; if someone was traveling, perhaps they found shelter in a cave, or at Ha'limra, then decided to make a run for Ticca when the weather abated. It has happened before, which is the reason for having the alarm."

"Mm." Getting to his feet, Tizu motioned for the off-duty warriors lounging around HQ to follow him out into the hall. "OK, Fadir, lead the way. I guess we had better see who it is," he grumbled, as the sound came again. Fadir saluted, and lead the way to the tunnel that came out by a small emergency side gate.

When they reached the entrance, Tizu waved his men to a halt. Turning to his Second he said quietly, "All right, Fadir, the Speir'dina will keep out of this for now. It's going to be up to you and your kin to welcome our 'guests.' And, we don't want them to get suspicious, right?" he eyed his scaly troop with a hard stare. "So stay alert—no mistakes, got that?" The Warlinga gave him toothy smiles and touched the bone knives at their waists.

Tizu grunted and said to Fadir, "Take the visitors to that cleansing room you told me about and keep them there till I have a chance to see what the Kashallan or the Khutani want us to do with them."

When the human Hunt Leader and his men were out of sight, Fadir opened the slit in the door and peered out into the gloom. "Who is there?" he shouted over the rising wind.

"Aju'an Meh'gach," a voice cried. "Now open this door, damn you, or have the blood of your kinsmen on your hands, and our ghosts to haunt your sleep!"

Fadir stepped back and motioned for two of his cousins to unbar the heavy door. Before the door was opened fully, the waiting hunting pack burst through, a blast of electrically-charged wind and lake water roaring in along with them.

When the door was wrestled closed behind them, Fadir stepped forward, motioning a Warlinga with a torch to precede him. In the torch's flickering light, he surveyed their *visitors*. What a bedraggled bunch. Drenched and exhausted, they didn't look like they were capable of putting up much of a fight, if it came down to that. And until they had given their fealty, he would prefer to keep it that way.

When they had finished untying the ropes that bound them together and caught their breaths, a young man who was obviously their leader stepped forward and bowed. "I am Aju'an Meh'gach. A runner from this keep reached Meh'gach only a few days ago. As my father's representative, I have come in response to your Ima Matri's request for assistance."

And what a big help you would be in your present state, if we truly did *need you*, Fadir thought. Keeping his face expressionless and his head crest in a neutral position, he bowed in return. "I am Second Hunter Fadir. I have been instructed by my Hunt Leader to see to your needs. My Ima will be informed of your arrival. When you have washed off the corruption from your journey and rested, I am sure she will wish to see you."

Head crest in an assertive posture Aju'an faced the Second Hunter boldly and said, "You don't seem overjoyed to see us, Second Hunter. I think I should meet with Ima Ngeal as soon as possible. I would like to assure myself that the Ima and her people are well before I rest."

He noticed Fadir's twitching tail tip, and smiled. "Ah and what has happened to your strange pilgrims? Did you drive them off successfully, or were they harmless after all?"

Startled, Fadir wound his tail around his waist and bowed to hide his annoyance. The man was sharp, he'd give him that, though foolhardy and brash. He would not be easily deceived. Fadir decided he would have to tread carefully here, or risk arousing his suspicions even more.

"All in the keep are well, but your presence was unexpected, San Aju'an," Fadir said. "When no one came before the first storm hit, we had no way of knowing what had happened to our runner—we didn't think anyone would be answering our call so late in the season."

Fadir hesitated, then asked, "What did Temull tell you?"

Aju'an blinked. "Nothing. I didn't even know the runner's name. He was attacked and killed by a pack of vistri outside our gate. My men drove off the beasts, but not before the man had been slain.

"Judging that the news he carried must be urgent, I had our household priest open and read the message to me. There wasn't time to send it on to my father at Riath, so acting on his behalf I came as quickly as I could to your aid. When can I see Ima Ngeal?"

Most interesting, Fadir thought. *You have come here on your own; not at the High Council's, or even your noble father's, bidding.* Out loud, he said, "Soon, San Aju'an. I am sorry to hear of my kinsman's death. Temull was a good man, but I am also glad to know that he reached help before his passing."

"We brought back some of his bones for his kinsmen's death strands." Aju'an handed Fadir a pouch. "But to return to my original question—when can I see Ima Ngeal?"

Fadir sighed. "I am not deliberately trying to be evasive, San Aju'an, but it is not my place to make appointments for the Ima. It will be up to the Ima, or my Hunt Leader, to speak to you further. Now, if you and your men will come with me, I will show you where you may bathe, and I will have food and drink brought to you, if that meets with your approval." Then, without waiting for a response, Fadir started back down the tunnel.

Aju'an gritted his teeth, and quickened his pace to catch up with the other man. Grimly, he motioned for his pack to follow. He obviously wasn't going to get much more out of the man at the moment, so they might as well get cleaned up. Had he gotten his sister and his kinsmen into worse trouble by coming on to Ticca than if they had stayed at Ha'limra?

Fadir's attitude was scrupulously polite but strained, he could tell that. Looking around at the faces of the other Warlinga who accompanied them, he could detect nothing amiss, yet still his instincts warned him that things were not as they appeared.

Fadir, like every Warlinga would have known how dangerous it was to be caught outside at a time like this. And yet, It had taken them a long time to respond to the drum's summons. There were also too many armed warriors here to greet them, and they looked ready for a fight. Why? Who had they really been expecting—or were afraid might come, in answer to Ima Ngeal's letter? Had this keep been overrun by outlaws, or Umwira? Surely not—he hoped.

Just inside the main keep, Fadir paused outside a large room, and motioned for them to enter. "This is our cleansing chamber," he announced. "There is a conduit from an underground stream, so you can draw water to wash. I will come for you, San Aju'an, when my superiors are ready to see you."

Aju'an bowed and started forward, then froze as a shadowy figure stepped out of the doorway in front of them. Instinctively he took up a defensive posture in front of his sister. Behind him, he heard Chelka gasp, but paid her little attention, his eyes focused on the possible threat ahead in the gloom.

A moment more, and the shadow resolved itself into the figure of a large Warlinga, who stepped forward into the torchlight and bowed. Aju'an glanced at their "guide," who seemed almost as disconcerted as himself. But why?

Then, as the man rose from his bow, Aju'an caught a glimpse of the sigil on his face, and ice-water ran down his spine. Oh, Great Hunt Leader, a Wa'chassey'ul at Ticca!

Tail curling and uncurling in his agitation, Fadir stepped in front of Aju'an and addressed the big Warlinga. "Greetings, Cadrach. Is your Mistress within?"

"No, Cousin. But I have been sent by my Mistress to give her regards to San Aju'an and his sister Sa Chelka," he announced. Then, before anyone could stop him, Cadrach took Chelka's hand and looked into her eyes. "My Mistress bids you welcome, and asks that you attend her at some later time," Cadrach intoned in a hollow, expressionless voice.

Chelka stared in wide-eyed confusion at the strange mark on the man's face. Both Ticca's defender's and Aju'an's pack froze, eyes riveted on the pair. Finally she took a deep breath and said, "Y-yes, thank you—tell her I will be happy to visit her later." Then, pulling her hand out of the Wa'chassey'ul's grasp, she stepped behind her brother.

Aju'an glared angrily at Fadir, but the man seemed as dumbfounded as he was by the Wa'chassey'ul's invitation. In fact, perhaps more so, for it would seem that their host hadn't even noticed that there was a woman among them. Aju'an's mouth twitched in grim amusement, delighted that at least something had cracked the man's facade of controlled politeness.

Forgetting about Cadrach for the moment, Fadir stared at the vision before him. By all the Gods, she was beautiful, and so courageous, coming with a hunting pack on such a daring journey. She was just like a picture out of one of the old legends, standing there in her warrior woman's apron, spear in hand—right in front of him—her warm red eyes gazing at him boldly. She was so—beautiful!

Behind him, his cousin Byan cleared his throat, and poked him surreptitiously with the end of his tail. Startled, Fadir jerked, then, composing himself once more, he bowed to her. "Sa Chelka, forgive me. The Wa'chassey'ul has shamed me. I should have seen—I should have offered you welcome as well—please forgive me. Shall I have a separate room prepared, and send for a novice from the keep to attend you?" He broke off, head crest flattening in embarrassment.

Aju'an laughed, enjoying the man's discomfort. Then, suddenly feeling very protective towards Chelka, he decided he didn't want her to be separated from them. "That won't be necessary, Second Hunter, my sister chose to invite herself along on this journey. I agreed to bring her only if she came as one of my hunting pack. You need not trouble yourself—she will remain with us."

Chapter Fifteen

Nathan stopped by the edge of the kashallan pool, held up his lantern, and studied his sleeping friend. Dunnagh-Tani lay on his back, in the warm liquid, his red hair cloaking his bare shoulders like a ruddy shawl. His head lay on a headrest built into the pool's rim. He looked so peaceful lying there, until you noticed the angry, half-healed wound in his abdomen. Nathan's heart gave a lurch. Gods, he hated to see him looking like that, so weak and vulnerable—Gods, how it hurt.

Feeling anxious, he peered out into the mists that clung to the water's surface, wondering where the Maker was. He could hear the young playing somewhere out in the gloom, and saw a few smaller adults lounging in the shallows near the Kashallan, but there was no sign of the massive body of the Maker.

He'd been sent down here to ask for instructions, but after what happened the last time he'd faced Dievris, he dreaded another encounter—especially before he had a chance to talk to Dunnagh-Tani. And yet, Nathan hated to disturb him when he looked so in need of rest.

When the Khutani had pronounced the bondmates out of danger, a still-enraged Maker Dievris had demanded the presence of the keep's commanders for an accounting. That had been an experience that none of them were anxious to repeat. To go into the pool that time had been one of the most frightening experiences of his life.

And yet it had never entered his mind to refuse; he had known that the Maker could *force* him to come, if it chose, and be doubly enraged to have to have done so. Though Tizu and Fadir hadn't talked much about it afterwards, he guessed their experience with the Maker had been equally terrifying.

In the end, Dievris had grudgingly conceded that the attack hadn't been due to anyone's carelessness—and that was a relief. Probably the only thing that saved either Tizu or himself from being chewed apart was the fact that they acted so quickly in dispatching Tomina, and in getting the Kashallan down to the pools in time to be healed.

Nathan sighed, stripped off his clothing, and waded slowly into the pool. There was no help for it; he would have to wake him. When he sat down beside his friend, the nearby Khutani raised their heads, hissed a warning at him, and swam nearer. "Uh, Dunnagh-Tani?"

Dunnagh turned his head and opened one blue eye, trying to focus on his face.

"If you're feeling up to a visit, I need to talk to you, so would you mind telling your cousins that it's OK for me to be here?" Nathan said, eyeing the swarming Khutani uneasily. "They look like they might want to chew my ass off—literally—for disturbing you."

He grunted and extended a tentacled hand. Catching hold of one of the sinewy bodies, he made the link. When he released the Khutani, he yawned and slowly turned on his side to face his friend. "I'm getting hungry, so it would have been time for someone to wake me for a feeding soon, anyway. So what's the problem? I take it this isn't a social call."

Nathan grimaced. "No, it isn't, I'm afraid. We have company upstairs."

The Kashallan blinked. "Company? What are you talking about? The Sorins have begun—who?"

"Yeah, yeah, I know we thought we wouldn't be bothered till after the blue snows came and went, several months from now. But that isn't the case. A hunting pack from Meh'gach keep has arrived. Aju'an Meh'gach headed up the pack. His father is K'San Yargal, Fadir says, who just happens to be a member of the High Council. Apparently the family favors the Dingay cause as well."

The Kashallan's face darkened with anger at the mention of that hated name. Then taking a couple of deep breaths to calm himself, he nodded for Nathan to continue.

Nathan shrugged. "There isn't much more. His father hadn't returned from Riath, when Ima Ngeal's runner showed up dead at their gate. Aju'an, however, being a bright young lad, had the household priest read Ngeal's message and decided he'd take a stroll over our way, and come see what the Ima wanted."

Nathan grinned. "So, to make a long story short, Aju'an and his twin sister, who Fadir thinks is beautiful, by the way, and who apparently is a warrior herself, arrived with a well-equipped hunting pack about an hour ago, right along with the next storm. We didn't figure you wanted us to kill them outright, so Fadir has put them in what he calls the 'cleansing room,' awaiting further orders."

The Kashallan grimaced. "I'm not sure that my Elders would have agreed with you about not killing them outright, and especially if that family has anything to do with the Dingay cause. With the mood the Council has been in since I told them my suspicions about Tomina being a changeling—well, if you had asked, they would probably have told you to leave them to the tender mercies of the storms. But I'm glad you didn't kill them—we need more information about what has been going on in the Yeyen Banai Valley, and if this young Warlinga and his sister can be persuaded to join us—

"But in any case, if they are to remain alive, they will have to come down here and be tasted by Dievris and, if the Maker agrees, take the oath. I know that without even consulting the Elders—that will be a given."

"Mm, I figured that. Ima Ngeal is inviting San Aju'an and his sister to her apartment for refreshments. They should be there by now, in fact. She hopes to convince them to see the truth about who the Dingay really are, in hopes that they will join us voluntarily, once they hear our story."

He gave the Kashallan a sly grin. "But she also suggests that while Aju'an is absent, his men be served some drugged beer—compliments of the house, of course—to help them rest. Then, if Aju'an and his sister prove *difficult*, they can all be disposed of without too much trouble."

Dunnagh-Tani made a sour face, then relented. "Mm. I don't particularly like that kind of deception, but I see her point, so tell them to go ahead with it. It's probably for the best to keep the pack drugged till we decide what to do with them. After out-racing the storm to get here, they must need a good rest, anyway."

"Right, so—uh—when do you want me to bring them?"

The Kashallan sighed. He rubbed his face, his expression suddenly mirroring his weariness. "Give me time to eat, and to send someone to find Maker Dievris—then bring them."

Nathan touched Dunnagh's arm, a worried look in his eye. "Are you OK? Will this be too much of a strain on you? We could just keep them drugged for a while—or just kill them."

The Kashallan picked up his hand and kissed it tenderly, then released it. "I'll be all right. Bring them down in a while."

Nathan started to get up, then hesitated, a troubled expression crossing his face once more. Dunnagh saw it and asked, "There's something else, isn't there? Come on, out with it."

Nathan grimaced then sighed. "Well, I suppose I'd better tell you before somebody else does, since I guess, in a way, it's partly my fault." The Kashallan gave him a puzzled look.

Nathan sighed, and then went on. "After all the confusion was over down here, one of the priests found Conal's clothing stashed somewhere among the rocks over there." He motioned with his chin to the looming rock-face behind him.

"Come to find out that nobody's seen him in a long time, but with everything else going on, nobody exactly noticed he was missing until his clothes were found. Bennett thinks he must have committed suicide by drowning himself in the acid of the waste pit."

Nathan shivered at the thought. "I'm sorry, Dunnagh. We had our differences, but I wouldn't have wished him to end it like that. I wish I, or somebody, had noticed that he was getting that depressed."

The Kashallan nodded and patted his shoulder. "I know, Nathan, and he'll appreciate your concern when I tell him. He feels pretty bad about the fight, too."

"What?" Nathan blinked, his mouth dropping open in surprise. "Wait a minute—you mean to say he's not dead?"

"That's right."

"But where is he?" Dunnagh jerked his head towards the shadowed waters farther out into the pool. "Out there? But why—" Then suddenly his eyes went wide. "You mean he made a kashallan bond?"

Dunnagh-Tani nodded and smiled.

Nathan stared out into the blackness. "Damn. I would never have guessed—but why?"

"Evidently Tess-weh told him that if he wanted another hand, he would have to agree to a bonding. He finally worked up the courage to approach Dievris on his own to ask for one."

"Damn. How's he doing?"

"He's still pretty weak. His bondmate Tiel is having to do the reconstruction of his hand along with the other adaptations, but he's all right. Keep that bit of information to yourself, for the moment, though. Apparently the Khutani want to keep the fact that another kashallan bond has been formed a secret.

"They aren't saying very much about why, but they are still worried that the keep isn't safe, and both of us are still very vulnerable, should an enemy try again. They believe Tomina may have had an accomplice. Though personally, I can't see how."

Nathan continued to stare out into the gloom. "Yeah, sure," he said slowly. Then, remembering his mission, he jerked his head around and stood. "I'd better go. Have your meal and rest—I'll bring our guests down in a while." Still shaking his head about Conal, he left.

Chapter Sixteen

Chelka sat glumly, watching her brother pace. He was in one of his difficult moods again. She could tell he was worried, but he was being very vague about what was troubling him—and that made her furious. Instead of seeing her as an ally, he was treating her like a child who needed his protection, rather than a companion who could counsel with him. If they had been alone—she would have liked to—oh, he was so infuriating!

Glancing at Mar, Chelka noticed that he was watching her, his body language declaring his concern. When he saw her regard, he dipped his head crest and gave her an encouraging little grin. Comforted, she grinned back, then turned towards the door as a noise caught her attention.

She stood, along with the rest of the pack, as Second Hunter Fadir, a few of his men, and several Begta slaves carrying jars of beer and trays of food entered.

Approaching Aju'an and Chelka, Fadir bowed respectfully. "My Ima sends her regards, San Aju'an. If it would please you, she would like to offer you and Sa Chelka refreshments in her suite, so that she may speak with you personally."

Aju'an bowed. He glanced nervously around at his listening kinsmen. Catching Mar's eye, he said, "I want to talk to Ima Ngeal very much, but I think my sister should stay here with the rest of the pack for the moment."

Chelka's head crest flattened and she gave her brother a dagger's look. Then ignoring him she bowed to the Second Hunter and gave him a winning smile. "Thank you, Second Hunter Fadir, I would also be delighted to join the Ima for refreshments."

Aju'an gave her a murderous look, then reluctantly motioned for Mar to join them.

As they left the cleansing room, Chelka noticed that the Wa'chassey'ul fell into step behind Aju'an. Inwardly she shivered; still not sure what it was about the strange Warlinga that set her teeth on edge.

Aju'an and the others knew something about the man, and the sigil on his face, that she didn't. They were anxious—maybe even afraid, but when she tried to ask him, Aju'an refused to speak about it. And with the man still in the room watching them, she could hardly make a fuss about it. Later, however, she resolved to make him tell her everything he knew.

At Ngeal's suite, they were admitted promptly and seated on comfortable stools at a large table across from Ngeal and another Ima, whom Ngeal didn't introduce for the moment. They were expected, for spiced tea and food had already been set out on a side table, awaiting their coming.

Chelka noticed that Ngeal herself seemed nonplused by the appearance of the Wa'chassey'ul. But she recovered quickly, and made no objection to his following her guests into the suite and positioning himself discreetly by the wall behind them.

When her maid had served the food and poured the tea, Ngeal nodded to her visitors and said graciously, "San Aju'an, Sa Chelka, I haven't seen either of you since you were quite small, so I'm not sure if you remember me. It is a pleasure to see you now, though I wish our meeting could have taken place under better circumstances. It distresses me deeply that you risked your lives in this way to come to us."

"Though I was quite young, as you say, Ima, I do remember you," Aju'an said. "And—as my father's representative—if Ticca was in danger, it was my duty to answer your summons."

"Yes, well," Ngeal seemed a little flustered. "I am delighted that the Meh'gach line has remained so true to its breeding."

AS THE CONVERSATION dragged on in the same vein while they ate, Aju'an inwardly writhed in frustration. This polite banter was getting them nowhere. Ngeal glanced from time to time at the unknown Ima beside her, but still hadn't introduced her. The woman was being as evasive in person as she had been in her message. He decided that he would have to take the offensive, or be here for hours drinking tea and getting nowhere.

Laying his eating sticks across his empty plate, Aju'an said, "Ima Ngeal, I am not very good at polite conversation, I will be the first one to admit. I much prefer plain speaking to dancing around an issue. In your message, you said that there were strange travelers at your gate. They came from the Swamp, and you hinted that they might be the outlawed priestess and her alleged Umwira followers.

"I'm not inclined to believe without proof the ravings of that idiot Combaron, but your evasions aren't making me feel any easier in my mind. I came to offer you my support and that of my hunting pack, if it is needed. Why did you send that message? What has happened here?"

The two Imas exchanged worried glances, than the other one, to whom he hadn't been introduced, faced him squarely. "You are right, San Aju'an. I too prefer plain speech to circling around a topic. I haven't met you or your sister before; my name is Sagas Caltia."

Suddenly there was a knock on the outer door, but, before Ngeal could make a reply, the door was flung open and a strange creature dressed all in black stepped into the room.

Aju'an took one look at the man's long, brown mane, eerie gray eyes and flattened, ugly face, and knew with a sinking heart that the Dingay claims were true. Not only was Sagas Caltia here, but her band of demon Umwira were as well. They had taken over Ticca, and like a cocky fool he had blundered right into their midst.

With a snarl of rage, he leapt to his feet, Mar following his lead. Before he could do any harm, he was forced painfully back onto his stool, as Cadrach's muscular grip came down upon his shoulders like a stone wall. Enraged, Aju'an fought desperately to free himself, but the Wa'chassey'ul who held him was impossible to resist.

Beside him, his cousin was also being encouraged to take his seat, in his case by the Second Hunter. Chelka's astonished glance flicked from her brother to the ugly mutant still standing by the door. She shuddered, then mastering her surprise she started to draw her knife.

A menacing growl from the Wa'chassey'ul changed her mind about doing anything rash. Placing her hands on the table, she stared wide-eyed around the room.

"I don't know much about these things, but it's my understanding that the power of the Wa'chassey'ul is more than mortal. You'll save yourself a lot of grief, San Aju'an, if you settle down and relax," a cool voice from the bedroom doorway said.

Suddenly realizing that he was getting nowhere, and probably making a fool of himself in the process, Aju'an slumped back onto his stool and snarled at Mar to do the same. Instantly Cadrach released him, but remained close by his side.

Aju'an swiveled around so he could see the owner of the voice that spoke to him. He was a small male about the size of an Avairei, but more muscular of body than men of that race. Dressed in some kind of black clothing that covered almost all of his body, he had the same naked, flattened facial features as the larger male standing bemused by the outer door. The smaller man was watching the Warlinga with hard, obsidian eyes that missed nothing.

"That's better," he said and stepped fully into the room and crossed to the table. "I'm sure Cadrach here can handle you if you won't behave, but if you push me too far, I will kill you and be done with it." He touched the side arm at his hip.

Aju'an glared, but the little man ignored him for the moment, focusing his hard, angry eyes on the man by the door. "As usual, Nathan, your timing is impeccably bad," he growled in disgust. "Next time knock, then wait to be invited in."

"Yes, Sir," Nathan mumbled. Then turning to Ngeal he added, "Sorry."

Ngeal sighed then cleared her throat. Raising her voice, she called, "You might as well come join us, Clan Elders." Then, addressing Nathan directly, she said, "San Nathan, come sit down. I gather you've been to the pools, so I'm sure you have something to report, which we can get to in a moment."

Pushing himself off the wall, Nathan walked over and pulled up a stool, eyeing Aju'an and Mar warily. "I do, but it'll keep for a while."

After introducing the Warlinga to the Speir'dina elders and Ticca's hunt leaders, Ngeal said, "San Aju'an, Sa Chelka, as you said earlier, plain speaking is probably the best way to tell you what has happened here."

Aju'an snorted. "What is there to say, Ima? It is obvious. You are all traitors, and though I hate to admit it," he glanced contemptuously around at the Speir'dina, "it would seem that Combaron's claims are true."

Unable to control herself, Sagas uttered a vile barracks oath, which made Aju'an's head crest rise in surprise. "Damn the sniveling little pus-boil, I wish I had killed him when I had the chance. His lies—"

"Settle down, Sagas," Tizu soothed, taking a seat beside her. "You had other things to worry about at the time, so stop blaming yourself." Then, fixing his cold, gaze on Aju'an, he warned, "That name won't win you any friends in this keep. In fact, that kind of talk will get you killed faster than anything.

"The Dingay, and anyone championing their cause, is not very popular around here at the moment. So I suggest you mind your tongue, or your sister and your men may also suffer for your brash words."

"Why should I?" Aju'an shot back. "We're as good as dead anyway, so why shouldn't I speak the truth?"

"Because you don't know the truth, you insolent young fool," Sagas snapped.

Red eyes pleading, Chelka laid a hand on her brother's arm, digging in her claws to get his attention. "Aju'an, please. You said back at home that you would welcome the opportunity to hear the Ima Sagas's side of the story, and now's your chance.

"If these people wanted to kill us, they could have just left us to the storm, or murdered us long before now—please, brother, don't let your quick temper make more trouble for us."

Arishim smiled and nodded her approval. "That is very sensible advice, My Dear. And may I add that it is a pleasure to meet you. We haven't encountered any of the women of your species since coming to Timorna, and you are a most delightful surprise."

Glancing at Aju'an and Mar, she confided, "Our contacts with your men haven't always been very pleasant. It is reassuring to know that Warlinga women are so sensible. I will look forward to talking with you again later, I think."

Chelka murmured an embarrassed reply, then glanced sidewise at her brother. Aju'an sat rigid, head crest held belligerently high, arms folded on the table in front of him. She sighed.

Aju'an hated to admit it, but Chelka was probably right—he was being a fool. These demons, or whatever they were, could have killed them before now, if they'd wanted to. And if he didn't watch his tongue, he could still get them all killed.

Perhaps the wisest course would be to go along with whatever these traitors wanted, until they could make their escape after the storms were over. Turning to the outlawed priestess, he grumbled, "Very well, you said I don't know the truth—and my sister is right, I did say I wanted to hear your side of Combaron's wild claims—so I'm listening. Tell me."

Sagas nodded, her eyes meeting his boldly, without hesitation. "You called us traitors. I assume by that you mean that myself and everyone else in this keep have forsaken our allegiance and our duty to the Holy Ones in the pools?"

At Aju'an's curt nod, she leaned forward, her eyes fierce. "I am no traitor, Aju'an Meh'gach. My duty to the Khutani is the most important thing in my life. It always has been, and it always will be. I did not destroy Sulas, as Combaron claims. The Khutani themselves fouled and abandoned it, because of what Combaron *himself* tried to do to one of their sacred children."

Aju'an snorted, giving her a disgusted look. "I would agree with you that Combaron is a liar and a pervert, but I find it hard to believe that even that degenerate would go so far as to try and kill a Khutani. Did you really expect me to believe that? Your accusations are as wild as the Dingay's. By the Gods, maybe you're both crazy."

Sagas regarded the young man with jaw tight. "He did try, and if I hadn't gotten there in time, he would have succeeded." She waved her hand, drawing his attention to the Speir'dina seated around the table. "He tried because of the Speir'dina."

At their blank stare, Sagas sighed and asked, "Do either of you young people know what a kashallan bond is?"

Aju'an looked blank, but Chelka, who had always paid more attention than her brother to the old stories, said, "I think it has something to do with the Khutani and the old bonding they had with the Bebech, doesn't it?"

Sagas nodded. "You are as learned as you are sensible, it seems, daughter. These people you see here aren't mutant Umwira, as the Dingay claim—they are the new host species that the Khutani, with their magic, have brought to Timorna to host their symbiont children.

"Combaron tried to kill the first kashallan pair. That was why we fled Sulas, and why the Khutani deserted it. The Holy Ones have sworn to abandon all of us if we don't accept these new kashallans. And the accursed Dingay, who are not even Avairei, but Umwira changelings put among us by the hated enemy, are trying to destroy us."

Aju'an sat stunned. He glanced at his equally surprised kindred. Could this woman's wild ravings possibly be true?

"I know, young Warlinga, that it's a lot to take in at one bite," Bennett said, "but it is the truth. We can, indeed, host the Khutani, though not without great personal sacrifice for those of my people who have chosen to do so. The kashallan bond has been re-formed after many centuries. The Ima does, indeed, speak the truth."

Choosing his words carefully, Mar said, "This is all very hard to believe, Ima, clan elder—it goes against everything we have ever been taught."

"Yes, Warlinga," Sagas hissed, "and are you and your people happy with that state of affairs, hmm? Have the Avairei always dealt with you fairly, or is there an unspoken threat behind their gifts and their soft words? 'Do as I want or your house will suffer from an unknown plague, that, alas, is *incurable.*' Or more commonly, 'Do as I say, Warlinga keep, and Loti village, or there will be no red kavay available for your marriages."

Thinking of his own unconsummated marriage, that last struck too close to home. Aju'an slumped, hurt and bewildered, head crest flattened in despair.

"The Khutani are not happy about this," Sagas continued, "and that is why the Speir'dina have been brought among us to host their children, so they can see for themselves what has been happening in the world outside the pools. Now they will have a chance to restore the balance that has been lost since the death of the Bebech, but only if the Dingay and their Umwira masters can be stopped."

Aju'an didn't know what to believe, and said so, in a brittle voice that he couldn't keep steady as he spoke.

Nathan stood up and stretched. "Well, it doesn't really matter if you believe us or not, because we aren't the ones who will decide whether you live or die. Who you have to worry about is the Maker Dievris, and the Khutani Council of Elders. They make the decisions around here, and everyone in this keep has sworn to do their will. When you go to them, they will decide, and we'll do whatever they tell us to do with you.

"For you and your men to survive, Aju'an, you're going to have to convince the Khutani that you can be trusted. And the mood they're in at the moment, after Tomina Dingay nearly killed the Kashallan the other day—" He smirked. "Your taste had better be pretty sweet when you get into that pool."

He glanced at Ngeal and Tizu. "That's what I came up here to report, and it's later than I said I would be bringing them down, so maybe we should let the Kashallan and the Khutani take it from here. It won't improve Dievris's mood any if it has to wait for us. We should go."

At the door Aju'an paused. "What about the rest of my pack?"

"For the moment, they're well enough," Nathan said. "If they've finished off the drugged beer that the Ima so generously sent them, they're having a badly-needed rest. Whether they wake up again depends on you, and on what the Khutani decide."

"I see," he said, then followed his sister out into the hall.

AJU'AN, LIKE MOST WARLINGA, had never been permitted to go down into the great caverns that held the Khutani pools of an ancient keep like Ticca. He wished he wasn't so scared, for he had the vague impression that they were beautiful, and he would have liked to have had time and the peace of mind to enjoy them.

But as it was, he barely noticed his surroundings, as the big Speir'dina male and their Warlinga guards ushered them along the main walkway towards a secluded pool.

At its edge, they halted. Aju'an stared anxiously out into the clouds of mist that rose from the pool's surface. He shivered, in spite of the warmth of the air around him. Lowering his eyes to the faintly glowing liquid of the pool itself, he could see the sacred Khutani swimming, their phosphorescent wakes crisscrossing the pool's surface.

A short distance from the pool's rim, a Speir'dina male with a long red mane and eyes as blue as the kavay seemed to half stand, half recline within the massive coils of one of the Ancient Ones. Aju'an could see pink tentacles extending from the man's two middle fingers, where his hand rested lightly upon the Maker's sleek, gray neck.

Under a strange compulsion, Aju'an removed his belt and cloak and stepped hesitantly into the pool, trying to control his fear. Hard blue eyes studied him coldly. Then the hollow, otherworldly voice of the Maker spoke to him through the mouth of the man it held.

"Come to me, Aju'an Meh'gach. We have been informed that your house has in recent years favored the Dingay cause. I will taste you and know if the taint of their Umwira filth is upon you. I would learn if your breeding is true, or false. If you are worthy of my leniency, you may give us your oath of fealty. If not... Come!"

Trembling violently, Aju'an took one last look at his sister, bowed his head to the Maker and waded out into the pool.

Part Three: Uncertain Refuge

Chapter One

Dressed in some of their best clothing and finest ornamentation, Ticca's inhabitants filed into the large dining hall and took their places in the rows of benches that were lined up against the walls. Tonight was a special occasion, and an air of excitement filled the room.

This evening's entertainment was the culmination of much hard work by the Dymarian performers. To give the actors and dancers space to display their art, the room had been cleared of the long tables that usually crowded its interior.

When all were seated, Tomas Chambers, the director, walked to the center of the floor and announced the titles of the plays being enacted. The production would be presented in two parts. The first was the retelling of a very popular legend that the native Timornans knew immediately, and praised loudly when the performance was completed.

The second play, now being enacted, was a retelling of Dunnagh and his squad's capture by the Begta, their subsequent enslavement at Sulas, and the making of the first kashallan bond. The Kashallan sat with his wives and, watched the proceedings with a rapped attention. The cast were doing an amazing job, considering they had only makeshift stage props and costumes to work with.

Ah, but fine art was what the Dymarians were famous for, throughout the galaxy, after all. Dunnagh felt proud to number among his clansmen such talented folk, and, judging by the surreptitious glances he had been giving to the audience, the Timornans were both delighted and amazed by his people's craft.

The technology that they brought with them from the stars wouldn't last forever, the Speir'dina needed some way to support themselves and blend into the existing Timornan society. Offering entertainment to the rest of

Timorna's population during the confinement of the Sorin season might be a workable plan.

Such entertainment was a novel idea to the native Timornans. If their response to this performance was any indication, those of his people suited to such arts should have no trouble in the future finding patrons to support them.

Returning his attention to the drama being enacted, Dunnagh found it a bit disturbing to see himself being depicted upon the stage. As the first kashallan, it would be natural for him to become a figure of importance in his people's new history, but it still made him feel embarrassed and shy.

It was also disconcerting to see himself being portrayed by a woman. The actress was one of the tallest in the cast, which was probably why the director had chosen her for the role. With her long black hair and olive skin, she looked nothing like her redheaded, blue-eyed clan leader, and yet there was something about her performance that caught his attention and held it. She mimed his way of walking and his mannerisms accurately. It was obvious, that she had taken some care in her observations of him and had transformed them into a very moving performance.

The presentation had progressed now to the part of the story where the slave Dunnagh was being brought to the pools at Sulas Keep to make the bond. Dunnagh himself had suffered intensely during the process, and he tried not to think about The Transformation any more than was necessary.

But in some indefinable way, this actress had caught the essence of the ordeal, and was mirroring it back to him and the audience in a most unsettling way. He shifted uneasily on the bench, his concentration on the play interrupted by the painful memories invoked within him by the mime and dance she was using for this part of her performance.

<<Are you all right, Kasha?>> Tani asked. <<She is very good, but I can taste your distress. Do you want to go?>>

Dunnagh sighed. <<No, Shalla, I'll be all right. You're right; she is very good, and I wouldn't want to shame her by leaving. She would think I didn't like her performance, and that's not the problem.>>

<<Mm, well, you can close your eyes if you find it too distressing,>> Tani suggested. <<I am enjoying this, but I don't want you to be upset, either.>>

<<That's very thoughtful of you, Shalla, but I'll be fine. And I want to see this too.>>

Tani was silent for a long moment, then it said in a tiny mental voice, <<I'm sorry, Kasha, I'm sorry I hurt you like that when I was too young to know better—I wish it could have been done another way—I wish—>>

Dunnagh stroked his middle, his eyes still focused on the stage. <<Don't, Shalla, I've told you before, it's all right, I know you didn't mean to hurt me—it just happened. Don't think about it; it's over—and I love you.>>

<<I know, Kasha, and I love you too.>>

Dunnagh continued to watch, but slipped into a light trance to distance himself from his memories. At some point Sairsa sensed his pain, took his hand and squeezed. He turned to her and smiled, covering her hand with his own.

When the performance was over, the audience burst into applause and excited chatter. The Kashallan stood and stretched, glad it was over. He helped Sairsa to her feet beside him. She adjusted the sleeping baby into a more comfortable position in his sling. "Are you all right?"

"Mm hm." Sairsa gave him a searching look, which he ignored. This public place wasn't where he wanted to discuss his memories further. Diverting the conversation to a safer topic, he said, "The performance was excellent, though I couldn't help but wonder where the actors got some of the details for their portrayals."

She hesitated, then deciding to play along. "Oh, I wouldn't have any idea," she said, with a merry twinkle in her eye. "Maybe a little birdie told them."

"Mm—considering there are no birds on Timorna, My Sweet, I doubt it. No, I'd say it was some other kind of animal. Cute little bunnies' maybe, one with silky brown fur, and the other with pretty green eyes, gave away my secrets." He glanced at his Avairei wives, now also standing beside him, including them in his witticism.

Sairsa shook her head and laughed. "Couldn't be rabbits, there aren't any of those creatures on Timorna, either. Are there, Tani?"

"What is a bunny or a rabbit?" Tani asked.

Dunnagh laughed. "Oops, I forgot."

Pela and Amril, smiled, but he could see in their eyes that they hadn't understood the joke. Pela was near her birthing time, her sleek, rounded belly large with the Kashallan's other son.

"I think you are happy, husband," Pela said. "You must have liked the performance."

The Kashallan nodded, noting out of the corner of his eye, as he did so, that others around them seemed to be listening to his opinion. "I did, Sweet, very much, though it was a bit disconcerting to see myself portrayed on stage."

"You'd better get used to it, Love," Sairsa said. "This is only the first of many renditions of that historical event."

"I know, and it's going to take some getting used to."

To avoid further comment, Dunnagh turned towards the stage area where admirers were surrounding the performers. He watched for a moment, then asked, "Sairsa, who is the woman who—uh, played me?"

"Her name is Tasheyna Margannal."

The Kashallan nodded, looking thoughtful. He wanted to go over and join the admiring crowd and talk to some of the performers, and yet— His eyes slid over to his pregnant Avairei wife. She looked weary. "Pela, Sweet, are you getting tired?"

"A little," she admitted, "but if you wish us to stay—"

He considered, his eyes scammed the room, taking in the lingering clusters of chatting people. "I should probably stay for at least a little while, so that no one will think I am displeased with the show, but you should go back to our suite and rest." Right on cue, Tameh woke up and began to complain about the slow meal service. Dunnagh smiled at his son and winked at his other Avairei wife. "Amril, would you mind escorting your sister-wives back to our rooms and seeing to their comfort for me?"

Amril, too, had been watching Pela, a worried frown on his face. He bowed to the Kashallan. "Yes, husband, I will be happy to do that for you," he said, and dropped his eyes.

"Thank you." The Kashallan kissed the women, and watched as the young man, in his long woman's kilt ushered his sister-wives through the crowd and out into the hall. He sighed. He'd spent so much of his time convalescing in the pools, since he'd married the young man that they hadn't had time to become comfortable with each other.

Amril was still nervous around him, and that in turn made the Kashallan feel uncertain about his role as his husband. In spite of his assurances that he didn't want Amril for himself—and that he really did approve of Pela and him enjoying themselves together, Amril still seemed overwhelmed by the strangeness of their group marriage.

"Great play, eh?" a voice at his elbow asked. Turning, Dunnagh saw Nathan grinning at him; Aju'an standing uncertainly at the big man's side.

The Kashallan grinned, displaying his sharp, white triangular teeth. "A bit disturbing, actually. And how did *you* like seeing yourself out there?"

Nathan grimaced. "It was a bit—uh—embarrassing."

Inwardly Dunnagh sighed and turned to Aju'an. Here too was another who seemed nervous in his company. Giving the Warlinga an encouraging nod, the Kashallan asked, "What about you, San Aju'an? Did you enjoy my people's performance, and do you think, in the future, our players will be able to find willing patrons among the other Timornan clans?"

Aju'an bowed, tail twitching. "I enjoyed it very much, Holy One. I can't speak for the Avairei, of course, but the boredom of being confined to the keep while the poisonous storms rage outside our walls, is always difficult for the Warlinga. Such entertainments would be a welcome diversion for us, to be sure."

The Kashallan gave him a crooked grin. "I trust you haven't been too bored yet this season?"

Aju'an laughed nervously. "No, I have had no time to be bored, even without such excellent entertainment. Hunt Leader Tizu and San Nathan have seen to that, I can assure you."

Aju'an was referring to the literacy lessons and combat training that Ticca's new Hunt Leader, Tizu, had set up for Ticca's combined fighting force of Warlinga lizardmen and Lann Gheal armachda. As an outlawed keep, Ticca would need all its warriors trained and ready by the Renewal Season, in case other hunting packs from the capital were sent to attack them.

When Aju'an's attention was diverted by Tizu joining them, Nathan took his friend's arm and steered him out of earshot. "Timma has managed to—uh—find another bottle of that good brandy, like we drank on your wedding night. He just so happened to leave it lying around in my quarters yesterday. You want to come by and sample it with us?" He motioned with a jerk of his head to Aju'an and Tizu.

The Kashallan chuckled softly. "You had better speak to the lad about that kind of thing. If Ngeal finds out he's been rifling keep supplies—even for such a good cause—he might be in for a bad time of it. Although he has your and Tizu's patronage, he would be subject to her discipline for such a violation.

"She still isn't sure she likes the unconventional idea of Avairei doing anything but what they were bred by the Khutani to do. And our allowing him to receive warrior's training and become a medic hasn't endeared him to her, if you take my meaning."

"Yeah, I see what you mean. I'll speak to him." The big man sighed. "Well, I guess it's back to mushroom beer after this, so we better enjoy it while we can. You coming by? Aju'an's been telling us some things that I think you should hear, before you start making your plans for after the Sorins."

"What makes you so sure I'm going to do anything, hmm?"

Nathan snorted, and gave him a disgusted look. "Yeah, right. This is me you're talking to, remember? You're planning something, and you're not about to wait around for Enaju Dingay's Warlinga to box us in for a long siege here at Ticca. I figure we'll be gone soon after the blue snows melt."

"What about the Elders? They haven't let me get very far out of their sight so far," the Kashallan countered.

Nathan gave him a toothy smile. "You'll figure out some way to talk them round. The way I see it, we have to go, and the Khutani got Conal-Tiel to fuss over now, and maybe Philip is a kashallan too, somewhere out there in the Swamp. That makes two others so far that have made the bond. You're not the only kashallan any more—but you are the only one who knows what the Umwira taste like, so you'll have to go."

The Kashallan laughed. "You know me too well, Nathan, but you're right—I have to go to Riath, for all our sakes. It's one thing to breed herd-beasts and talk about plans to seek patronage for our actors and musicians among the other clans, but all that will mean nothing, if the Dingay and their Umwira masters destroy everything the Khutani have created. None of us can survive on this world, let alone have a future, until that threat to our way of life is ended."

"I know," Nathan said, "and that's why I'm coming with you, and also why I think you need to sit down with Aju'an and talk to him. Tizu has sort of put me in charge of training him and his men, so I've gotten to know him pretty good while you've been sick. He was in Riath when Combaron Dingay and the survivors from Sulas showed up at the capital. His sister Chelka also told me he got sent home in disgrace by his father for insulting Combaron, which gives him high marks in my book."

"Yes, and mine too."

Combaron had been another of the Dingay clan who had tried to kill him. The way the Kashallan saw it, Combaron was responsible for their status as hunted fugitives, and had a lot to answer for when next he and the Dingay priest met.

Glancing briefly at Aju'an, who was now talking to Tizu and Fadir, Nathan lowered his voice and continued, "Maker Dievris gave him a pretty rough time of it before it took his oath. He's still overwhelmed by what he and his men stumbled into when they came here.

"That's sort of why I hinted to Timma about the brandy; I figured Aju'an might be more at ease talking to you if he was—" He shrugged expressively, then repeated, "So you coming by for a drink, or not?"

"I'll come in a while, but not for a drink. I may be back on a liquid diet since Tomina's attack, but not that kind," he said. "First I want to congratulate the cast, check on Pela then have my—uh—meal, and then I'll come by, so don't get him too drunk before I get there."

Nathan grunted, then went back to Tizu and the two Warlinga.

Noticing that the crowd around the performers was thinning at last, the Kashallan joined them to offer his congratulations to the director and his cast. The actress Tasheyna Margannal was near the end of the line of players. When he approached, she broke off another conversation, and went to greet him, smiling. "I hope you were pleased with our show, Ce'awn."

Returning her smile, he reached out and took her hand, but didn't form the link. "I liked both productions very much. Though, to be honest, I found this last piece, and especially your portrayal of me, very disturbing." His voice trailed off as once again the old memories rose up to confront him.

Tasheyna seemed aware of his distress, and searched his face carefully for a sign of his disapproval. "Have I given offense? If so, I am deeply sorry."

He shook his head, then raised her hand to his lips and kissed it. "Not at all," he assured her. "You are a very skilled actress, Tasheyna. It was obvious that you worked hard to perform your part. Please don't misunderstand me, my unease has nothing to do with your portrayal. No, it is more a problem of sorting out my own feelings about that time.

"I could tell from your dance, you have already guessed much of what it was like to undergo the Transformation and make the bond. Your performance was good." He smiled. "Too good, perhaps, but nonetheless I appreciate, and pay homage to, your art."

"Thank you, Ce'awn, that means a lot to me. I have been giving a lot of thought these last few weeks to the concept of the bond. It is a very noble thing, to offer so much of oneself to help others, in spite of the personal suffering that will come with such a decision.

"I have tried to imagine—to feel in my mind and body—what it would be like—" Her voice trailed off and she looked down, suddenly embarrassed. "Forgive me; that sounds very presumptuous. I'm sorry."

"Don't be sorry, Dear Lady—I appreciate the skill you took in your portrayal of me." Looking around and seeing the waiting line of people, he said, "I should go—your admirers will be annoyed at my monopolizing your time."

As he turned to leave, Tasheyna impulsively reached out and clutched at his arm. "Ce'awn, please—"

The Kashallan paused. "Yes?"

Now that she had his attention again, Tasheyna hesitated. She licked her lips, then said in a rush, "Ce'awn, there is something I need to talk to you about. I will be finished here soon—could I please talk to you then? If you aren't too busy, or tired"

"All right, I need to go check on my wife Pela first, then, I must go eat. If you don't mind going with me to the pools, we can talk down there."

"The pools?" Her lip quivered, then she took a deep breath and nodded. "I will meet you at the entrance to the pools, as soon as I can."

Chapter Two

Back in their suite, Pela sank down with a sigh of relief in a comfortable wicker chair. Resting her head on the back of the chair she closed her eyes. She had been so tired and uncomfortable lately that she could hardly wait for her pregnancy to be over. And, it would be so much more enjoyable to hold her little Jorran in her arms and play with him.

Pela looked up at a soft touch on her shoulder. Amril smiled down at her tentatively, his eyes troubled. "Are you all right, My Love?"

Pela nodded. "I'm fine, just a little tired," she assured him, "but I would like some spiced tea, if you would get it for me, please."

Amril crossed the room, took the pitcher from the tray on the side table, and shook it. Pela swiveled around and asked, "What's wrong, Love?"

"The pitcher's empty, but I could have sworn that Nona filled it earlier."

Pela sighed an expression of annoyance crossing her pretty Avairei face. Damn, Sairsa's obsession was getting intolerable. "You'll probably find it in the waste pot again."

"What! Why would the contents of the pitcher be in there?"

"Because our sister-wife has some silly notion that our maid is trying to poison us," she snapped, barely able to contain her irritation. She was tired and didn't need this—not now.

"But that's crazy," Amril said. "I've known Nona for years—she couldn't possibly do anything like that. There isn't a kinder person in this keep!"

"Try telling that to our Sairsa."

"I saw Nona hovering out in the hall when we came in. Would you like me to send her for some more refreshments?"

"Yes, please do."

Amril walked to the door and spoke to someone unseen out in the hall. Returning, he sank down into a chair near Pela. Reaching out, he took her hand. "It will be over soon," he predicted, eyeing her swollen belly.

"Mm, I suspect so," she murmured, with eyes closed. "Did you send the maid for tea?"

"Yes, it should be here shortly."

Coming out of the bedroom, Sairsa paused, closing the door quietly behind her.

Amril smiled. "Is the little one asleep again so soon?"

"Yes, unfortunately, which means he'll probably be up later wanting to play." Sairsa yawned, then crossed to the wall, picked up the pitcher, and headed for the door.

Pela opened her eyes. "Don't bother, Sairsa'meh," Pela said in a tightly controlled voice. "Amril has already sent Nona for some more tea."

Sairsa froze, then turned to face her. She took a deep breath. "Pela, I thought I told you I didn't want that little chit coming around here anymore."

Pela sighed. "Sairsa, please don't start this again. We've been through this before, Nona is Ngeal's niece. It would give great offense and make a lot of trouble for everybody if we dismissed her without good cause."

Sairsa stared at her wide-eyed, incredulous. "Pela, we *have* cause—"

Pela sat up straight, her temper flaring. "No, we don't. I've spoken to Dunnagh-Tani about this—he is very sorry, both for upsetting the girl and for hurting you by his inexcusable behavior. He swore to me that it would never happen again—"

Sairsa snorted. "Oh, what does that big boob know?" she insisted, her voice beginning to rise. "The girl was using the red kavay, or something else like it, I tell you—he was totally under her spell. Then, after he left with Oglas, she tried to do something to my mind too!"

"But that's impossible," Amril blurted, "Nona wouldn't be allowed to use the red kavay—she's not even promised yet."

"Damn it, I know what I saw," Sairsa said angrily. "The little witch was sitting on his lap with her hand under his kilt—and the tea she was trying to make him drink was poisoned."

"But we can't prove that, now, can we, hmm? Because you threw it into the waste pot before it could be checked, like you keep on doing. Dunnagh-Tani made a mistake, you made a mistake—damn it, Sairsa, let it be."

Suddenly the door was pushed open and the Kashallan walked into the room. At his appearance, his wives fell silent, glaring at each other. He paused, puzzled. Looking from one to the other, he asked, "What's wrong, Loves?"

They looked away, each unwilling to answer. He waited with growing impatience, finally he repeated, "What's wrong? You could cut the tension in here with a knife; it's so thick. What are you trying to keep from me? I know there's something; I've felt this before—come on out with it."

Blue eyes demanding an answer, he fixed his stare on Sairsa, who seemed the most agitated, willing her silently to speak. She flushed, her mouth beginning to tremble as her eyes filled with tears. But, before she could give way, the baby began to cry in the bedroom.

Seeing her escape route open before her, she turned and fled inside the bedroom, closing the door hard behind her. Arms folded across his chest, the Kashallan turned to his Avairei wives. "Care to enlighten me about what's going on?"

The Avairei exchanged glances. Finally, Pela said, "It isn't anything, really, husband. It's not uncommon for women, when they are breeding, to get upset over nothing."

"Mm, that's very interesting, Pela Sweet, but not very informative. I repeat, what's wrong?"

"Our Sairsa has some crazy idea that the maid Nona is trying to poison all of us," Amril blurted.

Pela gave him her dagger eyes look. He flinched. "Please, husband, don't worry yourself about this. Sairsa'meh is just tired—the baby keeps her up a lot at night. She isn't thinking clearly—it will pass," Pela assured him.

At the mention of the maid, the Kashallan's face clouded. He glanced at the closed bedroom door. "Maybe I should go talk to her," he suggested.

"Husband, if it will make Sairsa'meh feel better, I will do the maid's chores for a while," Amril offered.

"No, that wouldn't be seemly. And besides, you have your studies with Ata Hobral to occupy your time," Pela protested.

Startled, Amril looked at her, now thoroughly confused. "It's all right, Pela, I don't mind. There isn't that much to do around here, anyway, and, as junior wife, it is perfectly *seemly* for me to see to my senior sister-wives' needs."

He stood up and headed for the door. "If it will ease our Sairsa's mind while she is recovering from her birthing, I will be glad to do it."

"Thank you, Amril. That might be best until I have the time to straighten this out with her."

Out in the hall, Amril almost ran into the maid Nona, who was hovering by the door. "Sorry, Nona—here, I'll take that," he offered, reaching out for the tray.

Nona smiled demurely, then handed it to him. Amril hesitated, then he said, "Nona, please don't take offense, but I'll be seeing to the needs of my sister-wives for a while."

Nona stared at him with moist brown eyes. She blinked, and a tear rolled down her cheek. "What's wrong, Ata, have I done something to displease the Holy One?"

"No, no, you've done nothing wrong. It's just—well, sometimes women, when they're breeding, take strange notions—it would just be better if I do your work for a while, that's all."

"All right, Ata Amril, if you say so. I'll be here whenever you need me."

Amril nodded. "Thank you for being so understanding, Nona, I'll let you know if we need you. Now I should go." Smiling, he turned and hurried back inside the suite.

"DAMN THE SPEIR'DINA witch!" the maid snarled under her breath, as she retraced her steps down the corridor. She had been listening at the slightly-ajar door long enough to learn that the troublesome woman was interfering again.

Now what was she going to do? Ima Tomina and the Master had told her that this evil kashallan and his kin must die. Her beloved mistress had gotten her assigned as maid to the Kashallan's suite, so that she could be in a position to carry out the Master's orders and kill the hated enemy.

But now Tomina was dead, her magics and potions destroyed, and the Master. Nona had tried to contact him through the pendant Tomina gave her, but she hadn't been able to succeed. And now this *witch* had gotten her dismissed.

Her guts knotted as she felt the compulsion laid upon her by the Umwira sorcerer awaken to torment her. She hadn't been able to put anything in this last jug of tea, because the kitchen had been full of people, and now she had lost the chance.

The Master would be furious with her. Nona gasped and leaned against the rock wall, as a spasm of white-hot pain tore through her body, leaving her dazed and disorientated with its passing. Oh, what was she going to do?

Chapter Three

Tasheyna was waiting for him, by the stairway that led down to the Khutani pools when he arrived. Giving her a reassuring smile, he motioned for her to follow him down the dimly-lit stairs. As they stepped out into the main cavern, an expression of pleasure lit up her intense face. She took in a deep breath, inhaled the warm, spice-scented air, and smiled.

"Is this your first time down here?" the Kashallan asked.

"No, I've been here a few times before, but it is so beautiful, I could never take it for granted, I think, no matter how many times I came."

"Yes, it's like that for me, too," the Kashallan admitted. He glanced around once again, saw Timma waiting for him, and frowned. To Tasheyna he said, "Excuse me a moment. Timma?"

Timma bowed to them then stood respectfully a couple of paces away, toying with his warrior's braid. The Kashallan raised an inquiring eyebrow. "Are you here to see me, too?"

"Sort of, Holy One. I went to the kashallan pool to find you for the blood gift; you weren't there and the Khutani sent me to look for you."

"Mm. He sighed and turned back to Tasheyna. "It seems our talk is going to have to wait until after my—uh—meal. I hope you don't mind. You're welcome to wander around and wait for me, if you like, or we can talk another time if you have to be back upstairs soon."

Tasheyna took a deep breath, her body tense. "I'll wait, Ce'awn, if you don't mind; I would like to have a look round; take as long as you need."

"All right." The Kashallan pointed towards the far edge of the main causeway. "Give me a few minutes, then come down there—I should be finished by then, and we can talk."

TASHEYNA STROLLED THROUGH the maze of walkways that criss-crossed the main cavern and tried to dissipate her nervousness. Here in this underground world the Khutani lived, and created the almost magical substances that kept life alive on this wounded world.

Near the entrance were shallow ponds in which the Khutani deposited the medicines they made within their own bodies. These healing potions were, in turn, taken away by the Avairei priests and distributed to the other inhabitants of Timorna.

Each pond was color-coded, glowing with a faint phosphorescence that helped the Avairei identify which substance to use for which ailment. In the larger, deeper pools, further along the causeway, Tasheyna caught sight of the Khutani, their sinewy gray bodies gliding effortlessly through the dark water, long opalescent wakes trailing out behind them.

Pausing by one large pool where a number of the young were playing, Tasheyna watched in fascination as they twisted and dove in the azure depths below her. The creatures had such a simple bodily form, so primitive by her people's standard, and yet they were the engineers and creators of the new life that sprang up on this world after the great wars had almost destroyed it. She breathed in the fragrant warm air and wondered what it would be like to call this place home.

Sinking down to the stone, she sat cross-legged on the causeway, allowing her mind to drift into the familiar meditations that had been her comfort and strength since her girlhood. The mists from the pools flowed around her, and caressed her face with a fragrant dampness. Tasheyna closed her eyes and took several deep breaths, letting them out slowly. The sights and sounds of the physical world around her shrank away, as she reached out with her psychic awareness.

Her spirit danced within the ghostly tendrils of vapor that hugged the water's surface, delighting in the currents of air that moved her along. As she drifted, she became aware of others gliding through the etheric mists nearby. She sensed their curiosity, but they made no effort to detain her, allowing her to explore as she would.

Floating further into the darkness, she searched for a communion with the grotto's spirit. So peaceful—so wise, she could almost taste the power of the ancient stone.

Sometime later, she was startled out of her reverie when a furry hand touched her shoulder. Tasheyna opened her eyes and looked around. The warrior priest Timma was standing beside her. "Excuse me, Sa Tasheyna, the Kashallan is waiting. He sent me to find you. The Maker wants him to rest a while, but if you would be comfortable joining him in the kashallan pool for your talk, he would be happy to speak with you now."

Tasheyna swallowed hard, suddenly feeling her nervousness rise up again in spite of her meditation. Taking a moment to center herself once more, she nodded and rose to follow the Avairei back down the causeway.

The Kashallan was reclining on the stone ledge that ran along one of the pool's sidewalls. As she paused by the water's edge, she smiled in appreciation at the sight of him; he was a good-looking man. Though he had seemed healthy enough upstairs in the dining hall after the performance, here she could see the long, half-healed scar on his abdomen, and had a clearer sense of how close they had come to losing him from this latest Dingay attempt on his life.

Though some of the Dymarians found the semi-nakedness that many of the Speir'dina now adopted when not exposed to the weather uncomfortable, Tasheyna herself wasn't one of them. Without waiting to lose her nerve, Tasheyna stripped off her few articles of clothing and waded into the pool to join him. He opened his eyes and smiled up at her. Sitting down beside him, she returned the smile, and held out her hands, palms downward, inviting the link.

Startled, he gave her a questioning look. "Please," she begged. "For what I need to say, I would like to be in the link with you. I want you to taste the sincerity of my words."

"All right." Sitting up and swiveling round to face her, he picked up her hands and formed the link. "I'm listening. What is it you wish to say to me?"

Tasheyna looked down at their joined hands, staring with a certain fascination as his tentacles extended and sank into her flesh. Taking a deep breath, she said, "Ce'awn, I have come to offer myself for a kashallan bonding."

He blinked; then without speaking he closed his eyes, the bondmates taking counsel with one another. At last, he sighed and opened his eyes, studying her for a moment before he cleared his throat, and said, "Tasheyna, this is a very honorable offer, and I am both startled and pleased, but my Elders—well, with so few breeding Speir'dina females with which to create a viable gene-pool— I'm sorry, but they feel it would be better for only the men among us to make the bond at this time."

To his surprise, she nodded, agreeing with him. "I understand. I suspected it would be something like that, and I agree with their reasoning, in principle. But in my case, having more children shouldn't be a consideration. You see, after my second baby there were complications—my uterus was removed, so I am unable to fulfill the Elder's charge, whether I make a bonding or not."

"I see. You say your uterus was removed after your second child—what happened to your family?"

"My husband was killed in the first invasion of Dymar, and my two girls were on the Freedom's Chance with my sister when—" She looked away, tears suddenly coming to her eyes.

Through the link, he could taste the deep sadness that this loss had meant to her, and marveled at the calm strength and determination that he also tasted there.

After a moment to compose herself, she continued, "I have given this a lot of thought over the past few months, Ce'awn. I want my life to have some greater meaning. I want to help this world heal.

"Oh, I know that all the Teh'lach family groups will need extra hands to care for the children and help with the chores. But I want something more for my life than being an aunt to other women's babies. It's too—painful."

Through the link, he could taste her sorrow, and knew how hard it would be for her to be around breeding women, at least for a few years. And there were certainly a growing number of them in the keep now.

Since there were more men than women among the Speir'dina, it had been agreed upon by all the humans to trace descent through the mother's line, as the Avairei, and Caldoni among them did. This meant that women were the heads of the households now.

To avoid disputes among the men, the new clan laws stated that sexual contacts were solely up to the women to arrange, but a woman would be allowed to have more than one spouse, if she so chose. This had seemed like a reasonable compromise between the Timornan custom in which the Ima

Matri of a keep controlled breeding arrangements in her area, and human traditions.

A childless woman would have little place in this new scheme of things, and he could understand and sympathize with her wish to absent herself from the whole situation. "What of your art?" he countered. "You are very good at what you do. As an actress, you could contribute a lot to our world in that way."

She sighed. "That's true, and I've considered that. And certainly, if my petition is refused, that's what I will devote my time and energies to." She looked at him then, her eyes imploring, begging him to understand.

"I don't know if I can explain this to you, but, for me, my dancing and acting are something that comes too easily for me. I had already given up my career on Dymar to have a family before this, because there was no joy in my craft for me anymore. I want—no, *need*—something to challenge me—to take my mind off my grief. Oh, Ce'awn, I want to do something more useful with my life than pretend to be other people. I want to *really* help others." Her voice trailed off, as she feared his refusal.

Releasing her from the link, the Kashallan sat back. "Tasheyna, this isn't a decision I can make on my own; it is up to the Elders to consider such a weighty matter.

"You have some valid arguments, and I can taste your sincerity. If you are sure that this is what you want, the best I can offer you is to go with you to the birthing pool, where you may put your case directly to the Khutani, then you will have to await their decision on the matter."

"That seems fair enough, Ce'awn. I am ready; if you are rested enough to go with me, I'd like to go and speak to them now."

He blinked. "Now?" She nodded. "Mm—what about your other performances? Not everyone has seen the show yet—surely there are more shows to come?"

Tasheyna chuckled. "Yes, there are, but my understudy has been dying for a chance to show what she can do. Tomas will be annoyed, but I am not indispensable. Please," she begged, "this is much more important than a play—and if I don't do it now, I may lose my nerve, in spite of my good intentions!"

He gave her an approving smile, then stood up. "All right; if you're sure, let's go for a little swim." Taking her hand, he helped her up, then led her out into deeper water.

TASHEYNA SWAM, DELIGHTING in the feel of the pool's azure liquid against her naked flesh. It wasn't long before they were joined by a growing number of the Khutani. Curious, the little ones swam close, sliding their sinewy bodies over, under, and around her. As curious about them as they were about her, she allowed them to touch and nuzzle against her as she glided through the gloom.

As they swam into the growing shadows, Tasheyna realized that they were entering a portion of this watery world that belonged completely to the Khutani. The busy activity and phosphorescent glow of the ponds near the entrance to the keep above seemed far away now, as if a part of another lifetime, in another world.

Pausing briefly to rest, she stroked one of the sleek gray bodies that had wrapped itself companionably around her torso. It raised its head, its mouth tentacles brushing against her cheek. Tasheyna smiled and rubbed its head. What would it be like to call these fascinating creatures her kin? What would it feel like to host one of them inside her, sharing her body, a constant companion, until death should part them?

She had carried life before—would it be like that? If her request was granted, Tasheyna supposed that she would find out. Gently untangling herself, she began to swim once more.

<<SHE'S VERY BRAVE, KASHA, don't you agree?>> Tani said. <<Our cousins like her, and she isn't afraid of them like so many of your kin are. I hope our Elders let her make the bond; I would be proud to call her amsi.>>

<<Yes, Shalla, she is a very courageous person. I am sorry that she has suffered so deeply, and I wish her well, whatever happens out here,>>

In a dimly-lit, out of the way part of the cavern, the Kashallan stopped swimming and stood; Tasheyna followed his example. The water was growing shallower again, and the sunken shelves and padded headrest seemed to be the mirror image of the kashallan pool on the other side of the cavern.

Taking her hand, he guided her over to the ledge and drew her down beside him. "This is the birthing pool," he explained. "We'll have to wait here until one of the Makers comes to speak with us." Tasheyna shifted the coils of the two young Khutani who were curled around her, so she could sit without hurting them, and gave the Kashallan a nervous smile.

Watching her for a moment with his cousins he said, "I am pleased at how comfortable you are with the little ones. Most of our kin who have experienced Khutani touch aren't so relaxed about it. I see they have already formed a link with you. You aren't afraid—I am impressed—you are an amazing woman—"

"Amsi? Is that you?" a voice asked from the shadowy rocks beyond the pool.

"Ah, Conal-Tiel—yes, it's me. I didn't know you were out here. We have company—come over here and meet our visitor."

"My hand has been hurting a lot today—I was just resting—" Conal-Tiel broke off his explanation as he came close enough to see the woman reclining in the pool beside Dunnagh-Tani. He stared down at her mouth agape.

Tasheyna looked around. In the light given off by the glowing fungi on the stone wall behind them, she saw a tall man, but more angular and less muscular than his Caldoni relative Dunnagh. His hair was long and dark, and, braided none too carefully, it hung in a loose rope over one shoulder. Like the Lann Gheal armachd he had once been, he had a long, drooping mustache. Conal had mischievous green eyes, which at the moment were opened wide in surprise.

Tasheyna knew him vaguely, but had never spoken to him much on their trip across the Great Swamp. On the rare occasions lately when he had been allowed by the Elders into the keep above, he had been shy and reserved with his Speir'dina kinsmen.

Tasheyna got the impression that he preferred to be with the Khutani than to be among the Speir'dina. And, maybe that too was understandable; the memory of how he had been treated while disabled would take time to fade.

The Kashallan laughed. "Close your mouth, Amsi, and come join us." Conal-Tiel blinked, closed his mouth, and slipped into the water with them. "This is Tasheyna Margannal, amsi," the Kashallan said. "I brought her out here because she has asked to make a kashallan bonding. And though it would normally not be permitted, in her case, the Khutani might make an exception. I have sent word to the Makers, so come join us while we wait." Conal-Tiel nodded, and, without taking his eyes off Tasheyna, he sank down beside them.

Tasheyna smiled. Hoping to set him at ease, she asked, "You said a moment ago that your hand was bothering you—is it bad?"

"Not too bad," he said shyly.

"Let me see how it's coming along," the Kashallan said, and reached out a hand.

Conal-Tiel hesitated then held it out for Dunnagh-Tani's inspection. The regenerating hand lay limp on his other palm, but outwardly it appeared not much different from its companion. "It's complete in form," he explained, "but the new bone substance hasn't hardened yet. And of course it will take longer still for that pair of tentacles to form."

"Hmm." The Kashallan took the hand and examined it, carefully forming the link. Yes, he could taste the other's pain. Conal had been playing down his discomfort as he suspected. Releasing a painkiller into the other kashallan's bloodstream, Dunnagh saw the lines of tension relax in the other man's face.

"You should ask one of the others to help you, Amsi, when it hurts like this, instead of suffering the pain of it," he chided gently.

"I guess you're right," Conal-Tiel admitted. "I just never thought about asking—it seemed so unimportant."

The Kashallan snorted, releasing the link. "It *is* important, so ask. There is no reason to be in pain, Conal, just because Tiel isn't mature enough to handle the regeneration and deaden the pain at the same time, so *ask*, Amsi."

"All right, next time I will ask."

After that, they waited together in companionable silence, Dunnagh-Tani resting, Tasheyna seemingly absorbed in her communion with the little ones, Conal-Tiel with eyes closed, almost asleep now that he was no longer in pain.

Sometime later, the two kashallans sat up, something in the feel of the pool alerting them to the Maker's coming. Tasheyna looked from one two the other. "One of the Ancients is coming," Dunnagh-Tani explained. "Stay here for the moment while I present your request." Then he was gone, gliding out to meet the Elder.

Conal-Tiel reached over and took one of her hands. "Don't be afraid, Sister. The Elders are very large, but they are also very gentle with us, especially at first," Conal assured her. "It won't hurt you, and I'll stay with you and help you all I can—if you would like me to."

Tasheyna swallowed hard, then whispered, "Thank you, Conal-Tiel. I think I would like that very much."

It seemed like only a moment before the Kashallan returned and took her hand, drawing her up beside him. "Come," he said, then led her farther out into the pool. When the water was about to her chin, he stopped and turned to her. A massive gray Khutani floated in the water nearby. She swallowed hard in spite of herself. As Conal-Tiel had warned her, the creature was huge.

"This is the Maker Meyagus, Tasheyna. I have explained your offer to it, and told it why I think an exception to the Council's ruling should be made in your case. The Elder wants to taste you and talk with you about your offer. To do that, it will wrap itself around you and hold you while it makes the link with you. Will you be comfortable with this arrangement?"

"Yes, I think so."

"Good." He hesitated a moment, then said, "Tasheyna, would you feel OK about me leaving you here with the Elder and Conal-Tiel? It's getting late, and there is still something I need to take care of before I can sleep tonight. My Elder has given me permission to go, if you will not be frightened by my leaving you here alone with it."

She shook her head and touched his arm in gratitude. "No, go on, I know you need your rest. Conal-Tiel has said he will stay with me. Go do what you need to; I'll be fine," she assured him. "And thank you for everything."

Raising her hand to his lips, he kissed it gently, then swam off into the darkness.

When he was gone, Tasheyna took in a deep breath, then leaned back in the water, allowing herself to float freely, awaiting the Khutani's contact.

Within moments, she felt it wrapping its coils around her, allowing her slowly to get used to the feel of its mass. Tasheyna relaxed, leaning her head back on a sleek gray coil, letting it float with her out into deeper water, where it would be more comfortable.

She closed her eyes and took several deep breaths to center herself, as she waited for the Khutani to form the link. She lay back, relaxed, feeling warm and secure. Losing track of time, she drifted. This felt like being a child again, held by a wise and loving parent.

———————————

THIS YOUNG ONE WAS a marvel, Meyagus thought. Certainly it would seem that the females of the new host species had much to recommend them for the bonding. It was a pity that there were so few of them, and that they were needed as breeders. It had noticed this ability to trust and accept its touch with little fear among other females it had tasted.

Swiveling its gray head around to face her, Meyagus brushed long, sensitive mouth tentacles down over her face and neck. It explored the feel of her, and she gave no sign of fear.

When Meyagus was satisfied, it bent to her shoulder, its sharp triangular teeth gently biting down to create a shallow wound, then it inserted a slender tentacle and formed the link. She shuddered when it bit into her flesh, and then relaxed once more. <<You are a wonder to me, Little One. I felt your spirit when you sat upon the causeway. Do many of the females of your kind practice such ancient disciplines?>>

<<Some, Elder. I learned to meditate when I was young, as part of the religious training of my family. Later I explored other paths of awareness on my own. But I wouldn't say that the women among my kin are any more skilled at such things than our men.>>

Meyagus gave a rumbling laugh. <<Perhaps, but there is a difference among the sexes, though its taste is too unfamiliar for me to categorize it. We haven't had many opportunities to learn about your people, and especially the females of your species.

<<You, I think, will teach us much about your kindred, if you do indeed choose to make the bonding.>>

<<Then have you decided to accept my offer, Ancient One?>>

<<I have not decided to refuse it,>> the Maker countered. <<Your taste is sweet to me. But before I make my final decision, I would like you to tell me in your own words why you wish to do this thing. I believe you are intelligent enough to know that making the kashallan bond doesn't come without a great deal of pain and personal sacrifice. Are you willing to accept that as well?>>

Tasheyna took in a long, calming breath, allowing her awareness to sink deeper into her trance. How to explain to this Ancient all the pieces of the puzzle that finally fell into place for her, when she decided in her own mind that she wanted to become a kashallan? She knew it would be painful. Having the little one carve out a place for itself within her living flesh would be a hundred times worse than the most painful childbirth that she could imagine.

It wasn't a pleasant thing to contemplate—and yet, the joy of serving others, of helping to make this world grow and bloom—that would bring with it a great deal of satisfaction as well. Then there was the Shalla, that other who would share her flesh, and her life's work. That communion would give her a lot of joy and contentment too. All of the gains seemed well worth the risk to her.

<<As my Ce'awn has, I'm sure, told you, my husband and children are dead, and I can never have any more, because of the complications that occurred after my youngest child's birth. At first, when I truly understood that they were gone and I was left alone here, I wanted to die, the pain was so great.

<<For a long time, I felt nothing but the pain. I just went about my daily routine, uncaring. But over the months since my loss, the old pattern of prayer and meditation that I learned in my youth reasserted itself, and I began to heal.

<<And as I came alive again, I looked around me and saw the pain and suffering, not only of my kin, but also of the other Timornans among us, and of the land itself. While we traveled across the Great Swamp, we were separated into small groups. Among the members of my Teh'lach were two Loti.

<<I got to know them quite well, because I discovered early on that, like me, they loved working with growing things. When my children were young and I had to stay home with them, working in my garden gave me much pleasure.

<<When I realized that I wanted to do something more with my life than wallow in my grief, or channel my energies into my acting career again, I knew then that I wanted to offer myself for a kashallan bond, and that I would like to work among the Loti, to help make this world bloom again. That is, if you'll have me.>>

When she finished, Meyagus was silent for a long moment. <<Your account was very moving, Little One, and I needed a moment more to savor it, before I gave you my answer,>> it finally said. <<You have obviously given your request a lot of thought. I taste that you aren't doing this to run away from your grief and loneliness, as I first feared. If it is truly what you want; I will accept your offering, and prepare the Shalla myself for the bonding.>>

<<Thank you, Elder,>> Tasheyna said. <<It *is* my wish. What must I do to prepare?>>

<<I will give you something now, myself, that will cleanse you,>> the Khutani said. <<Later, we will give you the green kavay to relax you and open your awareness to receive the Shalla. Then you need only rest in the birthing pool and wait. When it is time, I will come for you. And I will remain in the link with you until the little one is old enough to make the first contact.>>

Meyagus released her from the link. Tasheyna opened her mouth, and the Khutani placed a rubbery tube between her lips. She swallowed repeatedly as she felt her mouth fill with an oily liquid that must be the cleansing agent. When it judged she had swallowed enough, Meyagus pulled back, and began to slowly uncoil itself from around her.

After it had gone, she floated where it left her, a bit disoriented, and unsure where to go or what to do next. "Conal-Tiel?"

"I'm right here, Tasheyna," he said, touching her shoulder. "Come; I'll show you where you can rest. The shelf is just over here." Swimming close beside her, he guided her back to the shelf, and lay down next to her. He was silent for a long moment, then asked softly, "Are you afraid?"

"A little," she admitted, then fell silent again.

Conal-Tiel hesitated, then asked shyly, "Would it help any if I hold you?"

Tasheyna considered, then whispered, "Maybe."

Moving closer, he pressed his chest up against her back, and enfolded her in his arms. Leaning her head against his shoulder, Tasheyna let out a long sigh. "Thank you."

"Rest if you can. It will be hours yet before your Shalla will be ready. Try not to worry—I'll be here, and some of the other kindred. We won't leave you to face this alone."

Tasheyna's mind drifted, unable to come to grips with the fact that what she had wanted for her life was actually going to happen. It was one thing to daydream about being a kashallan, but it was a different matter entirely to know that such imaginings were going to become real. Now it had begun, and there was no turning back. Not that she wanted to, and yet—was she strong enough to endure the ordeal to come? Oh, by all the Gods, she hoped so.

Sometime later, a sharp pain in her abdomen awakened Tasheyna. At first she wondered if while she slept the Elder had come, and given her the Shalla. Then, more awake, she realized she had a violent need to relieve herself.

Gasping, she struggled out of Conal's embrace and sat up. Now she felt the urge to vomit as well. She had to get out of here before she embarrassed herself completely. Tasheyna gagged, and tried to push herself to her feet.

Conal-Tiel was awake now too, and helping her to stand. He seemed to know exactly what was happening, which was a good thing, because she suddenly found herself without words to explain her situation. Wave after wave of cramps swept through her tormented body. He guided her to a place in the rocks where she could relieve herself, and held onto her as her body cleansed itself. Caring for her like a parent with a young child, he seemed neither embarrassed nor disgusted as he helped her with this most intimate task.

When it was finally over, she clung to him in a daze, her head reeling. He led her back to the resting shelf and made her comfortable. "Thank you," she breathed. "I'm sorry I've made such a mess."

He chuckled, brushing back her damp hair. Lifting one of her hands, he extended his tentacles and formed the link. "No need to apologize, Dear Lady—the cleansing is a part of the process."

"What's next?" Tasheyna asked.

Conal-Tiel drew her into his arms, this time facing him. "The green kavay comes next, and the Maker has honored me by allowing me to give it to you. Then we wait for Elder Meyagus to come for you." He smiled at her, a mischievous light coming into his green eyes. Then, before she knew what he was about, he pressed his lips to hers. When she opened her mouth for his kiss, he surprised her by pouring green kavay into her mouth instead.

Startled at first, Tasheyna choked, then, recognizing what he was doing, she swallowed the bitter-sweet substance. When he finished, she gasped, catching her breath. "My, that was a most *interesting* kiss, I don't think I've ever had one like it."

Green eyes twinkling, he touched her lips briefly once more. "Ah, but that's only because you've never been kissed by a kashallan."

Tasheyna laughed softly, burying her face against his chest. "True enough," she admitted. "True enough."

A short time later she gasped, as green kavay began to take effect. Tasheyna was dazzled as the world about her exploded into a wealth of color and new sensations.

Conal-Tiel studied her a moment, then smiled. "You're beginning to feel it, hmm? Ah—but this is only a poor imitation of what you will experience when you and the Shalla are united." Settling her more comfortably within his embrace, he said, "Rest and let the green kavay carry you where it will. There is nothing to do now but wait, and conserve your strength for the Transformation to come."

Chapter Four

Dunnagh-Tani heard them as he rounded the corner into the section of the keep that the Warlinga and Lann Gheal armachda claimed as their own. It was later than he had hoped to arrive, and judging by the volume of noise coming from Nathan's quarters, the party was well under way.

Pausing in the doorway of Nathan's room, he saw that Aju'an, his kinsman Mar, and Ticca's commanders were sprawled comfortably on cushions against the wall. Several empty pitchers that had probably contained mushroom beer were tipped over on the floor, and the infamous bottle of brandy now stood half empty on a low table in the center of the room. The boisterous talk and the mess gave evidence of the amount of alcohol consumed and the lateness of the hour.

<<I hope they're not too drunk to talk to us,>> Tani said.

<<Mm, I hope so too, but the delay couldn't be helped,>>

Looking up, Nathan spotted him and waved him in. The Kashallan picked his way through the litter and sank down with a sigh on a cushion beside him. Nathan glanced at him anxiously, searching his friend's face for signs of trouble. "Everything all right?" he murmured, for Dunnagh's ears alone. "We'd just about given up on you." His eyes flicked to the lowering level in the bottle.

The Kashallan gave him a lopsided grin. "Yeah, everything's all right. I just got held up longer than I planned down at the pools—I'll tell you about it later."

Tizu leaned across and studied him owlishly. "You're late, Bright Eyes. Nathan here said you'd be by, but we expected you earlier." Reaching for the brandy bottle, he topped up everyone's drink then looked at the Kashallan, eyebrows raised.

Dunnagh shook his head with regret. "I'm still on a liquid diet, but unfortunately not that kind. So drink up while you can; it'll be all you get for a while."

Tizu smirked. "Ah, you never know about that. I've lived among you Caldoni for so long that I've begun to believe in fairies. So when Nathan tells me that a fairy just might magic up another bottle when this one's empty, I believe him."

The Kashallan gave him a wolfish grin. "I had a talk with your little 'fairy,' so don't count on it."

"Shit!" Tizu grumbled. Then, raising his bowl philosophically, he drank. Reaching out to the remaining bowl on the table, he handed it to the Kashallan. "After all our effort, I was hoping that this wouldn't go to waste."

Dunnagh raised his eyebrows, glancing around at the eager faces watching him so intently. They were up to something, but what? "What's in this?"

Nathan chuckled. "Drink some and find out."

The Kashallan glanced once more at his eager audience, then shrugged, raising the bowl to his lips. He took a cautious sip, then laughed and drank again.

Tizu grinned. "Nathan told us that you were back to your formula and the Blood Gift since the assassination attempt. And being the generous, good-hearted lot that we are, we didn't want you to totally miss out on the party. So the way we figured it a while ago, when we made up that cocktail, was that our blood alcohol level is probably high enough by now to give you a little buzz, at least. So we passed around the bowl for a donation."

The Kashallan toasted them and drank some more. When the bowl was empty, he leaned back and relaxed, allowing the talk to continue on around him. It was late, and he probably should be in bed, but this opportunity was too good to pass up. And their half-sloshed condition just might help relax the young Warlinga enough to get past his fear of giving offense to one of the sacred Khutani, so the Kashallan could talk to him openly.

Catching Nathan's eye, he made a slight nod, telling him to go ahead with his plan. Giving Dunnagh a covert hand sign of confirmation, the big man gradually shifted the conversation around so that they were talking about military actions in their old life, of which Dunnagh had been a part.

During the course of the talk, Dunnagh himself came in for a great deal of good-natured teasing by Tizu and Nathan. Fadir, who had been around the Speir'dina longer than Aju'an, and was getting used to his new commander's ways, was included in the ribbing, and returned their banter, though a bit hesitantly. But after a while, the Kashallan could tell, by the way Aju'an and his cousin Mar held their head crests, that they were becoming more and more uncomfortable.

<<This isn't working, Kasha,>> Tani complained, <<not that it isn't very interesting; I never knew you did all those silly things—but this isn't telling us what we need to know, and I'm getting very tired. Maybe we should go, and try something else later when they're sober.>>

Dunnagh sighed. <<Maybe you're right, Shalla. Nathan and Tizu's idea isn't working. Timornan ways of doing things are just too different; Aju'an doesn't understand the free and easy camaraderie that, as Lann Gheal, we accept as the normal way of things between men of different ranks.

<<Trying to show him that I was just another Warlinga officer, no different than himself is too alien a concept for him to understand. I feel our tiredness too. Let me try one last thing, and if that doesn't work, we'll go to bed.>>

ON THE FLOOR BEHIND him, Aju'an's tail flicked in agitation. How could these men talk to one of the Sacred Ones like this—and why wasn't the Khutani angry? Since coming here to answer Ima Ngeal's message, everything seemed so confusing. Most of the time he felt like he was drunk, but whether it was with ecstatic excitement over the rebirth of the kashallans, or stone cold terror over what the Dingay would do to them after the Sorins, he wasn't sure.

He glanced sidelong at his cousin. Mar was shifting nervously on his cushion, probably as shocked and uncomfortable by now as he was himself. Maybe they should go. It was getting late, and they had had a lot more than was prudent to drink. Yes, they should go before they did or said something stupid.

"—San Aju'an?"

Aju'an blinked. He'd been so engrossed in his own troubled thoughts that he'd missed what the Kashallan just said to him, and now the host was studying him with those eerie blue eyes of his, waiting for an answer to a question that Aju'an hadn't heard. Aju'an's head crest slumped in shame. "I'm sorry, Holy One—what did you say?"

Leaning forward Dunnagh rested his arms on his knees and said, "Aju'an, please, it isn't necessary for you to use such a high term of respect to me, and especially not now, when we're sitting around this room drinking. It seems a little formal, don't you think? Kashallan, or Dunnagh-Tani, will do just fine."

Aju'an blinked again. "I'm sorry, Hol—Dunnagh-Tani, I didn't mean to give offense."

"You haven't given offense," he assured him, "not at all. If one of us should be apologizing to the other, it should be me, not you."

Aju'an shook his head in bewilderment, trying to clear away the alcohol fog from his brain so he could think. Had he heard the Kashallan correctly? "I don't understand."

Dunnagh smiled. "I know this can't be easy for you and your men, Aju'an. For whatever were your own personal reasons, you risked your life, with the Sorins so near, to try and help Ticca. Unfortunately, when you arrived, you got caught up in events that were far more complicated than you expected.

"To have the beliefs of a lifetime shattered, then to be forced into outlawry or die, well, I'm sure it wasn't easy for you to forsake home and kin and give me your oath. I sincerely wish that it didn't have to be like this, believe me.

"I am sorry that my convalescence hasn't given me the time, before now, to get to know you and your kinsmen as I would have liked. In the time coming, I will need your advice and support. But I would also like to call you friend, as well as being your new Ce'awn. Can you accept that?"

"You do me a great honor, Kashallan, of which I will try to be worthy. What *are* your plans—can you tell me?"

"To be frank, I haven't made any definite plans as yet. I need more information, and that is where you can help me."

Aju'an's head crest lifted. "Of course, Kashallan, I will do whatever I can, as will the rest of my hunting pack." Aju'an glanced at his cousin, who nodded his agreement.

"What I need most at the moment, is information about what might be going on in the Yeyen Banai Valley, and the Capital at Riath in particular. I need to know a little more about the people who make up the High Council, and what they are likely to do when I go there—"

Aju'an's head crest rose a little higher. "Is that wise, Hol—Kashallan?"

"Probably not," he said, "but it is what I intend to do. I don't plan to stick around Ticca, waiting for Enaju Dingay to send Warlinga troops to box us in here for a long siege, while the Umwira continue to carry out their plans for destroying us."

Aju'an nodded. "This information doesn't surprise me. I suspected as much, but one thing still puzzles me, Dunnagh-Tani. You mentioned just now the Hated Enemy. Others have talked before about the Umwira being in control of the Dingay clan—how could that be? Surely the sacred Khutani would have known about such a thing, if it were true." He froze, his head crest drooping. "I'm sorry, Holy One, I meant no offense—I didn't mean to question your word."

"Don't apologize, Aju'an, that is a perfectly reasonable question to ask," the Kashallan assured him, "and one that will be asked by many, when I make such a claim before the High Council."

Taking over the explanation, Tani said, "You see, Aju'an, I am the only one who knows for certain that the Umwira control at least some of the Dingay, because I am probably the only one of my Khutani kindred to actually have tasted the Hated Enemy in centuries."

The Warlinga blinked, then stared incredulously. The Kashallan nodded. "It's true," Tani continued. "When we fled Sulas, we ran into a warband of the Ghostland Umwira in the underground passages as we escaped. My Kasha and I fought the Umwira war leader.

"Mostly we used the mind magics to fight him, because physically we would have been no match for the monster, unarmed and weakened from the Transformation as my Kasha still was. But at the end of our combat, when the war leader was defeated and wanted only to run away, my Kasha and I were still so enraged that we pursued him and physically tried to kill him. It was at that time that I tasted him, when my Kasha bit into his arm.

"That foul taste is something that I could never forget. And later, here at Ticca, when I checked Tomina Dingay's injuries, I tasted that same taint again. She was what my elders call a changeling—half Umwira, half Avairei."

"But surely the traitorous woman was acting on her own," Mar blurted. "A few of that clan may have been corrupted, but how could such a changeling achieve the High Matri's seat? Surely the Ancient Ones would have known—"

"Not necessarily," the Kashallan countered. "Obviously the Umwira have ways to mask their true selves from us, at least for a short time, while they are in the link. Tomina went for years here without being discovered by Avairei or Khutani. She did that in part by pretending to make the blood gift and commune with the Khutani, when she was actually giving her 'gift' to the waste pit.

"Remember, there isn't usually a Maker in the Avairei keeps. The ancients, beside myself are the only ones of my kindred who could have discovered the lie. My other kin would not have recognized the Umwira taint when they tasted it, even if she had given the blood gift honestly. No, I am sorry to say, it could be done—and was."

He sighed and rubbed a hand across his face; it really was getting late. "For too long my Khutani kin have been confined to the pools, and have had to accept on trust that the society they helped to re-create was evolving as they planned.

"We never even considered a deception like that possible—so they didn't look for that kind of treachery. The Elders only knew that something was wrong, but never thought to consider Umwira changelings as the source of the problem."

Aju'an's whole body trembled. *The High Matri, herself, perhaps an Umwira changeling—oh, by the Great Hunt Leader, that was too terrible to contemplate.*

"Having Umwira help and backing would go a long way to explaining how the Dingay have managed, in such a short time, to go from a relatively unknown border clan twenty years ago, to having one of their own sitting in the High Matri's chair today. With everyone trying to curry their favor, or too frightened to oppose them."

The Kashallan nodded. "It would indeed."

"This is so terrible, I don't even want to think about it. But I know in my soul that it is true. I have, without knowing it, feared something like this for quite some time now. It would account for so much—all the strange new plagues that afflict only rebellious families, the unexplained accidents and disappearances, and the numerous blasphemy trials—all of it!"

He looked down into his empty bowl, paying little attention now to his audience, lost in his own dark musings. "And we're all so afraid—so damned afraid, because we know that if we object, or don't do what the Avairei want, they can wipe us out in one generation, by simply claiming that the Holy Khutani have denied us the right to have the red kavay for breeding. And so we bow to their will, one by one. I've tried to tell my father—" He broke off, unable to go on, the vision of his beloved Latiya coming before his eyes, and choking off his speech.

Tizu reached over and poured the rest of the brandy into his bowl. "Drink up, Aju'an, it'll help a little."

Aju'an glanced at him, then down at his bowl, and did as Tizu instructed.

"My cousin is speaking from personal experience, Kashallan," Mar said. "Once our clan supported the Dingay cause wholeheartedly, but in the past couple of years, my K'San Yargal has taken a more moderate course. He has not come out publicly and defied the High Matri's will—but Enaju Dingay has made it clear, in many subtle ways that she is not pleased with us.

"At present, all of Meh'gach's folk are unable to obtain the red kavay. This unfortunate state of affairs came about just after my Cousin Aju'an's marriage contract was signed. His marriage to Sa Latiya hasn't been consummated, and the bride's family is making noises about wanting the woman back if things are not resolved soon."

The Kashallan's face was as dark as a thundercloud by the time the Warlinga finished their tale. He shifted on his cushion, barely able to control his mounting fury. Taking a few calming breaths, he finally said, "We knew some of this from Sagas, but neither myself nor my Elders, realized things were so far out of control. Abuses like this are the reason I must go to Riath.

"And as to the situation of Meh'gach, I promise you that I personally will make for you, and the rest of your folk, as much red kavay as is needed."

Aju'an looked at him stupidly for a moment, then blinked as a new idea exploded in his mind. By the Great Hunt Leader, he had never considered that possibility.

This alien carried a Khutani symbiont coiled inside his middle. By his sacrifice, the Khutani were freed from their confinement; the kashallans could give his people what they needed, without having to submit themselves to Avairei tyranny. The enormity of this revelation was so overwhelming that for a moment he could hardly breathe.

By the Great Hunt Leader, with the kashallans come amongst them once again, Warlinga, Loti—all Timornans—they were free! And with that knowledge, he began to tremble once more, and this time with fear. For if the Dingay, and their Umwira masters, knew what had been done, they would stop at nothing to destroy these newly bonded kashallans, and all who supported them.

The Kashallan nodded, as if aware of the path Aju'an's thoughts were taking. "The Umwira filth can't be allowed to destroy, once again, all that has been so dearly won back. They must be stopped, and I am the only one who can recognize the taint. I have to go, no matter what the risk is to me personally."

"The question is, the way I see it," Nathan said, "whether your father, Aju'an, and others like him will support the Khutani and the new kashallans. Or will they be too afraid of Dingay threats, to accept the changes that this new order will bring?"

"That is a good question, San Nathan." He sighed. "And one to which I have no sure answer."

Tizu laughed. "Well, they had better think about it with care before they give their answer, for like you, upon your arrival here, they may not have a second chance to decide."

Aju'an's head crest flattened. He looked from one grim Speir'dina face to another, puzzled. "I—I don't understand."

There was a long silence, before the Kashallan finally said, "My Elders have sworn to abandon all who do not accept the new kashallans and give us their fealty. Once they know who we are, if the people of the Yeyen Banai defy their will and try to harm me or the other kashallans, the Makers may go back to their pools deep within the bedrock, and wait for another time to make a Renewal.

"The Elders made that declaration after the attempt on my life at Sulas. Since that time, however, things have become very *complicated*, and I don't know what they will do ultimately. Like yourself and my Speir'dina kindred, there are now those native Timornans whose breeding has run true and who have given me their oaths, and there is an obligation on the part of the Khutani, as well, not to forsake those who have been loyal."

The Kashallan shook his head, and raised his hands in a hopeless gesture. "It is all a tangled mess," he admitted. "I am telling you this, Aju'an, not just to frighten you, but to make you understand how deadly serious my Elders are. They are appalled by how corrupt some of the Avairei and Warlinga families have become in the absence of their direct supervision.

"I truly don't know how far they are prepared to go in setting matters right. No one, I believe, wants to let the Umwira destroy what has been reclaimed, which is why I must go into the Yeyen Banai to try to convince those who will listen of the truth. But before I begin, I need to know who will be willing to hear me, and support us."

Aju'an shook his head in horror. This was too terrible to contemplate. But he knew from personal experience with the Maker Dievris that the Kashallan was probably right. He stole a glance at his cousin. Yes, he could tell by the way Mar held his head crest that Mar understood the danger, as well.

"My father and older brother can be very stubborn at times, and right now I think they are very afraid," Aju'an said. "But that is because my father sees no way out of the trap that the Dingay have laid for us. He doesn't want our people to be destroyed.

"But if you could come with me to talk to him—when he understands—when he sees you, and knows what you are—"

He broke off, shaking his head in frustration. By the Great Hunt Leader, Aju'an hoped his father would listen to reason, hoped they could get to Meh'gach in time, before Yargal and Varrod left for the Capital again.

"I would like to talk to your father, if you think he will hear me, and not put me under arrest without listening to my message. But I know what

I look like to the native-born Timornans," the Kashallan said. "It is far easier for most of them to believe that I am an Umwira mutant, rather than to accept that I and my people came out of the sky and can host the Khutani symbionts."

Aju'an sighed. "That is very true. There are many who would dismiss your claim out of hand, if they saw you." He took another drink from his almost empty bowl, giving himself a moment to consider. At last he said, "I think it would be best to go in secret into the valley at first, rather than coming to the Council openly.

"There are those, both Warlinga and Avairei, who have too much to lose to accept your claims at face value. You would be put under arrest the moment your alien features were seen near the Capital.

"Enaju Dingay would know the truth, of course—that you are not an Umwira mutant—but that wouldn't stop her from having her pet Warlinga K'San, Drucas Segoi, seize you, torture you, and publicly execute you in front of the populace at the next high festival.

"And, outside of open warfare among the clans, there would be no way for my father, or anyone else, to stop them."

"I would like to avoid bloodshed, if I can," the Kashallan admitted. "The idea of clan fighting clan appalls me."

Tizu leaned forward, fixing the Warlinga with hard obsidian eyes. "You'd better understand this, too, Aju'an. The Ce'awn here doesn't want violence, and I respect that, but my men and I won't stand by and let him be taken and mistreated. If the circumstances force me into it, I will use our off-world weaponry to ensure his safety. And if I do that, many will die."

The Kashallan glared at him angrily. Tizu met his gaze, and nodded. "I know you don't want to hear that, but I already went over your head in this matter. I have Khutani approval, if it comes to that."

The Kashallan swore under his breath, giving his commander another black look then he decided to drop it. Turning back to the Warlinga, he said, "You haven't seen an example of what my Hunt Leader is talking about, but I can assure you that our weapons are most terrible indeed. And to prevent their use is yet another reason why I need to convince the people of the truth of my claims."

Aju'an nodded. He had no doubt of these creatures' assertions. He had seen enough of their alien ways to believe almost anything about them. He scratched his jaw, thinking.

"I suspect we would have a better chance at convincing many of the clan elders if we meet with them privately first. There are many, I believe, who hate the Dingay, but are too afraid to challenge them openly, as long as they fear the High Matri will order the Avairei to cut them off from obtaining red kavay and other medicines.

"Once they realize that—a kashallan can give them the kavay, as well as the priests—once they know that, I suspect you will gain a great deal of support among the clans. It would be far better for us to come into the valley in secret, and try to win the allegiance of as many of the Warlinga and Avairei clans as possible, before going to Riath.

"Then, when you do go to the Capital, there will be enough warriors at your back to ensure that you are not arrested, hidden away, and disposed of in secret."

"That is how I see it, too. You are smart, and see the situation quite clearly." Dunnagh-Tani glanced around the room at the rest of his commanders. One by one, they gave him their nods of agreement.

Aju'an looked down at his now empty bowl, then spoke into the silence. "I am humbled by your praise, Holy One. No matter what my father or the rest of my kin decide, I want you to know that my hunting pack and I will be true to our oaths of fealty. We are at your command, and I would offer you my protection and my services as your guide for your journey into the valley, if you will accept it."

"I will, gladly, Aju'an, and I hope that your father and brother can be convinced to join us."

Aju'an gave his cousin an anxious look; their eyes met. "So do we, Kashallan, so do we."

"So," Nathan said, "now that that's settled, when do you plan to leave?"

"As soon as possible after the blue snows begin to melt," the Kashallan said. "I agree with Aju'an's assessment of our situation—we will travel light, fast, and as much in secret as possible, until we can gain the support we need to confront the Dingay openly.

"I'll take Aju'an, his hunting pack, and, perhaps three or four of our smaller Speir'dina warriors, like Oglas, Briyenn, Ellis, and a couple more of the women. They can pass for Avairei at a distance, if need be."

At Nathan's frown, Dunnagh-Tani smiled and added, "And I guess you, because there's probably no way to leave you behind, short of throwing you in the pools for the bonding."

"Damn right," Nathan grumbled, "and don't even joke about that. It's not funny."

The Kashallan laughed. "All right, Nathan, all right. I was just teasing to see if you were paying attention." Nathan glowered, but said nothing further.

Tizu let out a startled curse of protest. "And just what do you think you're doing? I'm the Hunt Leader here, remember?"

The Kashallan turned to him; his expression softening. "Yes, I do remember; you are my Hunt Leader—my best Hunt Leader. I know you would prefer to go with me yourself, but I need you here. K'San Yargal will probably send Ima Ngeal's message on to Riath after the Sorins, without waiting to hear from his son.

"For that reason, I need you at the keep in case Ticca is attacked. With so many of our people left behind here, not to mention a kashallan or two, I can't afford to leave this fortress in the hands of any but my most experienced Hunt Leader. I'm sorry, Hukiyo."

Tizu didn't like it, but finally he nodded his agreement. "All right, I can see the sense in what you want. You've made your point, but hear mine. I'll choose who goes with you, and they're going to be armed to the teeth, just in case you need some back up—is that clear?"

Dunnagh-Tani chuckled, then stood up and stretched. "Fair enough, Hunt Leader, fair enough; you can choose them, if you wish." He yawned. "And now, if you'll excuse me, I've got to get some sleep."

Aju'an stared at the closing door, his head crest flattening with worry. Turning back to the men in the room, he asked, "Is he going to be able to make the journey? The country between here and Meh'gach is very rough—not suited to a litter, unless we go slowly. But we will need to travel very fast if we are to catch my father before he leaves for Riath."

Nathan laughed. "Whether he's strong enough or not, he'll go. There'll be no stopping him; I can promise you that. But as to a litter—no need to worry; he won't need it. We know how fast a hunting pack can travel, and to be quite honest, even in top condition, we probably couldn't keep up with you. But we have already solved that problem. We won't slow you down."

At the Warlingas' puzzled looks, the Speir'dina grinned. "We may not be able to keep up, but most Loti can," Nathan explained. "We'll bring them along."

When they continued to stare at Nathan in bewilderment, Tizu added, "In our old home, we had four-footed animals whose backs we rode on. In our journey here across the Swamp, the Kashallan and others among us rode the Loti in the same way. I don't think we'll have any trouble getting volunteers to carry us when we need them, so don't worry about that."

"It seems you have thought of everything, Hunt Leader. So I will leave the preparations in your most capable hands." Aju'an stood up and bowed, motioning for his cousin to join him. "San Tizu, San Nathan, San Fadir, if you will excuse us, it does grow late."

Chapter Five

Nona moaned, and tossed restlessly upon her narrow bed, but she was unable to wake. There was no escape. Even within her dreams, a kaleidoscope of frightening images tormented her. She writhed helplessly, crying out—begging for someone, anyone, to save her. She would do anything—promise anything. Just make them stop—go away. Oh, please, make them stop!

Nona whimpered, then relaxed as she was engulfed in a swirling violet mist. The terrifying images were suddenly gone, leaving her breathless in their wake. <<There, there, Little One,>> a smooth, oily voice spoke into her dreaming mind. <<You needn't be afraid any longer. I am here, and I will protect you—if you please me with your report,>> the voice assured, with just the slightest hint of threat in its tone.

<<Master? Oh, Master,>> Nona murmured, <<thank all the Gods that you have finally found me. I—I have been so alone—so afraid—and the dreams—>>

<<Never mind all that foolishness, Avairei Filth, tell me what has been going on within Ticca,>> Barak snarled.

Nona gasped, shrinking away from the Umwira's harsh words. Barak ground his teeth in frustration, silently cursing his impatience. For just a moment he had forgotten that this young Avairei wasn't one of his changelings accustomed to the cruel treatment their Umwira masters inflicted. She was a true Avairei, one of the Khutani slaves, and his hold over her mind and body was tenuous at best.

Sending a soothing, pleasurable feeling down the link that bound them, Barak cooed, <<Now, My Child, be easy. I am not displeased with you, so don't be anxious. I wish only to know what has been happening—there is an evil spirit in your keep that has tried to prevent me from coming to you, and Tomina—>>

<<Oh, Master, they've killed her—>> the girl blurted. <<I tried to—>>

<<What are you saying, Child—>> Barak demanded, feeling his temper rising once again. <<Who—how?>> Realizing, too late, that she was shrinking away from him again, he relaxed. This would be easier if he could gain a stronger hold over the girl, but the demon—damn it to the Fires—had been very watchful; it had taken him some time to find a way past its power, even to communicate with the girl through her dreams.

If that filth Tomina was indeed dead, as the child claimed, that would explain why he hadn't heard from the changeling. He would have to go cautiously here, or lose his last hope of destroying his adversary by stealth while he was still within the keep.

He must handle this one carefully, indeed. <<This news is very upsetting to me, Little One, as I'm sure it is to you. Tell me everything, My Dear, so we can decide how to make them pay for the evil they have done. Come now, you would like to see your beloved mistress avenged, would you not?>>

<<Yes.>> then she told him about Tomina's death and her being barred from the Kashallan's suite, because of his wife's suspicions.

As Nona related her tale, Barak had to work hard to control his rage. Damn the Avairei filth for bungling the job. The quick death she had been given was an unexpected mercy that she didn't deserve.

But how had the mutant slime, or his western wizard master, known about the Dingay changelings? That piece of information was a closely guarded secret that only a few of his Ghost Land colleagues knew. How had this western bred, Khutani-enslaved, vermin known—how?

Had the Sweh'an demon told them? No, Barak doubted it. Somehow, these mutants' master had managed to gain the loyalty of a Sweh'an, but he didn't think the demon would volunteer that information to its new master. It did have a certain code that it lived by, and to weigh the scales of the future so heavily in one direction would go against its pact. The Sweh'an had probably not told them, though he was sure it knew.

But if it had not given away his secret, how had they found out? Now it was even more important that these enemies be stopped, before they could spread the news of the Dingay corruption beyond the walls of Ticca.

The maid fell silent, waiting submissively to know his will. She was in his control at the moment, but he would have to strengthen his hold upon her in the waking world or all might be lost. She was his only tool left within the keep now, and if she was right about Tomina's magical items and potions being destroyed along with the priestess herself, then he would have to be very careful not to lose this weapon as well.

<<My Poor Child,>> the wizard soothed, <<how terrible this time must have been for you. If I had only known earlier, I would have come to help you.

<<It is a pity about your mistress, and together we will avenge her—you and I, I promise. For we can't let the evil ones go unpunished, now can we, hmm?>>

<<But, Master, there is nothing I can do,>> Nona wailed. <<I have no magics, and they won't let me near him anymore!>>

<<What are you saying, child?>> the Umwira demanded. <<You must kill him, as we planned.>>

<<But I can't do it, Master,>> she protested. <<I couldn't poison him now, even if I could get to him, because I've used up all the poison my mistress gave me.>>

<<Hmm.>> This was yet another frustrating complication. <<Does anyone else but this one troublesome woman suspect you?>>

<<No, I think not. I have given the Kashallan my oath—they don't suspect me. They only humor her because she is breeding, and they fear it will sour her milk for the child if she is upset too much.>>

<<And what of their leader?>> Barak pressed. <<You told me that he liked you. Can't you lure him away from the others?>>

<<I know he likes me,>> the maid said, savoring the taste of her growing feminine appeal. <<But since that first time, when his wife discovered us, he has been avoiding me—whenever I try to speak to him alone, his naked face turns all red and he hurries away from me.>>

Barak considered; damn these stupid, indolent slaves! This was just another setback to plague his mind. It was a good thing that he had sent his warbands west to hairy his rivals. Their meddling could not be allow to spoil plans that had taken centuries in the making. The western clans would pay—how they would pay!

Finally he remembered the waiting girl, and said, <<You told me that they destroyed all of Tomina's things—her potions and powders—>>

<<Yes, Master.>>

<<What of Khutani drugs within the keep? Are you familiar with their usage—do you know which can be used to kill?>>

The priestess hesitated. <<I know some of them,>> she admitted.

<<Good, that is very good, Little One,>> Barak cooed, <<this pleases me very much. I think we will yet be able to have our revenge upon your mistress's murderers. Here is what you will do. First you must get rid of this troublesome woman and his Avairei wife.

<<So you will find the proper drug from the keep's stores and poison them. This Kashallan, as you call him, will be grief-stricken by such a terrible tragedy. He will need comforting; someone to take away the pain of his loss, hmm? He will not run from the sweet release you can offer him, then. No, I think under the circumstances, he will welcome you into his bed. Then, when he is oh-so-trusting and vulnerable, you will do what is necessary to obtain my revenge.>>

<<But, Master, I am forbidden to go into their suite—>>

<<Don't worry; now that I have found you again, I can help. With my magic, I will help you get the poison, and get into their suite,>> Barak promised. <<The fact that you are not allowed in those rooms makes it even better,>> he chortled, <<because no one will suspect it is you.>>

Nona tossed restlessly. <<No, no, please, no. Killing the strangers—Master, if you say they are evil I will do it. But killing an Avairei—no, no, I couldn't—it would be too terrible—>>

Feeling the girl pulling away from him, Barak growled a curse. Reaching out to gather the power of the Sorins about him, he focused the full force of his will upon the unsuspecting girl. She cried out once, then the last shreds of her consciousness were torn apart under the wizard's onslaught.

When Barak was finished, only a soulless shell remained, the spirit of the young Avairei having been driven out of her mortal flesh. Now the soul could only cower in some dark limbo between the worlds, until death claimed her body. She was no longer able to interfere with his plans. The Kashallan would die—all the enemies of the Real People would die!

Chapter Six

Eyes still heavy lidded with sleep, Dunnagh-Tani watched his son's frantic efforts to find his mother's nipple and get started on breakfast. On her side facing him, with the baby between them, Sairsa lifted a heavy white breast, and guided the erect, rosy tip of her nipple into the baby's searching mouth.

Seeing him awake and watching the operation, she smiled. "I'm sorry, Love, did he wake you? He's so impatient sometimes." She glanced down at the now contentedly sucking baby.

The Kashallan smiled. "No, I've been dozing on and off since Pela and Amril left a while ago." He returned his attention to his new son, a twinkle in his blue eyes. "Impatient? Or is he just greedy?"

Sairsa made a face, then, laughed and looked into the baby's eyes. "Pay no attention to him, My Little Seal. He's just jealous."

The Kashallan laughed. "True enough, My Sweet, true enough." Rising up on one elbow, he kissed her tenderly, then bent and took her other creamy breast in his mouth and sucked, savoring her milk's rich warm taste upon his tongue. Between his parents Tameh squirmed, his confinement not to his liking.

Laughing, Sairsa pushed Dunnagh away. "Leave that alone, you big Amadan—your son will want that one in a minute."

He lay back, smiling. "Mm hmm, like I just said—greedy."

Sairsa sniffed, but her green eyes sparkled. In a few minutes, it was as she predicted—the baby finished at one breast, and complained loudly for more. Turning her back on her mate, Sairsa put Tameh to her other breast, then wiggled her firm buttocks up against Dunnagh's russet crotch as she settled herself once again.

Feeling his sex harden with interest, he chuckled and put an arm about her. "Mm, do that again, after the baby goes back to sleep." He licked her neck beside her ear, and rocked his hips gently against her backside.

Sairsa purred deep in her throat, and pushed back. She reached up and clumsily caressed his face. "Mm, keep doing that and I can hardly wait."

"Mm, maybe I will—if you ask me nicely." Sairsa made a rude noise. Dunnagh-Tani flopped on to his back before he could get too interested.

Shifting the baby to a better position, she looked over her shoulder at him. "I'm all right now, you know—it's been long enough after the birthing. You aren't going to hurt me. Or," she broke off as a new thought occurred to her, "it would be nice, if *you're* feeling up to it."

He grinned. "Mm, Truly I must be on the mend. For the first time since the attack I do feel—uh—interested, and I'm glad to know that you are better. But let's wait till later. I need to see about some things this morning, and if you tempt me into staying in bed with you—I'll never get them done."

"You're talking about your trip, aren't you. Do you have to go so soon after the snows melt? Are you sure you'll be well enough for such a hard journey by then?"

"I'll be fine. The snows won't be gone for several weeks yet and I'll be well enough to travel by then, so don't worry about me, Love." In spite of his repeated reassurances, he could see the fear lurking in the depths of her green eyes. Leaning over he kissed her tenderly. By all the Gods, he would like nothing more than to stay here with her and his growing family—but he couldn't, and they both knew it. He had to go to Riath, for all their sakes.

She nodded, answering his unvoiced thought. "I know, you have to," she said with a slight tremor in her voice, "though I wish it were otherwise."

When the baby was finished, Sairsa sat up, and without looking directly at him, she placed his son atop his chest and crawled around him to the edge of the bed. Dunnagh grunted in surprise.

"What? You can watch him for a moment." She smiled. "He's been fed; I have to pee." She glanced around, looking for the chamber pot.

"Amril took it with him, when he and Pela went to chapel."

Hearing an odd note in his voice, she turned back to face him, her mouth tightening. He sighed. "I don't want to spoil the good feelings between us this morning," he said, "but I have to say this. Sairsa, I know I behaved like a beast—and I hurt you very much—but you've got to stop this. Pela's right—Amril can't go on doing a maid's work, just because of my stupid behavior on one occasion—"

Sairsa jerked as if he'd slapped her. Hands on her hips, she glared down at him, face flushed. "Damn you, Dunnagh-Tani, damn all of you," she said, voice shaking. "You all think I'm just a stupid breeding woman having delusions. Well, I'm not. I know what I saw—know what I felt—and damn the lot of you for not believing me—"

"Sairsa, please—I'm truly sorry, it won't ever happen again—"

"Damn it, you big boob, it isn't what you did that's the point here, it's what *she* was trying to do both to you—and to me. That's the problem," Sairsa cried. "And why can't I make any of you believe me? That girl is not what she seems!"

He sighed, trying to maintain his calm. "Sairsa Love, I tasted her, I took her oath; she's just a young Avairei girl, nothing more. I would have tasted—"

Blinking back tears, Sairsa swore one of Nathan's favorite Caldoni curses, then, giving him one last murderous look, she grabbed her cloak off a chair and stomped out of their bedroom.

When she was gone, he let out a long troubled sigh. <<She is very stubborn about this, Kasha, what are we going to do?>>

<<I'm not sure, Shalla. You're right, she is being very stubborn. I suppose we could just taste the girl again.>>

<<We could, if we have to,>> Tani agreed, <<but if we do that, it will create all kinds of trouble for everybody. And we would have to explain to Ngeal why our Sairsa is so against the girl, and—>> Breaking off, Tani left that thought uncompleted, but its bondmate could imagine the problems that retesting Nona would create for them. Ngeal would not be pleased—not pleased at all.

Dunnagh let out another deep sigh, privately wondering why women had to make things so complicated. Well, maybe if they just let it be for a while she might give it up herself.

Sprawled atop his father's chest, baby Tameh gurgled then burped loudly, droplets of bluish milk drooling down his chin and onto the Kashallan's chest. "Well spoken, My Son," the Kashallan said, and reached for a rag to wipe the baby and himself off. "Your opinion of your father's bungling efforts to understand your mother has been duly noted." He stroked the baby's cap of red fuzz and smiled at his son again.

Tameh stared back at him with unfocused green eyes, he burped again and swayed like a drunkard, trying to keep his head up. Letting it fall at last, he sucked a pink thumb furiously for a moment, then raised his head once more and looked around. Dunnagh chuckled and lifted his head to kiss his son on the forehead.

When someone opened the door he looked up. Expecting Sairsa, he opened his mouth to resume their conversation then saw it was Amril and the words died on his lips.

Amril crossed the room and set the now empty chamber pot down in the far corner; he straightened and glanced over at their big bed. When he saw the Kashallan alone with his son, he hesitated then came over to them.

Dunnagh smiled, and patted the edge of the bed beside him. Amril sat, his eyes watching the baby. The Kashallan cleared his throat. "I've been meaning to ask you. How are your self-defense lessons coming along? I heard from Nathan that Timma managed to talk you into letting him and Chang teach you."

Amril laughed nervously then shrugged. "All right, I guess. I'll never be as good as Timma, but I see the sense in them, and I am enjoying the exercise."

"Mm, good. I'm glad you're taking them. I hope that in time other Avairei will agree to be taught as well. I don't necessarily want all the young to start braiding their manes in a warrior's braid, but it doesn't hurt anyone to know a little bit about how to defend themselves if they are attacked. And you can tell them so for me."

Amril looked down shyly at his hands; he twisted the fringes of his sash. "I will tell them if you wish, husband, but it is Ima Ngeal who must be convinced. My Ima is still not sure she approves of all this change. I think most of the Avairei will not attend any classes and risk offending her, unless you order them to do so."

"Mm, Ngeal—I know how she feels about a lot of things." His eyes flicked to the kilt and marriage bottle Amril was wearing. "But I hope with time and a little more patience, I can convince her to broaden her opinions on certain subjects."

At the tone of annoyance in his voice, Amril glanced sharply at him then down at his woman's kilt. "Don't trouble yourself about me, husband, I don't mind—truly."

"Mm." Changing the subject, Dunnagh-Tani turned back to his son. He ruffled Tameh's silky hair one more time. "Seeing him is such a wonder to me," he murmured, his eyes still fixed on the little one. "It's a marvel to me, knowing that a part of me helped create him." He chuckled. "I don't think I could ever get tired of watching him. Isn't he beautiful?"

"Yes, I guess so."

The Kashallan heard the hesitation in Amril's voice and laughed. "Don't mind me. Every father thinks his own babies are beautiful, whether they are or not. It's probably the fault of our male egos or some such. But you'll understand better, when Pela gives you your first child."

Amril dropped his eyes, twisting his sash again. "You have hinted at this before, Dunnagh-Tani. Truly you wish me and Pela to have children together?"

The Kashallan nodded, his expression suddenly serious. "Yes, I meant what I said. Maker Dievris thinks that Pela may have a difficult time of it during this birthing. But in a couple of years, there would be no reason why you and she shouldn't have a child of your own. Of course, officially, I will be its father, but that shouldn't stop you, should it?" He smiled slyly up at the priest, and winked.

Amril gave him a tentative laugh, his body relaxing. "No, it shouldn't stop us at all."

Dunnagh smile widened and he stroked the other man's velvety fur. "I'm glad." He pulled the young man down beside him on the bed, and laid the baby atop his chest for a better view. Tameh gurgled, flexing his tiny fingers in Amril's fur. Amril reached up a tentative hand and stroked his smooth pink cheek. "He seems very strong—he can hold his head up very well for such a young one. Is that normal for your species?"

"Mm, I'm not sure actually. But I think you're right. Probably all the swimming he's been doing with my younger cousins has made him stronger than usual."

As the baby began to pull at his fur, Amril picked him up and laid him on his back between them. Both men fell silent, watching the little one play with his fingers, and babble happily till he fell asleep.

SAIRSA HADN'T RETURNED when Dunnagh-Tani left the sleeping baby with Amril and Pela and headed down to the pools. Leaving his clothes and lamp on the walkway, he swam out into the waters that the Khutani claimed for their own.

Dunnagh swam slowly. Before he reached the birthing pool, he needed to set aside his annoyance with Sairsa and calm his thoughts. It had been two days since he had been able to take the time away from his other responsibilities to come out here and check on Tasheyna. And now that he was making the time, it would never do to go to her with his emotions in turmoil.

That would only upset the young Shalla. The Makers and his other relatives would be very cross with him, too—and they would show him their displeasure in some very painful ways.

Slowing his pace even more, he lay back and allowed the sensuous feel of the water to envelop him in its azure peacefulness. Lettimg go of his troubles, he drifted in a place out of time....

Startled out of his reverie a while later, the Kashallan grunted as several sleek gray bodies slammed into him, jostling and knocking him about in their excitement.

<<Amsi, silly Amsi, what are you doing?>>

<<Are you sleeping?>>

<<This is no time for sleeping—come, oh, you must come see them!>>

Dunnagh-Tani sat up, treading water, as a cacophony of young Khutani voices exploded into his mind. <<All right, all right, slow down, I hear you—the kashallan bond has been successful?>>

<<Yes, oh, yes, Amsi, you must come see them now.>> they said as they entangled themselves about him.

<< I'm coming,>> he said, almost as excited as his young cousins. Dunnagh's progress was slowed as the pod nipped and nuzzled him in their

eagerness. He stopped. Still chuckling to himself he said, <<Stop. How can I swim if you tangle in my legs and arms. I will get there much faster if you let me swim by myself.>>

<<But you swim too slow, Amsi,>> they cried. <<No, no, hold on to one of us—we will carry you much faster.>>

<<Come, oh come, Amsi. That's right, hold on—>>

Dunnagh relaxed, laughing, allowing the largest of his exuberant cousins to bear him along.

In the shallow water of the birthing pool, he found the Maker and the two kashallans. Tasheyna rested quietly in the Maker's coils, her mouth molded around the Maker's rubbery feeding tube. Her eyes closed she was swallowing repeatedly as the Maker fed the young Shalla.

Dunnagh-Tani smiled to himself, suddenly recalling his own early days at Sulas with nostalgia. To be young and cared for, cradled protectively in the Khutani's massive coils; such days of innocence were too soon past. He hoped she would be able to enjoy them without interruption.

As before when he visited, Conal-Tiel was hovering near Tasheyna and the Maker. Like a proud father with his first child, he gazed at this new miracle with a mixture of wonder and concern. When he saw Dunnagh-Tani approaching, Conal-Tiel smiled and swam out to greet him.

"The kashallan bond has been safely formed then?" Dunnagh-Tani asked in a low voice, glancing over anxiously at Tasheyna.

Conal-Tiel nodded. "Yes, not long ago. Maker Meyagus is feeding the young Shalla, Rinn, for the first time."

"And Tasheyna, how is she?"

Conal-Tiel beamed. "She's weak and still in some pain, as you might expect, but she's awake, and excited. Yes, I'd say she was doing quite well.

"She was braver about it than I was, that's for sure," Conal confided. "She kept joking with me, when she was conscious during the worst of it—said it wasn't much harder to bear than childbirth, so I shouldn't be so afraid for her." He shook his head in admiration.

"Mm, I guess neither of us would know about that, would we?"

Conal made a face then grinned. "True enough, Amsi, and I'm glad I don't have to know, if child birth hurts like the Transformation."

Dunnagh chuckled and together they swam into the shallows.

When the Maker finished the feeding and uncoiled itself from about her, Conal-Tiel hurried forward to guide her into shallower water where she could rest. Dunnagh-Tani started to follow them, but one of the Elder's coils wrapped itself about his legs, halting his progress. <<Since you are here, Young One, I will feed you, as well, and taste how your injury is healing.>>

He lay back, and allowed the big Khutani to envelop him in its coils. Leaning his head back as Tasheyna had just done, he opened his mouth then swallowed the creamy, sweet-tasting liquid when he felt it trickle onto his tongue.

When the Kashallan was finished, the Maker removed the feeding tube from between his lips, then reinserted a mouth tentacle against his inner cheek to form the link. Meyagus tasted him in silence for a while, then said, <<You are healing nicely, Young One. You should be able to resume your normal way of eating and begin your own healing work again soon.>>

<<I am glad to hear that, K'amsi,>> Dunnagh-Tani said. <<Then I will be able to travel into the Yeyen Banai, as we planned?>>

<<Though I wish it wasn't necessary for you to go, you will be well enough by the time the blue snows melt to travel,>> it said. <<None of the Council of Elders likes the idea of you taking such a risk, but your argument is a valid one.

<<You are the only one of us that has tasted the corruption and is free to travel upon the land, so it will be as you want. But you are still so young, and oh, so precious to us. We would not want to lose you.>>

<<I will be careful,>> the Kashallan assured it.

<<Let us pray to the Mother that, between your caution and your warrior's skills, it will be enough to keep you safe. Now stay here and rest with the young bondmates for a while; you need the sleep too.>> Then, with a final sending of affection, Maker Meyagus released him and was gone.

Dunnagh-Tani waded over to the two kashallans lying exhausted in each other's arms. They looked up at his approach, and Tasheyna smiled. "Ce'awn—" She broke off, laughing. "Amsi," she began again, using, for the first time, the Khutani word for a cousin of the same age grouping. "Oh, Amsi, I'm glad you've come."

Smiling tenderly at her, he sank down into the warm liquid beside them. "I am too."

Tasheyna carefully untangled herself from Conal-Tiel and turned to face him. He kissed her then enfolded her in a gentle embrace, careful not to cause her still-changing body more pain. When she was settled, he extended his tentacles and formed the link. She nuzzled him affectionately, the young Shalla welcoming the contact with its older symbiont cousin.

Dunnagh-Tani caught Conal-Tiel's eye and said, "Amsi, I will stay with her now. Go find one of our relatives to feed you. If you stayed with her the entire time, which I'm sure you did, this transformation must have been almost as hard on you as your own. I will care for her. The Elder wants me to stay here and rest. You look exhausted, so go on—she'll be all right."

Conal-Tiel gave Tasheyna-Rinn one last anxious look, then nodded and swam slowly out into the pool. The Kashallan turned his attention back to the woman in his arms, but she had drifted off into an exhausted sleep. He closed his own eyes and dozed.

Chapter Seven

"All right, you bunch of lay-abouts, listen up," Tizu shouted. In the large room that they had made their practice area, both his Speir'dina and native Warlinga fell silent. "First matches for the day." Tizu read off the sheet in his hand. "In eric one," he pointed to a roped-off oval to the far left of the room, "Waluk and Tarla. Eric two, Ross and Byan. Eric three, Nathan and Meh'gach."

From her place on the bench between her new friends, Chelka rose and stepped out onto the combat floor. About halfway across the room, she halted as she saw her brother Aju'an step into the roped-off eric beside San Nathan. Confused, she hesitated, unsure what to do next.

Seeing her standing there, Second Hunter Fadir bent and spoke hurriedly to his commander. Startled, Tizu looked around, then, catching sight of her, he waved her back to the bench against the wall.

Chelka's scales turned an intense shade of green. Feeling as if every eye in the room was on her, Chelka bowed stiffly and walked back to her seat. At that moment she wished the floor would open and swallow her.

Without turning to face her, Moraga laid a hand on her arm. "Don't let him upset you none," she murmured out of the side of her mouth. "The Hunt Leader just forgot he has another set of twins under his command again. He used to do that to my twin brother and me too. He'd shout out 'Fe'an,' and when both my brother and I reported, he'd look confused like, then say which one of us he wanted."

"It would be simpler if he used everyone's personal name, like we do, since most of the hunting packs in a keep all have the same family name," Chelka said.

Moraga nodded. "Oh, it would, and he knows that—he just probably forgot. Old habits sometimes are hard to break."

From Chelka's other side, Marti laughed. Then, leaning across her friend, she grinned at Moraga. "But she has such a good sounding name; almost like one of ours. Think about it—shouting out 'Gretoc, MacFe'an, Meh'gach,'" as she spoke she emphasized the guttural sound of their names, "it's so satisfying and—sexy!"

Moraga snorted, but Chelka could tell she was amused. Chelka hadn't known until just now that the big, yellow-maned Speir'dina woman was a twin like herself. Never having seen anyone at Ticca who looked like her friend, she said, "Moraga, I didn't know you are a twin like me. Where is your brother—does he look like you?"

For just a moment, a look of deep sadness came over Moraga's face, then it was gone. Without meeting her eye she said, "My brother died soon after we came to Timorna."

Chelka would have liked to ask more, but she could tell the subject pained the other woman, so she held back her curiosity. On her other side Marti hadn't seen the look. Not thinking about Moraga's feelings, she spat out, "That Gods-cursed, black-hearted Gormach Tragar killed and ate him—may he rot in a cesspit."

Chelka lowered her head crest in shock. She didn't know what to say—what did the woman mean? Why would Gormach, who was no kin to these people, partake in the feast of a dead clansman? Then the awful truth struck her—Marti had said "killed and ate." The Warlinga K'San had killed and eaten Moraga's brother, like he would a lowly Begta! Her head crest shot up and her red eyes opened wide. Marti nodded grimly.

"My father says that all the Tragar clan are a bunch of misbegotten, lazy drunkards. He won't have anything to do with them," she offered, hoping to placate the women's feelings.

"Ah, well, that was true enough for Gormach," Moraga agreed, "but young Tobrach's a good laddy. He's sworn the oath to the Ce'awn like the rest of us, and he'll make a fine K'San of Tragar, if he can break the rest of his kin of the bad habits they learned from Gormach."

Chelka blinked. What was Moraga talking about? Seeing her confusion, Marti gave a bark of mirthless laughter. "You understood her right, Sister—that Butcher Gormach's dead, and good riddance."

"How?"

"The Ce'awn killed him," Marti said with grim satisfaction. "He fought him in some duel called a Ci'awa-something."

"Chi'awari'ga?" Chelka suggested.

"Yeah, that's it," the dark-skinned woman agreed. "Tobrach's head of his clan now, out in the Broken Lands. Though I doubt if he was in any hurry to let them know that fact in the Yeyen, before the storms confined them."

No, Chelka thought, he probably wasn't. Well, this was indeed a new state of affairs, and she wondered if Aju'an knew this. If not, he should be told, because it might change how their father and other Warlinga lords saw things. She would have to speak to him privately, at the first opportunity. Leaning forward, she started to ask another question of her willing informant, when a Speir'dina officer, named Goronwy, frowned at them as he passed. "Stay alert, you gossiping bunch of old hens, you might learn something."

Marti ran her tongue over her lips, and gave him a toothy grin. "Come and see me later, Dillwyn, and you'll definitely learn something too, hmm?"

Chelka watched in amazement as the man only laughed softly instead of getting angry with her for her insolence as a Warlinga would do. Turning his back so that Tizu and Fadir couldn't see him, he asked, "Is that a promise, My Lovely?"

Marti's smile widened, becoming even more predatory. "If you think you're man enough for the job, Boyo."

He scowled at her, then, shaking his head, he moved on.

Moraga's pale eyes gleamed with amusement. "Marti, you're a terror. Ever since your woman decided to take the Ce'awn's none too subtle hints and get herself pregnant, you've had every man in the outfit scared shitless. You'd better have a care, or Marnez won't be the only one rocking a cradle after the renewal."

Marti made a face, then grinned. "Not a chance. My birth control implant is still good for a while yet, so I intend to enjoy myself while I can. But," she sighed to dramatize her point, "I suppose eventually I'll have to do my duty and have a babe or two, just to keep the Ce'awn and his Khutani Elders off my back. And," she added slyly, "now that Nathan's *available*—"

Moraga snorted. "Give it up, Marti. You'll not have any better luck in that direction than you ever had, especially now that that Dymarian woman with the Caldoni name—Briya—be spending so much time in his company."

"Maybe, maybe not. This is Timorna remember; the Khutani and the Imas might have a thing or two to say about where our handsome lad be dropping his pants, now, mightn't they?"

Moraga gasped, then laughed giving her friend an admiring look. Marti affected an air of wide-eyed innocence, then laughed herself.

Standing by the ropes of the second eric, Goronwy turned at the sound of their laughter and gave them another murderous glare. Deciding not to press their luck any further, they turned their attention once more to the practice combats.

Chelka stared out into the room, pretending to be paying attention like her friends, but her mind was elsewhere. Coming here to Ticca with her brother and his hunting pack, meeting these, alien warrior women, and being accepted as one of them had opened up a whole new world to her. It was like a dream come true, and sometimes she had to scratch herself just to prove that she was awake, and not asleep and still dreaming.

At first Aju'an hadn't been happy with this new state of affairs, probably thinking of their father's wrath when they returned to Meh'gach Keep. But there wasn't a lot he could do about it. Both the Kashallan and his Speir'dina officers accepted that it was perfectly natural for a woman to be a warrior, if she so chose.

They treated her like any of the other fighters, judging her worth by her skill in combat, not by her sex. And though it went against the way things were done in the Yeyen Banai, Aju'an had not been able to stop her, and so with good grace finally resigned himself to her new position.

Being the only female of her species, and a warrior as well, had made her both a curiosity and a celebrity to her new-found Speir'dina friends, a role which she was not unwilling to fill. She had blossomed under the tutelage of the tall, muscular, dark-skinned Marti. Accepted as just another one of Ticca's outlawed defenders, she had willingly taken her place among them without a backward glance.

This was what she had always wanted and prayed for—and she was good at what she did; even Aju'an had to admit that, and praise her. If she had any regret at all, it was only that the old Hunt Leader Overn, who had encouraged and trained her in secret, wasn't here in person to share her triumph.

Much to her surprise, as well, Hunt Leader Tizu himself praised her, and like her brother, Chelka's opinion was sought, when they were plotting the best way to combine the Speir'dina and Warlinga into one fighting unit. The future, to be sure, looked grim and uncertain for all of them.

But whatever it might hold, Chelka knew she would face it with a calm certainty that she was doing what the Great Hunt Leader and the Mother had intended for her, and that was all that mattered.

Chapter Eight

"Sairsa'meh, where are you going?" Pela demanded.

"Anywhere, as long as it's away from here," Sairsa cried. She adjusted the sleeping baby in the shawl upon her back, and stepped closer. Pela remained where she was, back pressed against the closed bedroom door. "Move, Pela, and let me pass."

Pela folded her arms across her chest and stubbornly refused to budge. "No, we need to finish this," she insisted.

Sairsa let out a bark of a laugh, her body quivering with anger. "What's there more to say, Pela? You went behind my back and told that little chit Nona she could resume her duties as our maid. You and the rest of this family think I'm just a crazy with no sense—well, damn the lot of you! Now let me out, or I'll do something we'll both regret later."

"Sister-wives, please!" Amril begged in a high-pitched anxious voice, and stepped between them. Looking from one angry woman to the other, he said, "I'll go tell Nona that we changed our minds again—I really don't mind doing Nona's work. Please don't quarrel, this isn't good for either of you in your conditions—our husband will be very cross with us—please."

"Shut up, Amril, and stay out of this," Pela snapped, without taking her eyes off Sairsa's flushed face.

Sairsa swore a vile Caldoni oath then looked at the worried young man. "Why should he—he's got a right to his opinion, and if he wants to do Nona's work, why should you care so damn much?"

"Because it's not proper, and he really doesn't want to—he's just doing it because you're being unreasoningly stupid about all this."

Sairsa glanced at Amril again. He looked away, unable to meet her blazing green eyes. Her expression hardened, and she nodded to herself, seeing the truth of Pela's words on his face.

Suddenly icily calm she said, "So that's the way of it. Now that you have your love, Pela, you don't care about me anymore. You're back among your own people and you have your man, that's all that matters, hmm? Never mind all that we shared on our journey here—now that we've reached Ticca, all of a sudden my words and opinions are nothing.

"The all-knowing, all-wise Avairei have the answer to everything. You've made a united front against me—because what do I know, a stupid, ignorant stranger to this world who doesn't understand, hmm? Shit, you two make me sick. Now get away from that door and let me out!"

Pela's face crumpled and without another word she stepped away from the door. Sairsa had said what she did in anger. Her remarks had been meant to hurt, but there was also enough truth in her words that Pela could offer no defense against them. When her sister-wife was gone, she sank down on the edge of the bed. Ignoring Amril hovering by her side, she buried her face in her hands and began to cry.

EYES STINGING WITH unshed tears, Sairsa hurried away from their suite. She wasn't sure where she wanted to go or what she wanted to do, but she knew she couldn't hang around and hear all this dragged up again when Dunnagh-Tani came back. They were all united against her, and she felt so alone.

She wiped a tear of self-pity off her cheek. It was true. Pela had her Amril, and Dunnagh had Tani—there was nobody left to love *her*. *Except the baby, and he'll grow up and leave too.*

Sairsa reached around and touched the baby's rounded form against her back. Yes, at least she still had Tameh, for now, and that might have to be enough, because if they were all going to treat her so—so badly, then maybe she should just go.

Rounding the corner of the corridor, Sairsa let out a startled cry as she slammed into a hard, scaly body. She staggered and might have fallen, but the other reached out and steadied her. "Are you all right, Speir'van?" someone asked.

Sairsa blinked, trying to clear her eyes and focus. "Ah, Sa Chelka, I'm sorry. I should have been paying more attention." She stepped back a pace into the shadows, still blinking back tears and hoping no one would notice.

Chelka murmured an apology and gave her a nervous bow. She would have gone on, but Moraga, who was with her, frowned, and followed the other Speir'dina woman into the dimness. "Sairsa? What's wrong?"

Sairsa wiped her eyes, and sniffed. "Nothing, really, Moraga. I'll be all right."

Moraga snorted and put an arm around her shoulder. "You're not crying for nothing, I am thinking. What happened—did you and Dunnagh have a fight? He may be the Ce'awn and the Kashallan and all, but he's still not too high and mighty to get a good tongue-lashing from a Caldoni clanswoman if he needs one."

Sairsa laughed in spite of herself, feeling suddenly better. "Oh, Moraga, you are a dear. No, it's not just him, but everything and everybody. But I don't want to talk about it at the moment. And thanks for your support. I'll let you know if I need any help, in the future—" Sairsa broke off as a new thought struck her.

Suddenly she knew where to go, someplace where none of her mates would come seeking her—a place where she could relax and calm down for a while. She smiled, a sly twinkle coming into her eye. "Moraga, what's Tessa doing right now?"

Moraga blinked at the abrupt change of subject. "I'm not sure. Chelka and me just came from the practice room. I haven't been back to our suite for a couple of hours—why?"

"Oh, I don't know. I just thought I might pay her a visit."

"Mm. When I left, she and Ata Doyan were studying some old manuscript. I don't suppose they'd mind—" Suddenly she laughed, startling the Warlinga beside her. "A safe refuge—is that what you be a-needing', hmm?"

"Something like that," she admitted.

"Come along, then. Chelka and me were going to get something to eat, but that can wait. We'll go see if she wants to take a break from her studies."

Chelka fell in beside them, her head crest flattened. Moraga glanced over at her new friend. Dropping behind Sairsa, as a group of boisterous young Avairei passed them, she said, "I'm starting to understand the complex language of Warlinga facial expressions, tail movements, and head crest positions that you use to communicate with one another. I've seen this expression of yours before. What's wrong, have we confused you again?"

"A little."

Moraga chuckled. "It's quite simple, really," the big woman explained. "The Speir'van there has had a quarrel with her man, and maybe one of her other co-wives. Sairsa needs some place to go and cool down. Tessa is her friend, but she is also the bonded host of the Sweh'an. The Ce'awn and the Spirit don't get on, to put it mildly. Visiting Tessa is the safest place she can go if she wants to avoid her man, because he won't go there unless he absolutely has to. Now do you understand?"

Chelka's head crest rose, and she nodded, giving her friend a faint smile. "I think I do—thank you." Moraga touched her shoulder, then she quickened her pace to catch up with Sairsa. Chelka let the women precede her, still lost in her own musings. She wasn't sure that she wanted to go with the other women to see this Tessa.

They were entering the Avairei part of the keep now, a place where she never went, unless invited by the matriarch, or one of the other Imas. It was much quieter here; a solemn air of contemplation and prayer had replaced the boisterous talk and frantic activity of the rest of the keep. The sound of a hymn wafted towards them from a crossing corridor. All this piety made her feel uncomfortable and out of place.

Thinking of the Sweh'an also made her blood tingle. She recalled with some chagrin that first day, when the Wa'chassey'ul met them. The Spirit's slave had singled her out and addressed her by name. She hadn't really understood what a Wa'chassey'ul was then, but the meeting unnerved her all the same.

Later, when she finally wormed it out of her brother what a Wa'chassey'ul was, she had been even more resolved to avoid the man if she could. But now, here she was trailing after her friend to the very place where that unnatural creature lived. By the Great Hunt Leader, why was she doing this!?

Though she had known Moraga, along with the other warrior women of the Speir'dina, for some time, Chelka suddenly realized that she had never seen the big woman outside the practice room or their mess. She had just assumed that Moraga lived somewhere among the many crowded dorms, even though she had never seen her in any of them.

Until this moment, she hadn't realized that the sturdy, unflappable Moraga was also the sometime servant and female companion of the woman who was the demon spirit's host.

As they approached Moraga's quarters, Chelka could see the Wa'chassey'ul standing silently on guard in the hall outside the suite. Chelka shuddered in spite of herself and hung back, falling even farther behind. At last, noticing that something was wrong, the other two women slowed, waiting for her.

"What's the matter?" Moraga asked when she came up to them.

"Nothing," Chelka said, but her eyes flicked nervously to the Wa'chassey'ul, noticing with macabre fascination the magical sigil on his forehead.

Moraga took her arm, urging her forward. "Don't you be worried about the poor laddy there; he won't bother you none. He be missing his Mistress powerful bad today, and probably won't even notice you." Stepping up to the door, Moraga greeted the big Warlinga. "Hello, Cadrach, we have company. The Speir'van and Sa Chelka have come a-visiting. Is Tessa inside?"

"Yes, Sister Warlinga, the little mistress is within, studying with Ata Doyan, but *my* Mistress is not here," he said, and Chelka shivered at the tone of utter despair that came into the man's voice as he said those last words.

Moraga patted his arm. "I know, Laddy, you miss her very much, but she may come to us anytime, so don't be too sad."

"Do you think so?" he asked hopefully, the light of anticipation once again animating his scarred face.

Moraga shrugged. "Who can say, Cadrach? Your Mistress comes and goes as she pleases, and who are we to know her mind?"

Cadrach nodded solemnly, and opened the door for them. "That is true, Sister, that is true. I must learn more patience—that's what the Ata always tells me, anyway, and I'm sure he is right."

The apartment given over to the Sweh'an and its entourage was a luxurious one. The heavy wicker tables and chairs were of the best quality, and the intricately woven rugs and tapestries were of the finest Loti and Warlinga women's craftsmanship. Ima Ngeal was taking pains to show the

Demon Spirit how much its presence was valued among them, by letting its host live in such accommodations.

Chelka's attention was next drawn to the full-breasted, dark-haired Speir'dina woman sitting at a large worktable strewn with books and writing materials. A middle-aged Avairei priest, the host's companion and teacher, was seated beside her with an open manuscript laid out between them. As the door opened, the two looked up from their work. Recognizing Sairsa, the woman rose, holding out her hands and calling her by name.

Sairsa smiled wanly and crossed to her friend, embracing her for a long moment. At last releasing her, Tessa held her friend at arm's length and surveyed her with a critical eye. "You've been crying," she observed. "What's wrong?"

Sairsa let out a nervous laugh, but was unable to meet her friend's gaze. She wiped at her eyes and sniffed. "Is it that obvious?" She shrugged, trying to make light of it, but not convincing anyone, not even herself. "I just had an argument with Pela, and this morning Dunnagh and I-I needed to take a break."

Tessa's face clouded at Sairsa's unspoken implication, and she let out a mirthless laugh. "Well, never mind that for now," she said briskly. "I'm glad you've come. Doyan and I need to take a break ourselves. We've been at it for hours, and a bowl of spice tea would be very welcome. Please sit down, everyone."

Doyan rose and bowed to their guests, then, addressing Tessa, he said, "I'll see to getting the tea, My Dear."

"I can get it, Ata," Moraga offered.

He shook his head and smiled. "No, sit down with our guests. I'll see to it this time." As he moved to go, Tessa reached out and touched his arm. "Come back and join us," she suggested.

He hesitated. "Yes, do join us. That is, if you aren't too busy, or intimidated by the company of so many women," Sairsa said, her green eyes sparkling.

Doyan laughed softly, and shook his head. "No, I am not intimidated, as you suggest. That would hardly be the case, serving here at Ticca as I have done for so many years. I merely thought you might prefer that I leave."

Sairsa shook her head. "No, I just need a break from my family. There are no deep feminine mysteries that I want to share. So if you would like, come back, please."

Doyan considered a moment, then bowed to them. "Thank you, I believe I will come back. I must confess, I haven't had the pleasure of talking to Sa Chelka since her arrival, and you, Speir'van, are always pleasant company."

When he was gone, Tessa resumed her seat and turned to her Warlinga visitor. She smiled. "Though we haven't been formally introduced, I have heard much about you from Moraga and other visitors. I'm very glad to meet you in person finally, Sa Chelka; you are most welcome here."

"Thank you, Sa Tessa."

Sairsa shifted the baby from her back to cradle him in her lap. He was awake, and was making his usual frantic noises as he searched for her breast. Sairsa sighed. "Just a minute, Little Seal, it's coming," she assured him, as she laid aside her shawl and put her nipple in his mouth. Sairsa leaned back and let out a contented sigh, settling herself more comfortably in her seat. She looked around at the other women, and smiled at the expressions of fascination upon their faces.

Tessa watched the baby nurse with a mixture of envy and longing in her eyes, finally she said, "Sairsa, it's been a while since you've brought Tameh with you on one of your visits, and you know how my bondmate likes to see the little one. Would you mind if I summon it?"

Sairsa shook her head. "No, I don't mind, but give him a minute to finish his meal first. He won't take long; he thinks he's starving, but he ate just a little while ago, so he won't want much." She looked down at her son, her eyes soft and loving. "He's probably upset, the poor dear, hearing his loved ones fighting, and can't understand why." She sighed, sinking back into her earlier despondent mood.

Moraga sniffed with indignation. "I know what you said before 'bout letting him be, but I think I had better have a serious talk with my Caldoni kinsman. It's obvious to me he needs one. Getting far too big for his britches, or should I say kilt, he is, to make you feel so bad like."

Sairsa giggled, shaking her head in amusement at an image of the big woman turning her husband over her muscular thigh and giving him a well-needed spanking for his behavior. "Oh, Moraga, you are wonderful," she gasped. "You do make me feel better."

Tessa smiled in sympathy. "I can't say the idea of seeing Dunnagh-Tani get a comeuppance doesn't have its appeal to me too, and—" she gave Moraga an appraising look, "I'd bet money that you'd be the one to teach him the error of his ways, Moraga, but I'm missing something here." Turning back to Sairsa, she asked, "What's he done now to get you upset, and Moraga snarling like a protective mama bear?"

Sairsa sobered. Removing the now pacified baby from her breast, she rose and laid him in Tessa's waiting arms. Glancing at the closed door, she sat down and said, "It isn't just him, it's all of them. They all think I'm a crazy breeding woman with delusions, and I'm getting sick of arguing with them about it."

"I don't understand," Tessa repeated.

"It all started several weeks ago," Sairsa said, "before the Dingay woman tried to kill him. Anyway, I came in one day, and I found Dunnagh-Tani sitting with our new maid on his lap, and the little chit had her hand up under his kilt."

At a strangled sound from Moraga, Sairsa held up her hand. "I know what you're thinking, and at first I thought that too, and was terribly hurt and angry, but—I don't think it's his fault. There's something odd about that girl—she's not what she seems. I'm sure of it. When I caught them together, she was also trying to get him to drink something—and I'm sure it was poisoned—but no one will believe me!" she cried.

"And after it happened, like a fool I dumped the drink into the chamber pot before anyone could test it; so now everyone thinks I imagined it."

"But why, Speir'van, do the Holy One and your co-wives think you would lie about such a thing? Attempts on his life have been made before," Chelka said.

"They don't think I'm lying, exactly, Sa Chelka. They think that because of my 'delicate condition' I was mistaken. You see, Nona is Ngeal's own niece. Pela and Amril think it would cause all kinds of trouble if we dismiss the girl. And my husband, the big boob, thinks he's to blame for what almost happened that day, so he doesn't want to talk to Ima Ngeal about the girl, either.

"Dunnagh-Tani thinks, because he has tasted the girl and she gave him her oath, that what I say about her couldn't possibly be true. I don't know how she's managed to trick even the Khutani, but she has. There's something wrong with that girl, and I don't care what Tani or my Avairei co-wives say—I don't want her in our suite.

"For a time, Amril was humoring me, and was doing the maid's chores himself, but today Pela informed me that she asked Nona to resume her duties, because it wasn't *seemly* for Amril to continue to do a maid's work. When I protested—we had a big fight. I don't know what to do now—"

Sairsa broke off as Doyan reentered the chamber, carrying a large tray of refreshments. He set his burden down on the worktable and turned to face them. Studying their intent faces, he hesitated before sitting down. "Am I interrupting something important?"

Sairsa shook her head, but was reluctant to continue the conversation in the Avairei's presence. When she remained silent, Moraga said, "Sit down, Ata. We were talking about the Speir'van's maid Nona. Maybe you can help. What do you know about the girl?"

Doyan took a moment to consider while he played host and passed around the tea and cakes he brought. When they were all served, he sat down next to Tessa, and looked at their expectant faces. "I know very little of the girl," he admitted. "She is Ngeal's niece, of course, but I had little to do with the training of the novices; my work here was with the old Lore Master before he died.

"When I used to visit him in his room, I would see the girl occasionally. She was Tomina's maid then, and—" He broke off as Sairsa choked, then set down her tea-bowl with a loud thunk.

Sairsa rose without being aware that she did so. She glanced around wildly, her whole body trembling now. "Sairsa, what's wrong?" Moraga asked, but the woman ignored her, her attention focused on some inner vision.

Suddenly Chelka felt a cold chill run down her spine. The atmosphere around them had suddenly changed. Something had come into the room—an invisible presence that nonetheless dominated its ambiance with a power that set her blood to tingling, and her teeth on edge.

Chelka turned her attention from the Speir'van to the one called Tessa. The Warlinga woman swallowed hard as she saw cold obsidian eyes watching her speculatively. No, this wasn't the woman Tessa—the Demon Spirit had entered its host. Her hand shaking Chelka set down her tea bowl and bowed to the Spirit.

Tess-weh gave her a feral grin, then turned her hard eyes away from the Warlinga, and focused her otherworldly gaze on the woman standing in the center of the room

"Sairsa'meh, My Jewel," the spirit cooed. Tess-weh hadn't spoken much above a whisper, but Sairsa jerked as if she had been startled by a loud noise.

She turned, wide-eyed, trying to focus her attention on the possessed woman's face. "Tess-weh?"

"Yes, My Treasure. I am here now."

"What—" she began, but the Demon cut her off.

"You must remember, My Precious. I have told you already what you need to know. I can say no more—think!"

Sairsa shuddered, and closed her eyes. Remember—yes, there was something— She strained, trying to pull the memory out of the quagmire of her churning thoughts. Something—

That first day they had entered Ticca—there had been an argument between her husband and Tess-weh that had ended in physical violence—Sairsa had stepped in—and when things were settled, the spirit had given her a kiss and a gift before it left its host...

When you are in doubt, always trust your inner feelings. No matter what others do or say, trust in yourself, for you do have some of the gift, my Sairsa-meh. Always believe that. The words thundered into her awareness, as if they had been spoken to her by the Sweh'an just moments before. And Nona had been Tomina's maid— Sairsa gasped, her eyes going wide. "Ata Doyan, was Nona Tomina's maid just before the Ima assigned her to our suite?"

"I'm not sure. She may have been. As I said, I have never had much to do with the training of the young. Why?"

Instead of answering him, she glanced back at Tess-weh. Her eyes flicked down to the baby still held in the other woman's arms, her indecision plain upon her face. "Tess-weh—what should I do?"

Tess-weh shook her head. "I can't tell you that, My Jewel. You must decide for yourself—and soon."

Sairsa swallowed hard, then, making her decision, she nodded. She glanced down at her son. "Will you take care of him for me?"

"You would trust me with him?"

"You're my friend. Yes."

"Then go do what you must. The babe will be safe with me—I swear it to you."

"Thank you, Tess-weh—for everything." Then, before the two warrior women had time to register their surprise, she was out the door and gone.

"What—" Moraga began.

The Spirit let out a mirthless chuckle. "Your wits are slow today, My Sweet, but perhaps you and Sa Chelka should follow—she may need your assistance."

Moraga clamped her mouth shut on any further questions and rose. Motioning for the bewildered Chelka to follow her; they raced after the retreating Sairsa.

When they were gone, Tess-weh looked down at the baby she was holding. She caressed his silky red cap of hair and chuckled to herself. "Oh, My Pretty Little Jewel, if your father only knew where you were right now—he would definitely not be pleased." She laughed even louder, and kissed his cheek. "But of course knowing that pleases me, very much indeed. And if my Sairsa'meh is quick, he will once more be in my debt, and I will be sure to let him know that, won't I, hmm, My Treasure?"

The baby looked at her owlishly for a moment, then closed his eyes and put his thumb in his tiny pink mouth, sucking lazily as he drifted off to sleep.

Bemused, Doyan refilled his bowl and sat back down beside her. As he sipped the spicy drink, he studied the spirit-possessed woman and the baby out of the corner of his eye. Still watching little Tameh, she reached out a hand and caressed Doyan's velvety fur with a slow sensuous motion. He shivered, but didn't pull away. "That was most cleverly done, My Treasure," she purred.

Doyan laughed nervously. "Thank you for the compliment, Honored Spirit, but I don't know what I have done to deserve your praise."

She looked at him then, her dark eyes smoldering with unreadable emotions. "You gave her the key she needed to unlock an enigma."

When he still continued to frown in bewilderment, the Sweh'an shook her head and chuckled deep in her throat, letting her hand slide over his silky shoulder and chest, rhythmically stroking him, aware that her seductive behavior was now adding to his confusion. Cradling the baby in the crook of one arm, she rose, pulling him to his feet beside her. "Come, lie down with me while the baby sleeps."

He hesitated, his eyes flicking to the outside door, where the Wa'chassey'ul was waiting. The poor creature would have been aware of his Mistress's presence from the first moment she manifested in this physical reality, and would be longing to be with her. "If you need to—I could keep the baby with me out here—"

"No, Ata, I will see to my slave later," she snapped. Then, softening her tone, she added, "This is for my H'an as much as it is for me." She looked down at the sleeping Tameh and smiled. "We wish to pretend—to imagine—what it would be like to be mother and wife for this stolen moment—not what we are. So you will come, hmm?"

Doyan nodded, his eyes moist. He lifted her hand to his lips. "Your will, Honored One, I am yours to command as always," he breathed, and followed her into their bedroom.

Chapter Nine

Sairsa hurried down the hallway, driven by an uneasy sense of urgency, only vaguely aware of the two warrior women pounding down the corridor in her wake. Nona had been the Dingay woman's maid—and Pela, trusting, blind Pela, asked the girl to return to her duties in their suite. Oh, Holy Mother, Sairsa prayed, she hoped that she would be in time!

She didn't know what the maid planned, or how Tomina managed to corrupt her and fool the Khutani, but all that didn't matter now. What mattered was that she had regained a fading confidence in herself.

She wasn't crazy, or mistaken about her suspicions—and the Sweh'an tried to warn her weeks ago. Oh, Gods, how had she forgotten—she must tell them—make them listen...

Almost running by the time she reached her quarters, Sairsa burst through the door and stopped, looking around wild-eyed. The room was empty, but on a low table in the center of a cluster of chairs, a jug of spiced tea and several tea-bowls, along with a tray of sweet cakes, lay waiting as if someone expected company.

Sairsa held on to the doorframe, catching her breath. Where was Pela, or Amril? Sairsa closed the door, and listened. Was that a noise in the bedroom? "Pela?"

Behind the closed door the noise stopped, but there was no answering response to her call. "Pela," Sairsa called in a louder voice. "Damn it, answer me. I want to talk to you about—" She broke off, feeling suddenly uneasy. *I'm not imagining things; I heard someone in there. Why doesn't whoever it is answer me?*

Crossing the room in several quick strides, she flung open the inner door. Her next question died unvoiced; Nona was standing motionless in the center of the room. The girl must have been changing the sheets when she heard Sairsa call. Now she stood clutching an empty pillowcase in one hand, a pile of dirty bedding on the rug by her feet.

"You," Sairsa's voice dripped with contempt.

Nona fixed her with a look that was as impenetrable as stone. She bowed, then said, "Speir'van?"

"Get out," Sairsa growled.

The maid smiled. A mocking gleam coming into her obsidian eyes; she dropped the pillowcase, but remained where she was. "I think not," she purred. "The first wife has given me permission to resume my duties. And there is nothing you can do about it." Her mouth twisted into a smirk of disdain as she saw Sairsa's face flush.

Growing suddenly calm, Sairsa stepped further into the room, and gave a derisive bark of a laugh as she met the Avairei's eye, and held it. "You mean there's nothing I can do, because you're the Ima Matri's own niece, and because they all think I'm crazy. Is that it?"

Nona's smile widened, suddenly becoming predatory. "Yes, something like that. They won't believe you, and they are tired of humoring your *delusions*."

Sairsa nodded. "You're very clever," she agreed. "I haven't been able to figure it all out yet, but I think I know enough already to make them listen to me, especially when I remind them whose maid you were before you got your aunt to assign you to us." At the look of fear that crossed the Avairei's face, Sairsa smiled in triumph. "Yes, I think that bit of information will interest the Khutani Makers very much. My husband and co-wives will listen to me this time."

"I think not, Meddlesome Witch," the maid snarled, in a voice much deeper than was her wont. "I have been told how you spoiled this slave's other attempt to carry out my will, but this time you will not succeed."

Sairsa's eyes widened, suddenly realizing her mistake she cursed herself for a fool, and backed towards the door. The maid laughed and raised her arm; the door slammed shut behind Sairsa with a loud bang. She jumped, glancing in astonishment at the door, then swung back to face her adversary.

The maid drew another sigil in the air between them; Sairsa felt her body grow rigid as if she had been turned into stone. "Your meddling can't be permitted to continue. You and your troublesome kin cannot be allowed to spoil plans that have been centuries in the making. You and the rest of the traitorous western slime will die—and most painfully," the wizard promised.

Sairsa's green eyes flashed with defiance. She couldn't speak, but Barak felt her resistance and the wizard growled an angry curse. "You need to be taught a lesson, insolent slave, for that. You will beg me to kill you before I am through, mutant."

Sairsa gasped; pain exploded in every part of her being. Her body felt as if it was on fire, while horrible images of torture and dying flooded her mind. The Umwira's magic was tearing her apart; drowning her in a sea of agony. So much pain, so much fear—never had she dreamed that something like this could be possible, let alone be happening to her.

Desperately she fought, searching for something to cling to, something with which to re-braid the unraveling strands of her sanity. In the chaos, a fleeting image of her son swirled by—oh, Gods, Tameh! If this monster defeated her, Dunnagh-Tani, her baby, Pela—all those she loved would be lost. She must hang on—fight him—

FLINGING THE DOOR OPEN, Moraga grunted in surprise. "Sairsa?"

Chelka stepped into the room behind her friend and closed the door. Her head crest rose. "Where did she go? We stopped for only a minute to answer San Nathan's question. How could she have gone anywhere else without us seeing her?"

Moraga shook her head. "I don't know." She glanced around the empty room again, feeling a cold chill run down her spine. "Sairsa?" she called, louder this time. She listened. Nothing. This was odd, very odd indeed.

"Maybe we should return to your quarters, Sister Warlinga, and ask the Spirit to help—"

"Tess-weh wouldn't tell us any more than she already has. No, we have to figure this out for ourselves—"

Both women turned, as a noise out in the hall caught their attention. The door opened; Pela stopped just inside the doorway, Amril and his sister Sagas right behind her. All three Avairei stared in surprise at the two women already in the room.

Chelka's head crest dipped and her scales greened in embarrassment. "Ima Pela, Ima Sagas—uh, we were following the Speir'van back to her suite. She was not far in front of us—we stopped for only a moment—but when we arrived—she was not here."

Sagas scowled, eyeing the unexpected guests suspiciously, but Pela herself seemed unperturbed by the women's appearance. She took a seat by the table laden with refreshments and waved all her guests to comfortable chairs around the table.

"If Sairsa'meh was just ahead of you, I'm sure she will be here soon. She probably saw a friend she needed to speak to. Please join us," she said with a gracious smile, and began to pour out the tea into the waiting bowls.

The two warriors exchanged anxious glances, but remained where they were, still uncertain what to do. Looking at the closed bedroom door, Chelka whispered, "Could she be in there?"

Moraga shrugged, then raised her voice and called once more, "Sairsa?" Hearing no reply, Moraga started towards the bedroom when the door opened and Nona walked out, the bundle of dirty bedding in her arms.

Bumping the door closed with her hip, the maid bobbed her head at the Imas, shifted the pile of bedding in her arms, and glanced down shyly as all eyes in the room focused upon her.

Sagas transferred her frown to the girl. "Nona, have you seen the Speir'van?"

The maid looked up and shook her head. "No, Ima, I haven't—perhaps she came and went away again while I was gone to fetch the tea."

Pela smiled, then addressed her unexpected guests once more. "Please sit down, Sa Chelka, Moraga; have some tea. I'm sure my sister-wife will be back soon." Setting down the pitcher, she brought her bowl to her lips.

Chelka hesitated, ice water was still running down her spine. There was something wrong here; she felt it, and she knew Moraga did too, but what? Well, maybe if she sat for a moment and had some tea—

Tea!

"Ima, no!" Chelka shouted and leaped to slap the bowl from Pela's hand as she began to drink. Pela stared down at the spicy liquid forming tiny droplets of light on the velvet darkness of her fur; then she glanced up at the Warlinga, a bewildered expression on her face.

Sagas and Amril jumped to their feet. "Sa Chelka, what's the meaning of this?" Sagas spluttered.

Chelka blinked, astonished by her own daring. She had reacted without conscious thought, but why? She shook her head; her scales becoming even a brighter shade of green. Hesitantly, she began to apologize—

Suddenly Moraga muttered a curse and lunged for the bedroom door. She shoved the maid aside, knocking her to the floor in her haste. Nona let out a squawk of protest, the bundle of bedding scattering about her as she fell. Ignoring the maid, the big woman flung open the bedroom door and stepped inside.

With a strangled cry, she disappeared, returning in a moment with a half-conscious Sairsa supported against one shoulder.

Sagas gaped, starting forward then stopped. "What's going on here? What's the meaning of this?" she snapped, her eyes flicking from Moraga to the now sobbing maid.

"What's going on is murder, or at least an attempt at it," Moraga snarled, her blue eyes cold with menace as she helped the gasping Sairsa into a chair. "Sairsa, what happened? What did she do to you?" Moraga demanded, shaking her gently, trying to get the dazed woman to focus on her face.

Sairsa gazed blindly into space, her eyes haunted, unable to speak. Moraga shook her again, this time with more force, but her vision still remained focused on some inner terror that only she could see.

Moraga swore in Caldoni. Letting Sairsa sink back into the chair, she rounded on the maid who, though still sniffling, had picked herself up off the floor and was gathering the bedding while watching her intently out of the corner of one eye.

"Umwira Bitch, what did you do to her?" Moraga clenched her fists, and took a step towards the now cowering maid.

"What are you saying, Stupid Warlinga?" Sagas cried. "This child—"

Moraga swung back to Sagas her fist raised. Eyes wide, Sagas stepped back. Moraga lowered her hand, but continued to glare at the angry priestess. "Stupid, am I?" she snorted. "Sometimes you Avairei can be so blind that you can't see what's right in front of your own pointy noses. Look at the Speir'van, Ima, LOOK AT HER! Seen that expression before? Like after the attack by the underground river, maybe?"

Sagas narrowed her eyes in annoyance, but she did as the big woman demanded. For a long moment she gazed at the vacant-eyed Sairsa. "Yes, by the Holy Mother, I have seen that look before. It is the mark of Umwira sorcery," she muttered.

"But how is this possible—she is Ngeal's own niece—" She swung back to the Avairei maid, her stern expression commanding an answer—an explanation.

Nona shook her head, sobbing even louder. "No, oh, no, Ima, don't believe her—I would never hurt anyone, especially not the Holy One's wife! I would never hurt the Speir'van—"

Totally bewildered, Sagas looked from the sobbing girl to the angry warrior woman then to the dazed Sairsa. She shook her head. "This is all crazy. I don't know what's happened here; why would Ngeal's niece harm anyone? She's taken the oath and is as loyal as the rest of us."

"Ima Ngeal's niece might not have a reason, but Tomina Dingay's maid might have, don't you agree, Nona? I certainly do," Chelka said. "The blue snows will be here and gone soon, then we can leave and tell the world what we know. Does your Master grow impatient because the Kashallan isn't dead yet, hmm?"

That last had been a lucky hit, and Chelka was caught off guard by the maid's swift reaction to her remark. Hurling the bundle of unfolding bedding into the Warlinga's face, Nona lunged at her, gripping a very lethal-looking dagger that she produced out of the folds of her kilt.

The mass of bedding hit her squarely, blinding her in its smothering folds. Snarling, Chelka grunted in surprise and stepped backwards, tripping over one of the chairs. She sprawled, clawing desperately at the sheet covering her face.

That fall had been a blessing in disguise, Chelka decided a moment later as she felt a slight breeze above her and saw the maid's blade pass harmlessly overhead. She rolled, flinging off the fabric and springing to her feet, the overturned chair, for the moment, between her and her adversary.

The dagger was one of the Speir'dina blades, long and extremely sharp. How had the maid come by such a precious thing? In itself, the dagger was a formidable weapon, but had the girl poisoned the blade as well? *Best be careful* Chelka warned herself as she sidestepped another slash. Best play a waiting game until she saw a good opportunity to disarm her.

The wizard who was controlling Nona's body leapt over the chair and attacked again. With a strength that was far more than that of a small Avairei priestess, the Umwira pressed the Warlinga mercilessly with the dagger and the mind magic. If she had not been warrior-trained, the wizard would have finished her in the first unexpected onslaught.

Trying to keep one eye on her opponent and the other on her surroundings, Chelka circled, dodging around the furniture and other obstacles in the room. It wasn't easy; the maid was fast—incredibly fast.

The Warlinga was unarmed, and in the cramped conditions of the chamber she couldn't use her tail, or greater physical strength to best advantage.

Chelka fought on with a grim determination; the Umwira's horrible images of torture clouding her mind and slowing her reflexes. If the Umwira wizard had been using a stronger body, Chelka suspected that her inexperience would probably have cost her, her life by now. But even with the Umwira's strength and cunning, the Avairei's body wasn't good enough to do more than hold its own against her warrior's skills.

Neither of them, for the moment, was able to gain the upper hand and finish the struggle. So they continued to circle, using the mind-magic even more than their physical bodies to determine the outcome of this uneven combat. Feeling her body and mind respond instinctively to the challenge, Chelka fought, her blood singing. She reveled in the combat, meeting the Umwira's physical and mental attacks head-on, knowing that for just such a conflict her race had been bred.

Chelka leapt over an obstacle, then hearing a strangled cry from somewhere out of her line of sight, Chelka hesitated, her attention caught and held for just long enough for her opponent to get in under her guard and thrust the dagger at her unprotected side. With a startled yelp, Chelka flung herself backwards and tripped over the table, upending its contents.

Her hand flew out, groping for something to stop her fall. At the same moment, Nona gave a triumphant cry and lunged forward, intending to make the kill.

As she felt herself losing her balance, Chelka's outstretched hands closed over the dark stone pendant that hung around the priestess's neck. Her body a dead weight, Chelka fell, snapping the pendant's cord from around the girl's neck as she came down hard on her back, the maid sprawling on top of her.

Snarling in sudden panic, the Warlinga rolled, shoving the maid off her, and sprang to her feet, still clutching the broken necklace in one hand. She stepped back, and, kicking out at her, slammed the half-risen Avairei to the rug. Nona hit the floor hard, sliding several feet backwards, the dagger flying out of her hand.

Letting out an unearthly cry, Nona staggered to her feet, breathing heavily. Chelka tensed, but the Avairei ignored her, making no attempt to resume the combat. Nona put up a hand, and touched her lacerated throat. She whimpered then looked around, wild eyed, as if searching for something.

At last she spied the pendant she sought in the Warlinga's hand. "Give it back," she cried, and lunged for the valued prize.

Chelka stepped back, red eyes mocking, dangling the pendant just out of reach. The possessed girl whined and made another attempt to regain the jewel. But without the dark stone, the Umwira had little control over the Avairei's body, and Chelka fended off her attempts easily.

Circling around the wreckage of the room, Chelka taunted the maid as she inched closer and closer to her goal. Finally she stopped, holding out the necklace in invitation. "Want it, Umwira Filth? Come take it, if you can."

Nona let out a strangled cry and rushed forward, but just before her hands could close over the stone, Chelka turned and tossed the jewel into the brazier near the wall.

Nona screamed, and suddenly a blinding flash of light and a deafening roar rocked the room. Chelka felt herself being picked up, and flung across the room. A chair splintered under her as she landed. In the silence that followed, the Warlinga blinked up at the ceiling, taking in great lungfuls of air.

When she could breathe again she picked herself off the floor and looked around. Was anyone else hurt—where were Moraga and Sairsa? The room was a mess. Broken crockery, splintered furniture, and other items were strewn everywhere. Gods, what was that thing—what had she just done?

From out in the hall she could hear excited shouting; nearby someone was sobbing, but she couldn't see who it was.

Sagas was sitting in the far corner, looking dazed but uninjured. Chelka broke off her inspection of the room as Moraga poked her head around the bedroom door and peered in awe at the chaos. She gave Chelka a crooked grin. "Are you all right?"

"I think so." Still listening with a part of her mind to the quiet sobbing somewhere nearby, she asked, "Where's Sairsa? Is she all right?"

"I brought her back in here when the fighting started, but as to whether she's all right—" Moraga shrugged. "The Umwira has done something to her—I seen the signs before. The Ce'awn or the Makers will have to see to her before we can know for sure."

Chelka shivered, then saw something out of the corner of her eye that returned her attention to the outer room. Nona was standing over the brazier, looking down into the ashes, an eerie keening coming out of her throat. Chelka shivered; the sound sent cold chills down her spine.

Unable to move she watched in helpless fascination as the grieving Nona raised the dagger and plunged it hilt deep into her own chest. As the girl fell, her face contorted with such a despairing agony that Chelka knew the sight would haunt her nightmares for years to come.

Chapter Ten

"What the— Gods!" Nathan stood in the outer doorway, staring at the wreckage and shaking his head in bewilderment. Behind him, several other people crowded into the doorway. Spotting Moraga and Chelka standing in the mess, he snapped, "What happened?"

Chelka stared at him speechless for a moment. "Umwira." She shook her head, trying to get the rest out, but unable to explain any further.

"The Kashallan's maid tried to kill Sairsa. Chelka fought her—then threw some Umwira magic thing that she had been wearing into the fire. It exploded," Moraga supplied. "We need to tell the Ce'awn—get some help—" She motioned behind her.

Nathan swore and crossed the room in a few quick steps, kicking aside obstacles that got in his way. In the bedroom door he stopped, gazing in horror at the woman sitting on the edge of the bed. She looked up at him, her eyes haunted, barely aware of his regard. He felt his guts knot in fear. Oh, Gods, he knew that look—knew what had happened to her. For just a moment he clung to the doorframe, remembering another woman, another attack. Tessa—Sairsa—oh, Gods, why?

Suddenly looking around, he demanded, "Where's the baby? Did that creature—"

Moraga shook her head. "The babe wasn't here, thank the Gods. He's all right."

"Where is he then?"

"Sairsa left him with Tess-weh before she came back to warn Pela about the maid."

Nathan swore. He didn't even want to consider what the Kashallan would have to say about that little turn of events. Dunnagh-Tani wasn't going to like it, but he had too much else to deal with now to worry about that little problem.

"San Nathan, help me—somebody help me," a tear-choked voice behind him cried. "Pela, my Pela, I think she's dying!"

Nathan swung round, spotting Amril finally where he sat in the corner behind an overturned chair, a shuddering Pela clutched in his arms. He looked up at the big man, frightened eyes pleading. Nathan crossed to him and crouched down beside the priest. He reached out a tentative hand and touched the woman's arm. She was trembling violently, her breath coming in ragged gasps, her pregnant belly heaving with effort at every breath. "What happened?" Nathan demanded, but the distraught young man could only shake his head in bewilderment.

"I don't know—I'm not sure," Amril finally choked out, shaking his head once again, oily tears streaming down his face.

"She must have drunk some of the tea before I knocked the bowl out of her hand."

Nathan glanced up frowning. Chelka was standing over them, looking down at the Avairei her tail flicking back and forth anxiously. "What tea—make some sense, woman."

"The Speir'van told us that she suspected the maid of trying to poison the Kashallan once before—but she said no one would believe her, because Nona was Ngeal's niece. When I saw Ima Pela start to drink some tea that the maid had just brought I-I thought—I tried—" She broke off, glancing once more at the suffering woman.

"Shit!" He would be damned if he'd let the cursed Umwira win this round. Not without a fight anyway. Looking over at the curious people in the doorway, he caught sight of a large figure at the back of the crowd. "Tarla, get in here, now!"

Pushing past the onlookers, Tarla hurried to his commander's side. Looking down at Pela clutched in the priest's arms, he blinked, his mouth falling open in surprise.

"Don't just stand there, you big Amadan, pick her up," Nathan snapped impatiently. "We need to get her down to the pools and the Khutani for help. Now move!"

Tarla bent and gently took Pela from Amril's unresisting embrace. He straightened and headed for the door, the priest scrambled to his feet and followed.

When he was gone, Nathan sighed and rubbed a hand across his face. He looked at the women. "You two all right?" They nodded. "Where's the maid?"

Chelka pointed to a crumpled form on the floor by the still smoking brazier. "She killed herself after I threw that necklace of hers in the fire."

Nathan grunted and walked over to look down at the body. When he satisfied himself that she was dead and would give no further trouble, he returned to the women. "She'll keep, but we'd better collect Sairsa and get down to the pools. She needs some looking after, too." He made a sour face, feeling his guts knot up even tighter at what else he needed to do. "And I'll have to make a report to the Maker Dievris as soon as things settle down, so you can tell me what happened on the way."

When they were gone, Sagas rose shakily to her feet. Stepping around the wreckage she crossed the room and peered down at Nona's tortured body. She hugged her arms to her thin chest; she felt so cold, and empty inside. Sagas could hear other people in the room now. Speaking in hushed voices, they moved about quietly, clearing away the mess. She paid them no heed, continuing to stare down numbly at the girl, her own body as rigid as stone.

Lost in her dark reverie, she started as she felt a hand on her shoulder. Sagas jerked her head around, an angry retort dying on her lips as she recognized who had come over to her.

"Sagas," Tizu said gently, stepping closer and drawing her into his strong arms. She held herself rigid in his embrace for a long moment, but when he refused to pull back and leave her to her grief, she gave in and slumped against him, laying her head on his shoulder. Enfolded in his capable arms, she let go for a moment, her body trembling, wracked by silent sobs.

Finally she forced herself back under rigid control, and pushed herself far enough away to look up into his ugly alien face. Sagas stared up at him, her eyes searching for an answer that she knew he didn't have. She asked anyway, "Oh, Hukiyo, how? Nona was Ngeal's own niece. She wasn't an Umwira changeling. And she was so young and innocent, to end up like this. Oh, Mother, if the enemy is so strong that they can do something like this to our children, no one is safe—what's going to happen to us?" Sagas broke off, shaking her head, trying to hold back her tears.

Tizu touched her face with an aching tenderness, pushing back her tangled braidlets. "I don't know, Sagas," he said, his voice dull with weariness. "Since coming to Timorna, I'm not sure I know anything for certain any more. Everything's in flux, changing so rapidly that all we can do is hang on, try to keep our sanity—and survive." He hugged her close, a tormented pleading in his eyes.

She nodded, suddenly feeling both shy and a little frightened by the unspoken implications of his offer, and her own growing response to it. She pushed away, releasing herself from his embrace, aware of his disappointment. "I've got to go," she murmured, unable to meet his eyes.

He sighed, letting his hands fall back to his sides. "Shall I have one of my men escort you back to your room, while I see to this mess?"

She shook her head, still not able to look directly at him, feeling the lump of grief clogging her throat once more. She swallowed, glancing down at the stiffening corpse of the maid. "I'd better go to Ngeal. She would have heard something of this trouble by now. I need to be with her—to tell her myself what's happened, and what the Dingay woman did."

"All right, she'd probably appreciate hearing this from you rather than from me or one of the others. Tell her to send me word about what to do with Nona's body."

She nodded and had started to turn away when he put a restraining arm on her shoulder, and turned her around to face him. Lifting her jaw, he forced her to look at him once again. "Give Ngeal my condolences. Tell her that I'll come to make my report as soon as I can. But when I'm finished, I'm coming to find you, and then I won't take no for an answer so easily."

He focused on her face as she took in his meaning; his eyes as dark and determined as her own. She met his look with an angry glare for a long moment. His expression never wavered, and at last it was Sagas herself who looked away. Without a word, she swung round and headed out the door.

DUNNAGH-TANI RAISED his head, listening. He'd been dozing beside Tasheyna-Rinn when he'd thought he heard someone calling him—

"CE'AWN, YOU OUT THERE?" Tarla's foghorn-like voice rang out across the cavern. In his arms, Tasheyna stirred, whimpering. "CE'AWN?"

Beside them Conal-Tiel sat up, yawning and rubbing his eyes. "What is it?" he murmured. "What's wrong?"

"I don't know," Dunnagh-Tani said; disentangling himself with care from the half-awake Tasheyna-Rinn.

"That was Tarla, wasn't it? Gods, I'd know that bellow anywhere," Conal grumbled.

Dunnagh grunted, but before he could speculate on what the big armachd wanted, he heard another, fainter voice crying out to him, its tone washing away the sluggishness of sleep, like being drenched in ice water. "Husband? Oh, husband, please answer—please come—Pela, our Pela—"

Dunnagh's head jerked up, focusing on the place where the sound was coming from. He squinted through the dimness of the swirling mists, trying to make out who was over there by the kashallan pool. "I'm here, Amril," he shouted, "what's wrong?"

Tasheyna let out a frightened wail. "Amsi?"

Cursing himself for his lapse, he laid a soothing hand on the new kashallan, murmuring his assurances that everything was all right. Conal-Tiel reached over and gathered the woman into his arms, his tentacles forming a link to comfort the young symbiont. He jerked his head towards the distant shore. "Go on, I'll see to Tasheyna-Rinn."

"Oh, husband, come," the priest cried. "Pela's dying—the Umwira—oh, please hurry!"

"I'm coming," he called out. With powerful strokes, he swam out into the dark water, afraid of what he might find when he reached the shallows on the other side.

Chapter Eleven

Ngeal stared numbly at the brightly colored tapestry against the far wall of her outer chamber. The Loti artist who wove it probably hoped to convey the merciful love of the Great Mother with her art. Usually Ngeal found the piece comforting, but not tonight. *Oh, Holy Mother, how could you have let such a terrible thing happen? Nona—such a good and innocent child—oh, by all the Gods, why?*

When Sagas came to her with this latest tale of Umwira treachery, she had been stunned—hadn't been able to take it all in. It was too terrible to believe. How could she have been so wrong about so many things?

She ignored the sendings of the Holy Ones when they tried to seek her aid. She lived and worked for years with an Umwira changeling as one of her trusted advisors, and she unthinkingly allowed a girl who was like a daughter to her to be used by the Umwira—right under her nose.

Ngeal took in a ragged breath, her throat tight. *I'm getting too old for this job,* she thought, hating herself for her failures. *Perhaps it's time to retire, let someone who hears the voice of the Khutani more clearly take over—someone like Sagas—*

"Mistress, can I get you something? You should eat, or have some tea," Sondi pleaded.

Ngeal made a face. *Tea, indeed.* The way she felt, it was too bad all that poisoned brew had been spilled in the struggle; she would willingly drink a bowl of it right now. "No, thank you, Sondi, I'll take some refreshment later."

"You should rest and eat, Teacher," Sagas said, adding her own voice to the maid's entreaties.

Ngeal scowled at them both, but was saved the effort of answering when they heard voices talking in the hall outside her door. Earlier, to allow her some privacy, Tizu had posted a guard outside her door to keep her from being bombarded with questions from other Avairei.

There was a knock, then, at Ngeal's answer, Tizu stepped into the room. Closing the door behind himself, he paused his dark eyes surveyed the Avairei sitting around a low table. His eyes lingered on Sagas's face for just a moment longer than was necessary then he returned his attention to Ngeal.

Stepping forward, he bowed and related the latest news from the pools. Ngeal listened, expressionless. When he finished his report, Ngeal nodded and thanked him. She was glad that the Kashallan's wives were out of danger—but this tragedy was still so hard to accept.

If the Umwira could do something like this to innocent breeding women, to a child—and right within a Khutani keep itself—none of them were safe until the enemy was destroyed. Anyone could be overpowered and used—anyone could be a traitor. She had to stop this, such nonsense would drive her insane.

There was one thing the Hunt Leader hadn't mentioned, and though she hated to learn the answer, she forced herself to ask. "Hunt Leader Tizu, what did the Holy Ones decide to do about my niece?"

Tizu gave her a measuring look; she met and held it. He cleared his throat and said in a low voice, "I asked, and they told me that because of the wizard's taint they couldn't allow the usual death feast, or the feeding of the Khutani young. They didn't feel that it would be proper."

Ngeal shuddered and looked down at her hands, clenching them painfully upon her knees. She sighed. "Then she was consigned to the waste pit?"

"No, Ima." She looked up, startled. "They directed me to have my people take her to a quiet place in one of the abandoned tunnels, away from the inhabited portion of the keep. We did that—laid her out nice and proper.

"The Khutani felt she was too young and wasn't to blame for what was done to her, but the taint was there all the same, so that was the best that could be offered, under the circumstances."

Ngeal nodded. "Thank you, Hunt Leader." Suddenly feeling totally drained, and unable to maintain her facade of calm control any longer. She stood up. "If you will excuse me, I will retire now."

Tizu bowed and stepped back to let her pass. "Ngeal," Sagas called after her anxiously, "are you all right? Shall I—"

Ngeal paused at her bedroom door. She shook her head, then, without turning, said, "Get some rest, Sagas, and I'll try to do the same. Go on; I'll be fine." Ngeal opened her door then closed it firmly behind her, leaving a stunned silence in her wake.

SAGAS STARED AT THE Ima's closed door, unsure what to do next. She should stay—Ngeal might need her. She began to tremble, suddenly aware of the Speir'dina commander's eyes upon her. Standing over her now, he touched her arm. "Sagas?"

She looked up at him, eyes pleading and shook her head stubbornly. "I'll stay. Ngeal might need me later—"

"You go ahead, Ima, you need your rest too. I'll see to my mistress," the maid assured her. "I can send for you if you are wanted."

Sagas shook her head, determined to ignore once again the compelling feelings that were making her body react to the man beside her.

Tizu's eyes flashed with annoyance. He sighed. Bending over, he startled both Sagas and the maid by picking her up in his arms.

Sagas gasped, stifling a cry. "Put me down, you ugly Warlinga," she demanded indignantly.

Tizu chuckled. "You aren't needed here at the moment, and I warned you—"

Sagas bared her teeth. "Put me down."

He glared at her, a warning plain for her to read in the depths of his dark eyes. "If you bite me, I'll hit you. I warned you about that before, remember?"

She returned his stare angrily, their eyes locked in a silent struggle. At last she lowered her eyes, conceding defeat for the moment. "All right, I'll go with you. But please, Hukiyo, put me down." She glanced at the closed outer door.

He understood, and nodded, setting her back on her feet. He took her arm in a possessive grip, making sure she couldn't change her mind, but allowing her to retain a sense of dignity in front of whoever was out there in the corridor. Motioning for the astonished Sondi to open the door, he escorted her from the room.

At the entrance to her tiny cell, he opened the door and stepped inside, with her still on his arm, giving her no time to dismiss him. He smiled, with satisfaction as he closed the door behind them.

Curious, he released her then and looked around. Votive altar against one wall, worn carpet on the floor by the narrow bed, worktable and single chair in the far corner, no tapestries, no bright colored accessories, the room's Spartan furnishings, were so like his own austere quarters.

Sagas glared at him murderously, but his smile only widened, his eyes still hard and determined. Finally she looked away, her body betraying her. She began to tremble again.

Tizu put an arm around her shoulder and guided her over to the bed. He sat on its hard mattress, pulling her down beside him. He studied her solemnly. Without speaking, she implored him with dark eyes, begging him to go—to stay. He shook his head slightly, denying the unspoken plea for him to let her be, as he always had before. Sagas looked away, her body shuddering with the force of her conflicting emotions.

Leaning forward, he took her face in his hands, tilting her jaw up so she had to look at him. He kissed her gently; then drew back, looking deep into her eyes. "I'm not letting you send me away, not this time—not after what's just happened. I think you need me to stay as much as I need you right now. Why is it so hard for you Avairei to accept physical forms of affection between a man and a woman, hmm?"

Suddenly all resistance gone, she slumped against him, sobbing. Tizu gathered her close, stroking her silky fur and murmuring soft endearments into her braids. He held her, letting her cry, until her grief was spent. Sagas clung to him like a child desperately searching for comfort. Surprisingly gentle, he soothed her.

"Go ahead, My Dear, cry it out. So much has happened—so much change, and you've been so brave. There's no one here to see—to know, so cry if you want to."

When she at last quieted, spent and silent, he held her a while longer, then pressed her back upon the bed. Looking deep into her eyes again, he allowed his hands to slide down her thin satiny chest and began to fumble with the tie of her belt. She stiffened as she felt the cordage part and her kilt loosen about her waist. Eyes frightened. She begged, "Don't."

Tizu paused. Sliding the fabric aside, he rested his hands, with an unspoken promise, against her warm fur. She shivered. "Is that what you want, Sagas, My Love? Rape isn't what I'm after, so I will go, if you really want me to."

He allowed one hand to drift sensuously downward, causing her to gasp. "But you are going to have to convince me that that is what you do want. Is it?" he teased, sliding his hand between the long outer lips of her sex.

"Oh, damn you," she cried, tears forming in the corners of her eyes. "This is so hard for me—please, why can't you see that—go!"

"Sagas, I know this isn't easy for you, but you've defied other traditions of your people before. Why is this one so tough? I can feel your wanting, and I want it too. Why are you fighting me and yourself so hard? I care for you, and I want to show you how much. Please, let me love you."

Oh, Holy Mother, this was so awful. She knew he cared, and by the standards of his own people what he was offering her wasn't perversion, or insult. Sagas knew that—had even counseled her own student Pela to ignore her upbringing, and give in to the desires of her kashallan-bonded mate.

Though Pela was reluctant at first, Sagas knew the girl had done what she advised, and now enjoyed her unconventional relationship. So why couldn't she herself— "I can't, Hukiyo," she breathed.

"Why?"

"Because—" She swallowed hard and turned her head away, unable to stand the hurt she saw in his eyes. "Please go."

He sat back, withdrawing his hands. "No, not yet, not until you tell me why—why you want to do this terrible thing to both of us," he said. "It's not just yourself you're hurting here, it's me too. What about *my* feelings, hmm?"

She turned back to him, her lip curled. "If you want to couple with someone, I'm sure you can find a willing companion among your own kind."

"You Bitch!" Suddenly his face contorted with rage, and she instinctively shrank away from him, fearing she had gone too far this time. He glared down at her murderously, hands clenching and unclenching as he fought for control. "Damn it, you are the most stubborn, infuriating woman!

"So this is the new tactic of our little amorous combat, hmm," he growled, his chest heaving. "Figure if you insult my pride—hurt me bad enough—I'll go and leave you to wallow in your own lonely misery." He laughed, his voice brittle and cold. "Well, if that's what you want, I'll go, and for good. Like you so crudely point out, I can find companionship elsewhere, but I still want to know why you're doing this, especially tonight—after all that has just happened.

"Don't you understand? I know what a blow this has been for you—for all of us—and I want to be with you. So why, damn it, why are you pushing me away like this?"

She knew she had hurt him unbearably this time. Oh, Mother, how could she explain—how could he understand— Heart sinking, body trembling, she whispered, "Because, if we—if I—oh, Hukiyo, why can't you understand? I care about you, too, but if I let you stay—let you—oh, Hukiyo, I'd be just like Combaron." Covering her face with her hands she began to sob once more.

Stunned, Tizu stared at her mouth agape. After a long moment he reached for her. She stiffened at his touch then allowed him to draw her close. He raised her face so she would have to look at him. "Sagas," he said gently, "what kind of nonsense are you talking about? You're not like Combaron Dingay. No matter what you did, you could never be like him."

When she started to protest, he shushed her and continued, "I never met the little shit, and I don't want to. For all the grief he's caused, I'd kill him without a thought. But from what Marti and others have told me about his 'appetites,' well, they're nothing like what we feel for each other.

"Neither of us are children, or master and slave, nor is one of us forcing the other by using drugs. We are two consenting adults who are looking for a little enjoyment and companionship.

"For my people, at least, that makes all the difference between perversion, rape, and a healthy relationship. Oh, I know you Avairei feel that sex without the need to have children is odd and perverted. That's what you've been taught, but it's just one way of looking at things, no better or worse than any other, and you don't have to accept it now that you've seen there are other alternatives.

"What we want to do isn't going to hurt anybody, either. We just want to share a little physical enjoyment and comfort with each other, and that's nothing at all like what that Dingay filth did to my armachd. And even you would have to admit that."

She nodded reluctantly. He chuckled and touched a finger to her nose. "So what do you care about what some stiff-necked old Imas in the Yeyen will say if they should hear some gossip about us, hmm?

"When the people in the Yeyen Banai learn about the Speir'dina and the outlawed Timornans, they're going to gossip about us anyway, most like. We're a pretty weird bunch, by Timornan standards, I gather. So we might as well follow our leader's example and give them something really juicy to talk about. I mean, why spoil our reputation as wild, uncouth outlaws?"

In spite of herself, Sagas chuckled, the sound coming out halfway between a sob and a laugh. Pulling up a corner of her kilt, she wiped the tears from her eyes. She sniffed, blinked, and then looked at him shyly.

Tizu enfolded her once more in his arms, kissing away the last of her tears. She relaxed against him, comforted by his strength and assurance that she wasn't a bad person or desiring something perverted and evil. And he was probably right—the Avairei might not approve, but she doubted if the Kashallan or even the Khutani would care if she and Tizu...

On the contrary, she realized with some surprise, Dunnagh-Tani would probably be very happy for them. Change, oh, Mother, more change—it was so hard to know what was right any more. Against his chest she nodded, surrendering to his way of seeing things. Smiling down at her, Tizu hugged her, burying his face in her hair.

He had won this round of their amorous combat; she would do whatever he wanted. But he could feel her trembling, and knew that if he made love to her right now, she wouldn't really enjoy it, and would resent him for his eagerness later. Well, he'd come this far; no sense in spoiling things now. He'd wait till she was ready for him.

Suddenly shy, he hesitated, unsure quite how to proceed. She wasn't Speir'dina, but Avairei—her culture, and even her biological rhythms, were different from his. What should they do— "Uh, Sagas, don't you need to do something before—I mean, don't we need that red kavay stuff, so we can—so you'll be more—so you'll be able to relax and enjoy yourself?"

She stiffened. Still unable to look at him, she nodded. Disentangling herself from his embrace, she stood up and walked across to her tiny altar. She picked up a small flask and pulled the stopper from the bottle.

Well, well, Tizu thought with some amusement, *she has some here, doesn't have to go elsewhere to find it.*

Sagas held up the bottle, then began to tremble violently, spilling some of its contents on the rug, almost dropping the flask in her agitation. Tizu took the bottle from her numb fingers as it began to fall. She looked up at him with frightened eyes, unable to speak. He lifted the flask and took a long drink. He made a face at its unfamiliar taste, then smiled and handed the red kavay to her. Taking a deep breath, Sagas took the bottle and drank.

Epilogue

Dunnagh-Tani sat in the shallow waters of the kashallan pool, staring blindly out into the mist hovering over the dark water. He felt numb, trapped in a nightmare from which he was unable to wake. This time the Umwira attack hadn't been directed against him, but against his unprotected and oh, so vulnerable family.

When he finally reached the kashallan pool after Amril's call, he found Maker Dievris and Maker Meyagus there before him. Through some uncanny ability of their own, they had known of the Umwira magic triggered in the keep above, and were waiting when Amril and the warriors arrived with his wives.

The Khutani hadn't let him go to Pela, or to Sairsa, however; they made him stay back, claiming that he was too emotionally involved, and still too weak, to attempt the healings.

Someone, Tarla maybe, had literally pushed the distraught Amril into his arms, and for a time they clung to each other, both caught up in a fear that was almost unbearable.

While they waited, he learned most of what had happened from Amril and the two warrior women. He glanced over at Moraga and Chelka still crouched against the cavern's wall, waiting, along with Aju'an and a few others. Gods, if they hadn't been there—he didn't want to think about it.

It was sheer luck that saved his first wife and their child. The poison the maid had used wasn't of Umwira concocting, thank the Gods. It had been one of the Khutani's own drugs, and so its properties, and the antidote, were familiar to his kin.

Pela hadn't drunk too much of the lethal tea, thanks to Chelka's quick thinking. But the poison created another complication, when it triggered the premature labor of her child, and for a long time it had been unclear if either of them would survive.

But, thank all the Gods of Timorna and Caldon, she and little Jorran had made it. They had allowed him into the link with the healers after it was over so he could be assured that both were well and resting peacefully. Yes, thank the Gods, they were all right—he should go rest—but if he left, he knew he wouldn't. He felt so guilty. He blamed himself, and knew that if he tried to sleep, his dreams would only torment him with his failures.

Now that Pela was out of danger, and was resting comfortably still within the Maker's coils, he had gotten Timma to take Amril away to rest. The priest hadn't wanted to go, but reluctantly went at last. The Kashallan remained, however, in spite of his people's urging for him to go with the young man.

"Dunnagh-Tani?" He looked up as Nathan sank down into the warm water beside him. Dunnagh saw that his friend's face looked haggard, and guessed his own probably didn't look much better.

Vaguely he recalled a grim-faced Nathan passing him a while ago, ordered out into the pool to make the link with one of the Old Ones, to give his report. Judging by the way he looked, the Elder must have demanded a lot from him.

"You should go rest," the big man observed, "you look like shit."

Dunnagh's lip twitched. "So do you. Maybe you should take your own advice."

Nathan grimaced. "Yeah, well, I will if you will."

Dunnagh snorted, then sobered once more, rubbing a hand across his face. "I can't, not just yet. I need to be sure how the baby and Pela are—I need to talk to Sairsa. I been such a fool—" he broke off suddenly, choked by a wave of remorse.

Nathan nodded. He glanced over at the Speir'dina woman, still resting, eyes closed, in Maker Meyagus's coils. She had stopped crying, at least, and that was probably a good sign. Whatever the Khutani was doing to mend her shattered mind must be working. He shuddered and looked away, settling himself more comfortably to wait beside his friend.

IMMERSED IN HIS OWN thoughts, the Kashallan lost track of time. He must have dozed off, however, because he was startled awake when a hand touched his shoulder. Dunnagh blinked, then, recognizing who was beside him, he sat up hurriedly. "Sairsa," he breathed. Pulling her down beside him, he enfolded her into a hungry embrace. "How do you feel, My Love? Are you all right?"

She nodded, resting her head against his chest. Burying his face in her damp hair, he held her close, rocking her. "Oh, Love," he murmured, his voice thick with emotion, "I'm so sorry. I didn't listen, and I almost lost you—both of you. Oh, Gods, I've been such a fool."

She looked up at him then, her green eyes tired but clear—freed from the Umwira's tormenting visions. "Don't, Dunnagh-Tani, stop blaming yourself. It just happened, so don't beat yourself up about it." When he started to object, she kissed him, silencing his protest. "There was no way you could have known, and the Avairei never thought it important enough to mention, that Nona had been Tomina's maid."

He shook his head. "Maybe, but if I'd listened to you, told the Makers about what you suspected, instead of— Oh, Gods, Sairsa—"

Sairsa lifted her head as an insistent wailing began from somewhere nearby. Rising hurriedly, she waded over to a drowsy Pela, still wrapped within the Maker's coils. As she leaned over, the Khutani raised its head and nuzzled her affectionately. Sairsa smiled, running her hand over its sleek gray skin.

She took the hungry baby from her sister-wife's arms and settled him automatically at her own overflowing breast. "The Elder has asked me to care for him, Love, till you're stronger," she said. "I'll be nearby, so don't worry."

Pela looked up, still half asleep. Sairsa repeated herself, and Pela nodded then lay back gratefully, closing her eyes. Returning to her husband and the half-awake Nathan, Sairsa settled herself companionably beside them, the little one now sucking contentedly.

Nathan rose up on one elbow and peered at the baby. "Well, one thing's for sure," he said, after an intent inspection of his friend's new son. "No one will ever be in doubt as to who his father is, with fur like that. I've never seen any Avairei quite that color."

Dunnagh laughed. "I suppose he'll be called Jorran Ru'a, at least by our people. But that's to be expected—both me and my older sister Shivon had red hair and were called Ru'a back home, if you remember."

Nathan nodded then smiled, looking once more down at the baby, as Sairsa laid him in his father's arms. "I remember—cute little guy," he said and reached out a hand to stroke the baby's damp red fur. Jorran blinked up at them sleepily, then closed his eyes and drifted back into untroubled slumber.

Jorran looked Avairei, even with his red fur, but his larger bone structure and more flattened facial features gave evidence of his mixed human ancestry as well.

Dunnagh-Tani looked down at his newborn son, again overwhelmed by the miracle he had played a part in creating. He shivered, then stroked Jorran's silky fur. Gods, he had come so close to losing both mother and child. Unable to help himself, he extended a pink tentacle, and slipped it gently into the baby's flesh, just to assure himself that all was well with the little one. Oh, Gods, if he had lost them—any of them—

Suddenly he glanced up, looking around as a new thought came to him. There had been so much to think about until now— "Where's Tameh?" he asked anxiously; looking from Sairsa to Nathan.

Nathan cleared his throat and looked away, unable to answer or meet his eyes. Dunnagh frowned. There was something going on here that Nathan didn't want to tell him about. Was Tameh—

"Tameh's fine, Love, no need to worry," Sairsa said. "I—"

"Look, here he is. They're bringing him now," Nathan interrupted with a relieved sigh. Rising quickly to make room for the newcomers, he waded to the shore and began to dress.

The Kashallan glanced over to where Nathan pointed. He scowled when he saw Tess-weh carrying his son, the Wa'chassey'ul following dog-like behind her down the causeway.

Ignoring him, Tess-weh waded into the pool and headed for Sairsa. Tameh was awake, but not fussing too loudly. Sairsa smiled up at her friend, her eyes conveying her gratitude. She reached up to take her child. "Thank you, My Friend."

When Tess-weh straightened, she glanced at the Kashallan. She smirked, the demon watching him with hard eyes.

Mouth tightening, he flushed a deep crimson. He met her stare, then looked away, and watched Sairsa put her son to her breast. The baby whimpered for a moment, then settled down to suck greedily at his mother's rich, bluish milk. He gazed down at Jorran in his arms. Two children and their mothers—almost lost to him...

He tightened his grip about the child. His face writhed, then softened as he came to some inner resolution. When he looked up and met Tess-weh's eyes again, he surprised her by bowing his head in respect. "Thank you, Tess-weh, for everything."

She held his gaze for a long moment, as if unsure of his sincerity, then she nodded, slowly turned and walked from the pool. Silently she passed the onlookers and headed for the stairs, the big Warlinga trailing at her heels.

When she was gone, Dunnagh couldn't help but breathe a sigh of relief. He caught Nathan's eye, motioning at the tired group of his people still huddled against the wall. Nathan glanced at them too then nodded, catching his meaning.

Moving over to the waiting Timornans, he spoke to them quietly, then ushered them ahead of him down the causeway and out of the cavern.

When they were gone, Dunnagh-Tani turned back to his wife. Sairsa was looking down at her son, lost in her own thoughts. She stroked the baby's head lovingly. She shivered, then, without looking at the Kashallan, she said, "When that wizard had me, and was showing me all those terrible things—I knew that if I gave in to him—if I let him defeat me—everyone I loved would be annihilated. I kept thinking of my baby, of Pela, and of you—I couldn't let him destroy it all."

Dunnagh-Tani swallowed hard, blinking rapidly. He knew what she meant—he had tasted the Umwira's mind magics before. His face crumpled. Gods, he hated to think of her having to endure that. "Oh, Love, I'm so sorry—"

Startled, she looked up, suddenly seeming to become aware that she had spoken out loud. She smiled at him tenderly and touched his face, her green eyes dark with her emotion. "Don't, Love—thinking of you gave me strength—I love you so much." She blinked, a tear rolling down her cheek.

Dunnagh-Tani leaned forward and kissed away the tear. "I love you too, My Love," he murmured. And when the blue snows melt, I will do everything in my power to see that you and our babies remain safe. The Umwira must be stopped; they will pay for what they've done."

The End

This story is continued in Book Five: *Prey of the Umwira*

Additional information for the Tales of the Kashallans series

Note to the reader: it is my hope that by reading the text of these fantasy books, the alien words peppering the writing are clear on their own. But for those readers who enjoy such things, and those who may get confused from time to time by the many foreign words from the various races and cultures on my imagined world Timorna, I offer the following notes to aid with clarity.

Best wishes and happy reading!

Celu Amberstone

Pronunciations of unfamiliar words:

Consonants
The sound [ch or kh] represents the ck in the word lock [lahkh].
Other consonants are pronounced like in English.
An apostrophe in a word represents a glottal stop.
Vowels
A – like father AI – like in ice AY – like in way
E – like in ate EI – like in island
I – like in see
O - like in low
U – like in too
Y – like in eat
H – when next to a vowel shortens and softens the vowel sound

Timornan words (general)

Timorna [tim-MOR-na] – The name of the uncharted planet where this story takes place.

The Great Destruction – A nuclear holocaust that almost destroyed life on Timorna, thousands of years ago.

The Burning Times – A time when the radioactivity was at its highest, just after the destruction.

Sorins [SOR-inz] – A weather condition in which the wind blows straight out of the north, picking up radioactive dust and other harmful substances as it heads south. During the Sorin seasons all life must seek shelter, or go dormant, to survive.

KHUTANI [KOO-TAH-NEE] – The ancient eel-like symbiotic race living on Timorna in its deep undergrownd waterways, who were responsible for storing the genetic patterns and keeping life alive during the Great Destruction and the Burning Times that followed.

Amla [AHM-la] – The term used by the Khutani and kashallans to refer to a parent.

Amsi [AHM-see] – A Khutani term used to address a peer of its kindred.

K'amsi [k'AHM-see] – A Khutani term of respect for an elder of that race.

Sh'amsi [sh'-AHM-see] – A Khutani term used to address a younger sibling.

kashallan [kah-SHAH-lan] – A host-symbiont bond. A partnership between two intelligent beings sworn to serve as guardians and healers of the planet Timorna.

Kasha [KAH-shuh] – The intimate name a symbiont in a kashallan pair uses for its host.

Shalla [SHAH-luh] – The intimate name a kashallan host uses for his symbiont.

The Kashallan – This term refers to a particular pairing, that of the human, Dunnagh Kai, and Tani, the Khutani symbiont. They are the first bonded pair in over seven hundred years.

Bebech [BEH-bech] – A native race that served as hosts of the Khutani, who were killed off by plague.

kavay [kah-VAY] – A blue substance created by the Khutani that when introduced into a living organism makes its survival possible on Timorna.

kavay alignment – The process by which the body is metabolically changed at such a deep level that, once alignment occurs, a constant supply of kavay must remain in the diet, or death will occur.

Sweh'an [SWAY'-ahn] – Another type of host-symbiont bond, this time between a mortal host and a spirit being from another dimension that will use its powers to aid a host, in exchange for possession of the host body at agreed times, so that it can experience a physical reality.

H'an [h'-AHN] – The host for a Sweh'an spirit.

Swe'a'sa [SWAY'-ah'-sah] – The intimate name the host uses to address her Sweh'an spirit companion.

H'an'si [h'-AHN'-see] – The name the Sweh'an spirit uses to address its host.

Cha'Han [CHA'hahn] – The Avairei priest who is bound to the Sweh'an bonded host as her companion.

Ba'etchat'seh [bah'-AYCHAHT'sah] – The Timornan version of a padded cell, used to discipline the Sweh'an when its behavior while taking its pleasures becomes too troublesome.

Wa'chassey'ul [wa'-CHSAY'-ool] – A Warlinga bound by magic to the will of the Sweh'an as both lover and mortal guardian.

AVAIREI [AH-VYE-RAY] – One of the four intelligent species bred by the Khutani. A furry, bipedal race with cat-like features and a long mane. They are the priests, scholars and healers of their society. Their function is also to care for the Khutani in their underground pools, and to distribute the medicines the Khutani make for the creatures they introduced to their world after the Great Wars nearly destroyed all life on Timorna.

Ata [AH-tuh] – (Father) A term used when addressing a male Avairei.

Ima [EE-muh] – (Mother) A term used when addressing a female Avairei priestess.

Ima Matri [EE-muh MAH-tree] – The priestess who is head of a Avairei keep like Sulas.

High Matri – The head, and ruler over, all of the Avairei family clans.

Ata Leyas [AH-tuh LAY-ahss] – (Healing Father) The male Avairei who is second in command of the religious hierarchy at a keep.

WARLINGA [WOR-LING-ga] – Another of the intelligent species bred by the Khutani. Large two-legged lizardmen naturally endowed with teeth claws and long muscular tails. Their function is to be warriors and hunters. They were bred especially to protect the Khutani-held southern lands from the Umwira, the mutated remnants of the original people who caused the Great Wars.

Chi'awari'ga [CHI'-ah-WAHR-ee'-gah] – An ancient Warlinga ceremony of single combat to settle a feud or other dispute.

Accavett [ah-cah-VET] – The women's quarters in a Warlinga keep.

Sa [sah] – A title of respect for female Warlinga.

San [sahn] – A title of respect for male Warlinga. The terms Sa and San are also used for humans as well because many of them are warriors, too.

LOTI [LOW-TEE] – A third intelligent species. They resemble centaurs with long, shaggy fur. Their function is to farm and care for the land of Timorna. They are also artisans, weavers and craftsmen.

Timornshaya [tim-morn-SHY-uh] – A term of respect offered to the Loti people.

BEGTA [BEKH-TA] – THE last of the four intelligent species created by the Khutani. Small, woolly-furred simian-like people with long arms. They live in the wilder regions of the south. The Begta are an outcast people, hunters and gatherers, who are notorious thieves. They are despised by most other Timornans, and often hunted for food, or sold as slaves.

Domail [dough-MAIL] – A Begta victory dance.

Begtanshay [BEKH-tahn-shay] – A term of respect given to the Begta people by the Khutani and the kashallans in earlier times.

UMWIRA [OOM-WEER-UH] – This is a name given to the mutated descendants of the planet's original intelligent inhabitants by their enemies. Also known as the Ghostlanders, they are the people who were responsible for the Great Destruction. They are the sworn enemies of the Khutani and wish to destroy all that the Khutani have created, so they can reclaim the more favored lands in the South.

Clans of the Western Umwira – The Western Clans are related to the Ghostlanders and descended from the original inhabitants of Timorna; being exposed to the poisons of the north and west where they live, they have mutated and interbred with slaves taken from the Khutani-held lands, so that they don't resemble the peoples before the wars.

The seven clans are: Blue Stone, Sand Mountain, Bitter Water, Red Wind, Rock Salt, Green Clay, Twisted Grass.

Plants and Animals on Timorna

Taba worm [TAH-buh] – A long, thin worm that lives among the liru reeds, in both the Swamp and the Broken Lands. Eaten by the Begta. The appearance of a bowl of taba worms is rather like blue spaghetti.

gumati [goo-MAH-tee] – A frog-like creature with four hopping legs, living in the Swamp. Eaten by the Begta.

budasen [BOO-dah-sen] – A stork-like creature with long neck and legs. It has big paddle feet for running across the surface of grassy ponds. Not a bird; it has scales, and can't fly.

pomong [puh-MAHNG] – A lizard-like predator with a long, sharp tail. It preys on the budasen.

snayga [SNAY-guh] – A small predator that swims in large schools. Eating habits like the piranha of old Earth.

vistri [VIST-tree] – A six-legged scaly predator about the size of a large dog, and like dogs hunt in packs. Very dangerous.

winglah [wing-LAH] – Any large creature of the western lands that has through the generations mutated into a dangerous monster because of exposure to the Sorins.

obeylem [oh-BAY-lem] – A large plant-eating creature, living in the Swamp. It has six limbs (four long legs for walking, two short arms for grabbing food), also a long tail and neck. Hunted for their meat.

bolacht [BAh-lach] – A herd beast introduced by the Khutani to meet the needs of the Speir'dina. Provides meat milk wool and can be ridden as well.

madag [MA-dag] – Timorna's answer to a herd dog. Looks something like a small armored dinosaur. Can fight vistri, but gentle with humans and other Khutani-bred races

shri moss [shree] – A short yellow moss, growing everywhere as ground cover.

liru reeds [LEER-roo] – A tall, brown bamboo-like plant growing in the canyons of the Broken Lands and parts of the Swamp.

kavalpa trees [kah-VAHL-puh] – Tall, black trees like weeping willows that usually grow up around a spring or other water source. When their long branches touch the ground, they root themselves, thus forming, over time, large thickets that give shelter to many of Timorna's inhabitants.

masa root [MAHS-suh] – A plant with a large edible root, eaten by most Timornans. Cultivated by the Loti.

lamra [LAM-ruh] – A corn-like grain developed from the liru reeds. A staple food in the diet. Cultivated by the Loti.

dahalli [Da-hal-lee] – A thorny shrub that can grow quite tall with purple broad leaves and bright orange berries that are sweet.

clamisa – A mutated form of masa root growing across the Shallow Sea in the West. A staple of the western Clans

oko – A small armored predator in the western lands it looks something like an armadillo. Thought to be sly by the Western Clans.

dhuura – A sea creature found in the Shallow Sea. It also is a food staple for the Clans of the coast.

leongon – An armored shark-like predator in the Sea.

nagril – A nearly transparent jelly/shrimp-like creature that feeds much of the sea life on Timorna.

cobura – A furred sea animal.

aluutae – A reed/grass-like plant growing in the West used for basket making.

Land features

Ghostlands – This is a wide peninsula of barren land that connects the Favored Southern land with the blackened and radio-active northern continent. Living mostly underground this is the land where a cabal of techno-wizards has control of what is left of the old technology. They also have tremendous Psy powers which they have gained through exposing themselves to mutations sought in the poisoned places in their land.

Broken Lands – A region of canyons and mesas where some of the Begta bands live, and where the humans set up their base.

Yeyen Banai [YAY-yen ban-EYE] – A large valley surrounded by a high rim of mountains. This is where most of Timorna's Khutani-bred population lives.

Rim Wall – The mountains encircling the Yeyen Banai.

Jeban Pass [JAY-bun] – The main route from the Broken Lands through the Rim Wall to the shelter of the Yeyen Banai Valley beyond.

The Great Swamp – A low-lying stretch of land to the south of the Broken Lands. Very dangerous to travel, since it is pockmarked with poisonous pools, and subject to constant earthquakes.

Lake Ticca – A large lake at the edge of the Great Swamp, out of which the Shaden river flows. In its center is the island fortress of Ticca keep.

Shaden Falls [SHAY-den] – The portage around this waterfall is the main southern route from the Swamp through the Rim Wall to the Yeyen Banai Balley.

The Shallow Sea – The straight between the land of the Western Clans of the Umwira and the northwestern edge of the Swamp.

Timornan Keeps and Fortresses

Avairei keeps:
  Riath [REE-ahth] – the capital
Sulas [SOO-luss]
Ticca [tee-KAH]
Shaden [SHAY-den]
Ha'limra [ha'-LEEM-rah]
Warlinga fortresses:
Tragar [TRAh-gar]
Meh'gach [MAY'-gakh]

Caldoni words adopted into the Timornan language

Speir'dina [SPEER'-din-uh] – The term chosen by the humans to refer to themselves after they accepted that they had become a part of Timornan society. Literally it means sky people.

Teh'lach [TAY'-lahkh] – A pseudo-family group among the followers of the Kashallan, containing members of several different species.

Speir'van [SPEER'-vahn] – Literally, "sky-woman." Used by the Speir'dina as a term of respect for a high-ranking human woman, such as Sairsa the first kashallan's human wife.

Other Caldoni words and phrases

Caldon [KAHL-don] – The world where Dunnagh and many of the Lann Gheal armachda are from.

Cumarsaid [KOO-mar-sayd] – A trance-like state in which the practitioner opens his awareness to communicate psychically with other life. This discipline was practiced as part of the ancient Caldoni warriors' training and is still taught today.

Lann Gheal – A term meaning "Bright Blade," it refers to a mercenary organization formed on Caldon. Their purpose is to keep alive many of the ancient warrior traditions of their race. They are not for sale to the highest bidder in a conflict, and will only fight for what they believe to be right.

armachd (plural: armachda) [ar-MAKHT, ar-MAKHT-uh] – Warrior.

Geish (plural: Gessa) [gaysh, GAY-suh] – A charge or compulsion laid upon someone that binds them to do a certain thing. A Geish is usually of divine origin, but also can be laid by one person on another.

Fir Gall [feer gahl] – A foreigner.

mo – This word means "my," but when used with other words often changes the sound at the beginning of the next word.

Cara [KAH-ruh] – Friend. mo hara [moh HAH-ruh] – My friend—my love. Mo hri [moh hree] – My heart. Mo gra [moh grah] – My love.

Ce'awn [kay'-OUN] – A chieftain. mo he'awn [moh hay'-OUN] – My chieftain.

Ceartachd [Keer-takht] – A word meaning the "rightness" of a thing.

Ca'companachta [kah'-kom-pah-NAKH-tah] – Literally meaning "battle companions," it is a relationship of lovers who also fight together.

Bacach [BAH-kakh] – An unlikable person, an evil man.

Amadan [AH-muh-dahn] – Idiot; can be used affectionately or as an insult.

Dina [DEE-nuh] – People.

kina [KEE-nuh] – Kin or kindred.

le'ayn [lay'-AIN] – Twin. Literally, "half of one."

shenahi [SHEN-ah-hee] – Ancient Caldoni storyteller or bard.

Pibroch [pee-BRAHKH] – A musical instrument like a bagpipe.

Faltia, cuj milla faltia [FAHL-tee-uh, coodge MEE-luh FAHL-tee-uh] – Welcome, a hundred thousand welcomes.

go ra my get [GOR-rah-MY-uh-get] – Thank you.

Ru'a [ROO'-ah] – "The red." It refers to a person with red hair; for example, Dunnagh Ru'a (Red-haired Dunnagh.)

colcannon [kohl-CAN-nun] – A native Caldoni dish made with potatoes, cabbage, and onions.

Don't miss out!

Visit the website below and you can sign up to receive emails whenever Celu Amberstone publishes a new book. There's no charge and no obligation.

https://books2read.com/r/B-A-YGQM-WFESB

BOOKS 2 READ

Connecting independent readers to independent writers.

Also by Celu Amberstone

Renewal
The Prophecy of Manu
Teoni's Giveaway

Rituals
Blessings of the Blood: A Book of Menstrual Lore and Rituals for Women
Deepening the Power: Community Ritual and Sacred Theatre

Tales of the Kashallans
The Dream-Chosen
The Hunted Kashallan
The Outlawed Bond
Uncertain Refuge
Prey of the Umwira
Blood Magic's Snare

Standalone
Refugees and Other Stories

About the Author

Celu is of mixed Cherokee and Scots-Irish ancestry. Celu Amberstone was one of the few young people in her family to take an interest in learning Traditional Native crafts and medicine ways. This interest made several of the older members of her family very happy while annoying others.

Legally blind since birth, she has defied her limitations and spent much of her life avoiding cities. Moving to Canada after falling in love with a Métis-Cree man from Manitoba, she has lived in the rain forests of the west coast, a tepee in the desert and a small village in Canada's arctic. Along the way she also managed to acquire a BA in cultural anthropology and an MA in health education. Celu loves telling stories and reading. She lives in Victoria British Columbia near her grown children and grandchildren.

About the Publisher

Kashallan Press is an independent publisher releasing books by author Celu Amberstone. Among her books are critically-acclaimed works now re-released by Kashallan Press, and new works showcasing her talents in writing both fiction and non-fiction.